Praise for Mesu Andrews

"Mesu Andrews is one of my favorite novelists. You can always count on her for an engaging, compelling read. She cuts no corners with her detailed research, and her stories always reach the heart."

Jerry B. Jenkins, JerryJenkins.com

"I am such a fan of Mesu Andrews and so grateful for each story she so artfully and masterfully brings to vivid life. No historical or biblical fiction fan's shelf is complete without all of Mesu's works on it!"

Tosca Lee, *New York Times* bestselling author of *Iscariot*

"In *Noble*, Mesu Andrews pulls back the palace curtains on Maakah, one of King David's overlooked wives. Blending vivid political intrigue with humanizing insight into the Warrior-Poet-King, this emotionally resonant tale is destined for your keeper shelf."

Connilyn Cossette, Christy Award–winning author

"Intriguing and filled with political and religious tension, Mesu Andrews pens yet another gripping tale of King David's wives. Nestled within the ongoing conflict between David, Saul, and the enemies of Israel, *Noble* showcases the good and faithful love of Yahweh for all who seek to follow Him."

Jamie Ogle, Christy Award–winning author of *As Sure as the Sea*

"*Noble: The Story of Maakah* is a richly textured tale of a foreign princess learning to trust in Yahweh alone. Mesu Andrews engages hard questions in her nuanced portrayal of flawed, relatable people. Maakah's journey into belief is compelling and excellently rendered in this next installment of KING DAVID'S BRIDES."

Heather Kaufman, author of the WOMEN OF THE WAY series

"Rich with historical texture and emotional depth, *Noble* offers a stirring glimpse into King David's world through the eyes of a courageous and conflicted princess. Mesu Andrews weaves faith, duty, and destiny into a story that lingers long after the final page."

Jenelle Hovde, author of *No Stone Unturned*

"Once again, Andrews has taken a lesser-known section of Scripture and expounded upon it with historical facts and her beautiful imagination to reveal the culture and political climate of the time. Readers of biblical fiction will be enthralled in this *Noble* tale."

Naomi Craig, award-winning biblical fiction author

"Mesu's *Noble* is, as always, a stunning work of biblical fiction. Her details make you feel you are part of the action, standing right next to David and the princess Maakah. King David's multiple marriages is a difficult topic, and Mesu has approached it with faith, caution, and sacred imagination."

Carole Towriss, author of the PLANTING FAITH series

NOBLE

Books by Mesu Andrews

KING DAVID'S BRIDES

Brave: The Story of Ahinoam
Noble: The Story of Maakah

King David's Brides

TWO

NOBLE

THE STORY of MAAKAH

Mesu Andrews

BethanyHouse

a division of Baker Publishing Group
Minneapolis, Minnesota

© 2025 by Mesu Andrews

Published by Bethany House Publishers
Minneapolis, Minnesota
BethanyHouse.com

Bethany House Publishers is a division of
Baker Publishing Group, Grand Rapids, Michigan

Printed in the United States of America

All rights reserved. No part of this publication may be reproduced, stored in a retrieval system, or transmitted in any form or by any means—for example, electronic, photocopy, recording—without the prior written permission of the publisher. The only exception is brief quotations in printed reviews.

Library of Congress Cataloging-in-Publication Data
Names: Andrews, Mesu, author.
Title: Noble: The Story of Maakah / Mesu Andrews.
Description: Minneapolis, Minnesota : Bethany House Publishers, a division of Baker Publishing Group, 2025. | Series: King David's Brides ; 2
Identifiers: LCCN 2024059581 | ISBN 9780764242625 (paper) | ISBN 9780764244933 (casebound) | ISBN 9781493450701 (ebook)
Subjects: LCGFT: Christian fiction. | Romance fiction. | Bible fiction. | Novels.
Classification: LCC PS3601.N55274 N63 2025 | DDC 813/.6—dc23/eng/20241216
LC record available at https://lccn.loc.gov/2024059581

Unless otherwise noted, Scriptures are taken from the Holy Bible, New International Version®, NIV®. Copyright © 1973, 1978, 1984, 2011 by Biblica, Inc.® Used by permission of Zondervan. All rights reserved worldwide. www.zondervan.com. The "NIV" and "New International Version" are trademarks registered in the United States Patent and Trademark Office by Biblica, Inc.®

Scripture quotations labeled NLT are taken from the *Holy Bible*, New Living Translation, copyright © 1996, 2004, 2015 by Tyndale House Foundation. Used by permission of Tyndale House Publishers, Carol Stream, Illinois 60188. All rights reserved.

Scripture quotations labeled ESV are from The Holy Bible, English Standard Version® (ESV®), copyright © 2001 by Crossway, a publishing ministry of Good News Publishers. Used by permission. All rights reserved. ESV Text Edition: 2016

This book is a work of fiction. Names, characters, places, and incidents are the product of the author's imagination or are used fictitiously. Any resemblance to actual events, locales, or persons, living or dead, is coincidental.

Cover design by Peter Gloege, LOOK Design Studio

Map design by Stan Campbell

Author is represented by Steve Laube.

Baker Publishing Group publications use paper produced from sustainable forestry practices and postconsumer waste whenever possible.

25 26 27 28 29 30 31   7 6 5 4 3 2 1

To Amanda Geaney

For the fourteen years of friendship, cheerleading, praying, and virtual assisting with all things detailed! I dedicate this book to you, Amanda, because not only could I NOT do this writing thing without you—I'm not sure I'd want to. Love you dearly, my friend.

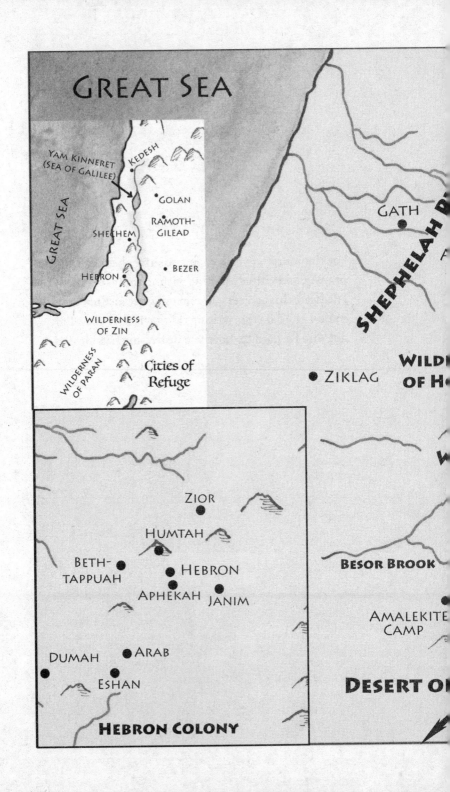

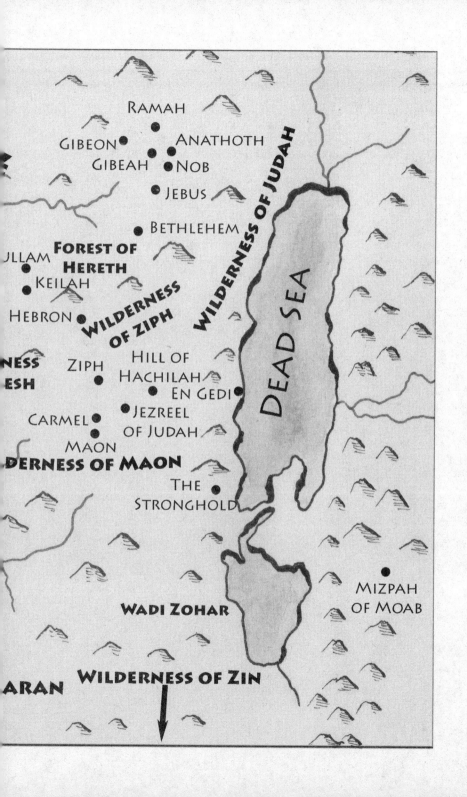

CHARACTER LIST

Abiathar—David's personal priest

Abigail—Nabal's wife; David's wife

Abishai—David's nephew; Zerry's middle son; Commander of the Three

Abital—Asahel's wife; Zerry's daughter-in-law

Abner—Saul's general

*Abraham—Patriarch of God's Promises to Israel

Achish (King)—Philistine king of Gath; appointed David governor over Philistine city of Ziklag

Ahinoam (Nomy)—David's wife; from Jezreel

Amasai—Kohathite (Tribe of Levi); captain of David's Mighty Men

Amnon—David's firstborn son

Asahel—David's nephew; Zerry's youngest son; one of David's Mighty Men

Attai—a Gadite scout in David's army

Azam—King Talmai's Captain of the Royal Guard

David—son of Jesse; anointed as Israel's next king while Saul remained on the throne; husband of Ahinoam and Abigail

Dobah—wife of Phinehas (a Mighty Man)

Noble

Eglah—daughter of Moabite maidservant (Keyalah)

Eleazar—one of David's Mighty Men; a member of the Three with Shammah and Abishai

Eliel—a Gadite scout in David's army

Eliphelet—one of David's Mighty Men; a Maacathite

Haman—Maakah's chamber guard

Jehoiada—chief priest at Hebron, presiding chief priest over tribe of Judah; Benaiah's father

Jesse—David's father; descendant of Ruth (a Moabitess) and Boaz

Joab—David's nephew; Zerry's oldest son; General of David's army

Jonathan—King Saul's crown prince; David's best friend

Joseph—the patriarch Jacob's eleventh son; sold into slavery by his brothers and became Egypt's second-highest ranking leader who saved the ancient world from famine

Joshua—Moses's successor who led Israel's troops into the Promised Land and assigned Yahweh's portions to the twelve tribes

Kepha—Maakah's first love

Maakah—daughter of Geshur's King Talmai; sent as treaty bride to marry David

Maok—Maakah's maternal grandfather

Michal—Saul's daughter; David's first wife

Nabal—Abigail's wicked husband, slain by Yahweh before David married her

Nakia—Egyptian slave discarded by Amalekite masters and given shelter among David's army

Nitzevet—David's mother (ima)

Noah (Japheth, Shem, and Ham)—they and their wives the only survivors of Yahweh's Flood

Paltiel—the man Saul gave his daughter Michal to in marriage after taking her away from David

Phinehas (*a Mighty Man*)—husband of Dobah

Raziah (Queen)—King Talmai's wife; Maakah's mother (ima)

*Samuel—a priest and prophet who anointed Israel's first and second kings

*Saul—first king of Israel

Shammah—one of the Three

Talmai (King)—Maakah's father (abba); ruler of Geshur, one of five Aramean kingdoms

Uriah—a Hittite; one of David's Mighty Men

Vered—Joab's wife; Zerry's daughter-in-law

Zeb (Zebadiah)—Asahel's son; Abital's stepson; Zerry's grandson

Zelek—Maakah's personal guard; an Ammonite; one of David's Mighty Men

Zerry (Zeruiah)—mother of Joab, Abishai, and Asahel; David's half sister

Zippor—Maakah's chamber guard; Geshurite escort

Zulat—Maakah's nursemaid since birth

*Characters with an asterisk beside their names are mentioned in the story, but they don't appear in the story.

Characters in **BOLD** are fictional.

NOTE TO READER

Second Samuel 3:2–5 introduces us to the women who bore David's first six sons while he reigned in Hebron for seven years—two years over Judah and seven years over all of Israel. Because the Bible focuses more on David's reign *after* he conquers Jerusalem, I wanted to explore David's life *before* he reigned in Jerusalem. In a four-book series called KING DAVID'S BRIDES, we'll meet all six women: Ahinoam, Abigail, Maakah, Haggith, Abital, and Eglah.

I began researching these underappreciated women in David's world and launched Book #1 of KING DAVID'S BRIDES in October 2024, *Brave: The Story of Ahinoam. Brave* introduces both Ahinoam and Abigail and gently eases us into a culture in which David, a man after God's own heart, would have broken God's law.

He must not take many wives, or his heart will be led astray.

Deuteronomy 17:17a

For today's reader, multiple wives can be an emotional trigger. Some women—and men—have been betrayed by a spouse and find David's sin too great and God's grace too freely given.

My biggest challenge when writing biblical FICTION is to remain 100 percent accurate to the Bible's Truth, and it's the one rule I guard with the most zeal. The Bible says Ahinoam, Abigail, Maakah, Haggith, Abital, and Eglah bore David six sons while he ruled in Hebron for seven years.

But why did he marry them? Was it love or lust? Was it to rescue them or an obligation to produce sons for a king's household?

The Bible doesn't tell us—nor did any resources available to me.

When there are few historical details (in biblical or academic resources), I have the joy and privilege of *imagining* David's and these obscure women's motivations for marrying. From the time David, his army, and their families fled from Saul at the Hill of Hakilah, to his escape to Gath/Ziklag, to the whole camp's transition to Hebron where David is anointed as Judah's king—I get to use clues in Scripture, archaeological findings, and some good ol' imagination to write these four books about David's marriages to these six women.

Some will ask, "No, but really—why did David marry six women?" Honestly, there is no definitive answer. David's and his wives' emotions and/or motivations—and even how much they knew of God's Law at this time—it's all a guess.

What we do know is the Truth from God's heart through the prophet Samuel when he levied Yahweh's judgment on King Saul. Remember, this prophecy was likely spoken *before* God knitted David together in his mother's womb:

> Your kingdom will not endure; the LORD has sought out a man after his own heart and appointed him ruler of his people, because you have not kept the LORD's command.
>
> 1 Samuel 13:14

Keep in mind that I'm writing a *novel*, not an academic report. In *Brave*, David's motivation to marry a second wife (Abigail) **seemed**

like Yahweh was in favor of David marrying Nabal's widow to provide for her (and her maids) and become their *protector*. You're reading the thoughts and desires from David's and Abigail's point of view, how *they* interpret God's will.

In the book you're about to read, David and his wives will meet a Geshurite princess. Again, David, Ahinoam, Abigail, and (spoiler alert) Princess Maakah will find a way emotionally, spiritually, and practically for Yahweh to confirm that David should marry the Geshurite princess.

But would God ever approve of breaking His own Law (Deut. 17:17)?

Surely not . . . would He?

The series, KING DAVID'S BRIDES, is a single story published in four books. With each novel, you'll see how each new bride brings conviction and more understanding that their own hearts may have misinterpreted Yahweh's intention for them because their own desires led them astray. This heart-searching conviction becomes the central issue of Book #3, *Loyal: The Story of Haggith*. Haggith, the daughter of Hebron's chief priest, has memorized the entire five books of God's Law. She's disappointed in Hebron's priests, including her father, when the whole nation of Judah anoints a lawbreaker as Judah's king. When she publicly snubs David and his three wives, the royal household is forced to seriously search their hearts.

What if they did misunderstand Yahweh's will for them, and their marriages broke God's Law? What should they do to make it right—after Nomy has a son and Abigail is already pregnant? Have you ever gotten in the middle of the creek and realized God didn't give you a paddle?

On the other hand, David was the LORD's chosen king. Did he have a special exemption from some laws because he had a 1-800-GOD phone to speak more directly with Yahweh than anyone else? I don't believe God would ever justify sin. For those who have read my earlier books, I hope you remain confident that biblical accuracy is nonnegotiable.

Can we set aside our twenty-first-century queasiness when David and his two wives *think* they hear Yahweh's approval for David to marry "many" wives? Can we also agree that the repercussions of sin don't always come immediately after the sin?

Read 2 Samuel 3:22ff to count the awful consequences David's household faces right before and after he conquers Jerusalem. David's and his wives' lifelong family woes can be directly linked to his early marriages.

LORD, save us from justifying our sins by finding ways to reshape Your perfect will into our own misshapen, earthly desires.

Follow me, now, out of the twenty-first century, and let's immerse ourselves in the Truth, facts, and fiction of David's life. To prepare your heart and mind, read 1 Samuel 27 through 2 Samuel 2:7, and come with me to the land of the Philistines.

Over a year ago, David, Ahinoam, Abigail, and David's army of six hundred men with all their families fled the Judean wilderness and now live under the protection of Gath's King Achish. David has been so successful in raiding outlying villages and returning plunder to Gath's king that Achish gives David and his camp the Philistine town of Ziklag—and appointed David governor. But life is never as simple as it seems . . .

PROLOGUE
DAVID

In those days the Philistines gathered their forces to fight against Israel. Achish said to David, "You must understand that you and your men will accompany me in the army." David said, "Then you will see for yourself what your servant can do." Achish replied, "Very well, I will make you my bodyguard for life."

1 Samuel 28:1–2

Sivan (May), 1010 BC
Ziklag, Philistine Territory

My wives, as different as the sun and moon, had each been as essential to me as those lights in the sky during our sixteen months in Philistia. Ahinoam stood two paces away. Those who knew her softer side called her *Nomy*, and I knew her scowl and crossed arms meant she was afraid.

"How can you follow King Achish into battle against Israel?" she snapped. "Against people you'll one day rule?" Her voice broke. She lifted her chin, swiped at her eyes, and waited for my answer.

It didn't matter that we'd discussed the matter privately a dozen times. My sister Zerry had asked the same question repeatedly, as had her three sons Joab, Abishai, and Asahel. So why had my feisty wife voiced her concern publicly, moments before I led my men out of Ziklag's city gate?

Because Ahinoam bat Toren, my brave Kenite wife, wanted everyone to hear the answer Yahweh had given me last night.

After sharing a knowing look with her, I turned to meet the expectant faces of six hundred soldiers, their wives, and the families who had gathered around the central well at dawn. Their eyes felt like hundreds of tiny arrows piercing me. Could I convince them to follow when even I wasn't sure of Yahweh's reason or purpose?

Follow Me. My Good Shepherd's whisper had woken me in the night. I'd been guided by His rod and staff for nearly eight years—since the night Saul's assassins first came for me in Gibeah—long enough to know His voice.

"The LORD is on His throne," I said for all to hear. "He examines everyone on earth. Those who love violence, He hates with a passion. The LORD knows the righteous because *He* is righteous. He loves justice, and those who are upright will see His face."

Silence answered. I'd hoped for a few nods of understanding, if not approval. Dawn's amber glow revealed not only weary faces but also my men's empty eyes. We were all exhausted from constant raiding, but the wary way they looked at me now had begun two days ago.

I had arrived in Gath with a small contingent of men, going straight to King Achish's court to deliver a large amount of plunder. We'd raided another Amalekite village, but I, of course, told the king what I always said: The booty had come from the destruction of more Judean villages. After praising our willingness to see what Achish called "the larger picture," he then informed us that my entire army would accompany his troops to Aphek. We would then join the four other Philistine nations to completely destroy Israel.

I'd fallen to my knees, head bowed to conceal my horror. "I'm honored," I lied, mind reeling. How could we fight our own kinsmen? But how could we not? What other choice did I have but to continue the deception with this king who had been our only protection from King Saul?

On our trek back to Ziklag, my small contingent had traveled in silence. Though we arrived well after the night watch had begun, I gathered my Mighty Men to ask if any of them could think of a way out. That was when I realized their empty stares had become their new normal. Only the silence was new. Though we'd obeyed God's command given generations ago to Joshua and destroyed our enemies in Canaan—the Geshurites, Girzites, and Amalekites—the ceaseless killing of every man, woman, and child had darkened our souls.

But, again, we had no choice. If we left a single one of those villagers alive, they could have told Achish, and it would have been our women and children who would have died instead.

I scanned my people's haunted faces in the brightening light of dawn. "Our tortured souls prove our righteousness before God." My voice quaked as I added, "We find no pleasure in killing, my friends, but we will *always* obey God."

"God didn't tell us to fight our own people!" someone shouted over the gathering.

"Why not fight Achish?" another cried.

Scattered grumbles rolled like a wave among the throng, and Joab leapt to the top of the well, startling the dissenters to a hush. "The King of Gath has given us this city, its surrounding grain fields, and orchards," he reminded them. "Would you like to return to the wilderness and survive on broom-tree broth and less than a cup of water per day for your family?"

I motioned him off the well, nodding my thanks. However, hearing Joab's fears pierced my heart. Had it really been Achish who saved us? Was it really my deceptions that had won his favor? *Forgive me, Yahweh.* I'd become too dependent on a Philistine king and attributed Yahweh's protection to merely human efforts.

"Under whose authority do I serve?" Wide eyes met my query. "I've acted as if I'm under King Achish's authority and relegated Yahweh's power to mere prayers at waking, meals, and bedtime. Well, no more!" The sounds of rustling stirred my whole camp. "I am a man under Yahweh's authority, and *He* hasn't yet commanded me to engage the Philistines in battle. I truly believe when we join the Philistine armies in battle against Israel, we will see a miracle on the scale of how God fought for Joshua and the Israelites."

"How can Yahweh expect our husbands to completely destroy the Canaanites in our Land when even Joshua and our ancestors couldn't do it?" This from Joab's wife, Vered, who always spoke her mind. My general lowered his head, unwilling as usual to correct his outspoken wife.

Ahinoam stepped between Vered and me like a shield. "Think of the generations of innocent Israelites who could have been saved if Joshua and the Israelites who wandered that desert for forty years had obeyed God's command. But obedience seemed too hard, God's commands too harsh."

"And it's still too harsh," Vered snapped.

"The LORD is on His throne," I thundered back at the presumptuous woman. "And with His eternal view of past, present, *and* future, He's far more equipped to determine justice than you or I." When she drew a breath to argue, I turned my attention to my men. "We march with the Philistines and watch for a miracle. Yahweh's king obeys His commands, trusting His righteousness and steadfast love to guide His reasons."

Silence met the sunrise, and I looked to Asahel, my youngest nephew, for support. "Do you trust Yahweh?" I asked.

"I do." He kept a possessive hand on his son's shoulder.

"And why do you fight for Yahweh?" I asked, coaxing him with a grin.

He inhaled a deep breath and bellowed his declaration. "Because my obedience helps save my children's future!" His son, Zebadiah, danced and clapped, spreading his excitement.

I shouted over the rising noise. "I would not choose a life of violence, but I will always choose to obey our God." Hoisting my sword overhead, I shouted, "For Yahweh!"

My nephews and captains gave a hearty war cry, and a few others joined them. Others drew their families close and still avoided my gaze. I opened my arms, beckoning Nomy and Abigail to nestle at my sides. As the noise settled into sad good-byes, a low hum snagged my attention.

Then, with the practiced resonance of a Levite anointed to worship, Amasai sang the words of a familiar chorus. "I keep my eyes always on the LORD. With Him at my right hand, I will not be shaken." The captain of my Mighty Men often led us in worship, and this morning, his loud, clear voice was more soothing than birdsong. Men's bass rumble added low tones while the women's lilting harmonies set the children to dancing.

Our wives had sacrificed much to keep their families strong during our years of fleeing Saul in Judah's wilderness. When Yahweh revealed that Saul would indeed kill me if we remained within Israel's borders, my men and their families followed to Philistia, leaving behind everyone and everything they knew.

Abigail, tall and willowy, slipped her arm around my waist and captured my gaze. "Nomy and I trust Yahweh to bring you home safely."

Nomy, petite but full of fight, turned my chin toward her. "You'd better come home safely." Placing her free hand on her rounded belly, she added, "Abigail and I don't intend to raise your son alone."

I pulled them both into a ferocious hug. Nomy had miscarried our first baby last year, and Abigail had taken the loss as if it were her own child. All of us poured out our weeping and groaning before the God who both gives and takes away. So when the Lord opened Nomy's womb for the second time, Abigail seemed as delighted as the woman who carried my child. Though Abigail's womb remained empty, these two women loved each other as sisters and allowed me to love each of them wholeheartedly. It seemed to me another of Yahweh's miracles—akin to the Red Sea's parting.

Nomy used the cloak draped over my shoulder to wipe her tears and runny nose.

"Stop that!" Abigail handed her a cloth from her waist belt.

Nomy waved away the offering. "I don't need it now."

With a good-natured huff, Abigail tucked the cloth back into her belt.

The two shared a grin, and my chest ached at the thought of leaving them for so long. Achish had said we'd meet with the other Philistine kings and their four armies at Aphek, which was a three-day march from Ziklag. They anticipated another day or two to reach the Jezreel Valley, where the battle would likely take place.

"We could be gone as long as a month if we're involved in the cleanup." A knot lodged in my throat. *Yahweh, please protect Jonathan.* Saul's crown prince had been kinder to me than any of my brothers and as dear as my closest kin.

Nomy held my face between work-callused hands. "Jonathan is Israel's best warrior. He'll be fine. You must concentrate on protecting *yourself*." She often could read my thoughts. It was sometimes annoying, but this time it was comforting. "If you must fight," she continued, "don't hesitate. Use spear and sling at a distance. Let the larger warriors fight hand-to-hand with sword and dagger." My Kenite wife was a better military strategist than my captains and the best dagger thrower in camp.

Thankfully, she no longer begged to fight beside me. When she conceived, the realization came that she could serve our army best by working the metal forges as her abba, Toren the Kenite, had taught her. They'd forged every blade our army carried.

I realized she was trembling and opened my arms to offer comfort if she wanted it. She came willingly, my little warrior. I heard her sniffing. "I'll be all right," I murmured.

She only nodded. Nomy hated to cry—hated even more when anyone saw her crying.

Before she could wipe her nose on my shoulder again, I nudged her forward and lifted her chin. "While the men are gone, you must keep the women's throwing skills sharp. You've made them as capable at wielding a blade as most farmers."

"Our women could best any farmer." She gave me a rueful smile, and I laughed with my sassy wife.

Too quickly, we were interrupted by nine quick shofar blasts— the official call to arms. Abigail's breath caught, and Nomy's eyes widened.

"Take care of each other," I told them.

Abigail offered Nomy the cloth from her belt. This time she took it and ran toward our stacked-stone home. Abigail remained. I knew she would. I brushed her cheek, silently thanking her.

When I turned away, I left behind all tenderness. My muscles tightened. My focus narrowed to a single truth. To stay alive, I must only be David ben Jesse, Yahweh's anointed. Forget all else.

I walked away from the families, through my army, and toward the gate. Joab called the men to ranks. The Three fell in step behind me, and the Mighty Men led their contingents in groups of twenty. I had barely marched a hundred paces beyond Ziklag's gate when my heart betrayed me and I glanced over my shoulder.

Abigail was standing at the gate. Of course she was. We kept marching. I kept looking back. Abigail remained until the distance pulled her beneath the horizon. Abigail needed to experience everything, the best and worst Yahweh gave us. Nomy needed to process hard things alone, and she loved more fiercely than anyone I'd ever known.

My wives. So very different. And I loved them both.

Lord God, be our Shield until we're together again.

PART I

The Philistines gathered all their forces at Aphek, and Israel camped by the spring in Jezreel. As the Philistine rulers marched with their units of hundreds and thousands, David and his men were marching at the rear with Achish . . . But the Philistine commanders were angry with Achish and said, "[David] must not go with us into battle, or he will turn against us during the fighting." So Achish called David and said to him, "As surely as the LORD lives, you have been reliable, and I would be pleased to have you serve with me in the army . . . but the rulers don't approve of you. Now turn back and go in peace; do nothing to displease the Philistine rulers . . ." So David and his men got up early in the morning to go back to the land of the Philistines, and the Philistines went up to Jezreel.

1 Samuel 29:1–2, 4, 6–7, 11

ONE

MAAKAH

Ner was the father of Kish, Kish the father of Saul, and Saul the father of Jonathan, Malki-Shua, Abinadab and Esh-Baal.

1 Chronicles 8:33

Sivan (May), 1010 BC

The girl in the mirror wasn't fit for a prince, not even King Saul's fourth-born. Staring at my drab reflection in the body-length polished bronze, the future of our Geshurite kingdom weighed heavy on my shoulders. "What if Prince Esh-Baal rejects me, Zulat?"

My maid stopped humming and looked up from packing our wooden trunk. "Prince Esh-Baal likely had no more choice than you did in the betrothal. Kings make those decisions to secure peace and power. A woman's power is strengthened when she brings pleasure to her husband, and Asherah's priestesses have trained you to do so."

I examined my reflection again. "The high priestess said, 'Women love with their hearts and men with their eyes.' Esh-Baal's eyes will not love a dowdy princess devoid of cosmetics who wears peasant's clothes."

"Those clothes will keep you safe," Zulat said, then looked over

29

my shoulder into the polished bronze. "Remember what your ima and I have taught you: 'Royalty is born, not worn.' Your prince will see your beauty soon enough, and then you'll do as every shrewd wife does. Allow him to believe he's in control, then slip a gold ring in his nose and lead him wherever you desire." With a tap on my nose, she added, "Focus on our new home. In five days our caravan will reach Gibeah, and you'll sit at King Saul's table as his honored guest."

"Or I'll skulk back to Geshur after his son rejects me."

"Stop that." Zulat turned my shoulders to face her. "Israel needs this alliance as much as Geshur. Israel needs our favor to send their trade goods through Damascus, and whoever wins Israel's favor controls the trade routes between Egypt and the East. A treaty with Israel strengthens our position among the other Aramean nations."

I fought the urge to roll my eyes. "It's barely dawn, Zulat. Too early for a lesson. Let's just say I'll be amazed if the marriage actually happens." *Especially considering Kepha died in battle only two weeks before we were wed.*

My longtime maid could see through my words and into the window of my soul. "How can you still be afraid to hope? It's been six years, Prin."

Shame sent a flame up my neck and into my face. "Why would I fear to hope? Simply because Prince Kepha chose to go to war and get himself killed rather than marry me?"

"No one chooses to die in battle. Any man, no matter how brave or skilled, is in danger on a battlefield." Waving away my emotions, she returned to her packing.

Again swallowing the pain—as fresh as it still felt six years later—I tried to tamp down thoughts of Kepha and returned my attention to the mirror's reflection. I looked worse than a kitchen maid in our palace. Kepha wouldn't even recognize me. No matter how hard I tried, the memories of him were everywhere and always haunting.

30

I'd been infatuated with the Damascus prince since childhood. I was barely twelve harvests old when he was declared a great warrior. He was only sixteen.

I watched for him at the annual Aramean harvest festivals and could hardly tear my eyes away when I found him among the other princes. When he was eighteen harvests old, broad-shouldered and wearing a golden jeweled crown, he caught me staring. Rather than the snide squint I expected from such a god among men, his mouth curved into an appreciative smile.

I'd quickly looked away, hoping none of the royalty in the crowded hall had noticed our exchange. Likely, everyone else was too busy enjoying Baal's priests and Asherah's priestesses sacrificing their firstfruits of harvest. Why did I suddenly feel embarrassed by the intimacy of their worship? I stole another glance at the handsome prince. This time, he was whispering something to his abba and mine. The men laughed together, and after all three gave a curt nod, both kings turned toward the crowd and clapped their hands, halting the celebration.

The Damascene king announced, "My son, Prince Kepha, has asked to begin betrothal negotiations with King Talmai in order to marry his daughter, Princess Maakah. It is our hope that such a union will strengthen the bonds of Damascus and Geshur, thereby increasing the power of our entire Aramean empire." The gathering erupted in applause while I covered a gasp.

I could only stare as Kepha left his family table and walked straight toward where I sat with Ima on the royal women's elevated dais. With three long strides, he bounded from the floor to the platform—skipping the three steps—and knelt before me while cradling my right hand between his. "If you agree to begin nego-tiations," he whispered to only me, "then I will visit you regularly in Geshur so we won't feel like strangers on our wedding night." His lips brushed the back of my hand, which somehow made my heart race yet calmed many fears. I had no words but emphatically nodded my approval. The whole banquet hall had erupted in celebration.

For three months, he'd made weekly visits to Geshur's palace. My training with the priestesses to ensure I knew how to please a husband increased, but the tenderness Kepha displayed during his visits seemed to contradict the lessons from the power-hungry priestesses, my ima, and Zulat. Could the two women who taught me all I knew of life be wrong about how to love *my* husband-to-be?

During Kepha's last visit, he'd said, "In one month's time, as soon as our Damascene troops quash the Syrophoenician uprising, I'll make you my bride."

So I waited. A week. Then two. On the twenty-third day after Kepha left me, Abba barged into my chamber, his face crimson with rage. "Your prince got himself killed! What sort of imbecile dies two weeks before his wedding?" He picked up an Egyptian vase and threw it against the wall, then marched out of my chamber.

The next day, when I appeared in Abba's courtroom for my daily lesson on judicial wisdom, my eyes were puffy and red-rimmed. Abba and Ima asked why I appeared out of sorts, and I'd barely spoken Kepha's name when they ordered me out of the courtroom. "Return when you've regained your royal composure," Ima said.

I fled the throne room, and when Zulat finally returned to my chamber, her knuckles were swollen and bleeding. "I've taken the beating for your lapse in royal behavior—as I always do." She straightened her spine and looked down her button nose. "The Damascene king has refused to offer another prince in Kepha's stead."

"I don't want another . . ." Emotion overwhelmed me.

"Good, good," Zulat said. "If you so much as mention Prince Kepha's name or shed another tear on his behalf in your parents' presence, I will be beaten again."

"Am I to forget he existed?" I shouted. "Can my heart forget how to beat?"

"Tears show weakness. If you must grieve, Prin, speak of him only to me."

Since that day, I'd seldom spoken his name—not even to Zulat. Yet Kepha still haunted my dreams. Studying the peasant girl in my mirror, I think he would have loved me even in this drab robe. "Perhaps the gods will send Esh-Baal to war before we marry."

Zulat slammed the trunk lid closed and stood to face me. "I should hope you'll never say such a thing outside these walls, Princess Maakah. You're Geshur's only hope."

Unfortunately, she was right. I was considered an old maid at twenty harvests and was Abba's only political bargaining power as Geshur's royal heir. But our nation's hope for an influential marriage had begun to wane. The betrothal to Esh-Baal was like piercing the bloated carcass of a long-dead camel. Though it relieved the building pressure, it also released a humiliating stench since my bridegroom was a fourth-born, second-generation donkey farmer who had refused to personally come to Geshur and escort me back to his home in Gibeah.

"I know leaving Geshur for the first time is frightening." Zulat placed a hand on my shoulder. "And every bride is nervous about that first—"

"I'm not afraid." I rushed toward the door, refusing to stir more emotions before my farewell to Abba and Ima. "It's well past sunrise, and I'm tired of waiting for Abba's summons to the throne room." I flung open the door, startling my chamber guards. Nodding curtly, I marched past them, trying not to think about this being my last journey down the harem hallway.

"Princess Maakah!" Zulat's angry tone halted me, but I refused to face her. "You will not enter the throne room uninvited."

"Sometimes you forget I'm no longer a child in your care. Can you

Noble

think of anything more important to Geshur than my betrothal?" I stared straight ahead, waiting for an answer from the tutor who had taught me of national politics. "Well? Can you think of *anything more important?*"

"Yes—*you.*"

I wanted to scream. *If I'm so important, why did Abba promise me to a fourth-born prince?* Instead, I resumed the hurried pace down the hall, determination driving me to the hardest farewell of my life.

Winding through the palace hallways, I approached the throne room and noted Abba's guards widening their stance. "Princess Maakah," said the ranking officer. "King Talmai has ordered that we allow no one to enter until he and Queen Raziah resolve a difficult matter."

With regal calm, I threatened deadly consequences. "My caravan waits to leave for Gibeah. How will King Talmai punish you if you're the reason for my late arrival in Israel, my canceled betrothal, and our ruined peace treaty?" I paused only long enough to lift an eyebrow. "My abba keeps no secrets from me. Open those doors immediately."

"Yes, Your Highness." The guard nodded to his partner, and they swung open the cedar doors.

I crossed the threshold, victorious, and only then heard Abba's angry voice. He'd descended the dais and stood with his back to the doors, face-to-face with a dust-covered messenger. The other man spoke Hebrew—the language of my soon-to-be husband—which I'd learned in order to rule and trade. Before I could interpret his words, Abba reached for his sword and swung backhanded. The man's eyes widened as a glint of bronze approached his neck. Then a terrible shoosh. Then a thud when his head hit the floor. His body slumped at Abba's feet. Blood poured out—a river of it—flowing over and between the mosaic tiles.

Abba spit on the dead man. Only when he lifted his head did he turn and see me.

I covered a sob. Swallowed back the gorge in my throat.

He flung his sword across the floor. "Maakah, come to me."

His open arms beckoned, but I couldn't move. I glanced at Ima, still on the elevated dais and seated on her small throne. She said nothing. Rather, with only a raised brow, she demanded, *Remember your training!* How many times had she staunched my tears or calmed a tantrum with the same silent stare? I was born royal, yes, but I would remain royal only by the same iron will.

"Maakah." Abba commanded my attention.

I looked at him again, this violent stranger.

He walked toward me, hands extended. "We have much to discuss." He looked like a monster, blood dripping from his beard.

"Wipe your face!" I stepped back and bumped into Zulat.

Cradling me in arms meant to both comfort and control, she whispered, "You must obey our king."

Abba stopped two paces before me, suddenly examining his blood-stained hand and chest. He pulled a cloth from his belt, wiped himself clean, and tossed his soiled cloth and breastplate aside. When he focused on me again, the slight crease between his brows forecast the gentleness in his voice. "You're trembling, little one. Let me hold you."

There he was. My protector. My champion. The dripping proof of the violent stranger wiped away, I fell against his muscled chest. Here was the safe place I'd found refuge from many storms. These were the arms that comforted me after Ima's miscarriages. His were the tender words that patiently corrected my frequent missteps as a princess learning Geshur's rules of law and social justice.

"Azam." Abba quietly addressed his captain over my head.

"Yes, my king?"

"Didn't I specifically say *no one* was to enter this room until my business with Saul's messenger was concluded?"

Noble

"You did, my king."

"You will execute the guards who allowed my daughter to enter."

"Abba, no!" I pushed away. "It was my fault."

He frowned. "Did you physically overpower the two guards at the throne room doors?"

"No, but—"

"Then my guards chose to disobey me. Their choice was not your fault." His small black eyes bored into mine. I looked away, ceding the battle to my king.

The captain's sandals made no sound as he strode toward the door. No one could save the guards I'd convinced to disobey. My regret bowed to birthright, and I embraced my royal acquittal: *Their choice was not your fault.*

So why did I feel as if I'd just killed two good men?

A commotion near the dais brought me back to the moment. Two royal guards dragged the dead messenger toward the throne room's side door, where four maids entered with buckets and rags to wash away the mess. Everyone seemed so proficient, as if their tasks were a common occurrence. With gut-twisting recollection, I recalled the many times before I'd been denied entry into this throne room.

How many people had lost their heads in King Talmai's court? How naïve I'd been to tell those poor guards my abba kept no secrets from me. Such a gullible princess would make a poor political bride.

Political bride? My breath caught. "Abba, did you say that man was King Saul's messenger?"

"He was." Abba held my gaze, allowing silence to dismantle my future.

I choked out a dry laugh, then glanced at Ima on her throne and back at the madman who beheaded King Saul's messenger. "Should I assume my betrothal to Prince Esh-Baal is now canceled?"

He produced a small scroll from his belt. "The messenger delivered King Saul's betrothal termination, so I thanked him for doing his duty."

"You killed a man simply for delivering a message?"

"Saul would have expected it and likely sent someone disposable."

His smile chilled my blood. I stepped away and whispered, "King Saul canceled the betrothal before he even saw me?"

Abba brushed my cheek. "You still haven't learned, Prin. Your marriage will never be based on your beauty or companionship. You are the tip of Geshur's sword and will lead your nation to greatness by your ability to manipulate the husband we choose." A slight grin curved his lips before he extended his hand toward the dais. "Let's join your ima to discuss our new plan."

"Come, Prin." Ima beckoned with an outstretched hand, wiggling her fingers as if I were a toddler learning to walk. Her perfectly applied cosmetics starkly contrasted her pallor. Was she ill? Or was she equally horrified at the violence and Abba's sterilized thoughts on marriage? Of course I knew my role as Geshur's only heir, but Abba had never described my life so austerely.

I ascended the few steps and sat on the plush tapestry between my parents' thrones. Examining Ima's pale features, I asked, "Are you well?"

"As well as any ima whose daughter is leaving today."

I turned to Abba. "I'm still going to Gibeah?"

"Of course not." He waved a dismissive hand where the dead messenger had lain, then handed me the small scroll from his belt. "In the interest of time, I'll summarize King Saul's message. The scroll says King Saul broke the betrothal out of concern for your safety during Israel's tumultuous time. He and his troops have already marched to the Jezreel Valley to battle the Philistines. His oldest three sons lead Israel's army, but his fourth-born coward was left to rule at the palace in Gibeah. However, my spies say

Noble

Saul broke the betrothal because he feared offending his priests and a dead prophet named Samuel. Yahweh's priests warned him that marrying a pagan princess would offend their invisible god. So, in hopes of appeasing them all, Saul canceled the betrothal and removed *Baal* from Prince Esh-Baal's name, now calling him, Ish-Bosheth." Abba leaned forward with a sneer. "Saul should have feared offending me because soon his fourth-born son shall be called *dead*."

My mouth was suddenly dry, realizing again the level of violence my abba was capable of.

"You deserve a warrior, my beautiful girl." He leaned back and exchanged a glance with Ima. "Our lovely girl will marry a man favored by all gods and many nations; a man who fights with the Philistines against Saul's weak leadership. You will marry David ben Jesse—the *next* king of Israel."

I recoiled. "You want me to marry an outlaw?"

"A *warrior*," he said sternly. "David ben Jesse is shrewd and worthy of a throne. He's avoided Saul's capture for years and won the favor of your *dohd*, King Achish."

Ima laid a hand on my shoulder, gently coaxing my attention. "My brother isn't an easy man to impress. Yet even after David ben Jesse killed Achish's champion, Goliath, several years ago, this Hebrew has somehow won my brother's trust."

"Your dohd Achish made David the governor of Ziklag." Abba tilted his head, features softening with the familiar tenderness saved only for Ima and me. "If this David has the courage and charisma to win Achish's approval, I believe he might even win your heart, Prin. So I sent a messenger with the betrothal proposal shortly after Saul's messenger arrived."

"Without my consent?" I turned to Ima for support. "David ben Jesse has no royal blood, and worse, no loyalty. He fights with the Philistines and betrays his homeland."

Her coloring still looked gray. "A betrothal to Israel's next king is better than a marriage to a royal coward."

"It's decided." Abba pounded the arm of his throne. "David has already marched north with the Philistine army. Our messenger will wait south of Jezreel until the battle is over. My spies say the Philistines will place David on Israel's throne when the Philistines destroy King Saul and his successors. In the meantime, my best guards will escort your caravan to one of our Geshurite villages in the southern kingdom, where you'll wait for David to return to his home in Ziklag."

"I'm going to the southern kingdom?" The thought of it soothed today's unrest. "Have you instructed the caravan leader which village we're to visit first, or may I decide?"

Abba grinned, revealing the single dimple at the top of his beard on his left cheek. "If you're to be Israel's queen, you must begin to rule."

I leaned up to kiss that dimple and tried to suppress a squeal. It had been nearly ten years since I'd seen the governor's family. "Alannah is probably married with children of her own by now." She'd been my favorite friend in Geshur before she and several other noblemen's families traveled into Dohd Achish's territory to expand Geshur's influence under Philistine protection.

"While you're waiting, you must do more than just visit with friends." Abba's dimple disappeared. "We've had reports that some of our southern villages have been attacked, probably by Amalekites, which is likely the reason their tribute payments have lapsed. You will summon the elders from each village and demand an accounting. Whatever their explanation, you must decide which is deserved—punishment or mercy—and then dispense it judiciously. Understood?"

"Yes, Abba." The responsibility felt like a sack of grain on each shoulder.

"After David ben Jesse has been anointed Israel's king and agrees to marry you, Achish will order him to fetch you from our southern villages. Israel's new king will recognize the brilliant work you've done with our southern villages and most likely declare you Israel's queen before your wedding week has ended."

Israel's queen. The title was a balm over my trepidation. I glanced at Ima again. Her pallor was more than concerning. "Are you sure you're all right?"

She exchanged an unreadable look with Abba. He nodded, and she smiled at me. "I'm with child, Prin."

Fear shot through me. "You're . . . No!" Her last miscarriage nearly took her life. "I can't leave until I know you're safe."

She cupped my chin. "You'll leave as planned and without argument. Your marriage to David ben Jesse will secure Geshur's trade and strengthen our role among the Aramean nations." She leaned forward and kissed my forehead. "Remember, royal blood means kingdom first—always."

When she leaned back, Abba reached for her hand and gave it an affectionate squeeze. "If we have a son," he said, returning his attention to me, "I'll have an heir to the throne. If we have a second daughter, you and David ben Jesse will inherit Geshur's throne."

More unknowns. And Ima's pregnancy had been another secret they'd kept from me. I stood, bowed, and etched my parents' hopeful faces into my memory. "I love you," I said, turning quickly so as not to be disappointed when they didn't reply. My parents had never spoken of their love for me. Knowing it was true had always been enough.

I walked on wobbly legs out of the palace, and Zulat steadied me as we descended the long staircase toward the grand entry. The morning air carried with it the freshwater scent of Yam Kinneret. I would miss Asherah's sacred sea amid our southern kingdom's arid lands. Though I'd never traveled beyond the walls of Geshur and my future felt as if I were grasping smoke, by the gods, I would make Geshur proud.

TWO

MAAKAH

Now the Amalekites had raided the Negev and Ziklag.

1 Samuel 30:1

I remained huddled inside my tent, shaking uncontrollably as dawn succumbed to morning sun and the sounds of death stilled. Zulat had commanded me to stay hidden no matter what I heard. *"And don't you dare look through the flaps."* She'd said it right before marching into the chaos. Would those be the last words I'd hear her speak? Who had attacked us, and why? I reached for the palm-sized clay goddess beneath my lamb's wool headrest and clenched it in white-knuckled fear.

The sickening sound of fist hitting flesh came just before the victim fell hard, jostling my tent flap open enough to see—

"Zulat!" I lunged to cradle her battered face.

A stick drew aside one flap of my shelter, revealing a muscular man wearing a braided red headscarf and a patch over one eye. I skittered backward. The tent collapsed on me, and as I fought to free myself, uproarious merriment turned my fear to fury. Finally pushing the offending tent aside, I found myself surrounded by a circle of marauders—well over a hundred men. The man with the

41

eye patch, presumably their leader, was now seated on a foldable wood-and-canvas stool. Zulat sat in the dust at his feet, her hands and feet bound. Her face was bruised and swollen, and they'd placed a gag in her mouth.

"What have you done?" I scurried toward my maid. "She's just an old woman!"

The chieftain kicked dust in my face, blinding me for the moment. "And you're not merely a peasant." He spoke in perfect Aramaic, the language of trade. Zulat whimpered, and I looked up through stinging eyes to see our captor yank her head back and speak through gritted teeth. "You lied to me, old woman. I knew a peasant girl and an old woman wouldn't travel with fifty soldiers." He shoved her away. I tried to catch her since she couldn't break her fall, but before my arms could capture her, I was propped on my knees in front of the despicable leader.

I tried to bite the rough hands that held me, but my neck was suddenly surrounded by huge arms that cut off all breath. I kicked and flailed, scratching at immovable flesh. More laughing stoked my fury, but I felt life seeping out of me.

"Release her!" I heard a voice from the edge of consciousness.

On my side now, I blinked away the darkness, I tried to rise on hands and knees but fell on my side. When I opened my eyes, I was looking at the blank face of a dead man—a Geshurite soldier. Trying to scoot away, I became too dizzy and fell again, tripping over another dead Geshurite. More raucous laughter came. I lifted my head, squinting, and realized our whole escort was lying in the dust. Dead. All of them.

My fight was spent. I lay on my back, tears washing the dust from my eyes. I watched the sky spin. Surely this was a dream, a nightmare.

Callused hands lifted, carried, and dropped me at the chieftain's feet. He leaned over me and smiled, revealing two missing front teeth and breath worse than Abba's gassy horse. "A peasant woman would never fight her captors." He wagged his finger as if I'd done something wrong. "You're royalty, and the old woman is likely your maid. She lied, and I won't abide a liar."

"Do you abide traitors?" My wits were rattled but steady enough to defend Zulat. Rolling to my knees, I sat back on my heels. He scowled, which I interpreted as confusion. "My maid lied because she feared for my life. Only a coward would have told the truth and betrayed her mistress. Surely even an Amalekite respects a loyal liar more than a spineless traitor."

He chuckled, scratching his bearded chin, and grinned up at the younger man standing beside him. "She's regal *and* shrewd. This one will be mine tonight and yours tomorrow."

"What? No!" I tried to stand, but two large men shoved me back to my knees. I fell forward, bracing myself with my hands, and kept my head bowed to hide tears. "Forgive me, my lord, but ruining me would be a mistake."

"Oh really?" More laughter. He was a jolly scoundrel. "Explain how bedding a lovely young woman could be a mistake? You would produce handsome Amalekite princes."

Overcome by nausea, I swallowed and steadied my voice. "Royalty runs through both branches of my family tree. I'm King Talmai's only heir and King Achish's niece. Return me unsullied and receive a ransom from both the Geshurites and the Philistines. Ruin me, and neither will pay for my return."

No laughing this time. Not a sound. I lifted my head to venture a glance at my captor and his lieutenant. Both stared at me like hungry jackals. I quickly lowered my head again, terror sending uncontrolled shivers through me. Where had I dropped my goddess? Could she hear me still? *Asherah, goddess of love and war, spare me from this degradation. Give me a warrior's heart and mind to protect myself and Zulat.*

Noble

Could I kill a man if given the chance? Kepha had killed many, yet he was as gentle and kind a man as I'd ever known. Abba's violence against the messenger flashed across my mind. The blood had run like a river and was so quickly cleaned away. As if the messenger never existed.

Wouldn't our world be better if Amalekites no longer existed? When word of recent raids in our southern kingdom reached Geshur, I begged Abba to send troops to guard our friends. He refused, saying the total destruction of men, women, children, and livestock could only be attributed to the Amalekites, and he couldn't risk sending more troops so far from Geshur's capital city.

The loss of my people ignited my fury. *Yes, Asherah, give me strength, and I'll kill any Amalekite in my path.*

"Take them." The chieftain's gruff command interrupted my vow.

As his men dragged Zulat and me toward a camel, I spotted my little goddess and snatched her from the dust. Two men hoisted us into a sort of basket atop the one-humped beast. Surprisingly comfortable, it was filled with blankets and cushions. I quickly worked to free the gag from Zulat's mouth, which was secured around her head. Her lips were split and swollen, as were her eyebrows and cheeks. Her right eye was nearly swollen shut. I hugged her and wept.

"My wrists and ankles, Prin," she whispered.

"Oh, of course!" I released her and began untying the hemp rope, finding bloody chafe marks on both wrists and ankles. "This is all my fault," I whispered, unable to staunch the tears. "You did this to keep me safe."

"And I would do it again—a hundred times—because you're the future of Geshur."

I enfolded her in a tender hug just as the camel stood on its front legs and rolled us backward against the rear pillows. Holding on tightly to the saddle's sidewalls, we were jostled again when the beast pitched forward to stand on all four legs. The camel driver paid no heed to our awkward tossing but merely clicked his tongue to prod the animal into line behind the chieftain's one-humped mount.

Zulat and I leaned against the rear cushions and snuggled close. "Where do you think they'll take us?" I whispered.

"They're Bedouins, so they never camp in the same place for long, but I overheard the men talking after they'd tied me up. I think all Amalekite tribes are meeting at a single camp to gather their resources and plan a raid on Philistine villages while their men are fighting Israel in the north."

I glared at the despicable men who would prey on unprotected women and children. "Cowards," I hissed.

"Shhh!" Zulat chided. "Even though your assessment is accurate, they're cruel cowards—which makes them the worst kind of men. No honor to defend. No one to impress. No standard too low."

The few words seemed to exhaust her. She laid her head on my shoulder and was almost immediately snoring. As the sun approached midday, Zulat repositioned, laying her head against the cushioned sidewalls, so I laid my head in Zulat's lap like I'd done as a child. She stroked my hair, and the camel's rhythmic gait lulled me to sleep.

I slowly grew conscious of a distant revelry and lifted my head from Zulat's lap. Peering over our soft-walled saddle, I saw a vast desert stretching in every direction, and as far as my eyes could see, raucous Amalekites were singing and dancing around their tents and cook-fires. Imprisoned by a fence made of brambles on the outskirts of the camp was a holding area filled with huddled, smaller groups— none of whom were rejoicing. All were women and children. Most quietly wept.

"Don't speak a word," Zulat whispered. She'd scooted close

enough to be heard over the celebrating. "They're taking us to join the other prisoners. Don't make a fuss."

Only then did I realize that the Amalekite leading our camel had veered away from his eye-patched captain and was walking toward the bramble enclosure.

"Now is not the time to flaunt your royal heritage," she continued. "The captives are likely simple townsfolk who have lost everything. They've probably never seen a silver hairbrush or polished bronze mirror. If they realize you're royalty, those women could become as much a threat to you as the Amalekites."

A little offended, I said, "Do you think me arrogant or stupid that you must warn me of something so petty?" I sniffed back more hurt when she gave me a chiding look.

"I know you would never intentionally offend, but you've never been outside Geshur's gates, Prin. You're naïve, not stupid. Like it or not, you can't know everything at twenty that I know at sixty." She brushed my cheek. "But you're far more intelligent than any other twenty-harvest-old I've known. Don't tell your ima I said that." She winked playfully. The old woman often compared Ima and me since she'd been nursemaid, counselor, and friend to us both.

"I'll be careful." I slipped my hand into hers and was suddenly grateful that Zulat had insisted I travel in peasant's clothes. She was wise, and I became wiser when I listened to her.

A tormented howl erupted amid the prisoners, and our camel driver halted twenty paces from the guard at the bramble gate. "What's happening in there?"

"They won't move out of the way for me to see, but I think a woman is giving birth."

"Asherah help her," Zulat whispered.

"Let us down," I said to our guard. "Zulat and I can walk from here." Eyes narrowed, he examined us in the fading light. I rolled my eyes. "Do you really think this old woman and I could run faster than an Amalekite guard and survive the desert?"

When the woman howled again, I shouted, "Make your decision today, sir."

"Bah!" He tapped the camel's shoulder, and the beast rocked forward to perch on folded legs, then back. Zulat and I climbed over the saddle walls to dismount.

I linked arms with Zulat, who wiped sweat from her brow and hurried with me toward the bramble gate. The guard wore heavy leather mitts on his hands to protect against the thorny branches woven into a gate as tall as a small child and the length of a man lying on his side.

"There must be over five hundred women and children in here," Zulat whispered as we entered the crowded enclosure.

Another howl pulled us into the mass of captives. We shouldered our way through unwelcoming glares and frightened children and abruptly halted at the center, where a tight ring of women had formed a prickly gate of their own. No thorns or brambles were needed; they simply leveled deadly stares to protect their own.

I tugged Zulat forward, but she firmly held me in place. "No, Pri—Maakah." Her eyes could have drilled a hole through me. "These women don't need us to interfere."

"It's not interfering when you're the best midwife in Geshur."

"A midwife?" one of the staring women asked.

"If you're a midwife, get over here and help us," said a voice from within the impenetrable ring.

One of the women stepped aside to provide a narrow opening.

"Go!" I nudged Zulat forward. "I'm coming, too. You can show me how to help."

"This is a bad idea," she muttered but walked toward a cluster of three worried women kneeling around the exhausted ima. One woman knelt behind the laboring woman, supporting her shoulders.

Noble

A second knelt at the side, holding the pregnant woman's hand, while the third knelt between the ima's knees.

"Are you going to help or not?" asked the short-tempered one supporting the shoulders. Her hair, streaked heavily with gray, hung in sweaty clumps over her face. She lifted her shoulder to rub her hair away but never took her eyes off Zulat.

"*We* will help." Zulat nudged me toward the laboring woman's side. "Hold her other hand, Maakah. Comfort her." Zulat's terse instruction was punctuated by a whimper from the frightened ima.

Four expectant faces stared at me until the laboring woman clutched my hand, clenched her teeth, and let out an otherworldly yowl. Her grip was so crushing, I almost cried out with her.

When the pain subsided, both hers and mine, the woman kneeling between the expectant ima's legs patted my shoulder. "Well done. My name is Abigail." Then, pointing to the soon-to-be ima, she said, "This is Ahinoam, my sister-wife."

Zulat nudged Abigail aside to examine Ahinoam. My maid's face clouded with concern as expert hands pressed all sides of her belly. Ahinoam groaned, and Zulat consoled her. "Your baby is in the perfect position to be born, my lady. You'll likely meet your child before dawn."

"Dawn?" Ahinoam lifted her chin to look behind her at the woman supporting her shoulders. "Zerry, I can't. I can't do this until dawn." She drew in a breath and let it out through gritted teeth, the sound a strange mixture of growl and whine, and she squeezed my hand again.

"We do what we must to birth a child, love. You're this baby's ima. He—or she—will cause you many sleepless nights and unutterable pain. But it's also the last night you'll ever feel alone." Zerry shifted her gaze to Zulat. "What is your name?"

"I am Zulat, and my young friend is Maakah."

Zerry examined Zulat intently, taking in her bruised and bat-

48

tered face. "The raid on Ziklag started Ahinoam's labor earlier than expected. You should know she lost her first child only halfway through her first pregnancy. My brother, David, was inconsolable. You can imagine how devastating it would be for us all if we lose—" She cleared her throat and bowed her head. Sniffed. Then met Zulat's eyes again. "When David ben Jesse rescues us from the Amalekites, we must present him with his firstborn son. Do you understand, Zulat?"

Zulat glanced at me and back at Zerry. "Forgive me, but may I clarify? You're saying David ben Jesse is your brother, and this child—if a son—would one day become his crown prince."

My heartbeat sped, pounding so loudly I was certain the small gathering heard it. *David ben Jesse already has two wives—and a firstborn by dawn?*

Zerry's eyes narrowed. "You've heard of my brother? From what nation or tribe have you come?"

Ahinoam cried out, "I must push!" This time she bore down, obeying a guttural impulse that seemed to surprise even her. "Aaahooohhheeeyooowwww!" Her face turned the color of ripe grapes. Veins swelled on her forehead and neck. Her eyes bulged. All sound stopped as her arms began to shake, and her grip tightened, pulling both me and the other hand-holder toward her chest with amazing strength.

"Pull against her grip!" Zulat coaxed us. "Be her resistance!" I obeyed until the laboring ima sagged backward against Zerry's chest and waiting arms.

Both Zulat and Zerry congratulated her, encouraging Ahinoam she'd done exactly as she should. "When you feel like pushing, you push," Zerry explained. "Yahweh designed a woman's body to respond naturally to the birthing process."

Zulat rolled her eyes. "How could a male god know anything about childbirth?" she mumbled.

"Because Yahweh is the only God, who created both male and female in His image." This from quiet Abigail who sat between Zulat and me.

Only then did I notice her red-ringed eyes and cheeks wet with tears. Was she a second wife who would lose even more of David's attention now that Ahinoam was giving him a child? Or was she the first wife, who was about to lose the race of birthing David's firstborn? I leaned over to whisper, "Are you all right?"

Her eyes widened, as if no one had ever asked her the question. "Of course. I'm fine. It's Ahinoam we must—" Lips quivering, she bowed her head, undoubtedly hiding more tears.

I recognized her predicament instantly. Everyone expected Abigail to be "fine." She was placed between Ahinoam's knees because she was trustworthy, calm under pressure, and obviously a dutiful soul. How long since anyone had considered Abigail's heart? Her needs? I scooted near to her and whispered, "I hope we can become friends someday."

She nodded and sniffed, then gave me a lovely smile.

When I looked up, Zerry was watching me. I stared right back. "Where were you coming from—or going to," Zerry added, "when the Amalekites captured you and Zulat?"

"Leave her alone." Abigail came to my defense. "I believe both Zulat and Maakah are the answer to our prayer that Yahweh would bring someone to help Nomy deliver this baby."

Ahinoam groaned again, straining forward and pulling on my hand and the other woman's. When the urgent pushing passed, she relaxed against Zerry and said between heavy breaths, "Why didn't Yahweh send help while the Amalekites scaled Ziklag's walls?"

"Ahinoam!" Abigail scolded.

Zerry placed a kiss atop Ahinoam's head. "You're brave enough to say what everyone else is thinking."

I liked these women. Bold. Honest. Not afraid to challenge when a wrong is perceived—even done by their god. I turned to the woman kneeling across from me. "I didn't catch your name," I said, perhaps a little too boldly.

A kind smile softened her features. "I'm Abital, wife of Zerry's youngest son."

"The cutest child ever," Zerry inserted.

Ahinoam huffed. "Until mine is born."

The four women fell into good-natured banter followed by easy laughter that left me hungry for friendships like these. Zulat was my one and only friend. And could she be called a friend, when it was her duty to serve me?

Ahinoam's hand squeezed mine again and silenced the laughter around us. When the pain ebbed once more, the terror in her eyes drew everyone nearer even though she looked only at Abigail. "Don't let the Amalekites take my baby." She reached for her sister-wife's hand, and Abigail grabbed her wrist, as I'd seen soldiers do when making a pact. "If I die—"

"You're not going to die," Abigail said through tears.

"*If I die*," Ahinoam said, desperate and stubborn, "promise you'll never allow my child to live as a slave to Amalekites."

Abigail pulled her hand from Ahinoam's. "I'll promise no such thing," she said. "You're not going to die, and David will rescue us long before the Amalekites would ever take *our* baby." Her spine straightened with stunning courage. "You focus on delivering our healthy little bundle, sister."

Ahinoam reached for my hand again, panting and pushing through another pain. "I see the baby's head!" Zulat shouted—accompanied by a rare smile.

Ahinoam tossed her head from side to side. "David will be too late. They'll take my child."

"David will come." Abigail leaned over, holding Ahinoam's face with one hand while locking eyes with the despairing ima. "We will keep our child away from the Amalekites until our husband rescues us."

Our husband? How could Abba have promised me as a treaty bride to an outlaw with two wives? Did he know David was already married—twice? Or would my status as a third wife change Abba's plan for me to marry?

"Don't give up," Abigail whispered. "Only you can rally our women, but first you must believe Yahweh will send David to rescue us before these animals ruin our friends *and* their children."

"Abigail." Ahinoam paused, sweat dripping off ringlets of brown hair. "Think about the timing. David and our army probably haven't even reached the battlefield yet. The war could take longer than the normal forty days, not to mention their weeklong trek back to Ziklag. By then the Amalekites may have moved their camp. How will David ever find us? It's impossible."

"So was living in the desert for six years," Abigail said. "So was our escape from Israel to Gath and King Achish's favor. So is our love for each other and sharing the same husband. If we prayed only for the possible, how would we experience Yahweh's steadfast love?" She patted her sister-wife's hand. "Believe with me: David. Will. Come."

A commotion behind us drew my attention. The ring of women had linked arms and tightened our security.

"My master said I'm to deliver this bread only to David's wives, no one else."

"How do we know you aren't carrying a weapon?" one of the women asked.

"If I carried a weapon, it would have been buried in an Amalekite, and I would be dead."

"I like that one," Zerry said. "Let her in."

The protective ring parted ever so slightly, and a feral-looking young woman squeezed through with a tray of crusty bread. About my age and younger than the women of David's family, the woman needed a bath and a spritz of scented oil. Her hair hung loose in slender braids, decorated with feathers and beads. She wore a ring in her nose, likely declaring the master to whom she belonged.

As she approached David's family, she squinted through the darkness and halted abruptly. "Mistress Zeruiah?" Then, studying the laboring woman, her eyes widened even more. "Mistress Ahinoam?"

Before anyone could ask questions, Ahinoam's body demanded another push. To my surprise, the wild girl placed the tray of bread on the ground and knelt beside me at Ahinoam's shoulder. Tenderly stroking the pushing ima, she began a song in Hebrew. "In peace I will lie down and sleep, for you alone, LORD, make me dwell in safety . . ."

As Ahinoam's pain subsided, tears rolled from her eyes. "Eglah," she whispered almost reverently.

"Someone hug that girl!" Zerry instructed while supporting Ahinoam's shoulders. Abital practically leapt over the laboring ima and wrapped the sobbing Amalekite slave in her arms.

I turned to Abigail for answers, but she seemed as confused as I.

"Hug me too," Zerry said, so Eglah released Abital and embraced Zerry as if she were her own ima. "We thought Saul's men captured you," Zerry said, "when they raided Bethlehem and killed my ima and yours."

Eglah, silenced by heavy sobs, couldn't answer right away.

"Oh, Eglah," Zerry continued in a raspy voice. "I'm so sorry we took you and your ima from Moab. We thought we were protecting you, but perhaps—"

"You did protect us." She broke from the embrace. "Had we stayed in our homeland, I would have watched Ima die sooner and perhaps joined her." The girl turned to Abital. "Some of my best memories were with you and your friend Dalit. You two were never apart in Bethlehem."

Abital seemed uncomfortable. "Your memory serves you well.

Noble

Dalit was my best friend, but she, too, was killed in the Bethlehem raid."

"Oh no!" Eglah covered a gasp. "What happened to her little boy? I forget his name."

"Zebadiah." Abital beamed. "Thankfully, I'd taken Zeb on a walk just before Saul's men entered the city. I heard the screams and hid in my family's vineyard. I went with other survivors of Saul's raids to join David and his men in the desert. About a year later, Asahel and I married to provide an ima for Zebby." Her cheeks pinked. "Asahel and I miss Dalit very much, but we've found happiness in each other's arms."

"It sounds like Yahweh's perfect provision." Eglah seemed to be forcing a smile. She turned back to Zerry. "May I tell you the truth about that raid, Mistress Zeruiah?"

Appearing surprised and a little wary, Zerry nodded.

"A few of the raiders who attacked Bethlehem were Saul's men, but most were Amalekites who Saul's soldiers taught to fight left-handed. Saul wanted David to believe Israelite soldiers killed some in his family." Her eyes grew misty again. "The four years my ima and I served your ima were the happiest we've ever been. Those memories have kept me alive during these years with the Amalekites. At least as a slave, I can still pray that someday Yahweh will free me."

"And He will." Abigail leaned toward the girl for a clearer view. "I'm Abigail. It's nice to meet you, Eglah."

"It's very nice to meet you, Abigail." The girl then turned to Zulat and me. "Are you wives of David's soldiers as well?"

Zulat huffed. "Most certainly not."

Noting the offense on everyone's face, I quickly added, "Zulat never married. She was nursemaid to my ima and then to me. She's a trusted midwife in . . ."

"From where *exactly*?" Zerry asked again.

54

"We came from Geshur to visit some of our southern villages," I said, despite Zulat's angry glare. "The Amalekites killed our escort."

"You had an escort?" Zerry lifted one eyebrow. "Only someone important would be sent with an escort."

Zulat turned to me with fire in her eyes. "You've already said too much." Returning her attention to the anguished ima, she instructed, "On the next push, keep pushing even after the pain subsides. And no more noise. Sound only weakens your pushing. If you really push, I believe you can birth this baby with one or two big efforts." She patted Ahinoam's knee.

"You see! Another miracle," Abigail said with forced cheer.

"What was the first miracle?" Zerry challenged.

Abigail looked at Eglah. "Your master chose *you* to deliver our tray of bread. How many other serving girls could he have chosen?"

Eglah's smile was brighter than moonlight. "He could have chosen many, many others, but Yahweh directed him to me, Mistress Abigail."

Abigail produced a clean piece of cloth she had tucked inside her robe and held it at the ready. "Let's meet David's firstborn son."

"Son?" Zulat smirked. "Are you a prophetess?"

"No, but I believe Yahweh will encourage us with an heir tonight."

The anticipated push came, and Ahinoam pushed with all her strength, which was considerable, according to the squeeze on my hand.

"The head is out!" Zulat said with controlled enthusiasm. "Ease up on the pressure, Ahinoam. Gentle push now while I guide the shoulders out."

"Ooowww!" the ima cried.

"Yes, yes, you're through the worst of it." Zulat worked quickly, then said, "One more gentle push, dear. Gentle, very gentle."

And with a swish, Zulat held a slippery little creature in her arms.

"It's a boy!" Abigail shouted.

The captives erupted in celebration, but my focus remained on Zulat. She laid the silent newborn on her lap. Something like an unraveled lamb's intestine attached the baby to Ahinoam's insides. I'd seen something like the shiny, twisted rope whenever Baal's priests divined the future by reading the entrails of a sheep or goat. However, this strange cord was wrapped tightly around the baby's neck. Zulat worked furiously to loosen it, then slipped it over the newborn's head. He remained silent, and now his whole body was a dreadful gray.

"Give me the cloth!" Zulat demanded of Abigail, never looking away from the infant. A sudden pall settled over our small gathering while Zulat cleared the baby's nostrils and then vigorously rubbed his arms and legs with the cloth. She turned him over, holding the boy's tiny body with her left hand while whacking his back with hard blows.

"Zulat, don't—"

"Shh," Abigail placed her hand on my arm and leaned close to whisper, "Pray, Maakah. Our boy needs to take his first breath very soon or . . ." She bowed her head, moving her lips but without making a sound.

Pray here? Baal and Asherah were in Geshur. Who were the gods of this land? What sacrifices did they demand? Where was their temple?

"Yahweh, Maker of the heavens and the earth," Zerry said, "breathe life into our precious boy so we can know You are here and trust that You will rescue us."

Zulat was still alternately pounding then roughly rubbing the baby's back. I heard a weak cough, then a snort, and finally a wail. Zulat turned him around to face her and lifted him into the air. With tears in her eyes, she said, "Even this old doubter must admit you're a miracle boy."

THREE

DAVID

So David and his men got up early in the morning to go back to the land of the Philistines, and the Philistines went up to Jezreel.

1 Samuel 29:11

Eager to return home after being rebuffed by the distrustful kings, my men and I marched hard to reach Gath. We ate a meal prepared by the palace kitchen, bedded down in the empty garrison, and left the capital city before dawn for the last leg of a long and fruitless journey. I could almost hear the collective sigh as we veered off the crowded trade route and onto the less-traveled road to Ziklag. Every man among us was weary to the bone, and every one of us would be relieved to reach home before sunset. Trying to find something good about being sent home, I praised Yahweh. *Thank You, Lord, for at least now I'll arrive home before Nomy gives birth.*

"David, look!" Joab pointed into the distance at a thin column of smoke.

"What could produce that much—" Panic struck as our eyes met. Ours was the only city in that direction. "Run to Ziklag!" I shouted. "Ziklag's on fire!"

Noble

Six hundred crazed warriors ran for their lives. A full day's hike became a half-day's horrified sprint. The Gadites, my fleet-footed scouts, reached our hilltop city first. They skirted the northern cliffs and entered on the west, the only level approach. What had been our city gate, where I'd last seen Abigail waving goodbye, was now charred remains. The flames were dying to embers and ash, but anything that could be burned had been destroyed. Thankfully, I saw no bodies. No blood. No stench of death.

It was both good news and bad. A new sort of terror spread as men ran toward their homes, realizing our women and children had likely been taken captive. As I neared my small home, I heard a tortured cry—and realized it was my own. More wails and keening followed. The absence of our women, the sound of all-male grievers, was haunting. How could this have happened? I stumbled toward my home, blinded by tears, and found it like all the others—a shell of charred rocks and mostly burned beams. I fell over the threshold onto my knees and threw dust mingled with ash onto my head. *Why, Yahweh? Why allow our women and children to be taken?*

Someone outside cried, "Amalekites!"

I turned and saw Uriah the Hittite standing near the central well.

He waved a lightweight woolen cloth like a war banner. "Only those desert hyenas wear this." The raiders from the southern desert covered themselves head to toe in tightly woven, lightweight wool to protect against the punishing sun.

Yahweh, please no! The thought of my precious wives in the boorish hands of an Amalekite—another wave of grief passed over me. Wailing and grieving as never before, I poured handfuls of dust and ash over my head and pressed my face against the floor of what was once our modest but lovely home.

How could this have happened, LORD? Our women knew how to protect themselves. They would have fought hard to keep raiders outside our walled city. With deep ravines on three sides, my wives and the women Ahinoam had trained with bow and blade would never have opened the only city gate on the west side.

"We should never have left them alone!" an angry voice, probably Uriah again, shouted in the street.

I pressed my face into the dust and ash, groaning to the only One who knew the depths of my pain. *LORD, Nomy . . . our child . . . Abigail . . . gone. Please, LORD! Our women and children are the heartbeat of the city.* Though my nephews and captains were loyal friends, knowing even my deepest failings yet still willing to follow, my wives were a part of my very soul. *Yahweh, You must help us find them!*

"We should never have followed Achish!" A different voice this time, closer to my doorway.

I didn't even look up or try to defend myself. Perhaps he was right. Why had I acquiesced to King Achish's command without trying to invent an excuse? Why not add one more deception to the countless lies I'd told him since arriving in Gath?

The two lines from the new praise chorus came to mind. *You destroy those who tell lies, Lord, and detest the bloodthirsty and deceitful.*

But I'd convinced myself—and my men—that we had no other choice. Just like I thought we had no choice when Achish commanded us to march with the Philistines and fight our brother Israelites. I'd lied to Achish, but worse, I'd lied to myself and my men. God could have protected us.

Yahweh, did You take our women and children as discipline for my deception? The thought roiled in my belly, nearly making me retch. Just as quickly came the next line of the chorus. *But I, by Your great love, can come into Your house. In reverence, I bow down.*

Tears became sobs, but my tight chest relaxed. Perhaps the raid on Ziklag had been Yahweh's discipline, but because of His great love, I felt a surety that we'd rescue our families.

Noble

The shuffling of sandals—many sandals—drew my attention outside.

"David, get up!" Joab nudged me with his foot.

I shot to my feet but remained silent as angry men closed in on every side. Joab and his brothers, Abishai and Asahel, stood like a shield in front of me. "Don't speak," Joab commanded. "You'll only make this worse."

"I'm not sure how this could get worse." I stepped around my general and met Uriah three paces from my doorway. He seemed to be leading the mob.

"The women and children taken from us are gone forever," he shouted over my angry men. "We know what the Amalekites do to their captives. Someone must pay for the lives ruined by the careless leadership that cost us everything!"

"David is no longer fit to lead!" came a bold shout from the back.

"Under his command, we've ignored Sabbath and committed murder!" The second accusation broached death-penalty crimes.

Within moments, my six-hundred-man army—men who had risked their families' lives and their own to protect mine—became more like a writhing, hissing viper, ready to strike.

Abishai signaled his two compatriots, and the Three became my shield once again, while Joab and Asahel called more of my thirty Mighty Men to create an outer ring in front of them. They would provide two significant barriers but would never withstand a serious attack from the rest of my skilled warriors.

"Stone him!" cried an anonymous voice. Then another. And another.

"Stone David! Stone David!" Uriah the Hittite, one of my Mighty, led the chant, pounding his fist against his breastplate, mocking the salute he'd often given. "Stone David! Stone David!" The air throbbed with the demand, but no one had stepped forward to volunteer as the two witnesses necessary to convict and cast the first stones.

Encouraged by their hesitation, I shouted over the noise, "Abiathar! Where is Abiathar? Bring your ephod!" Nudging aside my human shields, I watched our High Priest shoulder his way through the quieting crowd.

His pallor and wide eyes proved his wariness. "My king, I don't believe you've done anything deserving of death."

"Thank you for that," I said, placing a hand on his shoulder. "My men are bitter and distressed about their wives and children—as am I—but I believe Yahweh intends to help us find them and will give us victory over the Amalekites. Let's make sure I've heard the LORD correctly, shall we?"

Whispers fluttered through the mob, but when Abiathar removed the black and white stones from the pocket behind his breast piece, all fell silent.

Without delay, I asked for Yahweh's guidance in a voice everyone could hear, "Should we pursue the Amalekite raiders?"

Abiathar threw the black Urim and white Thummim. Toppling end over end, it was the Thummim that landed upright, confirming the prompting I'd sensed earlier. Nods and banter showed my men's approval, but they were still too tossed by emotion. I lifted both hands to command quiet and said, "We must all consider the cost. I have one more question to ask Yahweh before we pursue the Amalekites."

Abiathar quickly retrieved the lots and held them in his trembling hand. "I'm ready, my king."

"Yahweh, will we overtake the Amalekites and *succeed* in this rescue?"

Murmurs of approval preceded Abiathar's toss, and six hundred men collectively held their breath. When the white Thummim stood tall atop the flat Urim, my men released a war cry.

Thank You, Yahweh. "Gather only what food you'll need for a two-day hike," I shouted over the noise. "We march before dusk."

As the crowd dispersed, Joab whispered, "We should exile Uriah for his treachery."

"True, but we'll need every one of our fighting men to rescue our families."

Cursing under his breath, he agreed and added, "We have no idea where the Amalekites are camped. If they've gone deep into the southern desert, we'll need more than two day's provisions."

"Yahweh will provide." I truly believed it for the first time in months. The cloud that had descended over my soul and blocked the warmth of God's presence was gone. Something bigger than a raid was happening in our midst—something even greater than the Philistines' war against Israel. My men had never turned against me. They needed to see God's greater plan unfolding, and somehow I knew we were about to witness His great power while saving our families.

Nightfall

My legs felt as heavy as Hittite iron. My eyelids, too. But the thought of my wives held captive by Amalekites kept my feet moving amid the unsteady footing of dust and rocks. We'd traveled east from Ziklag into the desert to avoid trade routes and cities. The western sky glowed orange on our right now that we'd veered south to skirt the mountains. One of our Gadite scouts appeared in the distance and lifted two red flags overhead, then crossed them—the sign of a city or trade route ahead.

I'd issued a command of silence for our rescue mission. We had no idea where the Amalekites were camped, only that since ancient times they'd been a Bedouin people who moved to various locations throughout the Negev, raiding peaceful villages in the more fertile

Judean hillsides and *Shephelah*. Not knowing where the Amalekites might have taken our families, I dared not take a chance on entering a city where an Amalekite scout or spy could return to camp and alert their warriors that we were coming. A surprise attack was our best strategy.

Our scouts were placed on surrounding hilltops. Joab and I walked at the head of our army, alert to any message they might give with red, yellow, or green flags.

"Joab." I pointed to one of our Gadites who waved his red flags to the southeast. I showed approval with a single clang of spear against shield.

Without breaking stride, my general turned to face our Mighty Men. "Signal to your contingents and scatter." He kept his voice low. "We'll travel in the desert to avoid trade routes in Gerar and Beersheba. Follow Besor Brook until Yahweh gives us more direction." All thirty captains slammed a fist against their chests—even Uriah, whose anger seemed to have cooled.

Uriah the Hittite was one of the few men in my ranks who refused to follow Yahweh—or any god, for that matter. He and his brother had been my middle nephew's best friends since childhood, and I'd seen Abishai castigating him after the lots spoke Yahweh's will. I'd decide Uriah's future service after we rescued our families.

The captains scattered right and left, each of them lifting his arms and chopping the air in the direction his contingent should follow. Joab locked eyes with me, silently questioning which contingent he should join. I pointed toward Uriah's men. My oldest nephew nodded and ran toward the Hittite's squad. I scanned the remaining groupings and chose to join Amasai's contingent. The Kohathite who joined us in Moab had not only become the leader of my Mighty Men but also the greatest encouragement to my weary soul. I needed that encouragement tonight. His musical ability had been a gift from the line of Levi, and he used it often to lead our whole camp in worship.

Amasai led us southwest into the desert, skirting the edge of the busy city of Gerar. We traveled the grueling wilderness in silence and felt the one-of-a-kind relief when we reached the Brook of Besor. Though only a trickle as summer approached, it was deep enough to fill our waterskins and wash the dust from our bodies and beards. The extra caution had conquered my sleepiness. Or was it a sense of imminent battle?

I heard the slightly altered caw of a desert jackdaw, four quick squawks in a row. I answered with the same. From the west came another adjusted nature sound, and someone answered southeast of our position. Amasai kept us moving southeast toward the guiding calls. We'd used the system for years to communicate in the desert while fleeing King Saul. A lone Gadite was running toward our group, likely Attai, judging from his stride and height.

Without using flags this time, he ran all the way to greet me and braced his hands on his knees while delivering his message. "We've found a half-dead Egyptian slave who was discarded by his Amalekite master. He saw the Ziklag raid, and when he fell ill on the way to the Amalekite camp, his master left him in the desert to die."

"Can he lead us to their camp?" I asked.

"We've given him some food and water, hoping to revive him." Attai pointed in the direction from which he'd come. "If we run, it won't take long to reach him and the other contingents that have gathered."

I scanned Amasai's weary men, trying to assess if running would use up crucial strength they'd need for battle. Amasai stepped between me and his contingent. "You set the pace, my king, and we will follow."

Always faithful. I gripped his shoulder, a lump in my throat making it impossible to voice my appreciation, then swallowed hard and turned to Attai. "Lead us."

The Gadite ran as if the desert were a fire beneath his feet. Like a gazelle, more bounding than running, I ran faster than ever and still lagged behind. Attai's pace was exactly what it needed to be, and I pushed myself to the limit. If this Egyptian could lead us to the Amalekite camp, we could travel faster and quieter, attacking without any warning. Always faithful. Always faithful.

Thankfully, Attai slowed as we rejoined other contingents that had reached the Egyptian's location before us. Several warriors lay on the ground, heads cradled in their arms, sound asleep. Others guarded the perimeter, and twelve men formed a circle around our prisoner.

The Egyptian sat on a reed mat, propped against a boulder, his arms hanging lifelessly at his sides. When he looked up and saw me, he gasped and instinctively pressed his back against the boulder. If that was his attempt at escape, he certainly didn't need a dozen guards.

"Do you speak Aramaic?" I asked while approaching.

"Yes, my lord," he answered. His voice was scratchy and weak, likely due to a lack of water.

I crouched beside him. "Who do you belong to, and why are you here?"

"I was the slave of an Amalekite chieftain who left me here three days ago." It was a miracle he was alive after three days with no water in the desert.

Joab stood at my left shoulder, so I motioned to his shoulder bag. "Give him a cake of your pressed figs and two raisin cakes."

"But I—I'll only have one fig cake left."

Should I remind him that I hadn't taken *any* fig or raisin cakes when we'd left Gath so my men could have more provisions? Through clenched teeth, I reminded my general, "When we rescue

Noble

our families and reclaim all the Amalekites stole from Ziklag, you'll have all the fig cakes you can eat."

Joab growled his protest while offering the treasures to our Egyptian friend.

"Thank you, my lord." The man ate the sweet treats as if he hadn't eaten in three weeks.

"Can you lead us to the Amalekite camp?" I asked while he still savored our offering.

He stopped eating and lowered the cakes. "If you will swear to me that you won't kill me or hand me over to my master, I will take you to them."

"We all serve a master," I said. "I serve Yahweh with all my heart. If you lead us to the Amalekites, we'll kill the master who abandoned you, and you'll be free to choose whom you wish to serve."

A slow smile brightened his countenance. He had only a few teeth, in various stages of rot. "Their camp is less than a day's walk. If we leave now, we can be there by dusk."

Dusk. Not the best time to begin a battle. *I'm trusting this is part of Your plan, Yahweh.* I patted the Egyptian's shoulder and stood.

Joab leaned over to meet the man's gaze with less than a handbreadth between their noses. "David ben Jesse is Israel's next king. He has saved your life and offered you freedom for your information and service. Don't betray us."

The Egyptian swallowed audibly. "Never. I would never—"

"Good." Joab lifted him to his feet. "You can eat on the way."

I turned to address my men and found even more of them lying on their mats, sound asleep. "Get up!" I shouted. "Gather for your orders!" Only a few even woke to my command.

Abishai, my middle nephew and leader of the Three, who were my best spies, hurried to my side. "They're exhausted, Dohd. Look at those still sleeping. They're our older warriors, many well past forty harvests. We haven't slept for two days. If they fight in this condition, we may lose a third of our warriors to Amalekite swords."

I wanted to argue, but something inside me said Abishai was right. *LORD, how can we fight the whole Amalekite nation with less than six hundred men?* How I wished for a burning bush like Moses had so I could actually hear the voice of God and know His plan. Abiathar had cast the sacred lots, and Yahweh had promised us success. Should I cast the lots again to ask about leaving my exhausted men behind?

Gideon.

The single name came to mind, and I was suddenly certain of God's answer without casting lots. The Angel of the LORD came to Gideon and told him to attack the Midianites. Yahweh then directed Gideon and his army to drink from the Spring of Harod. Then He said, *"You have too many men, and if you win, Israel might believe they conquered the Midianites by their own strength."* So Yahweh began winnowing Gideon's army from twenty-two thousand down to only three hundred.

I turned to Abishai. "How many are too exhausted to join the battle?"

He scanned our men, as did I. Even those who had stood at my command had already laid on their mats again and fallen asleep.

"Two hundred," Abishai said. "We would conquer the Amalekites with only four hundred warriors—and Yahweh's promise of success."

I nodded, smiling. "Gideon was given only three hundred."

My nephew's eyes sparked with mischief. "Perhaps we should let a hundred more enjoy a much-needed rest."

"Are you trying to get me stoned?" I grinned at him and said, "Send Joab over. I'll give him the order and let him tell the men we'll attack with an army of four hundred."

Abishai saluted, fist to chest, and met Joab near Uriah's contingent.

Noble

I heard Uriah's protest from twenty paces and Joab's immediate response. "If you can't fight believing in Yahweh's promise for success, you're dismissed from service in *King* David's army." He turned in a full circle. "That goes for the rest of you. Those who are too weary to fight will remain here to guard our supplies. Those who still have the strength to rescue our wives and children—and believe we fight with Yahweh's strength—follow King David." He thrust his sword in the air without the battle cry that usually accompanied such a challenge. Four hundred men lifted their swords, including Uriah.

Joab grabbed the Egyptian by his collar and guided him rather roughly to the front of our procession. The Mighty Men numbered their contingents and evenly dispersed the men in ranks to march. Within the time it might take to set a table and serve a meal, we were on the move.

"Which one is your master?" I asked the Egyptian.

At the mention of the man who had abandoned him, the Egyptian's countenance hardened. "He's their leader and wears a patch over one eye." Focusing on the path ahead, he added, "If you give me a sword, I'll kill him myself."

FOUR

MAAKAH

Whoever sacrifices to any god other than the LORD must be destroyed.

Exodus 22:20

I wrapped my arms around my waist and rubbed the clay goddess tucked in my belt. Could the Queen of Heaven hear my silent begging to stop the torture that started at dawn? Amalekite warriors had entered the enclosure and, before anyone could fight or flee, they'd held daggers to women's throats. Those held captive by the blade helplessly watched their friends, sisters, and daughters dragged into tents beside our holding area.

Shrieks from the tents proved the Hebrew women were warriors. But the repeated blows and the sickening thuds brought inevitable silence. No woman could match a real warrior's strength. When those women emerged from the tents, they were bloodied and broken, heads and shoulders bowed by shame not theirs to carry.

Another group of soldiers came to claim their turn with the spoils. The bravest of captives nudged their children toward the back and faced our captors with brazen courage. They, too, returned beaten and bruised, while more of their friends were abused. All day long, the desert dogs feasted on their spoils, and the wounded

Noble

women of David's camp continued to protect David's wives, his closest family, and the two strangers who had helped deliver David's newborn son.

I'd thought watching my abba kill a man was the worst thing I'd ever see. Or perhaps bearing the guilt of the two guards' deaths at the throne room would be the heaviest burden I'd ever bear. I, the spoiled princess, was so certain there were no secrets between me and my royal parents. I hated my ignorance. And I hated even more the world outside Geshur's walls.

The cries of Ahinoam's infant sliced through my grim thoughts. "Shh, love." Ahinoam opened her robe and held him to her breast. "We can't let them know you're here," she cooed through trembling lips. Dusk had settled over the camp. Would we live through another night of terror?

A commotion amid the captives meant another group of Amalekites had entered the enclosure and was moving through to choose their next victims. I was shaking so violently, I scooted away from Ahinoam so I wouldn't bump her and perhaps disturb the little one's meal.

But she put an arm around my waist and pulled me closer. "David will come," she said. "Abigail is always right. We must trust Yahweh." Her voice broke when she spoke her god's name.

"Did you say that for my benefit or yours?"

She raised an eyebrow. "Both." Then pulled me closer still.

Zerry, Abigail, Abital, Zulat, and Eglah stood around us, shielding us from the Amalekites' sight. "I should be standing with them," I whispered. "Why protect me when you don't know me?"

"We know that Yahweh brought you and Zulat at just the right time to help us deliver my son, which means you're important to Him—so you're important to us."

I shook my head and realized I was shaking a little less. Would she be so welcoming if she knew I'd been sent to marry her husband?

"Where is Geshur's princess?" a deep voice called out, and I recognized it right away as the captain with the eye patch.

I started to stand, but Ahinoam grabbed my wrist. "No!" She blinked tears down her cheeks. "Let us keep you safe."

"He won't touch me," I said, trying to match the certainty she'd proclaimed in David's rescue. "That man and I have an agreement." Pulling my arm away before courage failed, I stood and rushed through our shield of protectors.

"Prin, no!" Zulat lunged for my arm, but I was already moving through the crowd.

I passed by so many wounded women. Some were treating each other with torn strips of their already-tattered robes, and while everyone else was backing away from the imposing Amalekites, I pushed toward them.

"I'm here," I said, reaching a clearing near the bramble gate. The sight of the captain weakened my knees. *Remind him of your royalty and ransom from both Geshur and Gath if you're returned unsullied.*

Before I could speak, the captain smiled and said, "I've decided making you my fifth wife is better than any ransom."

"No!" I turned to run, but two large guards lifted me between them. Their grip bit into my arm. "Please don't do this! Please!" I begged. "My abba will pay handsomely but only if—"

A strange swish flew past each ear, and my captors fell beside me. Sudden chaos exploded with piercing shrieks encircling the Amalekites' perimeter. The Amalekites in our enclosure ran into their camp, leaving the gate wide open. I turned in a circle, scanning every direction, and saw archers as well as spearmen and . . . were those slingshots? I'd only seen Geshurite boys use the sling and stone as toys, but these men were whirling the cubit-long weapon and hitting Amalekites squarely between the eyes. *Asherah, could this be David ben Jesse and his men?*

I ran through the captives to reach David's family and Zulat.

Ahinoam was standing, and all but Zulat were beaming. "I told you David would come," Abigail said in greeting.

Ahinoam laughed. "She gloats sometimes. You'll get used to it."

"I thought you said he had six hundred in his army," I said. "It looks more like half of that—or maybe two-thirds—have come to rescue us. They'll never free us when there are thousands of Amalekites in this camp."

"Watch what our God can do." Zerry folded her arms. "David and his men aren't alone in this fight. Yahweh fights *with* them."

Out of respect, I kept silent, but none of the gods interfered directly in human battles. If they did, it usually went badly for the humans they tried to save. "What should we do to help?" I asked.

"Believe me," Ahinoam scoffed, "I've tried for years to join my husband in battle, but he never allows it. Our job is to watch and pray."

I turned toward the center of camp and saw that most of the Hebrew captives simply sat in small clusters with their children and friends. Many pointed toward certain warriors. Some even clapped and shouted encouragement. When I finally sat down beside Zulat, I looked for a man who might be David ben Jesse. Saul was reported to be the tallest—and most handsome—man in Israel when he was anointed king forty years ago. I scanned the battle, feeling a little nauseous at the rising noise and stench that came with the blood and excrement of death.

Finally, I found the tallest man among David's warriors and leaned over to ask Ahinoam, "Is that your husband?"

"Oh, no. That's Uriah the Hittite." She searched the camp, which had become a battlefield, and pointed to the southern perimeter. "That's David with the sling. He's doing what I always beg him to do—fight from a distance because the sling is his best weapon." She smiled with a shrug. "I can hardly believe he's heeding my advice."

He was broad-shouldered and muscular, fierce and accurate with his sling, but how could a man so short become Israel's next king? I tried to mask my surprise but evidently failed.

"Don't let his stature fool you." Ahinoam grinned at me. "Yahweh has given him the passion of a giant."

I watched him and wondered if he had enough passion for three wives, then chided myself. I had no intention of becoming David ben Jesse's third wife and would send Abba a message explaining exactly that as soon as David provided an escort for Zulat and me to one of our southern villages. Israel's next king need never discover that I was offered to him as a treaty bride.

A terrible thought crossed my mind. What if Abba's messenger had already reached David with the betrothal contract? What if David had already signed it? *Oh, Asherah, Queen of Heaven, let it not be so.*

The noise and violence raged into the night. Children slept on imas' laps while wives of David's soldiers kept vigil by moonlight. Our rescuers fought valiantly. Every one of them, now with sword in one hand and dagger or spear in the other, kept their arms whirling and their bodies twirling like a death machine working its way through the enemy camp.

"How do they do it?" I asked Ahinoam. "Aren't they exhausted?"

"I'm sure they are," she said. "But that's part of how Yahweh intervenes. He gives our men supernatural endurance and strength. Yahweh has a special hatred for the Amalekites because, without provocation, they attacked the children of Israel right after they escaped from Egypt. It was Israel's first battle. They'd been slaves for four hundred years, so no one knew how to fight. But fight they did, and they were winning—as long as Moses kept his hands raised to the heavens. When Moses grew weary, his friends found a large rock for Moses to sit on and then supported his arms aloft until the battle was won."

"Remarkable." I turned my attention to the continuing violence.

Somehow my senses had become dulled to it. No more nausea. I didn't even notice the stench anymore or wince at the death cries. I grew detached from this new reality outside my small world. My eyelids grew heavy as dawn tinged the eastern horizon. The Hebrew's god hadn't given me special endurance. The last thing I remembered was Zulat's gentle hands pulling my head onto her lap.

"Why kill women and children?" Zulat's panicked voice brought me upright.

"What's happening?" Still dazed, I looked around and saw the sun now in the western sky. Had I really slept all day?

"How can you kill everyone who doesn't worship your god?" Zulat rocked to her feet and stabbed both fists at her hips. "Does King Talmai kill foreigners who refuse to worship Geshur's gods?"

Abigail stepped between Zulat and Ahinoam. "I'm sure he would if he believed your false gods commanded it."

"False gods?" Incredulous, I stood beside Zulat in protest. "How dare you?"

Ahinoam nudged Abigail aside. "I've never needed a protector," she said, "and I certainly don't need your defense against the two women who helped bring my son into the world." She locked eyes with me. "Do you remember our conversation last night about Yahweh's special hatred of the Amalekites?"

I did, but . . . "That doesn't excuse the killing of women and children."

"Actually, it does. Those women will have more children, and those children will grow into either warriors or women who give birth to warriors. Amalekite warriors kill Israelites, and God won't allow it. The Amalekites are *herem*, consecrated by Yahweh for destruction. He made it clear to our ancestors years ago, and then again to King Saul, that the Amalekite nation must be completely destroyed. Our ancestors and Saul failed to obey, which cost many Israelites their lives and Saul his place on Israel's throne. Our God chose David instead—a man who pursues Yahweh's heart. My husband will obey the LORD no matter how difficult the command."

I was stunned that she would defend such butchery. In the camp beyond our enclosure, Amalekite soldiers lay in piles. Shrieks of women and children drew my attention to the south side of camp, where David's men had separated the women. They'd moved the children to the north side so neither group could see the other.

But everyone heard the screams cut short by the victors' blades.

I turned my back, covering a gasp of horror and fighting tears. *Will Zulat and I be next?* I glanced at my maid. Tears ran down her cheeks, but she hadn't looked away. I could count on one hand the number of times I'd seen her cry. She continued watching, her breaths coming more quickly, and her face growing redder as her anger intensified. I needed to intervene before she did or said something to seal our fate.

"What if we agree to worship your god?" I asked Ahinoam, who seemed most likely to negotiate.

"You're lying." Slowly, she turned a threatening look my way. "Don't lie to me, Maakah—ever. I've tamed my temper considerably since joining David when he first fled from Gibeah of Saul, but my daggers still fly straight and true toward anyone who deceives my family or tries to harm us."

Abigail stepped forward, gently cupping my elbow to draw my attention. "David has allowed a few men to remain in his army— foreigners who worshiped foreign gods—if they agreed to discontinue that worship and remain open to learning about Yahweh."

"If you can look us in the eye," Ahinoam added, "and vow to Abigail and me that you won't bring an idol or worship a false god while in our camp, we'll intercede with our husband on your behalf." She turned to include Zulat. "And on your behalf, my friend. Perhaps

Noble

when my baby becomes a full-grown prince, he can make the journey to King Talmai's court and meet you both." She must have heard the captain's call for me and deduced I was Talmai's daughter.

I reached for Zulat's hand and squeezed before she could tell them such a vow was impossible. Placing my hand over the clay goddess in my belt, I steadied my voice. "We'd like that very much."

My maid bowed and walked away, which was probably best. She'd always been a terrible liar, so I must learn to become the political weapon Geshur needed to secure our future.

DAVID

Completely destroy them. I'd repeated God's command since yesterday at dusk. With every sling throw and sword swing, I'd reminded myself of Yahweh's directive to our forefathers: *Completely destroy the idolators in the Land I will give you.* They had disobeyed. I would not.

Looking into the terrified eyes of the last young woman standing, I swung my sword. Her body slumped to the ground. Her head rolled, halted by another dead body.

I walked away, nauseous, and scanned the destruction around me, then dropped my sword and dagger and fell to my knees, retching. But I spit out only bile. The fighting had raged more than a full day, and we'd eaten nothing. My whole body shook from hunger and exhaustion, but this battle had been a righteous one.

It is finished, LORD. I would never fight for the Philistines or place my men in a position where they were forced to choose such an alliance.

"Master David!" The Egyptian who led us to the camp came bounding toward me. "Four hundred Amalekites escaped on camels. Your general asks permission to pursue them."

Panic tinged the edge of his voice. I fell back on my heels and looked up at him. "No, not tonight." How could anyone have the strength to chase an enemy on camels? "We'll find them later. We did our best, and Yahweh knows the intent of our hearts."

"But, my lord, what if . . ." Eyes wide, his fear spoke what he dared not speak. *What if my master is among the survivors and somehow finds me?*

I struggled to my feet, groaning like an old man. The Egyptian supported my elbow as I stood. "Thank you," I said, patting his shoulder. "You're safe in my camp. What is your name?"

"Nakia, my lord."

"What does it mean?"

"Faithful one."

I offered my hand. "Remain faithful to me, Nakia, and resist the gods of your heritage, and you'll always have a home in my camp."

Nakia hesitated only a moment before he gripped my wrist. "I will serve you well, my lord, and worship any god you say."

I studied him. He'd acquiesced a bit too quickly concerning a foundational tenet of life and existence.

"I'll do anything," he said again. "Please, my lord. Don't sell me to another tribe."

He couldn't have been much older than I'd been when I'd slain Goliath; sixteen, perhaps seventeen at most. Perhaps I, too, would be desperate if I'd lived this boy's life. "I'll never sell you, Nakia." *You'll live faithfully or die as a traitor.* He released my hand and bowed deeply before rushing off to rejoin Uriah's contingent.

I heard shouts and happy wails in the distance and knew the

reunions had begun. *Yahweh, let our faith to fight for this victory serve as our sacrifice to satisfy the ceremonial Laws since we have no Tabernacle in which to rightly worship.*

Feeling the heavy burden of responsibility lift as quickly as it descended, I released a sigh. Why was I so suddenly concerned about following Laws that we hadn't been able to keep for years? We'd fought many battles, raided villages, and touched countless dead bodies. Yet, somehow, tonight was different. Even sacred.

Joab's booming shout rose above the rest. "Vered, my love, where are you? Where are my sons?" Three little boys ran headlong into his arms, his wife not far behind them. They, like other families, seemed blind to the war stench on their valiant protector, who looked as if he'd been dipped in blood.

"David!" Abigail weaved through the happy reunions and wiped the dried blood from my lips before kissing me. She'd developed the practice when welcoming me home after our raids. Eyes closed, I inhaled her scent—cinnamon and cloves. "I'm so glad you're safe," I said, but in the next moment, panic struck. "Where's Nomy?"

"I'm here" came a soft voice behind Abigail.

I looked up and found Ahinoam bat Toren with a newborn in her arms. "Meet your son." Her smile was radiant, though she looked as exhausted as my warriors.

I loomed over the sleeping babe, and my chest tightened. "He's so tiny, Nomy. Is he well?"

Her beaming smile answered, and I drew them both into a gentle embrace.

We looked down at the miracle between us. "He's well because Yahweh sent two women who helped with the birth." She motioned toward the older woman first. "Zulat is an experienced midwife who saved our son's life when he came with the birth cord tightly wrapped around his neck." Nomy reached for the younger woman's hand, but she pulled away, remaining one step behind Zulat. The shy one's hair was unbound, long and curly and as black as the night. Her hands had fading henna stains, something Israelite women did only on their wedding day. She was no Israelite bride. Her clothing was that of a peasant, but her hands and face appeared softened by the lotions of a royal house. *Like Michal's had been.* How long had it been since I'd thought of Saul's daughter—my first wife?

"It's okay." Ahinoam nudged her forward. "David won't harm you."

"I can't make such a promise," I admitted.

"David!" Abigail and Nomy said together. Startled, my son began to wail.

While my wives tended the baby, I explained to the two strangers, "You could be shrewd Amalekites trying to escape my sword by taking refuge with my family."

Eyes narrowed, jaw set, the stout old woman stepped closer. I suddenly wished my dagger wasn't lying in the dust outside the enclosure. As exhausted as I was, she might best me in a wrestling match.

"Maakah is the daughter of Geshur's King Talmai," she said, "and the niece of King Achish, the man who has protected you from King Saul for over a year." Chin held high, she added, "Until a few days ago, my mistress had never left Geshur's high walls but has since witnessed more cruelty and bloodshed than any princess should. The least you could do, *King* David, is show my lady the deference she deserves."

King David? "Why would you suppose me a king?" I lifted my arms and turned in a slow circle to display my wretched appearance. "Do I look like a king to you, woman?"

The princess nudged the old woman aside. "You look more like a *shedim* from the netherworld. Have you no compassion? No conscience? I would never marry you!" She clamped a hand over her mouth, her indignation cowed by her shocking declaration.

"Marry? Why would we ever marry?"

She tried to step behind her maid, but I reached for her arm. She pulled away with surprising strength and gave me a bold glare. "I am Princess Maakah, Geshur's only heir. Correspondence between my abba and Dohd Achish led Abba to believe that after the Philistines defeated King Saul's army, they would place you on Israel's throne. In order to maintain the profitable alliance between Geshur and Israel, Abba sent a messenger to Jezreel with instructions to await King Saul's defeat before presenting you with King Talmai's betrothal proposal." Princess Maakah turned to my two stunned wives. "Please forgive me for not mentioning the betrothal, but once I learned David already had two wives, I was determined to nullify the contract."

My wives exchanged an enigmatic look in their silent language that I still didn't understand. Though Abigail was normally the spokesperson, this time it was Nomy who addressed the princess. "You are a lovely and tenderhearted young woman, Maakah. If our husband were ever to take another wife—" she turned to me with murder in her eyes—"which he won't"—and then returned her attention to the princess. "You would be a fine choice." Both Nomy and Abigail offered the girl a conciliatory hand in friendship.

My wives liked the princess? Nomy disliked everyone upon first meeting. Maakah had been brave to confess her true purpose among us, considering the slaughter she'd witnessed at my hands. She'd also placed her new friendship with my wives at risk. I was grateful for both her candor and that she'd ruled out a betrothal since I'd never marry an idolatrous woman.

"Thank you for your honesty," I said with a slight bow to Geshur's princess. Then I lifted my voice to explain our divinely timed rescue to everyone. "Though I don't always understand Yahweh's plans, I assure you His hand was at work even amid the awful circumstances of the past few days. When our army arrived in Aphek with Achish, the other four Philistine kings refused to let us join the Philistine army's fight against Israel."

"All praise to Yahweh for that rejection!" shouted one of my men. Murmurs of agreement joined an overall sense of relief. Even some women who appeared bloodied and bruised offered tentative nods. *Thank You, LORD, that they recognize Your goodness amid the strife.*

"Indeed," I said. "Had we fought with the Philistines, the Amalekites might have taken our families deeper into the Negev." I swallowed my emotions before continuing. "After a three-day march back to Ziklag, we found the city burned and our women and children taken captive. With Yahweh's assurance of victory, we set out immediately to conquer the Amalekites, though we'd had little sleep or food. We've left two hundred men at Besor Brook to guard our supplies, who we'll rejoin as soon as possible on our way back to Ziklag."

Many women who had gathered in a corner with their older children released a unified cry of relief. "Forgive me," I said. "I should have told you right away that your husbands were safe." They'd undoubtedly assumed their husbands had been slain in a Philistine skirmish or lay somewhere in the aftermath of our Amalekite battle.

A waterfall of exhaustion washed over me. *LORD, give me strength to finish this victory for Your glory.* I scanned the weary faces looking back at me and knew we must accomplish the work yet to be done but also regain some strength to return to our burned-out city.

"For now, I'll join a single contingent to take first watch around the perimeter of the camp. Joab will assign the middle and last watch for our three-day stay. Before we begin our return journey, however, we must sift through every piece of livestock and treasure to be sure we take nothing that originally belonged to an Amalekite. But first we praise Yahweh for this miraculous victory!" I released a victory cry and thrust both fists in the air. Every member of our camp exploded with praise, shaking the ground beneath us.

Noble

When we'd been rejuvenated by worship, Amasai's big voice continued to lead in praise while Joab used hand signals to direct our men to the central spring.

A light tap on my shoulder turned my attention to the princess waiting behind me. "Forgive me, Kin—I mean, *David*—but why sift plunder? Didn't your general say—"

"Joab. My general's name is Joab, and he's also my nephew."

"And my eldest son," Zerry added.

The princess seemed unimpressed. "Didn't Joab say that four hundred Amalekites escaped? Aren't we in danger every moment we remain in their camp?"

She might have been lovely had she not thought herself wise at such a young age. "We will leave behind anything the Amalekites didn't steal from a Judean village. We'll carry back to Ziklag all that belonged to us or our Judean brethren—pottery unique to our tribe, cloth woven with Judah's tribal colors, the curled-horn sheep and goats distinct to our Judean foothills."

A deep crease formed between her ebony eyebrows. I waited, certain another question was imminent. "If you don't want the Amalekites' wealth," she said, "why not at least sell it for a profit that could help your people?"

Tamping down a curt retort, I determined to teach rather than taunt this naïve foreigner. "We destroy everything belonging directly to the Amalekites and burn it with their dead bodies because it's all herem—consecrated unto God."

"Doesn't *consecrated* mean it's a good thing? Why destroy what's good?"

"Consecrated simply means *separated*," I explained. "It may be separated because it's good or separated because it's bad. In the case of the Amalekites, Yahweh commands us to separate ourselves from anything having to do with the Canaanite tribes or their cultures because we could begin to see it as ordinary. We might then be tempted to adapt it into our own practices. So, we obey Yahweh's commands, Princess, even when they seem harsh or unreasonable, because we know He sees the full picture of eternity, and we don't."

"You believe your god knows the future? Everything that will ever happen in eternity?" She gave me a cynical huff. "No god knows everything."

"No false god knows everything, but Elohim Adonai knows all things." All humor left me. "Yahweh commands that we completely destroy all herem," I continued, "so we kill every Amalekite man, woman, and child. We'll burn everything in this camp related to Canaanite gods or their culture, including what you might consider valuable, because it is an abomination."

Zerry, Abital, Asahel, and Zeb had joined us. Zerry glared at Maakah. "My brother is covered in the blood of obedience, girl. Any nation that dwells in the Land of Abraham's promise, and that worships any god beside Yahweh, is designated herem. Both they and all their belongings must be destroyed."

All color had drained from Maakah's face.

"I won't kill you and your maid," I reassured her. "Your abba sent you here in good faith, and I have no intention of starting a war with Geshur or offending your Dohd Achish, who has been our gracious protector for more than a year. Several foreign-born soldiers serve among my highest-ranking officers. I have no quarrel with those from other nations as long as those who live among us refrain from worshiping their gods. I also obey Yahweh's command to 'Love the foreigner residing among you as yourself, for you were once foreigners in Egypt.'"

"You weren't so kind to the Amalekites."

"They weren't *residing* with me." I was tired of arguing with an entitled idolater. "I will ask one thing of you and your maid, Princess Maakah, the same that I ask of my foreign soldiers: Never worship a foreign god while residing in my camp. In return for your cooperation, I'll allow you to send a message to King Talmai and will guarantee your safe return to Geshur."

I glanced over at Zerry and gave her an appreciative wink. "My sister is much like her son, General Joab. She'll tell you the truth even when it's hard." I returned my attention to the princess. "Our God taught us that life is in the blood. I don't enjoy ending a life. Yahweh shows us the severity of our actions by deeming us unclean for seven days, during which time we must wash thoroughly on the third day and seventh." I motioned toward Nomy and my newborn son. "Another Law says I can't touch my perfect child while I'm unclean. But Nomy and our son are also unclean—including all the women who aided Nomy in the birth."

"Me?" She inspected both arms as if searching for mud or stains. "How can I be—"

"It's symbolic," I said, trying not to laugh at her diligence. Was she always so genuine? "My point is, Princess—"

"You may call me Maakah."

"All right, *Princess* Maakah." Her cheeks flushed at my goading. "My point is, Yahweh gave our people laws to protect us and show us how to live safely with Him and one another. Some of those laws were impossible for our ancestors while they roamed in lands not their own—like my men and our families have lived for years. Since we can't follow every ceremonial detail Yahweh gave us, we search God's heart to know His motive for creating the Law. Then we obey according to the resources He's provided and trust His mercy is sufficient for our lack."

The princess studied me for several heartbeats and then said, "What a golden tongue you have, David ben Jesse. I still think your god is cruel to give the *unclean* label to babies and people who touch the dead. However, I appreciate your explanation." She leaned closer and added, "I also still think you're wrong to have harmed women and children, but I applaud your determination to annihilate the

Amalekites. I, too, have promised Asherah that given the chance, I would kill as many as possible." She straightened and waved me away as if the matter was settled.

My jaw dropped. Abigail covered a grin.

Nomy raised a single eyebrow. "You see why we like her?"

I laughed, loosening the tension.

Abital marched forward from a few rows back, dragging her husband with one hand and a wild-looking woman with the other. Abital and I had enjoyed arguing since we were children in Bethlehem, but I didn't have the strength for a verbal battle now.

I lifted both hands and said, "Everyone rest while you can. I must help my men with the sorting."

Abital stepped in front of me. "The women in your family have already sorted out one slave to keep." The disheveled woman stared at her feet.

"Why do you need a slave, Abital? You're one of the hardest-working women I know."

She tugged on the woman's arm to draw her close. "Eglah won't be a slave. Asahel said she can become part of our household and help me with Zeb and my chores."

"A slave," I reiterated, then saw Asahel slowly close his eyes—a sign I'd said something I was about to regret.

"She is *not* a slave!" Abital insisted. "Eglah is a friend who deserves this family's protection."

Eglah. Eglah. Why did that name sound familiar?

"I watched Joab kill Eglah's one-eyed master," she added.

We'd been looking for that brigand since he was identified as one of the raiders who attacked Bethlehem when Ima was killed—*Eglah?* Where had I heard that name? I tucked my knuckle beneath the slave's chin, but she flinched and pulled away.

Then, slowly, she lifted her head and met my gaze. "Forgive me, Master David. Since coming to this camp, my first instinct is to fight."

85

Noble

Immediately, I recognized the girl—who was no longer a girl. "You're Keyalah's daughter," I whispered. Her ima was my ima's maid while my family sought refuge in Mizpah's palace. Eglah's ima had bravely warned me about the king's conspiracy against our women in time to rescue them and escape. Eglah and her ima escaped Moab to live with my parents in Bethlehem. They'd faithfully served as ima's housemaids until . . . I couldn't bear to think of their deaths.

"I'm sorry our imas died at the hands of Saul's guards," I whispered.

"It wasn't King Saul, my lord." She bowed her head again. "It was the Amalekites who raided Bethlehem."

"But the raiders fought left-handed." Confused, I glanced at Asahel for affirmation. "Only Saul's Benjamite tribe does that."

"Eglah told Abital that Saul's royal guard taught the Amalekites to fight left-handed so we would believe Israelites raided Bethlehem. It was a double cross of a double cross. They'd tried to shift suspicion onto the Amalekites, dressed in their own Bedouin armor, fighting left-handed. For four years, we've believed they were Saul's royal guard disguised as Amalekites."

I stood speechless, duped by my worst enemies.

"I've been a captive of the one-eyed chieftain," Eglah said, bold enough to meet my eyes. "He's the one who killed both your ima and mine."

"I'm so sorry, Eglah, for what you must have endured."

When Eglah and her ima had traveled from Moab to Bethlehem to care for my ima, they'd agreed to never worship their foreign gods—but now her appearance testified against her. She was dressed like every other Amalekite woman, warding off evil shedim with feathered talismans in her hair. The shedim were thought to be roaming desert spirits, a superstition passed from the Chaldeans to the Canaanites, and the bandages on her upper arms were probably meant to cover self-inflicted wounds from worshiping Amalekite gods.

"I'm sorry about your ima," I said softly, "but no one who worships a foreign god will be allowed to reside in my camp."

Her head snapped up, eyes ablaze. "I worship only Yahweh." Her answer was instinctive—even defiant—but not desperate.

I pointed to the bandages on her arms. "What about the feathers and your wounds?"

"My master dressed me according to his pleasure and . . ." She raised her chin. "He liked to see me bleed." Her gaze held mine for only a moment before she bowed her head again. "But do as you wish, my lord. Death is preferable to being sold to any other master."

"David, she worships Yahweh!" Abital's lips quaked. "Eglah prayed when your son wasn't breathing. She stayed to comfort us instead of returning to her master, though she knew he would punish her for it." Abital looked at her husband, eyes glistening. "Say something, Asahel!"

Asahel wrapped his wife in a tight embrace and turned a soulful look at me. "Clan Jesse owes Eglah our protection. Her ima died trying to protect *Savta* Nitzevet."

"You owe me nothing." Eglah looked up. "It was my delight to care for your ima, Master David. She taught me about Yahweh, which is the greatest gift anyone has ever given me."

Asahel's son Zeb peeked around Abital. "I like her, Dohd David. She played with me while Ima was helping *Doda* Nomy push out your baby." Eglah gave him a coy smile.

Zeb's was the greatest commendation. He had an impeccable ability to assess someone's heart within moments. "Eglah," I said, commanding her attention, "if a rowdy seven-harvest-old boy approves of you, you must indeed be blessed by Yahweh."

"I like Princess Maakah, too!" Zebby pointed and then giggled, shyly hiding behind Abital.

At the compliment, Maakah's cheeks turned a lovely shade of pink, and even stone-faced Zulat gave him a smile.

"It's settled, then," I said. "We'll add Eglah to Abital and Asahel's household as a *helper*, not a slave. And we'll escort Princess Maakah and Zulat back to Ziklag."

"Why not simply take us to one of the southern Geshurite villages?" Would this princess question everything I said? "We'll be safe there until Abba can send a contingent to escort us home."

I dared not tell her we'd wiped out every Geshurite village—as well as most of the Girzites—for the same reason we'd destroyed the Amalekites. "I can't ensure your safety unless you're under my direct protection."

Without waiting for another protest or query, I hurried to join the first watch contingent and ignored her insistent shouts. *Thank You, Yahweh, that Talmai's daughter already decided to cancel the betrothal.*

King Talmai was a key ally of Israel. Northern Geshur was the gateway of trade from every nation north and northeast of Saul's kingdom. Had I known Talmai was related to Gath's King Achish, I might have hesitated to destroy its southern villages—but why hesitate? Were they herem, or weren't they? *Will I let political advantage determine my obedience, LORD?*

The thought slowed my pace to a stop, and I looked into the kohl-black sky dotted with glistening stars. Couldn't the One who created the great lights in the sky also determine the fate of nations? I would obey first and leave the politics to God.

A sudden and heavy anointing felt like hands upon my shoulders and drove me to my knees. I bowed my head as well, unable to bear the weight of what felt like a holy Presence. *You are my son.* A voice spoke inside me, not to my external ears. *Today I have become your Father. Ask me, and I will make the nations your inheritance, the ends of the earth your possession.*

Thank You, Yahweh . . . Abba. Tears wet my cheeks, consecrating the moment as holy. Maakah's boldness came to mind and the way her cheeks burned crimson when she grew angry. Her gray-blue eyes were an intriguing match to her long, black curls that cascaded down her back. Her inquisitive mind could be an affront to many rulers, but in retrospect, I found her refreshing. Had it not been for the feisty princess, I might not have searched my heart moments ago and reaffirmed my vow to obey. *Thank You, Abba, for Geshur's bold princess.*

Wiping my cheeks dry, I resumed my short journey toward Amasai's contingent. Of course, my singing captain of the Mighty would be the one who volunteered his contingent for first watch. After only a few steps, I heard Uriah's disgruntled complaints behind me. Looking over my shoulder, I found him grousing to his contingent about something, drowning out their reasonable explanations.

Perhaps I'd send Uriah back to the Hittites when we returned the princess and her maid to Geshur. Those who wouldn't follow Yahweh without question struggled to obey earthly authority without protest. Maybe when everyone focused on rebuilding Ziklag, we would criticize less and encourage more without his presence.

FIVE

MAAKAH

Then David came to the two hundred men who had been too exhausted to follow him and who were left behind at the Besor Valley. They came out to meet David and the men with him. As David and his men approached, he asked them how they were. But all the evil men and troublemakers among David's followers said, "Because they did not go out with us, we will not share with them the plunder we recovered. However, each man may take his wife and children and go."

1 Samuel 30:21–22

I'd hidden my blistered feet from Zulat during our first day's travel and overnight in the desert, but after this morning's hike over increasingly rocky terrain in my stiff peasant sandals, my blisters were the size of pistachios. I needed every drop of noble blood in me to walk without limping.

"Your feet are bleeding!" Zulat announced loudly enough for the whole caravan to hear.

"Hush!" But my chiding came too late.

Abigail and Ahinoam halted their donkeys. Abigail dismounted and knelt beside me. "Oh, Maakah, you're as stubborn as these beasts here. Why did you refuse when David offered you a donkey to ride?"

"I'm not one of his family," I explained again. "And I didn't want Zulat to walk alone."

"Look at my sandals!" Zulat pointed at her feet. "Am I bleeding?" Her worn, leather sandals looked as soft as Egyptian linen, but I'd never admit it.

"My feet will heal and—" I was suddenly lofted into the air and came face-to-face with David ben Jesse—and in his arms. "Put me down!"

"You're riding my donkey." The smirk on his face stoked my indignation.

"I'm not!"

General Joab held the reins of a white donkey, and David plopped me sideways onto the beast. I tried to scoot off, but he circled my waist and looked into my eyes, our noses less than a handsbreadth away. "You'll either willingly stay on the donkey, or I'll tie you to it."

"You wouldn't!"

His crooked grin stole my breath. "I most certainly would. What would happen if I returned King Talmai's only heir with scarred feet?" He lifted a single handsome brow.

I tried to ignore the cloves on his breath but found myself mesmerized by the green eyes speckled with gold. "Did you ask me a question?"

He chuckled, taking the reins from his general and transferring them to me. "I can't." My objection came out breathless. I cleared my throat. "Abba's guards always lead my mount."

He firmly cupped his hands, holding mine around the reins. "My wives told me the story of your capture and how you dealt with the Amalekite chieftain. I think you can command Victory."

"Victory?"

A low chuckle emanated from his chest. "Yes, my donkey's name is Victory. Would you like to choose another animal from our vast stable, Princess Maakah?" His mocking tone shamed me. Why couldn't I simply accept his kindness?

Noble

Lowering my head, I whispered, "Victory is a nice name. Thank you."

He released my hands and stepped back. "Simply cluck your tongue and gently press your heels into his belly when you want to move forward. Pull back softly on the reins when you want him to stop. He'll most likely follow the other donkeys, and you won't need to use the reins at all."

Fearing the whole camp had stopped to watch, I kept my head bowed. "I'll be fine. Thank you." Mortified, I could barely blink back tears.

He moved closer again and tipped up my chin. I turned away before he saw how he'd unnerved me. "I didn't mean to upset you." He spoke so only I could hear. "Please forgive me. You've been through a terrible ordeal, and I must be gentler with you. We're almost to Besor Brook where Zulat can help you tend your feet. We'll cross a trade route, see normal people doing normal things. You'll feel better, I promise. And, Maakah—" He paused, and I almost looked up—but still didn't trust my emotions. "You're safe with me. I want you to ride Victory all the way to Ziklag. Consider it a favor to the man you *almost* married."

With that, he walked away, his departure sending a shiver through me like a cold north wind. How did this man wield such power over women? Or was it only me who felt bathed in warm honey whenever he spoke?

"I'll take those reins." Zulat grabbed the leather straps from my hand and patted my leg. "What did he say? We must talk before you make any rash decisions."

"What rash decision?" My head jerked to meet her eyes. "I'm going back to Geshur."

"Shh!" She looked around as if checking who might have heard. "We must wait in Ziklag to discover if the Philistines defeated Israel. If so, David ben Jesse may still become Israel's new king, and your abba's betrothal contract will remain a viable match."

"What? No!" I kept my voice low despite my racing heart. "I will not now, nor ever, become a third wife or deny the gods of my ancestors."

"Do you think his first two wives had the training of Asherah's priestesses? Do you think they can please that rogue the way you can?" she asked with a cynical laugh. "That one likes women. With a little pressure from your abba, David won't consider you his third wife for long."

"But Ahinoam and Abigail . . . they love David—and each other. They're my friends."

"And the Geshurites are your responsibility!" she hissed. Her venom drew the attention of those walking past us. Gathering herself, she leaned close and lowered her voice. "Remember your training, Prin. 'Royal blood means kingdom first—always.'"

"Is everything all right?" Abigail reined her donkey to a halt beside us. Ahinoam and her donkey flanked the other side, both women appearing concerned.

"Yes," I said, "of course. Zulat sometimes forgets that I'm no longer a student under her tutelage but rather Geshur's heir in authority over her." Hardening my features, I instructed my maid. "I'll take those reins, Zulat. I'm perfectly capable of riding a donkey between my new friends." She hesitated only slightly before handing over the reins and then fell in step behind us.

Zerry and Abital flanked the outside of Ahinoam and Abigail. I felt wrapped in all four women's kindness and surrounded by their laughter. They asked about my homeland, and I asked about Ziklag. They asked about my family, and I asked Ahinoam why she hadn't named her son yet. She explained that all sons born in Israel were given names on the eighth day after birth, which proclaimed their lifelong character, on the same day they were circumcised. I thought it another cruel custom to maim a son's manhood on the same day they labeled him with lifelong expectations. How many other awful customs had their god forced upon them? Granted, both Egyptians and Ishmaelites also practiced circumcision.

Abigail explained that Egypt's reasoning was more because of hygiene than religion, but Ishmael's clans had inherited the custom from the same patriarch as Israel—a man named Abraham. Zerry clarified that Ishmael's tribes weren't included in Yahweh's promised inheritance of Canaan's land. Only Israel's descendants received "the Promised Land," which David was determined to completely conquer when he became king.

I wondered how the Amorites, Hittites, Perizzites, Canaanites, Hivites, and Jebusites would feel about that. Was David capable of seizing all that land? *How will Abba react to such a powerful Israel on Geshur's southern border?* The army I saw annihilate thousands of Amalekites could absolutely build Israel into a world power. Zulat's warning came screaming into my memory. *Royal blood means kingdom first—always.*

I glanced at David's wives, his sister, and her daughter-in-law, soaking in their easy banter and trying to imagine how I could betray my first-ever fledgling friendships. Placing my hand over the goddess in my waist belt, I acknowledged that deception might become my only choice. If David ben Jesse became Israel's new king, Geshur's future rested on my ability to convince my new friends that I would make a perfect third wife.

By midday, the desert terrain had become dotted with more and more green plants. In the distance, a large group of soldiers ran toward our caravan. I panicked. "Is it the Amalekites?"

"No, no," Ahinoam said. "We're approaching Besor Brook. Those are our own soldiers, rested and leaping with joy."

When the men reached our caravan, David addressed his united camp. "They look like new men, don't they?"

Their families ran to greet them, but before anyone could join in David's welcome, jeers came from behind us.

"They get no plunder!" someone shouted.

"Let them have their families and go!" The reunion quickly devolved into a roiling army of warriors forming battle lines against their own.

"No, my brothers!" David leapt onto a boulder overlooking the Besor Valley, where water flowed toward the horizon. "The LORD protected us and delivered the Amalekites into our hands. We must not be greedy with what the Lord has given us."

"But these men did nothing!" The tallest man in David's army shouted. He seemed the leader among the angry.

"They guarded our supplies so we didn't have to carry them into battle." David paused, scanning the effect of his words. "The share of the men who lightened the load will be the same as those who fought the battle. We. Will. Share. Evenly. Every man, woman, and child is important to Yahweh and to me."

Prickly flesh raised the hair on my arms. What kind of king would consider women and children of equal importance to his soldiers? A great shout rose, sending shivers through me again. David joined the celebration, and two hundred grateful men gathered around him, waiting for a turn to embrace their advocate. He may only be a shepherd and warrior, but David ben Jesse had done a very noble thing for his men. *Perhaps even royal.* I could see myself as this man's queen, but how could I ever convince Ahinoam and Abigail to accept me as a third wife?

"That's one of the reasons I love him." Ahinoam had ridden her donkey closer.

"He'll make a fine king," I said, not able to meet her gaze and not sure why.

"In Yahweh's time."

I sensed her watching me, though I didn't look her way. My cheeks warmed. Why did I suddenly feel so awkward?

"I don't know what Zulat said to you this morning, but I could tell it upset you."

I felt an overwhelming urge to confess Zulat's horrible plan but couldn't. She'd been right. My only duty was to my people. I must protect Geshur's future first and foremost.

"Zulat was scolding me about walking instead of riding a donkey 'as royalty should.' I get very tired of doing the things a princess *should*." At least that was the truth.

Still sensing her eyes on me, I lifted my head and met her gaze. She studied me carefully before responding. "You need not pretend while you're with us, Maakah; David does not abide deception. Please honor his request and set aside any other gods except Yahweh while you reside with us."

"Of course." I respectfully inclined my head. When I straightened, her donkey was already walking away. She was very perceptive. Perhaps too perceptive.

The little goddess suddenly felt like a boulder at my waist. If I was to spend more time with David's wives, I'd ask Zulat to carry the image. Who knew if Asherah could even hear our prayers in Ziklag. But we must continue to pray in hopes that our southern kingdom had provided enough sacrifices during their decade in Philistine territory to welcome the Queen of Heaven into this faraway land.

I continued toward the valley and brook below. Some of the other families were already splashing in the small stream. Zulat helped me dismount, and I yelped when my feet hit the ground. They felt as if they'd been dipped in fire. Leaning fully on Zulat, I bit my lip to keep from crying out with each step toward the brook. Surrounded by laughing children, David was playing with them in the trickle of muddy water. He looked up and caught me watching.

I lowered my eyes quickly and whispered to Zulat, "Royalty doesn't splash urchins in a muddy ditch."

"Indeed," she grumped. "Lean on me, Prin, and we'll find a quieter place to clean your wounds with my drinking water."

"We can't." I stopped, sending fire up my legs. "You need that water to reach Ziklag."

"I'll be fine." She coaxed me toward the ditch, but our path was suddenly blocked by a muddy David ben Jesse.

"Maakah is right, Zulat. You keep your drinking water." Without permission, he hoisted me into his arms again.

"What are you doing? Put me down this instant!"

"There's a spring not far from here. Few people know of it, but the water is clean, and Zulat can use it to tend your wounds and refill her waterskin."

I pursed my lips, not sure what to say. My hands felt awkward in my lap. The comfortable thing would have been to wrap my right arm around his neck, but surely I'd seem too forward. Zulat walked behind his left shoulder, giving me a bulgy-eyed look that only made me more confused.

"You could relax, you know." David looked down at me with that terribly wonderful smile.

If I ended up needing to marry this man, I should at least try to like him. So I slipped one arm around his neck, which drew our faces desperately close. I pulled my arm back to my side and instead sat like a bent stick in a sling. He offered no more suggestions, but his breathing quickened. Was it because I was a heavy load? Or might he also have been affected by our nearness?

I allowed myself to lean into the bend of his arm, comforted by his strength. "Thank you," I whispered, "for making me feel safe." That, too, was the truth, not mere manipulation. I hadn't felt this protected since I'd watched Abba kill Saul's messenger.

"You are safe, Maakah, and when we arrive in Ziklag, I'll make sure you have whatever you need until we can return you to Geshur."

My heart did a little flip. I felt his muscular bicep flex against my back with each sure-footed step. How could the arms that held me

Noble

now belong to the same ruthless warrior I watched murder thousands of Amalekites, their wives, and children?

When David said his god had given his army strength and helped them conquer the Amalekites, I'd almost believed him. What else could explain an army of four hundred killing fifty times their number of enemy soldiers? How had this god defeated the Amalekites who were under the protection of their own local gods? Had Yahweh traveled with his people and overcome a god in its own territory?

Impossible. The Aramean gods became increasingly weaker as our armies fought farther from home. Wasn't that why Kepha had been killed in the battle so close to Tyre?

Kepha. Grief hit me like a crashing wave, stealing my breath.

David stopped. "Did I hurt you?" His features, so full of concern, only added to the similarities I now saw between this warrior and the only man I'd ever loved.

"No, I'm . . ." I bowed my head and waved away the words choked off by the new revelation.

David resumed his march, his confident strides befitting a noble warrior who was certain he'd won his god's favor. If this Hebrew god could indeed save a baby's life, know the future, and strengthen his warriors to defeat their enemies, why shouldn't I worship him along with the gods of Geshur? If David became Israel's king and I his queen, our gods working together might empower Israel's troops to conquer every nation from Geshur to Egypt.

"Here we are." David gently sat me beside a scraggly broom tree and turned to go.

"Wait!" I said, startling him. He turned to face me but wasn't smiling this time. "I'm not sure what Zulat and I would have done if you hadn't allowed us to join your camp." I sounded pathetic.

"You're welcome as long as you abide by my rules." He turned again to walk away.

"I can learn to obey," I said playfully, flirting as the priestesses had taught me. "Perhaps someday you'll take another wife after all."

He halted again but this time didn't face me. "I was once married to a princess who also worshiped false gods. I should have stoned her when I had the chance." He strode away, which was good, because I had no words.

Zulat sat beside me and bumped my shoulder. "You did well."

Aghast, I slowly turned to face her. "Then why do I feel as if I've swallowed a scorpion?" So much for feeling safe. "Asherah's high priestess never prepared me for David ben Jesse, Zulat. David already has two beautiful, capable wives who worship his cruel god. Why would he agree to marry me?"

Zulat drew me into a reassuring hug. "He'll marry you because you're King Talmai's daughter and King Achish's niece. That's how alliances are struck, my girl. You would remember that if you weren't emotionally spent. After all you've been through, you've forgotten your training. But you'll remember after some rest and healing." With that, she gently propped my back against the broom tree's trunk and unlaced my sandals.

As she pulled the stiff leather straps off my feet, she inadvertently scraped a few raw and bleeding sores. I dug my fingers into the dirt to keep from crying out. When both sandals were removed, she patted my leg. "There we are. All done." Zulat lowered her waterskin into the spring, then poured the fresh, clean water over my feet, washing away the day's dust and dried blood.

Leaning my head back against the tree, I closed my eyes and allowed her to care for me. Zulat could be willful and opinionated, but I was truly grateful for someone I could completely trust. Compared to other women of twenty harvests old, I knew a great deal about reading, numbers, and politics, but Zulat always reminded me that knowing wasn't the same as experiencing. *"Knowledge is too easily swayed by emotion,"* she'd said many times, *"but wisdom is deeply rooted in experience and holds fast against the tempests of feeling."*

I needed time to sort out the harsh experiences of these past days so I could hold fast to the hard lessons they'd taught me. Perhaps then I could sort out the conflicting emotions awakened by David's similarities to Kepha. Maybe after a secret offering to Asherah, I'd gain the courage to once again believe marrying David ben Jesse was truly best for Geshur.

At the moment, I could see only disaster if I continued to pursue his affection. Why alienate Abigail and Ahinoam—my first true friends—by a treaty marriage with their Hebrew-warrior husband when their religious leanings hinted at madness? Perhaps I could somehow convince David to let me wait in one of our southern villages and hope for an elongated time frame to convince us all that Geshur's alliance with Israel's fanatical king could work in everyone's favor.

SIX

DAVID

Now the Philistines fought against Israel; the Israelites fled before them, and many fell dead on Mount Gilboa.

1 Samuel 31:1

I should never have held Maakah in my arms again. Did all royal women toy with a man's heart?

"I can learn to obey." Michal had given the same reply when I'd said she must set aside her foreign gods. I'd nearly run from Geshur's princess so she wouldn't see the wound she'd reopened. Most of Israel believed Michal to be a victim and I a traitor because she'd told her abba's council that I had threatened her life to force her assistance in my escape. She could have invented any number of explanations since I'd caught her in numerous lies and found her adept at deception. Instead, she accused me of a treasonous offense—threatening a member of the royal family— and placed a target on my back that meant anyone who aided my escape could also be killed as a traitor. I'd been a fool to marry Michal, to trust a king's daughter. I wouldn't make the same mistake again.

I must stay away from Maakah.

Waiting until the last of our camp left Besor, I walked among the flocks, feeling more at home with the sheep and goats than with any humans. The two contingents providing rear guard left me to my thoughts, but when I saw my general marching toward me, I knew my respite was over.

"Why are you hiding among the sheep?" Joab had never learned the art of social balm. What some called small talk, Joab considered a waste of time.

"If you found me, I wasn't hiding." I grinned, but he still grumbled something I couldn't hear.

He fell in step beside me. "I've sent a contingent of men ahead to Gerar to trade for supplies I'm sure we'll need for the rebuilding."

"Did you send enough to trade for all the supplies we need?"

"Not all the supplies we'll need," he said, "but enough to supplement the Judean plunder we reclaimed from the Amalekites."

"Good, but I intend to return some of the plunder to the Judean cities that have helped us through the years."

"Of course you do." Joab let out a long sigh. "Next, we need to assign duties for rebuilding before we reach Ziklag. Once the women see the destruction, they'll panic if we don't have a plan to make it home again."

"I don't think it will be home again." I shot a quick glance at my general.

"Has Yahweh told you we're to leave Ziklag?"

"Not yet, but it's coming."

His burning glare almost singed my beard. "Then we continue as if Ziklag is our home." Joab was abrasive, but he was also right most of the time.

"Agreed," I said. "Tell me the plan."

While our weary camp traveled through increasingly dry terrain, my nephew explained every detail of his well-crafted duty roster. "I've assigned each of thirty contingents to work details on all three daily watches. We'll ask Ima and your wives to assign the women and children tasks to keep hands busy so mouths can't complain."

"Very smart to let Zerry and my wives assign the women's duties."

He waved off the compliment and continued. "I've divided the contingents into three units: watchmen, workmen, and sleepers. The first two hundred men, those who rested at Besor, will take tonight's watch and allow the two hundred who were awake until dawn sifting plunder and slaves to get some sleep. The third unit—warriors who slept a little last night—will be assigned quiet tasks to accomplish tonight while others sleep. All three units will rotate with sun and moon, the daylight units doing demolition and rebuilding, while nighttime workers find quieter tasks."

I nodded my approval, wondering why he needed it. "You've thought of everything. Well done."

"Now, about King Talmai's betrothal proposal," Joab said as if it were just another item on his list.

"There is no betrothal," I said, refusing to look at him.

"Talmai doesn't know that." Before I could protest, he rushed ahead. "We should wait to see what happens during the battle. If Saul is killed and Prince Jonathan is offered the throne, you know the crown prince will defer to you as Israel's next king. He's the only one besides our family who knows Samuel anointed you years ago, and you two have been closer than any natural-born kin."

I stopped walking, and Joab faced me. "Hear me. I will not marry a pagan princess."

"You married an Israelite princess who worshiped her ima's idols. How is this different?"

A gut punch would have hurt less. "It's different because I've learned from that mistake."

"Think like a king for once. An alliance with Geshur could be the gateway to more alliances with other Aramean nations."

103

"I will be Yahweh's king." I ground out the words between clenched teeth.

Joab's features relaxed into something almost like compassion. "I'm not trying to offend. I merely wished to point out that marriage—even for a man wholly committed to Yahweh—isn't always about feelings. Yahweh can use politics to help you gain an advantage. Maakah is beautiful, smart, and resourceful. Win her heart, and you'll win her loyalty."

"She's loyal to her *gods*, Joab. You weren't there to see her face when I explained Yahweh's commands about herem. She showed nothing but disdain."

"Ima told me about it. But Yahweh's holiness can be a bit . . . *uncomfortable* when someone hears of His requirements for the first time. Don't you remember how strange it sounded when your ima first taught you about Yahweh as a boy?"

It had been Joab's ima who taught me everything because Abba had sent me to live with the shepherds, and Ima never spoke a contradictory word to Jesse ben Obed.

"We must give Maakah time to adjust," Joab was saying.

"We don't have time." I dragged my fingers through my hair. "If she discovers we've destroyed all their southern villages, she'll tell her uncle and her abba, which will bring down the wrath of two nations on our heads."

"If you're already married by the time she finds out, it will be in her best interest to keep our raids a secret. She can tell Achish and Talmai that it must have been some rival tribe that attacked the southern Geshurites."

"I plan to be the kind of king who trusts God to win the favor of his allies, not a king who trusts in his wife's deception."

Joab crossed muscular arms over his broad chest. "How do you intend to keep our raids from her?"

"I'll find a way."

"Hmph. Will you swear to secrecy our six hundred soldiers, their wives, and children? It won't work. No one can silence so many women, and who knows what a child will say at any given moment? If you marry her before her abba and Achish discover what we've done, they're more likely to show mercy to Maakah's new husband than to a deceptive Hebrew rebel."

"I don't need political advice or another wife." I marched away, bumping his shoulder hard as I passed.

"Princess Maakah could provide both," he shouted loud enough for the whole caravan to hear.

I whirled and rushed at him, hoping my whole caravan saw my reaction, and grabbed his breastplate to pull him close. "If you have more to say," I ground out through clenched teeth, "say it and be done."

After a moment's hesitation, he said, "I see only two choices, my king. Neither is ideal, but you must choose one. Either marry Princess Maakah to form an alliance *before* she discovers we've destroyed half her abba's kingdom . . ."

"It's not happening," I said. "Next option."

His features hardened. "Or we must kill her and her maid before they discover the raids to avoid the inevitable consequences from both the northern Geshurite troops and Achish's army."

I shoved him away, his options like a two-pronged fish gig in my belly. "Those are not the only options, Joab."

"Please, my king, tell me if you know of a way to avoid war with Achish and Talmai *when*—not if—Princess Maakah discovers the truth."

The tension drew tighter as the silence between us stretched like a bowstring. I could think of no other alternatives but refused to admit it or agree to either of Joab's terms. "Get out of my sight."

He gave a curt bow and lumbered through the flocks. My nephew also found solace among the sheep and goats since he, his brothers,

Noble

and I had been raised in Bethlehem's pastures. One of the shepherds approached my general and motioned toward the eastern hills. Joab hurried in that direction at a sprint.

Though I was curious what took my nephew away from our caravan, I trusted him fully. So completely, in fact, that I was compelled to consider his two options, though they were as repugnant to me as the Amalekite idols we'd happily thrown in the fire. I resumed the steady pace of my caravan and noticed that my wives, Maakah, and Zulat had halted beside the throng, no doubt having noticed my intense conversation with Joab. I forced a smile and waved them forward, trying to reassure them from afar. I wasn't yet ready to face the searching gray-blue eyes of Geshur's princess.

My wives must have commandeered a donkey for Zulat at Besor since the four women now rode away together. Still stunned that Abigail and Ahinoam genuinely liked the two strangers, I knew killing them was out of the question. But marriage? I remembered Ahinoam's murderous look after hearing Maakah's confession of the betrothal. My dagger-throwing wife may like the princess, but Ahinoam might kill us both if I ever broached the idea of another wife.

So what do I do, LORD? My family would never tell the Geshurite women about our raids, but they would eventually meet most of the camp women at the central well. Ziklag's plentiful spring was also the central source of plentiful gossip. I could hardly restrict Zulat from gathering water for her mistress. *Yahweh, can You keep women from gossiping?* That prayer would require more faith than I possessed at the moment.

Turning my attention to the flocks, I found my favorite lamb and lifted the two-month-old little ewe onto my shoulders. She was old enough to leave her ima, light enough to rest comfortably on the back of my neck, and tame enough to relax while I held her four legs under my chin with one hand. I pulled out my shepherd's flute with the other, and my dour mood left with the first sounds from my flute.

Not long after my song began, I saw advancing toward us a glint of metal from the corner of my eye. In one fluid motion, I placed the lamb and flute on the ground and was ready to defend with sword drawn. Both frustrated and relieved at the sight of Joab, I realized his metal wristbands had caught the evening sunset as he loped toward the flock carrying a lost lamb. My lamb ran back to its ima while I placed my flute in my belt. When I looked up, I expected to find Joab rejoining the troops. Instead, I found him walking alone, whispering to the no-longer-lost lamb cradled in his arms. The sight stopped me where I stood. My nephew—our fiercest warrior—was oblivious to all else but his favorite lamb. Once lost, now found. Once in danger, now safe.

Would King Talmai search as fiercely for his only child? But Talmai had sent his only daughter, his heir, with a maid in traveling clothes. From what the princess had told Abigail, they'd even begun the journey with a royal escort. What had Talmai been thinking? If he'd intended Maakah to be his heir, wouldn't he have disguised her as a man? Why not bind her hair and send her with only two or three highly skilled warriors? I glanced her way and felt an overwhelming need to protect her. What if King Talmai had no intention of putting his naïve daughter on Geshur's throne? *Yahweh, have You brought this Geshurite princess into our midst for protection?*

I shook my head, hoping the thought would somehow disappear. It didn't. I continued a loping pace, fighting stubborn thoughts about the Geshurite princess—and losing the battle.

We crossed the trade route near Gerar, and traveling merchants swarmed Princess Maakah's donkey, enthusiastically pointing to her luxurious, curly hair. How long before their gossip reached King Talmai that she traveled under David ben Jesse's protection? Perhaps

I was completely mistaken about Talmai's sinister motive for sending his only heir with an insufficient escort on the eastern edge of the Philistine-Israel conflict. Perhaps he was so confident in the Philistine victory and Geshur's security under Achish's protection that he was certain of Maakah's safety. Had he miscalculated the Amalekite threat? Or had he hoped for it, having never intended that Maakah sit on Geshur's throne?

I scrubbed my face to wipe away those thoughts and focused on the more pressing issue. What happens when Achish and the Philistine armies return from war? No matter whether the Philistines win or lose, Achish and his troops will have marched through Judean villages that I'd told him my men had raided. With his own eyes, he will have witnessed my deception and want revenge for being duped. *Yahweh, I know we must leave Ziklag before Achish returns with his army—and likely the rest of Philistia's troops.* But what could I do about Achish's niece—King Talmai's daughter? There could be no marriage. Even she knew that.

Shoving Joab's dreadful options aside, I must somehow return Maakah and her maid safely to Geshur—without divulging the annihilation of their southern kingdom.

Increasing my pace, I wove through the flocks and broke into a jog, slowing only as I neared my wives. They were deep in conversation with Maakah. I nodded a greeting to my sister and Abital. Eglah must have taken Zeb to play with other children.

None of my wives seemed to notice as I followed close enough to hear Abigail say, "The Lord struck my first husband, Nabal, with a paralyzing condition when I told him how close our whole household had come to destruction because of his foolish greed. He never harmed me again. Nabal died ten days later."

The princess gasped. "Does this god of yours kill everyone who displeases him?"

"If that were true," Zerry answered, "there wouldn't be a single person left on earth!" My wives turned to laugh with her, drawing everyone's attention to my presence among them.

Maakah and Zulat only glanced my way before exchanging a quizzical look between them.

Abigail sobered when she followed my gaze. "Elohim was my defender," she explained to the Geshurite women. "Nabal had beaten, bruised, and berated me since the day we were married. I didn't know men like David existed until the day we met in the Valley of Carmel. I saw compassion in his eyes and mercy. That glimmer of hope gave me courage to tell Nabal what his foolishness had almost cost our household." She cast a glance at me, and I nodded, reassuring her of what we'd promised every day since we'd married. *You're safe with me.*

She returned her focus to Maakah. "Sometimes we need only take one brave step, and Yahweh cares for the rest."

What steps should I take with Maakah when we reach Ziklag? Whether the Philistines defeated Israel or Yahweh miraculously helped Israel defeat their enemies, our time in Ziklag would be short. King Achish wouldn't care that we'd raided the Girzites and Amalekites along with the Geshurites. His wrath would come because my deception had made him look the fool. King Achish, the Maacathite, would have my head delivered to Geshur's northern kingdom in a basket.

Achish, the Maacathite? Realization struck like a bolt of lightning. *Princess Maakah of Geshur.* I scanned my army for one of my Mighty Men—Eliphelet, a Maacathite by birth, and my longtime friend.

In that moment, he glanced my way. I waved at him to join me among the flocks. Eliphelet had saved my life during the first weeks of my flight from King Saul. Upon hearing from my best friend, Prince Jonathan, that his abba had charged me with treason and was gathering all Israel's troops against me, I'd immediately fled to Gath with the mistaken belief that the enemy of my enemy might provide sanctuary. But Achish and his soldiers remembered me, the shepherd-warrior with no armor who had killed their hometown hero, Goliath, only a few years earlier. Achish would have executed me if his nephew, Eliphelet, hadn't helped me escape the city.

Eliphelet approached at a full sprint, panting when he stopped less than a pace away. "What is it, my king?"

"Do you know Princess Maakah?" I asked.

"Achish is both my dohd and Maakah's, my king."

"What can you tell me about her?"

Eliphelet's eyes widened. "I only discovered the woman's identity when we reached Besor Brook. My ima and Maakah's ima are sisters to King Achish. My family and I lived in the nation called Maakah, northeast of Geshur, and Doda Raziah was given in marriage to King Talmai when I was only a boy. I've seen Princess Maakah only once, at her newborn dedication to Asherah. Only weeks after, a coup in the capital city of Maakah displaced *Saba* Maok from his throne. He took all his sons—Dohd Achish among them—my ima, me, and several of Maakah's fiercest giants to Gath and took the throne from its Philistine ruler."

"So you didn't recognize her because you only saw her as a baby?"

"Yes, my king," Eliphelet said. "Princess Maakah has likely been taught Dohd Achish's history, including his rise to Gath's throne, but I doubt she knows a member of her family marches with David's Mighty Men." He looked up then, meeting my eyes. "I have pledged my life—my heart—to the one true God and to His chosen king. I serve you, my lord, and our people."

Our people. There it was. The loyalty I need not have questioned. I placed a hand on his shoulder and nodded. "Thank you, my friend, for helping me understand."

He stood and mirrored my stance. "Dohd Achish offered me forgiveness when he allowed me to return to Gath with you and your men—even after I'd helped you escape years before. I'm not sure he'll forgive me again if he discovers we've destroyed every Geshurite village entrusted to his care."

"We pray for time and Yahweh's protection," I said, letting my hands fall to my sides. "Then we listen for His direction on the next step of this journey."

"Indeed." Eliphelet inclined his head and returned to his unit.

I watched him go and felt dread creep up my spine like a hairy-legged spider. *I've struck a hornets' nest with my sword.* When Achish and Talmai discovered that I'd decimated Geshur's southern kingdom—and, as Joab said, they would discover it—me, my men, and our families would be hunted by Geshurites, Maacathites, and probably all five Philistine armies. That is, if Yahweh and Israel's troops didn't conquer the Philistines in the battle raging right now.

Closing my eyes, I focused on the choice before me: either rage at God or marvel at His sovereignty. Though a large part of me wanted to rage at Yahweh, the better part of me was convinced of His goodness. *LORD, the timing of this can't be coincidental. You revealed how these pieces fit together only days after I vowed to obey Your commands regardless of political consequences.* A smile came as I marveled with a heart full of praise.

"You're smiling." The princess had slowed her donkey to ride alone beside me.

"I am," I said, meeting her amused expression.

"Perhaps since you're in high spirits, you could assign a contingent of men to escort me to one of my villages tomorrow." She scrunched her nose, highlighting a smattering of freckles across its ridge and a few on her cheeks. Had I ever met a woman so confident at such a young age?

"I must disappoint you, Princess Maakah, but as you'll see when we reach the top of the next hill, rebuilding Ziklag will require our full attention for many days." The rebuilding would keep us occupied while waiting to hear Yahweh's guidance.

Noble

"Surely you could spare a few men to accompany us to—"

"The answer is no, Princess Maakah." I stopped and took hold of Victory's bridle. "You must be patient, which I suspect you haven't practiced as the only heir of Geshur."

Her cheeks instantly flamed. Her breathing quickened. To her credit, however, she held her tongue until she exhaled a calming breath. "Give me your word that Zulat and I will be escorted to a Geshurite village at the earliest opportunity."

While thinking of a way to answer without another deception, the shofar sounded a *shevarim*, three successive blasts.

"What does that mean?" Maakah's eyes widened as she looked toward the hilltop where our caravan had stopped to face the city.

I wanted to lift her off Victory and hold her again. Promise even more emphatically that she was safe with me. Why did she stir such a protective urgency? Perhaps it was her youth and the fact that I'd just become an abba.

"David?" A sheen of tears made her look even more vulnerable. "Are we being attacked?"

"No, no." I shook my head to clear the distracting thoughts. "The shevarim alerts the camp to a significant event, a call to assemble, or the king returning home. In this case, it's all three." I forced a smile that seemed to reassure her.

But when the sounds of mourning rent the air, her confusion returned. I took the reins from her and began leading Victory to the top of the hill. Joab's prediction couldn't have been more accurate about our wives' and children's reaction to their first sight of Ziklag's destruction. They'd likely been carried away while the city was still burning, so viewing the empty shell of our city across the valley on its high plateau was more than startling. Ziklag now looked more like a skeleton than the thriving city my army left behind to rescue our families.

When we reached the hilltop and came to a stop next to Zulat,

Maakah covered her mouth and whispered, "I had no idea. . . ." Tears rolled down her cheeks, and I marveled at this extraordinary princess who could care so deeply about the lives of a people not her own. "David, I'm so sorry."

Conscience bit into my heart, leaving it bleeding for her. I swiped a hand down my face, weary to the bone of living a life of deception when Yahweh so clearly detested it. How could I demand honesty from those around me, yet model deception every moment of every day? This young woman needed to know what I'd done to Geshur's southern villages—or perhaps it was I who needed to confess it.

Glancing at the princess, I realized her maid had been correct. Maakah had witnessed too much cruelty and bloodshed since leaving Geshur, and she needed to be home with her parents, the place she felt safest. Unfortunately, the land between Ziklag and Geshur would be filled with continuing conflict: battles between Philistines and Israelites, as well as raids by escaped Amalekites and other roving tribes. I must tell her the truth about the southern villages and somehow ensure that she still felt safe in our care until Talmai could send an escort to fetch her.

I placed my hand on hers, and she startled at my touch. "Forgive me," we said together. I offered a small cloth from my waist belt, and she nodded her thanks and then dabbed her eyes and cheeks. "May I lead you and Zulat away from the crowd to explain something to you both?"

Maakah exchanged a wary glance with her maid.

Zulat stepped between us. "Should we ask your wives to join us?"

"No," I said too quickly. The thought of facing their wrath and Maakah's seemed too staggering. "I'd rather speak to you and Princess Maakah alone."

The Geshurite women nodded to each other, so I led Victory to a clearing twenty paces from prying eyes and ears to speak the painful truth. Halting my faithful donkey, I circled his nose under my

Noble

arm, placing him between me and the two women, and released a heavy sigh. "Maakah, Zulat, what I'm about to say will be extremely upsetting, but I want you to know that you are as safe in Ziklag as my own family. I will protect you with my life until King Talmai sends a contingent to escort you back to Geshur."

"But why not just take us to—"

I lifted my hand to silence the bold princess. "Though I have greatly appreciated the protection King Achish has afforded us, I confess to you now that his favor is based on my deception. My men and I have raided several villages and considerably increased Achish's wealth."

"Why would that be upsetting?" Maakah asked.

I stared into her innocent face, feeling as if a boulder had rolled onto my chest. "Because—" I cleared the emotion from my throat. "Because I told him we raided Judean villages when, in truth, we began destroying Israel's herem enemies on our Promised Land— the Girzites, Amalekites, and . . ." I swallowed, my mouth as dry as the desert we'd crossed.

Maakah's lovely face turned ashen in dusk's fading light. "No." Her back stiffened. "You didn't." She drew in a slow, steady breath, her eyes growing larger until she lunged off Victory with a blood-curdling shriek. Instinctively, I stepped back, using the donkey like a shield. When Maakah's wrapped feet hit the ground, her angry cry turned to a yowl of pain.

Zulat caught her before she fell, but Maakah's focused fury remained on me. "They were my people!"

"I'm so sorry I've hurt you." I didn't know what else to say. We'd obeyed Yahweh's command—without pleasure in the task—and lived with the haunting of those faces in our dreams.

Maakah turned her face into Zulat's chest and continued her mourning more quietly. I was nearly overwhelmed by the urge to hold her, even knowing I was the last person on earth who could bring her comfort.

"Zulat," I whispered through a tight throat, "I'll provide you with anything you need to send a message to King Talmai with his daughter's location. I suspect he'll wish to send an escort as soon as possible to see her safely home."

Cradling Maakah against her chest, Zulat slowly lifted her head to face me. "We found writing materials in some of the plunder, my lord, but I'll thank you for providing a messenger to carry the missive as soon as we reach Ziklag." Holding my gaze, her eyes bored into me like a wood drill. "Perhaps now you have more reason to consider an alliance with Geshur than you realized."

"Zulat, no!" The princess nudged her away.

I was too stunned to speak.

The maid still focused on me. "Why must King Talmai know it was you who destroyed his southern kingdom? It could have been Amalekites or Girzites." She forced a smile, which seemed entirely foreign to her features.

Maakah fell to the ground, buried her face in her hands, and wept.

I locked eyes with Zulat, staring hard into her overconfident smirk. "My Gadites have gone ahead of us to set up Princess Maakah's tent near my family's quarters. I'll send a messenger before the moon's zenith to collect your message to King Talmai. You may tell Maakah's abba whatever you wish, Zulat, but do me the courtesy of telling the truth and honoring Princess Maakah. She has conducted herself admirably and represented Geshur as a noble heir."

With a curt nod, I strode away and set my sights on Ahinoam and my newborn son. Though my uncleanness from the killing was over, the maid's suggested deception flung an even greater defilement in my path. *Never again,* I promised myself. Even facing the uncertainties of the present or the potential dangers of our future, I would never willingly live a life of deception again.

Nor would anything delay me from holding my baby boy tonight.

PART II

When David reached Ziklag, he sent some of the plunder to the elders of Judah, who were his friends . . . to those in all the other places where he and his men had roamed . . . After the death of Saul, David returned from striking down the Amalekites and stayed in Ziklag two days. On the third day a man arrived from Saul's camp with his clothes torn and dust on his head. When he came to David, he fell to the ground to pay him honor.

1 Samuel 30:26, 31; 2 Samuel 1:1–2

SEVEN

MAAKAH

"Who can hide in secret places so that I cannot see them?" declares the
LORD. *"Do not I fill heaven and earth?" declares the* LORD.

Jeremiah 23:24

Zulat had found a small vile of soothing unguent in the plunder and
wrapped my feet when we'd arrived at our tent. *If only there were
ointments to heal my broken heart.* I couldn't remember a day in my
life when I'd cried so long or felt utterly empty inside. The mourn-
ful wails in Ziklag matched my grieving soul and overwhelmed the
pain in my feet. I looked down at the clay goddess in my hand. The
Queen of Heaven had done nothing to save our southern villages.
Was her power completely muted this far from Geshur? Or was
David's god too strong for any nation to stand against?

"Come over here, Prin, and help me craft this letter to your abba."
Zulat's callousness remained even while surrounded by a weeping
city. "All this grieving doesn't help secure Geshur's future."

My eyes, swollen and throbbing from prolonged tears and
Ziklag's acrid air, landed on my disrespectful maid. "Have you no
compassion for at least our fallen Geshurite villages?"

With a dramatic sigh, she placed the sharpened feather on the flattened saddle she was using as a writing table and looked up with condescension-weighted eyelids. "Of course I'm sorry the people in our southern villages were killed, but I hadn't spoken to any of them in over a decade. Had you? No. So, close that tent flap. You're letting in smoky air. And come over here to help me with this message to your abba." She picked up her feather and resumed the task.

"I will not hide my compassion! Put that stylus down and look at me!"

She obeyed but with another sigh. "I'm sorry the people of Ziklag lost their homes, Prin, but why not stop all this wailing and get on with the rebuilding? By all the gods," she said in a whisper, "you'd think these people would be accustomed to tragedy after following a rebel like David ben Jesse all these years. Now, may I?" She pointed to the stylus and waited only a moment before picking it up again to resume her work.

Grief turned to fury, and I wanted nothing more than to snatch the parchment from my maid and banish her from my presence. But at the mere thought of being abandoned, fear constricted my throat and kept me silent. The same fear that silenced me after David's confession. *Without Zulat, I'd be completely alone among people I barely know.*

"Think about it, Prin," Zulat continued as she wrote, "the tragedy of the southern villages could be your triumph. Your uncle doesn't know David did it. Your abba doesn't know it. You hold this secret over David ben Jesse's head like a village guarding the only clean-water spring, and David is a man dying of thirst." She chuckled to herself. "Did you see his panic when I told him we could allow King Talmai to believe someone else destroyed Geshur's villages?"

"It wasn't panic," I mumbled.

She scoffed. "Well, he tried to intimidate me, but he knows his little camp would never survive if I told your abba or King Achish what he'd done. If the Philistines win and make him Israel's king, you will be his queen, Prin. You'll hold that secret over his head and turn him like a mule with a bridle."

"Stop it!" I shouted, startling the stylus from her hand. She glared up at me but quickly softened when I rushed closer, towering over her. "I don't want to rule the man I marry. Must I tear out my heart because royal blood flows through my veins? Does feeling compassion make me a weak leader? Does weeping for Ziklag's losses disqualify me to rule in Geshur?" Zulat drew breath to speak, but I lifted a hand for silence. "Don't you dare say, 'Kingdom first—always.' Sometimes Ima puts kingdom first by showing mercy to our people. She willingly visits the poorest neighborhoods of Geshur and walks their sullied streets to help those who have no food, no shelter, and no healers."

"The Geshurites in our southern kingdom are *dead*," Zulat hissed. "They care nothing for your mercy or your grief. Make their deaths mean something, Prin! Use their sacrifice to secure a clear trade route through Israel and set Geshur apart from the other Aramean nations. Your abba will laud your political acumen. Set aside your emotions long enough to consider more than your own desires, your own *feelings*." She sneered as she said the last word as if it tasted bitter on her tongue, then picked up her stylus and continued writing as if our conversation was over.

I slammed my hand onto the scroll. "Like you set aside desire and feelings, Zulat? If I become like you, how can I become a queen?"

Her head snapped up, eyes full of fire. Calmly, she moved the saddle to her side, careful not to jostle the small pot of ink, then struggled to her feet. "You will only be different than me, Princess Maakah, if you do as you've been trained."

"Yes, yes. Kingdom first—always." I repeated the tired phrase with the mocking sing-song voice I heard in my head every time Abba, Ima, or Zulat reminded me of it.

"That wasn't what I was going to say." Her penetrating eyes

shamed me as they always did. "You will only be different than a peasant who has deadened their inner world if you do every royal duty with elegance and nobility—as does your ima—ensuring everyone understands their station. It is your privilege as a royal lady to show mercy and compassion beyond what your servants deserve. You, as the giver, bestow from a place of honor and celestial favor to the receivers in their position of degradation. They were placed there by their own poor choices or by the gods' determination. To blur the lines of station that the gods set in place tempts the deities to remove their favor from you and bestow it on another."

"Haven't you blurred the lines of station, Zulat, by insisting I marry David when I clearly refused him?" My voice broke, and I lowered my head. Why wasn't I a strong ruler like Abba and Ima?

A familiar gnarled knuckle tucked beneath my chin and gently tilted it upward to meet Zulat's tender gaze. "Your abba and ima sent me with you for this very reason, my girl. You're twenty harvests old, but you've never left the protection of Geshur's walls. You've never experienced the horrors we've seen during the past two weeks. *Two weeks*, Prin. You have a whole lifetime ahead, and I'm sorry to say, life seldom gets easier. I'm teaching you to think more quickly than your feelings can react. It's what elevates great rulers from a mediocre reign. I'm insisting because I see what happens if you don't take the lead. If you only react to what others do or say, you'll never get to determine the rules of the game."

Thinking of a lifetime filled with deception, wars, death, trade, and treaties felt like an avalanche that would bury me where I stood. I'd seen no such games or stations among David's women. Though Ahinoam, Abigail, and his sister Zerry were clearly leaders among the women, they never used their authority like a whip or prod. None of the three were designated a queen, but the women in camp willingly obeyed them as beloved friends. "I want to be more than a queen," I said quietly.

Zulat scoffed. "Only a king is more than a queen, and I don't believe David ben Jesse would relinquish a throne he's waited so long to attain."

"I don't want to rule David, his people, and definitely not Ahinoam and Abigail. I simply want to enjoy them as friends—perhaps someday."

Zulat's expression lost all warmth, every muscle in her face pinched and disapproving. "You expect too much, Prin. Set your sights on winning David ben Jesse's trust, but never trust any woman. A king's harem is more dangerous than a battlefield, and the grudges there last longer than any war."

"But Abigail and Ahinoam aren't like the women in Abba's harem. They don't seem jealous of each other like Abba's concubines are of Ima."

"We've never been alone with them. Of course they're polite when the whole camp is watching, but no woman can share her husband without making it a competition." Zulat waved her hand and reached for the scroll. "Enough talk about your rivals. Let's focus on your betrothal before we discuss how you'll best his wives and become David's queen." She unfurled the scroll. "May I read what I've written to your abba so far?"

I would never marry the man who killed hundreds of Geshurites, and I wasn't even sure Ahinoam and Abigail still wished to be my friend. But Zulat had employed the same tactic she'd taught me when reaching an impasse: *Delay. Defer. Deflect.*

"Go ahead." I sighed and looked away. She came nearer, placed the little clay Asherah in my hand, and read quietly so passersby couldn't hear.

"From the beloved heir to Geshur's throne.
    To the most honored King Talmai in the name of Asherah, Queen of Heaven.

Noble

I am safe and well in David ben Jesse's city of Ziklag, but I must report sad news. Every village in our southern kingdom has been completely destroyed by marauders. Thus, the cessation of tribute. In addition, David ben Jesse is currently wed to two common women. My match—as a third wife rising to queen—may still be prudent if the Philistines are victorious. Will wait for direction from Geshur's most esteemed king.

Also, I humbly request news on the queen's health. May the Mother Goddess protect you both."

Zulat lowered the scroll and pursed her lips.

Her restraint was surprising. "No more coaxing my approval?" I asked.

"I've presented you with the realities that surround us, Prin. At some point, you must reign."

David had asked her to tell the truth and honor me in the missive. She neither named the marauders nor disclosed that I had flatly refused to marry David. And she hadn't lied. I felt a measure of relief that Zulat's discretion had in some ways saved this city—at least for the moment.

"Your words represent me well," I said, "but Abba will still be angry when he hears about the villages and David's two wives." I was paranoid since I'd witnessed his violence against Saul's messenger. "To ensure he won't take out his frustration on David's carrier, perhaps add something like, 'Please send your reply with the bearer of this message,' so we can encourage his safe return."

"Of course." Returning to her spot and repositioning the saddle on her lap, she scratched a few more words on the scroll.

I waddled back to the tent flap, walking mostly on my heels to relieve the blisters on the balls of my feet, and watched the mourners disperse to their temporary homes. A commotion behind me stole my attention. Zulat was struggling to her feet again, a stick of wax in one hand and my seal in the other.

"Do you need help?" I asked, starting toward her.

"No, no!" She bent over the small fire at our tent's center and held the wax stick close to the flame. When the tip dripped wax, she smeared a small dollop over the scroll's seam and quickly pressed my seal into the wax before it hardened.

She brushed gray hair from her sweaty brow and set the scroll aside. "There. It's ready for whenever the messenger comes. Now, I'll fix us a light meal before . . ." She pointed to the goddess in my hand, then lifted her arms to the heavens to signal our first night of private sacrifice to the Queen of Heaven.

My belly clenched at the thought. Both David and the women of his family had been adamant about the penalty for worshiping our gods in their camp. Death. No trial. No mercy.

"Zulat, no," I said too loudly as footsteps passed by our tent.

Zulat pressed a finger against her lips, then, "You don't wish to eat now?" Her eyes bulged, silently reminding me that the last thing those outside the tent would have heard was our conversation about food.

I took a few steps toward her, picked up the scroll, and tucked it into my waist belt. Then I placed the goddess in Zulat's hand and said loud enough for the whole street to hear, "I'm not hungry. I think I'll go ask which messenger David has chosen and deliver our missive now."

"Prin, no! You can't go wandering by yourself."

I stopped at the tent's opening and looked over my shoulder. "Didn't you just remind me that at some point I must begin to reign?" I scurried into the night, ignoring her protests.

Stepping into Ziklag's wasteland alone was like a slap in the face. The desert heat had given way to night's chill, and I rubbed my arms to stir the blood. The sound of mallets pounding wooden pegs into place echoed in the air. Watchmen stood atop the suspended path attached to the high wall around the city to secure the patrolling circuit where they made their night rounds like sharp-eyed eagles.

Another contingent of workers scurried here and there, carrying buckets of charred waste to a pile outside the walls. I stood in the middle of our main street, between my tent and David's, allowing the pain in my feet to subside. Down the dusty street, left and right, were long rows of goat-hair dwellings on both sides of our thoroughfare. David's men had purchased enough in Gerar to line six more streets, which were arranged around the central well like the spokes of a wagon wheel. Within each goat-hair tent lived as many as three or four families. Behind the sturdy dwellings loomed the specters of Ziklag's burned-out homes.

The camp had settled into a peaceful hum. Scrumptious smells swirled and wafted through the streets, overpowering the lingering smoke and rekindling hope for better days ahead. I felt a stab of homesickness, missing Abba and Ima and the quiet meals we shared each day.

"Good evening, mistress," said a grimy soldier passing by. After three or four steps, he stopped, turned, and tilted his head. "Are you alone? Do you need help?"

I almost said, *Yes, I feel entirely alone,* but answered instead, "No, I'm fine." I awkwardly waved him away and turned to face David ben Jesse's tent. If I wanted to get my message to Geshur sooner, I must face the man who destroyed my southern villages, since only David knew who he'd chosen as the runner.

The sound of David's rich laughter drew me closer to his tent, where lamplight and shadows flickered through the slender opening. Abigail and Ahinoam answered with delighted laughter of their own. How could they laugh after so much death and destruction? Yet their contented joy beckoned me like a summons. I crept closer, hiding behind the right-side flap to peer inside.

Granted, I should have immediately announced my presence, but my hesitation was twofold. First, there was the practical consideration: How did one knock on a tent? Secondly, David had no guard to announce a guest's arrival, so what sort of protocol was appropriate for a woman alone to visit the chieftain and his wives after darkness fell?

Truth be told, I was mesmerized by the way this gentle yet fierce warrior interacted with his wives and couldn't bear to interrupt. Their easy banter was as lovely as Asherah's wedding dance. Both graceful and intimate, the three of them demonstrated their deep love through well-tended friendship. They spoke heaping measures of encouragement mingled with respectful poking at personal totems, intimate things known only to one another. Their words were careful yet chosen out of respect, not fear. Love, not manipulation.

Zulat had been mistaken. Abigail and Ahinoam were every bit as loving to each other while in their private chamber with their husband as they'd been during Ahinoam's terrifying birth. I saw the same adoration in David's eyes for both women that I witnessed in my own abba's eyes when he looked at Ima. But how could one man love two women with equal passion? And how could two women allow it? No, more than allow it—rather, *embrace* each other as sisters? Clearly, their strange god had cast a spell over them all, this god who empowered his people to love and kill beyond reason.

In that moment, I realized something as horrifying as David's confession. Considering the depth of sharing between him and his two wives, Abigail and Ahinoam had almost certainly known about the Geshurite raids all along. They could have told me the truth when they discovered I was Geshur's princess. I'd even mentioned going to the southern villages, and they kept David's awful deception from me.

I peeked inside again, watching the tender care with which Abigail transferred David's infant son into his arms and the satisfaction

Noble

on Ahinoam's features. *I thought you were my friends!* I raged silently. But as soon as the thought crossed my mind, it was silenced by the obvious: Their first loyalty was to their husband—as it should be. I wanted to hate all three of them for what David and his men had done to my people, but if Abba believed Baal had commanded that he go to war with the Israelites, he wouldn't hesitate to obey.

Life outside Geshur's walls was definitely more complicated than I had anticipated, with far more heartache than I had imagined.

"Phsst!"

Startled by the sound, I whirled, ready to scream—but saw no one in the street.

"Phsst!"

I stepped gingerly around the tent's corner, following the sound, and there found David's general leaning against a charred house. He wore a satisfied grin and pressed a single finger against his lips, then motioned for me to follow. He kept to the shadows, and I tried to keep up despite the pain in my feet while we walked toward the city gate.

Could I trust Joab? I suddenly wished I'd stayed with Zulat and let David's messenger come to us. But I'd insisted on doing this myself. *I'm reigning.*

Straightening my shoulders and spine, I hobbled like an elderly queen behind David's general. When he stopped in a small clearing behind the family's row of tents, cold dread lifted the hairs on my arms. What if he attacked me? I couldn't run away. "General, I don't know what—"

"Thank you, Majesty, for giving me this private audience." Joab offered a slight bow and continued in a whisper, "What I have to say would be best for you alone to hear."

Cautionary trumpets blared in my mind. "Shouldn't a loyal general be able to say anything to his king?"

"Everything I tell you now, I've already said to David. I realize

128

you may have decided against your betrothal to my lord since he confessed to the raids on the Geshurite villages, and that he already has two wives." His gaze never left mine. "The princess and only heir of Geshur must make a wise political match."

"Surely you agree that becoming the third wife of a murdering scoundrel ranks rather low on political wisdom."

One side of his lips twitched, threatening a smile. "I see your point, Majesty, but can *you* agree that Israel would provide a crucial trade partner for Geshur?"

"Of course." I'd known that much since I was five.

"Though my men may seem a meager army with only a passionate leader," Joab continued, "let me assure you that David ben Jesse *will* be Israel's next king. And he will rule *all* the land that Yahweh promised to our ancestors, the land of the Amorites, Hittites, Perizzites—"

"Yes, yes, I've heard the list. Why are you so certain David will sit on Israel's throne when Saul has four capable sons?"

Joab scoffed. "Saul has three capable sons and one imbecile in Ish-Bosheth. Saul won't allow his youngest to go anywhere near a battlefield, and the king's oldest son, Jonathan, is David's best friend. If Jonathan inherits the throne, he'll immediately turn it over to David."

At least Joab had confirmed my suspicions about Ish-Bosheth, but he had to be lying about Jonathan. "No crown prince willingly gives up his rightful inheritance, especially to someone outside the royal lineage."

"Israel has no royal lineage. Saul—a donkey farmer—was our first king, and Yahweh stripped away his throne because Saul refused to totally destroy the Amalekites when he had the chance."

"Your god would interfere in the reign of kings?"

"Our God was our only King until the Israelites demanded a human king on a throne like the rest of the nations. When Saul

Noble

disobeyed and then made excuses about it rather than repenting before the LORD, Yahweh promised to provide a new king, a man after God's own heart."

"How long ago was that?"

"God made that promise years before David was born and has since promised that David's throne will be an eternal kingdom."

"I don't understand."

Joab's twitching lips turned into a full-blown smile. "Nor do I, but this is what I *do* know: Saul's son, Jonathan, is faithful to both Yahweh and to David. Jonathan knows the prophet Samuel speaks the very words of God, and he anointed David years ago to become Israel's next king. Jonathan will honor Yahweh's choice for Israel's throne." Joab leaned closer, his eyes like onyx beads. "So, Majesty, if you wish to marry the king who will choose Israel's trade allies, you should honor your abba's betrothal proposal."

My mouth, suddenly dry, could barely form words. "Why tell me this?"

"Because David doesn't yet know how to reign like a king. You can teach him."

I almost laughed. "What makes you think he will listen to me?"

"To the contrary," Joab said. "He pores over your words slowly, like pouring honey on a cold day, rather than dismissing them like a honeycomb dripping in the sun."

A cynical huff escaped. "A general and a poet. Surely you know David ben Jesse better than anyone, with his charm and honeyed words. I suspect he acts the same with every woman he tries to persuade."

Joab sobered. "You're wrong, Princess Maakah. Yes, David can be charming, but he doesn't act falsely toward the women in our camp. The honor he shows you is real. He's capable of deeper feelings than any man I know. David loves Ahinoam and Abigail more than is healthy for any king. You see, he still believes marriage should be based more on the heart than political gain. He believes his wives' feelings are more important than his throne and that Yahweh will intervene on his behalf—even when Yahweh has given him wisdom and warriors to fight our battles."

"And you think he and I will incite battles if we break the betrothal contract?"

His brow lifted as if taking my measure before answering. "What I *know* is that David ben Jesse will be a better king with you at his side." He bowed and turned to leave me.

"General."

He stopped and faced me again.

"How can I trust him or you—or anyone in this city—who has killed hundreds of my countrymen?"

"Those villages were seeds planted in the land Yahweh promised to Israel. We have no arguments with your abba's Aramean kingdom—as long as he remains north of our God-given borders. And you can trust David because he told you the truth when he could have deceived you as he's done to your dohd Achish for over a year. David is a good man, Princess, and he's already a noble ruler." He grinned with a glint of mischief in his eyes. "David just needs your help to be royal."

I suppressed a smile and produced the scroll from my belt. "Where do I find the messenger David chose to carry this message to Geshur?"

He extended his hand. "I'll give it to him and the Gadite chosen to accompany him."

"Thank you, General, but no." I tucked it back into my belt. "The scroll will remain in my possession until the couriers fetch it from my tent. I'll then escort them to the city gate and watch them leave."

"You see?" he chuckled. "The wisdom of a royal wife could teach David much about the precautions of a king's court." He bowed again and walked away.

Noble

Standing alone in the darkness, I heard no more hammering. The night watchmen had begun their patrol on the repaired walkway above the city, and a sense of wonder passed over me. *Someday I could rule those men as their queen. I could be queen over all of Israel.*

The flutter in my belly shifted to a tightening ball of knots. But only if I lie to Abba about who destroyed our villages. Only if Dohd Achish never discovers the truth. Only if the Philistines conquer Israel and Dohd Achish convinces the other Philistine kings to place David on Israel's throne.

And I still needed to answer the biggest question of all: Could I marry David ben Jesse without feeling like I'd betrayed Abigail and Ahinoam, Geshur's southern kingdom, or the memory of my first love?

EIGHT

MAAKAH

Other members of the Thirty included . . . Eliphelet son of Ahasbai from Maacah.

2 Samuel 23:24, 34 NLT

I waddled slowly back to the tent, my feet throbbing after so much walking and the wrappings caked with dust. My heart thrummed in perfect rhythm with each thought of Kepha.

I let myself remember more about that night of our last meeting in Geshur's palace garden. *"I'll return in time to honor our wedding date,"* he'd promised, then kissed the back of my hand. Leaning close, he whispered, *"I hope you'll come to our marriage bed with the confidence of knowing you're loved."* He was so much more than a valiant warrior. He'd loved me with his gentle soul, and I believe the men who fought with him would have been as loyal to him as David's army was to the son of Jesse.

Too soon, I stood outside my tent and heard Zulat humming. Peering inside, I found her unpacking supplies that David's wives had shared from the Amalekite plunder. Mourners had quieted for the night, leaving the city still with a soothing peace. Perhaps I could quiet my grief, too. Though I might never love another as I

133

had Kepha, I realized for the first time that my sorrow had been that of a dreamy, fourteen-harvest-old girl. The feelings were real. Important, even. Because they enlarged my heart to embrace others who had experienced loss. *Like David.*

I glanced over my shoulder at his tent. I'd seen in him the ability to care deeply because of all he'd lost. Hadn't Eglah said that both she and David lost their imas when the Amalekites raided Bethlehem? I'd heard the merchants' gossip when King Saul gave David's first wife to another man. Had he loved her? Had he loved his ima? If so, how could he kill hundreds of innocent Geshurites, knowing he'd inflict that same pain of loss on families in Geshur?

My tent flap jerked open, and Zulat stared at me with a familiar frown. "Why are you standing in the cold? You'll catch a chill." She nudged me inside like a hen with a wandering chick. "I found dried fruit, crusty bread, and dried meat in the supplies. I'm sure we, along with David's wives, will be served something fresher in the morning."

I had just lowered myself to my reed mat when I heard, "Shalom to this tent." A male voice came from the opening and jiggled one flap.

Zulat lifted a silencing hand, then whispered, "You still have a maid to welcome your guests, *mistress.*"

Why did she only call me *mistress* when it suited her?

Zulat hurried to the entrance and yanked open the tent flap. Three men waited to enter. One was the Egyptian servant who led David and his men to the Amalekite village. The second I didn't recognize. The third made my insides feel like curdled milk. He was the exact image of Dohd Achish as he'd looked twelve years ago in Abba's courtroom. *He must be the king's son.* I stood on aching feet and joined Zulat in a bow. "Welcome, prince of Gath," I said, breathless. "We are honored by your visit."

I straightened, and Number Three's eyes were the size of our wooden plates. "No, no. I'm not a prince."

"But you look very much like—"

"I'm a Maacathite."

"Come in!" Zulat ushered all three men toward me. "Any relative of my mistress is welcome."

My eyes hadn't left Dohd Achish's lookalike, nor had he turned away. "You look very much like the king of Gath," I said, unable to mask my awe.

"And you look very much like my ima." His face lit with a kind smile. "She is King Achish's sister. I'm one of the messengers going to Geshur—"

I covered a small gasp, but Zulat stopped us. "How do we know this isn't a ploy? Will you convince us to follow you, pretend to escort us to Geshur, but instead kill us in the desert?"

The man let out a surprised chuckle. "Well, that's a very creative plan, but I have no intention of killing a cousin I just met." He returned his attention to me. "I'm sure you're eager to return home, Princess, but the journey northeast right now would be far too dangerous until we receive word on the war between Israel and the Philistines. Our scouts haven't yet located the escaped Amalekites, which adds to the risk. Those desert dogs will be especially desperate to raid any travelers since they abandoned all their plunder to us."

"You use the terms *we* and *us*," I said. "Are you a Maacathite or one of David's men?"

"I'm both." He respectfully nodded and began his introduction, "I am Eliphelet, son of Ahasbai. My ima's name is Razin. She is King Achish's youngest sister."

"My ima has no sisters," I said. "Only seven brothers."

"Leave!" Zulat pointed toward the tent flap.

Eliphelet looked puzzled, glancing from me to my maid. "But I'm here to pick up the message you've prepared for King Talmai." He stepped aside to introduce his companions. "Eliel is the Gadite

Noble

who will safely lead us through the wilderness, and Nakia is our new Egyptian courier who will learn all Eliel has to teach him."

"Have you visited Geshur often?" I asked. "When did you come to Gath? How did you become one of David's soldiers?"

"Wait, wait, one question at a time." His good-natured chuckle made me believe he'd be willing to answer whatever I asked. "As you may know," he began, "Saba Maacah was king of the nation that bore his name, sharing Geshur's northeastern border. He had just sealed a treaty with your abba Talmai by giving his oldest daughter, Raziah, in marriage to Geshur's young king.

"Only days after the wedding feast ended, rebels staged a coup in Maacah and dethroned Saba. He escaped with his life, his wife, seven sons, and one daughter. Unbeknownst to anyone but King Maacah, most of his army and a full contingent of Anak's descendants followed at a distance to ensure the protection of our fugitive family. When the Maacathite family reached Gath, we were given sanctuary by King Ahasbai. Unknown to Ahasbai, however, Saba's loyal warriors and Anak's descendants—"

"You mean the giants?" I clarified.

"Yes, the giants. They waited near Adullam Cave for Saba's signal to attack. Largely because of the Anakites' superhuman strength, Saba Maacah overthrew Ahasbai's throne. As a concession, Saba made Ahasbai governor over Ziklag."

"This Ziklag?"

Eliphelet nodded. "Saba also presented Ahasbai with a wife—his youngest daughter, Razin."

"No!" I said without thinking. "Why give his daughter to a defeated foe? Didn't he realize Ahasbai would take out his anger on her?"

"I was born five months after they were wed." Eliphelet waited until I nodded my understanding. "Ima never revealed my true abba's identity. I don't remember a day in Ahasbai's household that

136

I wasn't afraid. Ima bore fresh wounds or bruises every day that we lived in his house. When I was ten years old, instead of using his fists or leather strap to beat her, Ahasbai used a dagger on her face. I escaped before he came for me, joined a caravan, and worked my way to Gath in search of Prince Achish.

"A kind man delivered me to Dohd's chamber at the palace. When Achish saw my bruises and inspected the scars, he believed the story I told him about Ima's face. He hid me in his chamber and prepared for Ima's rescue. Late one night, he sent a spy to rescue her from Ziklag before the giants arrived at dawn. Dohd Achish gave us his chamber and sent the palace physician. He sewed her face and took care of her for months. I slept on a thick carpet beside her raised mattress every night—no longer needing to hide a dagger beneath my headrest."

"Oh, Eliphelet." I covered my quaking lips. "I'm so sorry. Where is your ima now?" My imagination spun all sorts of awful possibilities.

"She remains a resident of Gath's palace and enjoys a private life." His eyes grew sad, his lips pressing into a downward arc. "She has refused to see me since I rejected the Philistine gods. She stopped replying to my letters after I pledged allegiance to Yahweh and His chosen king."

I felt blood draining from my face. "You've rejected all the Philistine gods?" He began nodding. "Even Baal and Asherah?"

"Dagon was hardest for me to reject, but when I repeatedly saw the Hebrew God fight with us and for us, I couldn't deny that He was real and faithful, not only to David ben Jesse but also to anyone who chooses Him."

"That's enough." Zulat nudged me aside, standing toe-to-toe with Eliphelet. "Take the message and go but never speak to Princess Maakah again of your treasonous choices. You're no longer worthy to bear the name Maacathite."

Noble

He staggered back as if she'd stabbed him. "I meant no disrespect."

"Stop it, Zulat." I produced the scroll from my belt, placed it in his hand, and glanced over his shoulder at the other two men. "May the Hebrew god protect you all."

I stood back and noticed Eliphelet studying me. "You're not anything like them," he said.

"Not like who?"

"Not like Maacathite royalty—or any royalty. You notice people. You're interested in their stories, and you're far too compassionate."

Was he complimenting or condemning me? "And what about David ben Jesse? Is he like other royalty?"

He laughed, and the others joined him. "Oh, no," Eliel said. "David is a shepherd and a warrior. He cares deeply and protects fiercely, but he's not royal."

Eliphelet added, "He may not be royal, but he'll be the noblest king the earth has ever known."

NINE

MAAKAH

My frame was not hidden from you when I was made in the secret place,
when I was woven together in the depths of the earth.

Psalm 139:15

"Shalóm to all in the tent." Abigail's greeting was followed by long, slender fingers shaking one side of our tent's flap.

I'd dreaded this moment since David's confession about destroying Geshurite villages. My aching feet had kept me awake most of the night, giving more time to chase horrifying memories of dying Amalekites from my mind. I felt no pity for the Amalekite warriors, but my tortured thoughts placed a Geshurite face on each fallen woman and child I'd seen die at the Hebrews' hands. By the time I woke, my heart ached nearly as much as my feet.

"Hello?" came a second greeting from our tent flap.

I looked over the sparse meal Zulat had prepared to break our fast, but she ignored me and our visitor. I hadn't mentioned to her the increased discomfort of the blisters on my feet. In fact, we'd immediately gone to our mats after the messengers left last night. Neither of us had broached the topic of whether David's wives knew about the attacks on our Geshurite villages. Though I wanted to

139

believe they didn't know, the level of transparency David shared with Abigail and Ahinoam gave me little hope that my new friends were ignorant of the slaughter.

"Coming," I said when Zulat still gave no indication she'd move. "So much for the maid who insisted on greeting our guests."

She offered only a disapproving grunt when I pushed aside my half-eaten plate of goat cheese and hard bread. When my feet bore full weight, I sucked in a breath through clenched teeth. Spots dotted my vision.

"Prin?" Zulat stood to support me, but I refused her coddling and waddled on blazing stumps to meet Abigail.

Our visitor peeked through the tent flap before I reached her, brow creased and lifted with concern. "We're fairly informal in Ziklag," she said quietly, "even when we have homes with doors. May I come in?"

"Of course," I said, thankful not to waddle any farther. My belly began tossing and tumbling. Was it the pain or nerves about the difficult conversation we couldn't avoid? "I planned to speak with you and Ahinoam this morning."

"I'm sorry, Maakah," she said when I turned to face her. "David told us last night that he confessed what happened to your southern villages."

Our gazes held as I waited for her to say more. She didn't.

"What exactly are you sorry about?" I asked, sounding snarky without regret.

Her tentative features softened into—was it shame? Pity? Sadness? "I'm sorry for the loss to you personally and to your nation," she said. "And for the disappointment you must feel in David— perhaps even in Ahinoam and me for not revealing the truth when we discovered your identity."

Caught off guard by her directness, I spoke to her glaring omission. "Why aren't you sorry that your husband and his brigands killed hundreds of innocent people? How can—"

"They weren't innocent, Maakah." Her tenderness fled. "Our men returned from their assigned missions with only treasure that foreign villages stole from Judean cities. Every Geshurite town they destroyed had amassed significant Judean wealth by raiding *our* people."

"Geshurites don't raid." I refused to bear the grief of loss and the shame of false accusations.

Abigail's cheeks looked as fiery as mine felt. She paused, however, leaving the tension crackling between us. Inhaling a deep breath, she exhaled slowly and lifted her chin as regally as any queen. "Perhaps there's no need for your northern kingdom to raid other cities or nations, Maakah, but let me assure you that to live in this unforgiving desert, every town and village steals from another to survive the punishing sun and unrelenting droughts."

"Including David ben Jesse." I sneered. "How can you condone such—"

"I don't," she said sharply. "And David vowed to Nomy and me last night that he'll never again condone raids on villages for any other purpose than to obey our God's commands."

I proved my doubts with a huff. "Surely David doesn't think I'm so naïve to believe he'd make such a rash vow simply because of my tears."

The edges of Abigail's lips tipped up slightly. "The fact that you'd even think that David would make a vow based on your tears proves how little you know my husband. He made the decision after his conversation with our God while we were still at the Amalekite camp."

Struck dumb by the revelation, I would have been more willing to believe that David ben Jesse had been swayed by my grieving. "Are . . . are you suggesting that your husband actually speaks to a god face-to-face?" The hairs on my arms stood up as I voiced the question.

Abigail tilted her head with a forbearing smile. "Yahweh doesn't speak to David face-to-face as you and I are speaking now, but my husband does hear Yahweh speak directly. Not with his ears, but within his consciousness."

"That's enough!" Zulat shot to her feet and stood at my side. Though I expected her to mirror my indignation, she bowed slightly to Abigail and donned a poorly feigned smile. "Since the messengers likely won't return for at least a week—perhaps two, if they're delayed by the Philistine-Israelite conflict. I'm sure Princess Maakah would be willing to help you and Mistress Ahinoam. My mistress is adept at organization, recordkeeping, and whatever else is required of a chieftain's wife."

I glared at my maid. She was still acting as if I would honor the betrothal, but how could I marry the brigand who killed the men, women, and children in our southern villages?

"Thank you, Zulat." Abigail's smile widened when she turned to me. "Are you willing to spend time with Nomy and me even though you know what happened to Geshur's villages?"

"You still want my help after the way I've spoken to you?"

Abigail reached for my hands. "I can't imagine how hard it will be for you to live among us, knowing what our warriors have done, but David, Nomy, and I are deeply sorry for the loss you're feeling. We want to do all we can to help you feel safe and welcomed into our city, our home, and our lives. We believe Yahweh brought both you and Zulat to us for a purpose, Maakah. Maybe it was simply to help with Nomy's birth. But I hope you'll give us a chance to be your friends so we can discover together if there's more to God's purpose."

A lump of tangled emotions made it impossible to speak, so I nodded in agreement and squeezed her hands.

She returned the squeeze and then looked at Zulat. "Unfortunately, we have little recordkeeping to do, and Joab helped us organize the tasks for rebuilding last night." She looked back at me and asked, "How do you feel about making bread? Would you and Zulat like to join Nomy, Zerry, and me in our tent to bake bread for the camp?"

"The whole camp?" I asked. "Surely Ahinoam isn't sufficiently recovered after having her child to mix and knead bread all day."

Abigail released a tinkling laugh. "You're a natural ruler."

"You mean I'm bossy."

She put her arm around my shoulders to lead me out of the tent. "Not at all. I meant you consider others before you think of yourself. Someday you'll be a wonderful ima." She called over her shoulder, "Zulat, are you coming? Zerry would be especially disappointed if she couldn't argue with you about the recipes today."

"Zerry could be wrong and still argue the tail off a donkey," Zulat said, remaining where we'd left her.

Abigail stopped at the tent flap and glanced back. "So, you'll come?"

Zulat waved us out of the tent. "Not this morning. I'll unpack and make this smelly tent a home for my mistress, but I'll come after midday to instruct everyone on making the best bread south of Damascus." I cringed at my maid's hubris, but Abigail chuckled softly.

We left the tent, and I clenched my teeth against the pain, while trying to keep pace with Abigail's long-legged strides. "Is it awful that I'm relieved to be free of Zulat for the morning?" I asked Abigail in a whisper.

She glanced over her shoulder. "She seems very strict."

"You have no idea." Leaving it at that, I struggled with every step that felt like daggers piercing my feet. How could day-old wounds hurt worse than the day of injury?

"Will Abital be joining us today?" I asked to distract myself.

"Not today. She and Eglah are spending the day setting up their

Noble

tent to create a partitioned room so Asahel and Abital can have some privacy." Now two paces ahead, she looked back and then stopped for me to catch up. "Are you all right?"

I waved off her concern. "Yes, it's just those silly blisters from my new sandals. I'm sure they'll be scabbed over by tomorrow." We resumed our walk, Abigail slowing to remain beside me. "I've wondered why Abital was the only one of Zerry's three daughters-in-law who seemed to spend much time with you, Ahinoam, Zerry, and Abital. Have Joab's and Abishai's wives been banished, or do they choose to stay away for some reason?"

Abigail gave me a sideways glance. "You're extremely direct, Princess Maakah."

A burst of anger brought my head up, but Abigail's wry grin greeted me. My defensiveness was doused by her honest appreciation. "I was practicing," I said, "before I spent a whole day with Zerry and Ahinoam, the *queens* of directness." We laughed aloud, gaining the attention of passersby.

Abigail waved and called the women by name and then whispered to only me, "You'll fit quite well into our circle."

Her confidence gave me the boost I needed to enter the tent across the street from mine. Halting at the threshold, a thought suddenly pierced me: *Does everyone in Ziklag know about my villages? Of course they do.*

The realization quickened my heartbeat and deepened the throbbing in both feet. Zerry and Ahinoam had been overwhelmingly friendly to me before David had revealed his crimes against my southern kingdom. Had their acceptance been a ploy to hide David's secret or to lessen my anger when I learned the truth? Would they treat me differently today? Why was I so nervous when it was David who'd wronged Geshur?

Moving into the tent, I scanned the interior. Zerry leaned against a corner in the main room, paying attention to no one else except the newborn nephew in her arms. Ahinoam arranged sacks of wheat that David's men had purchased at Gerar's marketplace yesterday. The new ima straightened, wiped her brow with the back of her hand, and smiled at me. "Welcome, Maakah. I was so hoping you would come and we could start over on our friendship." She came close, offering her grain-dust-covered hand. "We'll start with grinding this morning."

"That's a lot of grain," I said, trying to calculate just how much bread we'd need to make to feed the entire city. "Is anyone besides Zerry and Zulat helping us?"

"We have five capable women and all day to make the bread," Ahinoam said. "We don't need help." She placed other ingredients on the low table, which I assumed we'd use for mixing and kneading. "David spent most of the night assigning tasks to the men with Joab and the captains while Abigail and I assigned the women's duties. Everyone has plenty to do, but no one is overburdened."

As Abigail began describing the bread-making tasks, my cheeks grew warmer. "Nomy will grind grain, a sitting-down job, so she can continue working while nursing the baby. Maakah, you and I will take turns grinding and kneading. Since Zulat is otherwise occupied this morning, she can help Zerry with the final step of baking later in the day."

Ahinoam had stopped placing things on the table and was staring at me, her eyebrows drawn in concern. "Don't you like to grind grain? Or is it the thought of kneading that makes you look like you drank a cup of vinegar?"

I couldn't confess how badly my blistered feet pained me, so I divulged another truth instead. "I'm more than willing to do anything you ask of me, but . . ." My mouth was parched by humiliation, but after a fortifying breath, I confessed, "I've never even visited the kitchen in our palace, so I know nothing about grinding or kneading or baking." The whole room fell silent, and I bowed my head, embarrassment turning to shame.

A comforting arm slid around my shoulders. "Yet you're willing to help us today?" Wonder laced Ahinoam's tone.

Abigail stood in front of me and tilted my chin up to face her. "You're the only princess I've ever met, but you're very different than stories I've heard about others. The royalty I've heard of places their desires above the needs of the people they rule. But not you, Maakah. You are willing to set aside your inexperience to learn and serve others. We're honored to have you helping us today." Abigail embraced me, and Ahinoam nodded her approval.

My knees nearly buckled. *If you only knew that I may still be asked to marry your husband.* Zulat's conniving strategy to hide David's attacks on Geshur's villages seemed ludicrous when she'd explained it last night. But now, with this dear woman's arms around me, I couldn't imagine telling Abba the truth. He would never make a treaty with the man who destroyed our southern kingdom, and he'd almost certainly incite Dohd Achish to join him in battle against the Israelite rebel who had deceived him for over a year.

Abigail released me to continue her preparations. Zerry cooed and nuzzled the baby in her arms. They all seemed oblivious to the danger coming if two powerful kings discovered David's reckless aggression against my southern villages. The thought of two armies marching into this city, killing these women and Ahinoam's precious baby . . . I couldn't bear it.

If I married David, his wives would hate me. But they would live.

If I refused to marry David, his wives would live—and remain my friends—but how long before Abba or Dohd Achish killed everyone dear to them before their eyes?

"Maakah?" Abigail stood before me and wiped a tear from my cheek.

I lowered my head and wiped my face. "Forgive me. I didn't realize . . ."

Head bowed, I noticed Ahinoam's sandals came to rest beside

Abigail's, and one of their hands rested on each of my shoulders. A commotion in Zerry's corner preceded another set of sandals halting at Abigail's other side. I swallowed faster, blinking away more emotion, wiping my cheeks that simply wouldn't remain dry.

"Maakah," Abigail said barely above a whisper, "can you tell us what's troubling you? Are you grieving your people? Or—you mentioned your feet. Are they so terribly painful?"

"What about her feet?" Zerry clearly aimed her question at Abigail. "Why didn't you say something?"

"What's happened?" David's voice behind me made me gasp, and the others stepped away. I tried to turn, but searing pain shot up my leg, causing me to stumble toward the low-lying table.

My friends reached out to steady me, but a strong arm slid around my waist and held me upright. Without thinking, I lifted my feet off the ground, desperate for relief, then pressed my face into both hands and wept. The awkwardness of dangling from David's left arm was excruciating but was worth the humiliation for the reprieve from pain. Though Ima had taught me grace and etiquette since I was four harvests old, all I'd learned was wiped away after only a few encounters with David ben Jesse.

"Bring her in here," Abigail said.

David toted me like a sack of grain toward the back of their tent. When he stopped, I wiped my face and saw Abigail pulling aside a curtained partition. The thought of David ben Jesse laying me on one of his or his wives' sleeping mats was unbearable.

"I can walk!" I cried and shrugged out of his grasp. But when my feet landed, my knees buckled.

Again, David grabbed my waist and tucked me against his side. "Allow me to escort you anyway." The playful grin caused my heart to gallop, which was a momentary distraction from the pain. "Easy now." He lowered me to the sleeping mat, and my first thought was, *How does he decide which wife he sleeps with on which night?*

147

Noble

I shook my head to dislodge such traitorous musings and then turned on my side to face the tent wall. David leaned over, bracing himself with a hand in front of me, while peering at my wandering eyes. Acutely aware of his hip pressed against my back, I closed my eyes and hoped he'd grow weary of mocking me.

"Forgive me, Maakah. I didn't realize your feet still pained you. May I check them?"

"No!" I rolled to my back. He was still leaning over me, so our faces were entirely too close.

"Should we fetch Zulat?" His voice was smooth, like well-churned butter.

"No, please," I begged, feeling emotion tighten my throat. "She'll make too much of it." He stared long into my eyes, and I could barely breathe.

"I've been treating wounded soldiers on battlefields for over a decade, Princess. So I *will* examine your feet," he said in a commanding tone, though his gold-flecked green eyes still sparked with mischief. As if bewitched, I nodded permission.

He motioned to Zerry for help. His hands, rough and calloused, cradled my ankle while Zerry unlaced my sandals.

"Ow!" I tried to pull away when Zerry scraped a blister, but David's grip held me in place.

"She'll be gentler." He turned to his sister, raising one brow. "Won't *she*?"

"Well, if she'd listened to us in the first place and ridden a donkey instead of trying to walk the whole way from—"

"Zerry." David waited until she met his eyes. "Show compassion to our guest." Her sigh was more of a snort, but she gave him a compliant nod. "Good," he said. "Have you found your herbal supplies in the recovered plunder?"

"Yes, and I'm quite capable of caring for a few blisters." She removed my second sandal and whispered, "Oh, David." Her face had gone ashen, and her brother's features sobered as they both gawked at my bare feet.

"Would someone please tell me what you're looking at?" I sat up and tried to pull one foot toward me so I could see what had so transfixed them.

David's hand was like an iron shackle on my ankle. "Your wounds have festered, Maakah." There was no mischief in his tone. No mocking. The concern on his features was far more disturbing.

"Go, David." Zerry nudged him aside and gently lowered my foot to the reed mat. "I'll care for Maakah's wounds, but you must get to this morning's assigned tasks." When he hesitated, she waved him out. "No arguing. Go!" She yelled for Abigail, who immediately appeared at the curtained partition. "Go to my tent. You'll find my basket of herbs, unguents, and lotions that I reassembled last night, anticipating we'd treat injuries during the rebuilding. Nomy's one and only job is to care for her son, but I'll need you to help me tend Maakah's feet."

Ahinoam joined Abigail at the partition. "I heard my name." She bounced the baby in her arms. Abigail rushed past her without a word, leaving Ahinoam with a surprised expression. "Did I say something to upset her?"

David, too, rose to leave and sheltered his wife and child under his arm, escorting them into the living area. Only a few moments passed when I heard Ahinoam exclaim, "Oh no!"

"Is it that bad?" I asked Zerry.

She raised her eyes to meet mine. "You'll live, Princess." It was the first time we'd been alone, and I hadn't spent as much time with David's older sister as I had with his wives. She began stippling her fingers up and down my calf, which somehow tricked my body into reducing the pain.

When the silence between us grew uncomfortable, I asked the first thing that came to mind. "Will Ahinoam pass off the burden of nursing to a wet nurse after the circumcision?"

Noble

Zerry's eyebrows dipped. "Our women consider it an honor to nourish their children with the bodies Yahweh gave them. We only employ a wet nurse if the new ima is physically unable to feed her own child."

"But isn't it important to set Abigail and Ahinoam apart from other women since they'll one day rule at David's side?"

Zerry's eyes met mine, half-hooded as she looked down her slender, curved nose. "Abigail and Nomy are already set apart because Yahweh chose them to become David's wives, and because of the place they hold in my brother's heart. I see the effect David has on you, little princess, but he has that effect on many women. You may get whatever you want as a king's daughter in Geshur, but your abba's contract means nothing here."

My cheeks burned with shame. "I didn't know he'd destroyed our southern kingdom when I agreed to the marriage," I whispered. "Nor did I know about Ahinoam and Abigail—or realize two women could love the same man and still love each other like sisters."

"And your maid?" She studied me so intently, I almost looked away. "I suspect Zulat is still trying to find ways to reinstate the betrothal for her princess."

Guilt washed over me, and I couldn't hide what Zulat and I had done. "It's true. We sent a message to Abba last night, asking for his direction." Zerry's eyes widened. Perhaps she hadn't expected that level of candor. "Regardless of Abba's answer," I continued, "because I respect the love between David ben Jesse and his wives, I intend to forgo a marriage contract."

"I've got the basket!" Abigail announced from the main chamber.

Without taking her eyes from me, Zerry called back, "Put on a pot of water to prepare the poppy tea." Lowering her voice, she said to me, "The tea will make you sleepy so you won't feel as much pain while I cut away the dead tissue and apply a mixture of honey, turmeric, and henna to your open wounds to fight infection. Then

I'll bandage both feet with a balm of animal fat mixed with meadow saffron and fenugreek to reduce the swelling and stave off infection. We must change your bandages twice a day until we see healing begin."

With a precocious grin much like her brother's, she added, "I'll make the process far less painful now that I know you're merely another maiden swooning over my brother rather than a viper among us."

TEN

DAVID

[The LORD said,] The first offspring of every womb belongs to me, including all the firstborn males of your livestock, whether from herd or flock.

Exodus 34:19

In the light of a new day, I woke to the sound of my son's hungry cry, Nomy's whispered comfort, and our baby's ravenous suckling. The single woolen curtain separating the two chambers was an adequate visual impediment but did little to muffle any noise.

Abigail turned over on our sleeping mat and grinned. "Isn't that a lovely sound?"

I pulled her closer and drew in the scent of her. She usually smelled of cinnamon and cloves, but this morning it was leaven and warm bread. "How did the bread making go yesterday after Zerry treated Maakah's feet? Did you find others to replace them and help you make the camp's bread?"

"Maakah wouldn't leave." She giggled, seemingly in an especially good mood already this morning. "Nomy and I urged her to rest in her tent, but she insisted on staying to help."

"How could she help?" I craned my neck to look down at my second wife. "She couldn't stand to mix or knead."

"But she did an admirable job of grinding the grain. Maakah sat on a mat, leaning against a full water jar, with a hand mill in front of her. We positioned a bag of grain on her left, so she could scoop grain into the mill's center and turn the wheel with her right hand. When the grain was crushed, Zerry removed the top wheel and scooped out the flour. They worked very well together."

"My sister *helped* the princess?" I couldn't believe it.

"Yes, and by the end of our day, we'd made enough bread to feed the whole city for three meals: last night, this morning, and midday today."

"*Zerry* welcomed this royal outsider?"

"Maakah doesn't feel like an outsider," she said. "It seems odd, but the princess from Geshur seems more like one of us than her maid."

I'd thought the same and noted Zulat's feigned smiles and forced happiness whenever I was near. She was an old woman who had likely served in Geshur's palace her whole life. She'd been more ingrained with proper regal etiquette than Talmai's spunky daughter.

"David." Abigail laid her hand on my cheek, drawing my attention back to her. "I have some surprising news for you." Thankfully, the gleam in her eyes said it was a good surprise.

"I'm listening."

"I wanted to tell you before you left with Achish for battle. After all that transpired, I'm glad I didn't. You would have been even more frightened when you saw that we'd been captured. Actually, I haven't told anyone yet, and I'm not sure now is the right time to share it, but I don't think I can keep the secret from you any longer."

Chuckling, I said, "So tell me!"

"Shh!" She giggled, covering my mouth. "I don't want Ahinoam to know yet, but—" Her cheeks bloomed a lovely shade of pink. "I'm with child, David."

I wrapped my arms around her in a cocoon of surprise and triumph. "Thank You, Adonai Elohim, Giver of Life and Maker of heaven and earth." We held each other like a lifeline, and I marveled at the goodness of God who had finally opened her womb. My Abigail had so graciously shared Nomy's joy throughout the pregnancy and loved my firstborn as her own. She'd seemed genuinely happy for her sister-wife to finally bear fruit—though her own womb had remained closed. It was closed no longer.

I whispered against her silky hair, "I love you, Abigail bat Eliud."

She lifted her smiling face to me. "And I love you, David ben Jesse."

"How long must I wait to meet my second-born?"

"I think I'm at the end of my fourth month, but I haven't yet been checked by a midwife."

"A midwife?" Nomy stood at the partition, holding my son. "Did I just hear you say *fourth month* and *midwife*?"

Abigail bolted to her feet. "I was going to tell you but after your son's eighth-day celebration. I wanted all focus on your miracle baby."

Tears formed on Nomy's dark lashes. "I'd say we both have miracles to celebrate!" She grabbed her sister and pulled her into a joyful embrace. My son, squashed between them, voiced his discomfort.

My wives moved together into the main room, laughing and chattering like morning larks. I sat alone on my sleeping mat, marveling at a third miracle they hadn't mentioned—the God-given bond between my two wives who were as different as night and day. *Yahweh, Your mercies are new every morning.*

I joined them in the main chamber just in time to see Nomy placing her hand on Abigail's stomach. Only then did I notice the slight bump beneath my second wife's sheer tunic. "Since Yahweh sent us a royal midwife," Nomy said, "we should have Zulat examine you to make sure everything is all right."

Abigail nodded, her expression growing serious. "I need to speak with Maakah, too. I was rather emotional during your birth, terrified that something would happen to your child and mine would become a constant cause for sorrow rather than the joy I hoped he'd be."

"He?" I joined the two women beside the morning food supplies. "What if I want a girl for my second-born?"

"Boy or girl," Abigail said, "we'll praise Yahweh because He knows the perfect child to add to our household."

I wrapped an arm around both my wives and gazed adoringly at my son. His circumcision and naming ceremony was only two days away. Had Nomy chosen his name yet? I dared not ask since it was completely her decision, but perhaps a little encouragement would relieve whatever pressure she might be feeling with that responsibility. "May I tell you something about my firstborn brother's name and the way I've seen it bless *others* in our family?"

A storm instantly clouded her features. "Why discuss it? I thought the privilege of naming our son was mine."

Abigail kissed my cheek and slipped back into the partitioned area, likely for the dual purpose of escaping the coming conflict and getting dressed for her day.

I gently braced Nomy's shoulders and offered what I hoped was a reassuring gaze. "The decision of our son's name is entirely yours. I only want to tell you how Eliab's name—which means *God is my abba*—has impacted more than just him. Many in Israel believe the firstborn son's name sets the spiritual course for all the siblings after him. By naming her first son, *God is my abba*, I'm sure Ima intended that Eliab would know the security of always feeling Yahweh's protection and love. Though I can't attest to my eldest brother's spiritual connection, I can absolutely tell you that several other siblings have experienced that undeniable blessing of recognizing Yahweh as their ever-present and intimate security."

"I don't understand. Didn't Mistress Nitzevet give all her children names that would have formed their individual characters?"

Yahweh, give me wisdom to speak gently and to do no harm. "I'm the youngest of Ima's ten children. My seven brothers were the sons of Jesse ben Obed, but my two sisters were conceived while Ima was held captive by King Nahash, the Ammonite. You witnessed my abba's blatant favoritism toward his successful sons and his neglect—and even malice—toward the sons who displeased him. He treated Zerry like a servant and never mentioned Abigal's name after she was taken captive by the Ishmaelites. Most of us who felt like we could never earn Jesse ben Obed's love have struggled through dark things in life and found the eternal Abba's love on the other side." I cleared the emotion from my throat and straightened my shoulders. "All I'm saying is that a firstborn son's name can also bless the siblings who come after him."

"So far, two of my brothers, both sisters, and I have learned through difficult circumstances that we couldn't rely on our earthly abba for the love and approval we sought while he lived. Shimea, Ozem, my sisters, and I have learned that only Yahweh can fulfill our deepest yearnings for an abba's affection. Eliab's name set the spiritual quest for all of Ima's children, and I pray our remaining siblings will someday discover the great Father in heaven."

Her face had turned a little gray. "What I've heard you say is Mistress Nitzevet cursed not only Eliab with that name but all her children as well."

"That's not at all what I meant, love. So far, two brothers and both sisters have discovered that *God is our abba.* What could be a greater blessing? Yes, it was a golden nugget refined by fire, but well worth any struggle. The name you choose for our firstborn son will set the direction for not only his life but also for the very foundation of my household."

She rolled her eyes and groaned. "Is that supposed to relieve the pressure I already feel?"

"Yes! Because I know you, Ahinoam bat Toren. We both realize our children will need to temper the stubbornness they'll inherit from us. So you've already been seeking Yahweh's guidance on a name to make our son strong yet teachable."

My prediction won a smile from my feisty wife. "I've been seeking those two qualities exactly," she said, "but I'm not telling you the name I choose before everyone hears it at the circumcision celebration."

Laughing, I embraced her and my firstborn. "I would expect nothing else. And we'll celebrate another birth in only a few months."

"Perhaps more babies after that." Such hope filled her tone.

"Of course." I turned away quickly, trying to hide my concern. "Joab will fetch me with a leash if I don't get to my morning tasks." I hurried away to avoid speaking of more pregnancies.

"But you haven't broken your fast!" Abigail said as I escaped the tent.

I didn't even look back. I couldn't bear the thought of losing either of them in childbirth. Both my wives were already thirty harvests old, and the dangers of childbirth increased significantly with a woman's age. I was completely satisfied with the miraculous birth of Nomy's son and the child in Abigail's womb.

ELEVEN

MAAKAH

> When David reached Ziklag, he sent some of the plunder to the elders
> of Judah, who were his friends, saying, "Here is a gift for you from the
> plunder of the LORD's enemies."
>
> 1 Samuel 30:26

I'd never sweat so much in my life, nor felt so completely alive. The balm and bandages Zerry applied to my feet had stopped the festering, and my new friends were invigorating my soul. The rest of my body, however, protested grinding grain both yesterday and today. My arms and shoulders felt like they were pinched in a vise, and my back felt as if I'd been trampled by a donkey. But my feet no longer throbbed, and the happy conversations with these women drowned out my aches and pains, filling me with unrivaled joy. I'd relished my pampered life in Geshur, but I delighted in how the women of David's family treated me as an equal.

How would they treat me if they knew I'd called his wives "common" in my message to Abba?

A groan escaped without permission, garnering a grin from Abigail. My cheeks immediately flushed. "Forgive me, Abigail. I—"

158

"You've been courageous to keep working despite the wounds on your feet."

"I told her she should rest," Zulat grumped from outside, near the oven.

"And she told you she was fine." Zerry waved off my maid's concern, and the two women bickered and bantered as they'd done all morning.

Abital, the only one of Zerry's three daughters-in-law who mingled with David's wives, watched the two women at the ovens. "I think Zulat might be the only woman in the world more stubborn than my husband's ima."

Amused, I said, "Zerry would need to be extremely headstrong to win a battle against Zulat. She was my ima's nursemaid from birth, but when my parents saw what a willful child I was, they put Zulat in charge of breaking me."

Abigail and Abital sobered, looking at me with pity.

I leaned close and whispered, "She hasn't succeeded."

"I'm glad." Abital's eyes sparkled when she smiled.

I'd been a little disappointed when I arrived this morning to find her here instead of Ahinoam, who had needed to return to her usual work at the metal forge. I couldn't imagine what sort of work Ahinoam could do in the hot, smelly men's world—especially with her newborn strapped across her chest. But if anyone could do it, David's first wife would.

As I had worked with Abital throughout the day, I discovered in her the same tender heart that I'd appreciated in Abigail and Ahinoam. Even Zerry now showed her softer side, once she knew I intended no harm to her family.

"Princess Maakah grew up in a palace with many benefits." Zulat peered around the side of the open tent, revealing her eavesdropping spot next to the oven. "I served her three meals a day and made sure my lady had anything a girl could want."

Noble

Must Zulat always emphasize what made me different?

Abital's eyes widened. "Is this the first time you've ground grain?"

"I ground grain all the time and made the bread for Geshur's palace," I answered.

Abital's eyes narrowed with uncertainty before Zulat chided, "She did not!"

We all fell into a fit of laughter—even Zulat—which did my heart good since she and I had barely spoken since my clandestine meeting with Joab. It seemed our day of bread making in Abigail's tent had even brightened her mood.

"We're finished for another day's cycle." Abigail covered the last bowl of dough with a clean cloth and dusted the flour off her hands. She glanced at Zulat. "I know you're still baking, but perhaps Abital could take your place at the oven while you and Maakah help me with another small task."

Zulat shot a questioning glance at me before answering. "Of course, Mistress Abigail. We're happy to help with whatever will rebuild Ziklag while we await word from King Talmai."

Abigail was already on her way to the partitioned chamber in their tent. We followed her inside, Zulat right behind her, and me still hobbling. When I entered the partitioned chamber, Abigail's cheeks were as red as fire.

"Zulat, I'm in need of your midwife services," she whispered. "I believe I'm about four months along with David's second child."

"Aahh!" I covered a squeal.

Abigail hugged me, laughing. "Shh! I don't want others to know until Zulat confirms it."

My celebration was interrupted by a memory. "You must have known you were with child when we were captives, so why were you crying as Ahinoam gave birth? I thought it was because you were barren."

"Prin!" Zulat scolded.

160

"I was afraid, not sad." Abigail smiled down at me. "I feared for Nomy's safety and her baby's because I love them but also for a selfish reason. If something terrible had happened to my sister or her son, our family wouldn't have welcomed my child with the same joy."

I was taken aback by her candor and honored our fledgling friendship with the same. "But aren't you David's second wife?" She nodded. "Then wouldn't it have been better for you if something had happened to Ahinoam or her son? If your child is a boy, he would have become David's crown prince."

Her lips pursed into a sad frown. "Surely after spending all this time with Nomy and me, you know we have no stations. There is no competition between us."

"Do you and Ahinoam believe it can remain so after you both bear David a child?"

"We not only believe it, but with Yahweh's help, we will make it so."

I pressed my lips tightly shut, trying to swallow the truth I'd seen lived out when each of Abba's concubines bore him a child. The new ima would flout her triumph in Ima's face and use the newborn to finagle more time with the king than was allotted.

Abigail straightened her shoulders. "I would understand if you and Zulat would rather rest in your tent at midday." The air between us had cooled, though inside the tent remained stifling. "I can seek out one of the women from camp to examine me."

"No!" I said. "Please forgive me, Abigail. I usually don't realize I've said something offensive until Zulat tells me."

My maid covered a smile, but Abigail laughed, lightening the mood considerably.

"All right, let's begin." Abigail lay down on the wide mat.

My heart galloped when I imagined David lying there beside her. I shook my head to clear my thoughts. "What can I do?" I asked much louder than necessary.

Noble

Zulat had just knelt at Abigail's feet. "Go to the food baskets, find an onion the size of a bird's egg, wash it, then bring it back." She held up her hand to demonstrate the size needed, and I hurried out to give Zulat privacy to do whatever a midwife does. I'd glimpsed Ahinoam's bare thighs while she gave birth but had managed to remain at her side and avoid seeing her intimate parts, which would have shamed both her and me. I'd never been allowed to attend Ima's miscarriages and had never seen her disrobed. As queen, her royal body belonged to Abba alone. I had no intention of dishonoring my new friends by gawking at their nakedness.

While searching through the vegetable basket, I heard footsteps enter the tent and assumed it was Ahinoam returning for her midday rest.

"Shalom, Princess." David's bubbly tone startled me upright. "How are your feet today?" He took two steps closer and brushed my jawline.

My breath caught. His face grew ashen, seeming as affected as I was by the contact.

"Flour." He showed me a dusting of white on his finger. "You had flour on your face." He gave me a curt bow and strode toward the partitioned chamber.

I stood like a statue of Asherah for at least five heartbeats, reminding myself to breathe. The warmth of his touch lingered unlike anything I'd ever felt. I wanted to run—or maybe hobble—to my tent and hide until the messenger returned with Abba's directive. *What if Abba says I must marry David?*

"Maakah?" Zulat called. "The onion?"

I opened my hand and realized I'd picked up the right-sized onion as David entered. But, by the gods, how could I enter the same room where David would witness his wife's nakedness? *They are married. He is soon to be Israel's king. He rules her body. It is his right.*

I poured a little water in a basin, washed the onion, and forced my feet to move. Halting outside the partition, I reached my open palm—with the onion perched on it—through the break in the curtain. "Zulat, here's the onion you requested."

"Stop being ridiculous, Prin. It's time you learned these things since you'll someday soon be with child."

Mortified to the bone, I inhaled a sustaining breath and pushed aside the divider and focused only on Zulat. In the periphery, I saw David perched by Abigail's head.

"Come, come." Zulat swatted my calf from her position between Abigail's splayed knees. "Kneel here beside me."

Thanks be to the gods, she'd tucked Abigail's robe modestly at the top of her thighs. But I absolutely could *not* kneel beside her.

"Princess Maakah!" Zulat whispered sternly, then shook her extended hand, demanding the onion.

I nearly threw it at her and ran, but her hard stare brought me to my knees at Abigail's side. I passed her the onion, then focused on the tent walls, a fly buzzing around the small enclosure, and then my gaze landed on David. He and Abigail had created a private world of their own. David cradled her against his chest, leaning over her as they whispered to each other in tones too quiet for anyone else's ears.

"Now, pay attention," Zulat said, "while I teach you one way to discover if a woman is with child."

At that moment, David ben Jesse leaned down and kissed his wife—thoroughly!

Unbearable! I bolted from the room as if shedim from the desert chased me. How could a soon-to-be king display such base desire in front of strangers? It wasn't proper. It wasn't regal!

I ran as quickly as my feet would carry me to my tent, which was sweltering hot inside. So I grabbed a shoulder bag, stuffed it with a crust of bread and hard cheese, then hurried in a hobble-hop to rest outside the city gate. When I'd gone as far as my feet would

Noble

allow, I settled under a copse of trees that would shade me against the blistering sun. Falling to the ground, I panted and rolled on my back. My feet felt dipped in fire, throbbing with every heartbeat, but my chest ached more. I rolled to my side, wondering how my insides could hurt more than my feet. Somehow I knew it had nothing to do with physical pain.

I'm falling in love with David ben Jesse.

I groaned at the thought and laid my forearm over my eyes. A prayer to Asherah might have been appropriate, but I was beginning to think she couldn't hear me in Geshur while I was in Ziklag. Should I pray to the Hebrew god? He was a male god, but Ahinoam and Abigail seemed to think him compassionate toward women. Yet how could a male god understand? I thought of Kepha and still felt an empty space in my heart. Perhaps what I felt for David was merely yearning for someone like Kepha.

Hebrew God, I want someone like David and Kepha so I don't need to destroy my friends' happiness to achieve my own.

Pounding footsteps drew closer and brought me upright. I looked toward the city and saw David less than fifty paces away. If I could have outrun him, I would have tried.

"Are you all right?" he asked, then braced his knees when he halted two steps from me. "You can't be outside the city alone, Maakah. It's not safe."

I stood to meet him. "Did Zulat shift her nursemaid responsibilities to your shoulders?" I might have been cordial were it not for his grin. "I see nothing funny about a man—a soon-to-be king—groping his wife in the company of strangers."

"Groping?" His grin disappeared. "What happens between a husband and wife, joined by Yahweh's marriage covenant, is something you can't understand until you realize He's the only God who joins a man and woman together as one flesh."

"What about a man and two wives, hmm? How does your god

make one flesh out of three or four or five? My abba has one wife, David. One."

"And how many concubines?"

"We're talking about marriage!"

"We're talking about intimacy. They're very different things and—" He stepped back and turned away. Placing both hands atop his head, he started pacing. "Why am I talking to a Geshurite princess about marriage and intimacy? Ahh! Yahweh, what are you doing?"

If this whole situation hadn't been so inappropriate, I might have laughed. But somehow I sensed my future and David's were linked. Perhaps I was to marry someone who would become his ally. Perhaps he would someday need an advocate in Geshur. Whatever the reason, the gods had brought us together in these most uncomfortable circumstances to speak of everything except the mundane.

"I am the daughter of Talmai and Raziah, king and queen of Geshur." My voice was controlled, my words clear yet quiet. "They have never displayed such affection publicly, nor in the presence of their only heir."

He turned slowly to face me, his anger changing to disbelief. "You've never witnessed affection between your abba and ima?"

"No, David!" Indignation spilled out again. "A king and queen belong only to each other and live completely private lives."

Pensive, he nodded. "I see."

"What do you see?"

"Not only are our gods different, but also our values and perspectives."

Values? What did kissing have to do with values? Before I could respectfully phrase another question, I noticed a large contingent of David's men leading a caravan of ox-drawn carts and flocks out of Ziklag. "That's all plunder you recovered from the Amalekites."

165

He followed my gaze, then returned his focus with lifted brows. "And?"

I shaded my eyes from the desert sun to count the carts. "Fourteen? Why would fourteen carts and scads of animals leave Ziklag when we'll need every piece of plunder to barter for building materials and food?"

His eyebrows shot up again.

"Must you do that?" I asked.

"Do what?" The faintest smile pulled at his lips.

"That." I pointed at his bouncing eyebrows. "Someday you'll be a king and listen to complainants in your throne room. A king's expression must remain impassive and impartial to the testimony given."

"How old were you when you began attending court hearings?"

"Why does that matter?"

"How old?"

"Five."

His eyebrows jumped.

"You did it again." I pointed at those expressive copper arches. "And you still haven't told me why you've allowed fourteen carts and half your livestock to leave Ziklag."

A scowl replaced the playful brows. "They're a sacrifice of praise to Yahweh. I'm sending the gift of Amalekite plunder to some of my friends in the tribe of Judah—elders in fourteen towns."

"A king doesn't need to buy favor from those he'll soon rule. We need those provisions to barter for winter supplies."

"Who is this *we* you keep mentioning? You'll be long gone by winter."

He sounded happy to be rid of me, but a foundational tenet of ruling a nation is the management of war provisions and victory spoils. "How will you purchase seed for summer crops? Or do you have another plan to fill your storehouses for winter?" I crossed my arms and glared at this man I'd thought was determined to protect his army and their families. "Have you gone completely mad?"

"I believe it is you who have forgotten your place, Princess." A vein bulged in his forehead, and his face flushed like red wine. "You have no right to question my decisions when you're barely weaned from your ima's breast and travel with a maid who instructs you."

"How dare you—"

"How dare *you* presume to know the etiquette between Israel's leaders, let alone the relationship I share with my Judean friends. Until you were escorted by your abba's royal guard, you'd never traveled outside Geshur's gilded cage. Do you think that a few days with my wives gives you the right to offer unwelcome advice on my political acumen? You know nothing about my life, my wives, or the nation I am to rule, so I'll thank you to keep your opinions to yourself!" Panting, his neck veins bulged as they had when I'd first glimpsed him—covered in blood and filled with fury in the Amalekite camp.

A shock of fear coursed through me, remembering Warrior David who had spun through the Amalekites with a sword in one hand and a dagger in the other, cutting down the enemy like a farmer cuts through his field with a scythe. I backed away, ready to run if he advanced with violence, my heart already beating like I'd started the race.

In the silence, his fury ebbed. Veins disappeared and the crimson faded to a dusty pallor. Perhaps he sensed my terror. Those ridiculous eyebrows were now pinched and lifted with concern. "Forgive me, Maakah. Your life has been only about ruling, responsibility, and meeting the requirements of others."

"I don't need your pity, David ben Jesse, and I most certainly don't want to marry you."

"What?" His confusion was like a lash, turning me toward a hasty retreat and chasing me toward the city.

Noble

Partly walking, half running, I chastised myself to block out his shouts behind me. Why had I mentioned marriage? Why had I ever believed such a coarse and common man could be a king? He and his people would be dead by next spring because he'd given away the treasure they'd fought to recover—and that was if my abba or dohd didn't come for Ziklag first.

After entering the city gate, I strode toward our row of tents and had almost reached mine when I met Ahinoam returning from her morning at the metal forge. A long cloth, wound snuggly around her upper body, held her baby boy nestled against her heart. Though she was drenched in sweat, the baby seemed utterly content.

"Maakah!" Her smile died when her focus settled on something behind me—presumably her husband's overly expressive face. He could never be an impartial judge.

She hooked my arm and pulled me to a stop. "What did David do now?"

I pulled away and shot through my tent flap. Perhaps David was right. I had been raised in a gilded cage. I'd left Geshur too young and allowed Zulat to rule me. When David ben Jesse sat on Israel's throne, he would need a wise queen who worshiped his god and could accept his strange customs.

TWELVE

DAVID

[Israel's king] must not take many wives, or his heart will be led astray.

Deuteronomy 17:17

"What did you say to upset Maakah?" Ahinoam had at least waited to challenge me until we were in our tent.

"She questioned my decisions as a leader." I sounded like a petulant child.

"You sound like a petulant child."

It was sometimes annoying that my wives knew me so well.

"She was upset before that," Abigail added, cleaning up the bread-making mess. She halted her task and told Nomy the original offense. "Maakah was embarrassed when David kissed me while Zulat was examining me."

The two women nodded as if completely understanding Maakah's reaction.

I drew a hand down my sweat-beaded face, convinced I might never understand women. "I realize she's young," I conceded, "but she's capable of offering valuable wisdom in one moment, then runs from our tent when I kiss my wife. What grown woman is offended when a married couple kisses?"

169

"Married couples don't often kiss in public," Abigail offered sweetly.

"I was in my own home!"

"With two strangers in attendance," Nomy answered in the same impatient tone I'd used.

"He was comforting me," Abigail offered, always the peacemaker. "Zulat was performing a strange midwifery procedure to tell us with certainty whether I'm pregnant or not."

"Of course you're pregnant." Nomy waved off the explanation and faced me. "Maakah is a virgin, David."

"We were all virgins at some point, but I never ran away when my parents kissed!"

Nomy growled her frustration, which startled our son. He began to cry, so she bounced and swayed with that innate ima motion they acquired while giving birth. "Shepherds raised you in pastures, and you helped ewes deliver their lambs from the time you were five harvests old. I grew up with a single abba after my adulteress ima abandoned us for an Amalekite soldier." She lifted both brows as if I should know what she meant.

"What?"

Her features softened to that of a patient tutor. "You and I understood life's harsh realities long before we were Maakah's age. Geshur's princess was protected under the watchful care of a royal household. And while we were taught Yahweh's heart for one flesh intimacy, Maakah was told lurid stories of false gods and their sexual escapades."

"Well said." Abigail clapped her flour-caked hands.

I'd never considered how deeply the lore of pagan gods could distort a child's understanding and then ruin every idolatrous adult's desire for married love and pleasure. I should know better than to argue with women about women. "How did you get so smart?" I reached for Nomy, but she stepped back.

"If we were observing the Law," she said, "you wouldn't be allowed to touch me or our son yet."

"I . . ." Dropping both hands to my sides, I wasn't sure what she meant by the declaration. "Does this have anything to do with why Maakah ran from our tent?"

"Not yet," Nomy said, "but it will eventually."

Even more confused, I looked at Abigail for an interpretation, but she shrugged one shoulder and returned her focus to Nomy—as did I.

"How do you decide which of Yahweh's Laws we'll openly obey and which ones we won't?"

"Are we still talking about you being unclean?"

Nomy nodded, still swaying our now-silent son.

"Mostly it's about resources and practicality." I paused, but both women's chins rose slightly as if waiting for more. "So because we had limited time and people to help sift the plunder of our enemies and help rebuild Ziklag, I sought God's heart of mercy when we didn't have enough time or resources to make everyone and everything unclean for at least seven days and you, Nomy, for a total of forty."

"Forty?" Her eyes widened. "I thought it was eight."

"That look is the reason I try *not* to focus on the Law and its consequences before I measure out Yahweh's motivation for the Law." She adjusted her expression to hide her initial reaction. "It's all right, love. The Laws of God are meant to cost us dearly, which is the reason I seek His heart for the motive behind them. For a new ima and her baby, I believe He meant to protect them from a boorish husband's forced intimacy. For warriors who come home covered in the blood of their enemies, I believe He meant to protect their families from spreading disease, which is the reason we didn't touch our wives after the initial reunion."

Realization brightened both of my wives' faces. "Is that the reason," Nomy said, "that you commanded our warriors not to touch their families again until they'd finished sifting plunder and then washed twice—once at the Amalekite camp, and a second time at Besor Brook?"

"Safety and clean water seemed to be Yahweh's motive," Abigail added.

"When we search the heart of God motivating the Laws of God, we can be certain of His mercy when our sacrifice of obedience doesn't quite measure to the Law's perfection."

"I'd never thought to search for the motive behind the Law," Abigail breathed. "I remember attending eighth-day naming celebrations where the new ima looked forlorn and angry."

"I tried the unclean Law." Nomy's announcement startled Abigail and me. "Perhaps neither of you noticed, but I haven't touched either of you. I've allowed you to hold the baby, but I haven't demanded a hug or any sort of touch since we left the Amalekite camp."

I hadn't noticed. Was I the worst husband in the world?

She looked at me then, and I wondered if I'd asked it aloud. "I wanted to see what it would be like for our next child." Her eyes glistened. "It's been hard, these first uncertain days of being an ima. I wanted nothing more than to lie in your arms and feel your comfort."

I opened my arms and stepped toward her. "Nomy, why—"

"Don't." She stepped back, but with a sweet smile. "My self-imposed law of uncleanness required me to turn to Yahweh for comfort instead of my husband or my friends. My 'practice' obedience has been the best sacrifice my circumstances allowed." Nomy turned to her sister. "I won't be a forlorn new ima at our son's celebration," she assured her. "I've never felt Yahweh closer than He's been during this time of seeking His wisdom for our baby's name."

She began unwinding the cloth from her chest. "I think it's dangerous to leave the interpretation of God's Law to anyone," she said, distracted by her task but still speaking profound truth. "But sharing Yahweh's heart behind the Law has meant more to me than listening to rule after rule after rule—as I heard one traveling priest recite it when I was only a girl."

While Nomy continued to unwind the binding cloth, I asked, "Is something wrong?"

"Nothing's wrong, but when you return from apologizing to Maakah, you should spend some time with your son."

This again? "I'm not going to apologize for showing affection for my wife in my own home."

"An explanation, if not an apology, then." Abigail crossed her arms, looking as determined as I'd ever seen her. "Later today, I'll also speak with Maakah and gently explain that she's too free with her opinions."

Nomy finished unwrapping the babe and held the soaking wet cloth aloft. The distinct scent of urine filled the air. "I was so busy at the forge, I forgot to change his waste cloth."

"Uhhh!" Abigail took the cloth with two fingers, holding it as far away from her as possible, and dropped it into a basket with the baby's other soiled cloths. "I'll launder them in the wadi this afternoon."

"I'll come with you and get a bath."

"Make sure a guard accompanies you," I said.

"There it is." Nomy pointed at me.

I shrugged, having no idea what she meant.

"I think Maakah is afraid, David."

"How does providing a guard for my wives mean Maakah is afraid? She marched outside the city gate *alone* and seemed quite content to remain there until I approached." I didn't dare mention the fear I saw in her eyes when I'd lost my temper. "I've promised not to send her back to Geshur without an escort, and I allowed her to send a missive to her father. Why would she be afraid?"

"Every woman is afraid." This from Abigail, whose neck was suddenly mottled with red splotches. "Few of us are blessed with husbands who love and respect us as you do." Her trembling smile proved the memories of her first husband, Nabal, still haunted. "I also believe Maakah is hiding something but not because she's a deceiver. I think she's hiding something because of her fear."

Inner warnings blared like shofar blasts. "If she's hiding something, I need to know—"

"The message to King Talmai included a request for his direction on the betrothal proposal." Abigail watched intently as I absorbed the news.

I turned to Nomy, my dagger-wielding wife, to see if she was surprised. She wasn't. "Who told you this?"

"Zerry."

"And Maakah is still breathing?" My sister protected me like a she-bear, and she wasn't one to spread idle gossip.

"Zerry said she didn't coerce her confession," Nomy explained. "Maakah added to her candor that she intended to refuse if her abba commanded she marry you because of her respect for the love she'd witnessed between us."

"Maakah could have been manipulating her." I raked my fingers through my hair, more confused with every word from my wives. "Why would Yahweh bring me an idol worshiper for a wife when the Law clearly says Israel's king must never marry a foreigner?"

Abigail dipped her chin, looking at me from a hooded brow. "It also says the king shouldn't marry multiple wives. Yet we sought Yahweh's heart—all three of us—and then stood united in a covenant with our God."

Nomy bowed her head. "I'll ask again. When do we follow the letter of the Law? And when do we seek God's heart behind the Law and adjust our obedience to the current reality?"

Only Abigail met my gaze. "Is she questioning our marriage?"

"We question everything."

"Are you in agreement?" I felt as if the ground shifted beneath me.

Abigail reached for my hand, steadying me. "We question everything and trust Yahweh for answers we don't have." She inhaled deeply and waited for me to join her. I did, and we breathed out a little more calm. I felt like a child, but we were standing on holy ground—the very bedrock of my faith.

"Since Saul killed the priests of Nob and has hidden the Tabernacle," Abigail began, "you've become the resting place of Yahweh's presence among His people and the channel through which His heart flows. Not everyone chases after God as you do, David. Not everyone has been given the access—or the passion—to speak with Him as you do. So please don't allow everyone to define their own interpretation of God's Law. *You* have been given that authority through Samuel's anointing and by God's public miracles and favor. It doesn't mean, however, that you'll never make a mistake." She lifted my hand to her lips with a momentary gleam of mischief, then released my hand as she grew serious. "Nomy and I believe, as you do, that Yahweh approved of our marriage covenant, and we believe He may have brought Maakah into our midst for the same purpose. We're asking you to speak with her privately to see if it's true."

Nomy's quiet sniffs drew my attention. "I don't need to speak to her now if you have any hesitation."

With her head still bowed, she said, "I pray that what I'm about to say is due to the morose post-birthing mood Zerry warned me about, but every time I see Maakah my heart flips over in my chest."

"Nomy, I don't want another wife."

"I know," she said, still not looking at me. "I absolutely believe you, David. Nor do I want to share you again." Her voice broke.

"Please let me hold you," I whispered.

She wiped her nose on her shoulder, which Abigail instantly protested, and finally met my gaze. "When I see you with Maakah, I get the same nauseous certainty that struck me when I saw you with Abigail the first time. If Yahweh has sent Maakah for you to protect, as He did for Abigail, we must not only accept her but also love her—as Yahweh loves her."

I couldn't have been more stunned if someone hit me in the head with a stone.

"But she must determine to follow Yahweh alone before she comes under your protection," Abigail added.

Nomy used the lazy-blink reprimand with Abigail—*of course that's what I meant*—whenever their differences clanged like dissonant cymbals. She then turned to me. "So, go. Apologize. Or explain. Or whatever. But remember that Maakah has a tender heart, and Yahweh may be trying to reach her through us."

I left our tent and waited in the sun for one of my wives to stop me. But deep in my tightening gut, I knew they wouldn't—because I'd sensed something different about Maakah, too. The moment I'd seen her in the Amalekite camp, I knew she was royalty. The sight of her reminded me of my first wife, Michal, and I poured all my ire against my first wife out on the princess and her maid. Rather than hide behind Zulat, she'd confronted me—the blood-soaked leader of four hundred warriors. She was nothing like Michal. My wives knew it before I did, calling her friend when they defended her in that camp.

Now, I must face something worse than Maakah's boldness. How could I explain the reason a husband passionately kisses his wife in their own home to a young woman who knew nothing of Yahweh's love? I halted outside her tent and heard a terrifying sound. Rather than Maakah's quiet weeping while she hobbled ahead of me into the city, she was now sobbing as she prayed—to her false god.

"Mother Goddess, can you hear me so far away? I beg you to hear and answer for I cannot fail Abba and my nation again."

Instant fury rose, and I wanted to barge into the tent and pour out my wrath on the idolatrous woman. Images of Michal raced across my memory, stoking the ire. But Maakah wasn't Michal. She was a young woman, cut off from her family, sequestered with a maid she couldn't fully trust, and terrified of what her future held. *Yahweh, give me grace to kindly show her the truth until she recognizes You alone are her salvation.*

"Please, Queen of Heaven," she said in barely a whisper, "provide for me a husband who can secure Geshur's future and bring us peace and prosperity. If Ima carries her child to full term, there may yet be hope for a second heir to rule. But what of your plans for me?" Weeping overtook her and pierced my heart.

I felt ashamed to have overheard her most private thoughts, yet shame bowed to compassion. She was pouring out her soul to a god who couldn't help, to a shedim cast to the underworld by Yahweh Himself.

"Am I doomed to live alone?" she continued her unheard prayer. "How many more broken betrothals must I endure? Am I so unappealing? So repulsive to men?"

Though I felt like a thief stealing Maakah's secrets, I also recognized the timing as divinely appointed. Abigail and Nomy had been right. Geshur's princess was afraid. But she was afraid of disappointing her abba and her nation. And afraid of being unloved.

Yahweh, I know You would never wish me to marry an idolater. I'd seen how Saul's wife, Queen Ahinoam, had refused to fully relinquish the Mother Goddess, and her apostasy had weakened Saul's faith in Yahweh. Such was the motive behind God's Law against many wives for Israel's king: He must not take many wives or his heart will be led astray. *Yahweh, if this princess will lead me away from You, remove the attraction between us. But if she can bring wisdom to build my royal household, then give her a heart open only to You.*

"Forgive me for intruding," I announced, peering into the tent but remaining at the threshold.

A gasp preceded a flurry of shuffling in the dimly lit space. "David,

Noble

I . . . what are you . . ." A quick huff. "Why have you come to my tent?"

There it was, the indignation of entitlement. "I've come to—" To what? In the silence, my wives' tender pleas replayed in my mind. "I've come to apologize." I glimpsed her puffy eyes before she bowed to hide her appearance.

"I need no apology. You may go."

I may go? Perhaps it was best she couldn't see my grin. "Abigail and Ahinoam seem quite fond of you, and I'm under strict orders to be nice. If I return without offering a heartfelt apology, I'm not sure they'll ever speak to me again."

No reply. Then I noted her shoulders shaking. The urge to embrace her overwhelmed me—for no other reason than to comfort—but even a shepherd-boy-turned-warrior knew she'd be offended. And I knew it was inappropriate. However, the urge remained strong, and I sensed Yahweh's hand in it.

How could I shove past the awkwardness without an offense? Perhaps offending her in a different way wasn't a bad idea. "Forgive me, but as I approached the tent, I heard parts of your prayer. I'm curious as to the names of others who have received a betrothal proposal from your abba."

She gasped and looked up, horrified. "You listened to my prayer?"

"I didn't intend to," I said, tying open one side of the tent flap before continuing inside. "However, I believe I can answer a few questions you asked Asherah."

Her whole countenance faded to gray. "I beg you to send Zulat back to Geshur, and please kill me now so I don't have to face Abigail and Ahinoam."

"We'll talk about consequences later. Right now, I'd like to know about those other proposals you mentioned."

I moved closer, and she scooted away. "You shouldn't stay here. Alone. With me." The tent's back wall blocked her retreat.

I perused their sparsely stocked dwelling. "Where's your maid?"

"I don't know." Her chin quivered. "We haven't been getting along. She's probably found a task that will keep her away from me until well past dark."

My heart broke a little more for her. "How long has Zulat tended you?"

"Why do you care?" She met my eyes. "I have no need to meddle in your business, nor do you in mine. If you let me live, you'll be rid of me as soon as your scouts return with Abba's message."

"I'm in no hurry to be rid of you, Maakah."

Her eyes widened. She hadn't expected that answer.

"As long as we satisfy Yahweh's modesty code," I said, changing the subject, "we can be alone."

"It's hard to imagine that you follow any modesty code." Her cheeks bloomed the color of poppies, but her eyes remained locked on mine.

There it was. Regal grit. A boldness in the blood.

With her confidence returned, I continued my approach and sat an arm's length across from her. "The Law of Moses makes provision for a married man and a virgin to be alone so long as the door of the dwelling in which they meet remains open and faces a main thoroughfare." I pointed to the flap I'd tied open. "You see? Modesty laws satisfied. And may I remind you that you were in *my* home when you witnessed me kiss my wife." Her eyes welled with tears again. Before she could look away, I pressed, "Please, Maakah, tell me about the broken betrothal agreements. You're a beautiful young woman. I'm sure the reasons had nothing to do with you."

She blinked a stream of tears down her cheeks. "There were two before you." She attempted a cynical laugh. "If a third bridegroom cancels the contract, I fear Abba will give up on his daughter completely."

"Who were they, Maakah?" I might find and kill them myself.

Noble

"The first was an Aramean prince." A soft sob escaped, and she wiped away a steady flood of tears.

"You loved him." I hadn't asked a question. It was obvious.

She nodded, inhaled deeply, and blew out a shuddering breath while regaining her composure. "He was a warrior," she said, then turned to meet my gaze. "With a heart not so different from yours."

Startled by her honesty, I probed, "And the second betrothal?"

She turned away and whispered, "Ish-Bosheth, King Saul's youngest son."

I could definitely rid the earth of Ish-Bosheth, and no one but his ima would mind.

THIRTEEN

MAAKAH

A perverse person stirs up conflict, and a gossip separates close friends.

Proverbs 16:28

Still shocked that he hadn't lopped off my head the moment he'd heard my prayer, I wasn't at all surprised by David's reaction to my broken betrothals. He lowered his face into his hands, unable to bear the sight of me.

"If you mercifully allow me to live, would you be willing to provide an escort for Zulat and me to Gath?"

His head shot up. "Why go to Gath when you sent King Talmai word that you're in Ziklag?"

"Why would David ben Jesse protect the idol-worshiping castoff of King Saul's son?"

Mouth gaping, he gathered his composure and said, "Don't you understand how fortunate you are that they canceled your betrothal to Ish-Bosheth? I met Saul's youngest son when he was twenty-five harvests old. He was a spoiled child then, and the only thing that's matured is his peculiarity."

"Joab hinted at a similar opinion."

I breathed a little easier at the sight of her rueful grin. "I doubt Joab hinted. He has no tact."

"He actually called Ish-Bosheth an imbecile."

"That sounds more like Joab." His gaze lingered, and I lowered my eyes. "Ish-Bosheth obviously never saw you," he whispered, "or he wouldn't have canceled the betrothal. Did Saul give a reason for reneging?"

I paused, remembering the poor messenger who delivered the reason. If David had been the king who received the same message for his betrothed daughter, would he have been so quick to end a man's life? Though I'd seen him kill more men than I could count, I no longer feared him as I had Abba on the morning I left Geshur—even though David had every right to kill me for worshiping idols.

Shaking the thought from my mind, I cleared my throat and said, "King Saul sent a messenger to inform Abba that he and three of his sons had already marched to battle the Philistines. He'd left Ish-Bosheth on the throne, so his son was unable to honor the contract. Both Abba and I recognized it as merely an excuse to break the contract. Abba was actually pleased because he'd heard from Ima's brother, Dohd Achish, what a great warrior you were and that you'd likely—"

David stared into the distance, far away though still in my presence. My silly betrothal had no bearing on his life. Empowered by their Hebrew god, David and his men had rescued their families from the Amalekites—and nearly exterminated the nation that mistreated their ancestors hundreds of years earlier. Perhaps Ima's assessment of the situation had been right all along: "A betrothal to Israel's next king is better than marriage to a royal coward." What encouragement would she offer me now, when I returned to Geshur after having been rejected by two Israelites?

A low groan escaped David's lips. Startled, I reached across the chasm between us and placed a hand on his forearm to startle him from the trance. "David?"

His focus returned. "Forgive me." He patted my hand that still rested on his arm.

I pulled back quickly. "No need to apologize, but you groaned. Are you well?"

His look was inscrutable; his features drawn and weary. "My chest feels tight with a terrible foreboding. Did the messenger mention anything about Saul's sons?"

"You mean did he mention anything about Prince Jonathan?"

His breath caught. "Did he?"

"No." I didn't think it wise to say Abba took off the man's head before we could ask any questions about the upcoming battle. "Are you a seer? Do you get these forebodings often?"

"Very seldom." He shivered, though the tent was stifling hot. "I feel Yahweh's presence," he said. "He visits at the most unexpected times and often speaks in ways I don't understand. But when He comes, I know something important is happening in the moment or will happen very soon."

My spine straightened like a measuring rod. "Is your invisible god here now? In my tent?" Angst rising, I asked, "Did my prayer to Asherah displease him?"

"Any allegiance to other gods displeases the one, true God. Yahweh is always present—in your tent, in mine, in Geshur, in Israel. He is everywhere, all-powerful, all-knowing, and eternal; living outside the bounds of time though remaining with His people in every moment of a lifetime."

Now he was playing on my fear. "No god is so powerful."

"Do you have another explanation for our victory over the Amalekites?"

I didn't. "If your god is so powerful—" Longing bubbled up from within, forming a lump in my throat. "Tell me what sacrifices your god requires to guarantee He'll provide me with a husband who brings stability and prosperity to Geshur. I cannot fail my people." I looked away and swiped stubborn tears from my cheeks.

"Yahweh isn't like your gods, Maakah. We don't use sacrifices

Noble

to bargain for what we want, and He doesn't play games with our lives. The LORD is forgiving and good. He created every human being, whether they worship Him or not, and He answers anyone who calls to Him. He is sovereign over all things, and, willingly or unwittingly, we participate in His plan. For those who choose to follow His commands, He works for their good and His glory."

"How can you still believe that? I've heard you were once Saul's greatest warrior and married to his daughter. But then he grew jealous of your fame and ordered your death, so you hid in the wilderness for years before asking my dohd Achish for sanctuary among the Philistines. How can you trust a god who allows you to be betrayed, who snatches away your fame, and who makes you a servant of your enemy?"

Instead of the anger I expected, his features relaxed. "You've described the process of a few years, but I was given Yahweh's promise for my lifetime, and His promises never fail." His lips curved into a broad smile, and his finger pointed in circles at my eyebrows. "Aren't you supposed to remain impartial while making a judgment?"

Instinctively, I covered my traitorous brow and matched his smile. The tension between us drained, and I ventured a deeper question. "I've heard rumors that the crown prince will give you Israel's throne upon Saul's death."

David's smile faded. "That rumor could get my best friend killed." He studied me with narrowed eyes. "That's the least politically savvy thing I've heard you say."

"Forgive me. I thought I was speaking in the confidence of a friend." Feeling my cheeks burn, I bowed my head. "It won't happen again." He tried to tilt up my chin, but I was too ashamed to meet his eyes. Who was I to speak so freely to this Israel's would-be king. "For worshiping an idol in your camp, David, I place myself at your mercy and await your righteous judgment." I pressed my hands together and lifted them to my forehead in a penitent pose.

184

"No, Maakah. Forgive me—again. I worry every day for the safety of my brother Jonathan. We've made a lifelong covenant, closer than any familial bond, to love and protect each other even to our future generations. If Saul knew our bond remained, I can't think of what he might do to his eldest son."

And you accused me of lacking political savvy? Rather than blurting out a judgmental declaration, I asked barely above a whisper, "Don't you worry about what Saul's descendants might do to your family when you take Israel's throne?" Daring to lift my eyes to meet his, I pressed, "Surely you know that a usurper must kill every wife and descendant of the previous king or forever live at risk of retribution on his family."

"Saul's family won't harm mine," he said as if it were true. "Jonathan won't allow it."

I placed my right hand to my throat and pursed my lips, restraining the arguments for Abigail and Ahinoam's safety that felt like wild stallions pawing for release. My Aramean lineage was rife with examples of new rulers whose whole families had been decimated because they'd shown mercy to their predecessors' kin.

With our eyes locked, I hoped to speak without words. I wanted to tell him how much I cared about Abigail, Ahinoam, and her new baby boy. I feared for them. Wanted the very best for them—especially for his firstborn son. I knew the eventual pressure the boy would face as the king's eldest child, the demands that would be made on him. The child in Abigail's womb would feel it, too. The danger of unseen enemies and the myriad expectations—spoken and unspoken.

David's gaze softened. His head tilted slightly. Lips parted as if he might say something, then closed again. Something inside me shifted. My chest ached again. This time I recognized the longing—and I saw it in his eyes, too.

"I must go." David shot to his feet and rushed to leave, nearly barging into Zulat at the open tent flap. "Forgive me. I—"

Ignoring his apology, she eyed him with suspicion. "What sins have I stumbled upon in this tent?" She gave me a disapproving stare and then returned her focus to David. "I certainly hope a chaperone was with you and my mistress. Surely the next king of Israel would never meet alone with Geshur's unmarried princess before they're wed."

David straightened, all geniality gone. "In my city, we abide by the Laws of Yahweh. I assure you, as a happily married man, I have taken every precaution to maintain the good name of Geshur's princess." He moved closer to my indignant maid, forcing her to step back. "And if I ever hear you or your mistress praying to your impotent gods or find an idol in your possession, the punishment will be severe." He strode to his tent without a backward glance.

In the afternoon light, I watched him disappear into the large goat-hair dwelling where I knew Abigail and Ahinoam would be waiting. He'd done as they asked and apologized to me, but would he confess to the longing we'd shared? My stomach involuntarily roiled, fear nearly driving me to my knees. *Hebrew God, if you can hear me, please convince my friends I would never do anything to hurt them.* No matter what my heart was beginning to feel for David ben Jesse, I would never come between him and the two women who loved him.

"You've certainly been busy." Feigned harshness aside, Zulat hurried toward me and sat on the cushion David had occupied moments before. "How did you manage to lure him into our tent—without his wives, no less?"

"I didn't lure him."

She rocked to her feet, poured a cup of cool water, and brought it to me. "Drink this. You look like a shriveled raisin." Long years of habit compelled me do as instructed while she resumed her seat. "You've been crying," she said. "Good. You've discovered tears are his weakness. A man who responds to tears is far more easily swayed."

I nearly choked on my last sip. "I wasn't crying to sway him, and the visit was his choice." A sudden thought made me grin. "Though Abigail and Ahinoam suggested he come."

"Why would his wives encourage their husband to spend time with you?"

I shrugged. "And you must keep the Asherah well hidden. We're within the Hebrew god's territory. Asherah seems to have little power here. So you would do well to speak respectfully of this Yahweh."

"Phsst." Zulat waved away my opinion, proving she was unable to reckon with me as an adult.

"You'll never consider my opinion as valid." It was a statement, not a question, and I was more saddened than angered. Without giving her time to argue, I changed the subject. "May I help prepare our midday meal?"

"It's not true, Prin."

"You don't want my help?" I knew she wasn't talking about food, but I didn't want a debate.

She huffed and drew breath to argue, but I cut her off. "You've proven incapable of respecting my wishes since we left the Amalekite village. I refuse to argue with you anymore. Now, tell me what we're eating."

Her cheeks were washed of color. "Everything I do is for you and the future of Geshur."

"Our meal, Zulat."

Expelling a breath, she set her jaw. "I added something extra to the message we sent to your abba."

I felt like she'd punched me in the gut. "You added to *my* message something I neither heard you read aloud nor approved?"

"I was sure you'd disapprove, but your parents needed to know you're becoming too easily swayed by the rebel David."

Noble

"I decide what my royal parents must know!" I exhaled the remaining fury, breathed in calm, and met my maid's ashen visage. "What *exact* message did you send without my permission?"

"I only said that King Talmai should intervene and that David and his army were a nest of vipers."

"Zulat! What if the messengers allowed Joab or one of David's captains to look at the message before it was sent?"

"But it bore your wax seal."

Now who was being naïve? "Don't you think a skilled spy could warm the wax, unseal the scroll, and replace the wax without damaging my seal?"

Eyes wide, she whispered, "We shouldn't have said David's two wives were common or that the betrothal could still be viable if the Philistines were victorious. If anyone from David's camp saw our message . . ."

"Joab wants me to marry David," I blurted. "If Joab discovered the contents, he'd believe I was working with him toward the same goal. Though I still don't understand why—if you wanted me to marry David—you would paint him and his men as vipers in Abba's mind."

"That's because you have no forethought." Her insult stung too much to reprimand her. "When Master David's men return with your abba's message, we'll know what your abba thinks of the three message bearers by their condition."

I'd begun shaking my head in protest. "You put those men in danger by accusing them secretly in that message." Panic rising, I replayed memories of Saul's headless messenger in my mind. "What if Abba kills them for no reason?"

"They destroyed our southern villages." Her features were cold as granite. "David deserves to lose a few men in the process of gaining Geshur as an ally."

I felt nauseous at the thought. Zulat rolled to her knees and busied herself with meal preparation.

I couldn't bear to work alongside her. By the time she placed a bird on a spit over our small cook-fire, I whispered, "You've made us spies among our friends."

She turned to me, eyes narrowed. "I've proved our undying loyalty to Geshur's king and kingdom. Or have you forgotten the reason we were sent to David ben Jesse?"

I chose my words carefully. "Have *you* forgotten whom you were sent to serve? Me, Zulat. You serve me. *I* was sent to marry a king. My mission was interrupted when the Amalekites killed our escort, but your purpose never changed. You remain at my side to follow my commands and do my bidding. Is that clear, Zulat?"

"Very clear, my lady." A slow grin curved her lips. "Now, that is the regal princess I'm proud to serve."

FOURTEEN

DAVID

A man arrived from Saul's camp with his clothes torn and dust on his head. When he came to David, he fell to the ground to pay him honor.

2 Samuel 1:2

Sweat trickled down my back though the eastern horizon barely glowed with the new day. The heaviness that descended on me yesterday in Maakah's tent at the mention of Saul and his sons in battle had intensified all day and into a restless night. *Yahweh, I need the peace only You can give.*

I rolled off my mat without waking Abigail and while Ziklag was still sleeping. Stepping through the partition, I found Nomy curled on her side in a corner of our main room with the baby nestled in the curve of her form. We'd been so devastated by the loss of our first child that this boy was even more precious. I stood staring at them for a long while, my throat tightening with gratitude to the Giver of Life. *Yahweh, You give and take away. Yet will I praise you.*

Snatching my lyre from beside the tent flap, I slipped outside. Guided by the last vestiges of moonlight, I jogged toward our city gate and veered left toward the narrow door, locked and guarded by two watchmen. They opened the child-sized exit for my departure, closing it behind me. I heard the heavy wooden plank slide back into place, keeping all inside the city safe. I started at a jog but increased my pace toward the tree where I'd found Maakah yesterday. Covering the short distance quickly, I settled beside the tree and rested against its knobby trunk. I strummed my lyre while watching the sunrise, praying while humming every song I knew. Still, the melancholy lingered. I pleaded with the LORD for a new melody, new words with which to praise Him and chase away the foreboding.

No words came and no new melody. Neither had Yahweh given us any direction on when to leave Ziklag or where to go.

On the edge of despair, I returned to the city to join the rebuilding. I knocked on the small door, and while waiting for admittance, was again struck by the destruction. Though the wall was intact, its charred stains told the story. When I entered Ziklag, the burned-out houses reminded me of our many losses through the years. Foreboding filled my chest. *Losses. Yahweh, are there more to come?*

I listened. Waited. Still no answer. I continued to my tent, where I would return my lyre to its place and resume the demolition of burnt homes. Abishai's unit would be demolishing a house behind the third row of tents today. Perhaps swinging a battle-ax and war hammer would relieve my angst.

Leaving my tent, I heard the shofar's t'ruah warning. Everyone stepped outside their dwellings, waiting for the watchman's shout. "Single man. On foot. Waving white flag."

Abishai ran from his tent near the well, and I joined him on our way toward the city gate. Joab met us less than twenty paces from Ziklag's only entrance. "Do we let him in?" my general asked. "Or should I meet him alone outside the gate to hear his demands?"

"Let him in." I lifted two fingers to my lips, whistling the call that several of my Mighty Men would recognize from our childhood together. I'd known and trusted them most of my life. Except Uriah. He'd wounded me deeply with his divisiveness. *LORD, should I even*

Noble

try to mend that relationship or release Uriah from my service? Again, no clear answer came. I'd watch and listen over the coming days for Yahweh's direction on the matter.

Four watchmen lifted the heavy wooden bar from its cradle and then four more swung open the heavy gates to allow the visitor to enter. I felt the reassuring presence of my Mighty gathering around me, weapons clanking. Why did I feel such fear when only one man walked toward us, waving a white flag?

At first sight, the man looked like an Israelite slave, but his darker skin tone and the gold ring in his nose proved him a foreign servant dressed in Israelite garb. He stumbled across the gate's threshold and fell to his hands and knees, panting as if he'd run a great distance. His clothes were torn, and he was covered in dust—all signs of mourning—and the foreboding I'd felt suddenly turned to panic.

Joab and Abishai hooked their arms beneath his and dragged the visitor toward me, dropping him at my feet. "Where have you come from?" I asked. Only then did I notice a bulging shoulder bag slung across his body.

The man reached for the bag, and ten warriors advanced toward him. "Wait!" He lifted both hands. "I escaped from the Israelite camp."

I shoved my men aside and grasped the collar of his torn robe. "Tell me what happened!"

"The Israelites fled from battle. Many fell dead—including Saul and his son, Jonathan."

Please, God, let it not be so. Releasing my grip, I stumbled back and tried to steady my breathing. "How do you know the king and crown prince are dead?"

"I was on Mount Gilboa and saw Saul leaning on his spear. As chariots and their drivers were closing in on him, he cried out to me. I ran to him and said, 'What can I do?' He asked who I was, and I told him I'm an Amalekite."

"An Amalekite?" I almost choked on the word. Was this a ploy?

"I've been a slave to an Israelite captain for five years. I think Saul recognized me because he said to me, 'Stand beside me, then, and kill me. Hurry! I'm in the throes of death but still alive, and I don't want the Philistines to make sport of me.' So I did as he asked since he could have never survived his wounds."

The murderer reached again for his shoulder bag. This time I waved off my protectors, wanting to see what he'd brought.

I gasped when he produced Saul's gold crown. He shoved it toward me, but I stepped farther from the Amalekite, refusing to touch the one-of-a-kind symbol of Israel's regent.

The man looked puzzled and then reached back into his bag and withdrew a second piece of gold. "I took the crown from Saul's head and the gold band from his arm," he said. "Take them, my lord. They're for you."

All I could see before me was an Amalekite who had killed God's anointed. Fury and grief congealed into an uncontrolled wail that sent me to my knees. Tearing the collar of my robe, I fell forward on my hands and tossed dust onto my head while others joined the mourning. I couldn't ask about Jonathan. I couldn't bear to hear the details of his death. The sights, smells, and sounds of too many battles came rushing in, and I saw Saul's and Jonathan's faces on every fallen soldier my mind conjured. I pulled at my hair and slapped at my head. *Please, Yahweh, please! Take these images from my mind!*

Gentle arms lay across my back. "Come, my love," Nomy whispered into my right ear. "Let us take you home."

How could I leave Saul's murderer unpunished?

"David, will you allow me to help you?" I looked up and found Maakah kneeling before me. "May I work with Joab to secure the Amalekite until later this evening, until you've had time to consider how to properly . . . *reward* his behavior?" Her half-lidded emphasis of *reward* assured me she knew he deserved the opposite.

Noble

I could only nod. Abigail, kneeling on my left, thanked her and ducked her head under my arm. Nomy did the same on my right side, and the three of us stood and turned toward home. Only then did I realize the whole city surrounded me. As we walked, every person knelt and bowed a dust-covered head. I couldn't stem my tears, but I didn't need to. The whole city wept with me.

As we retreated, I heard Maakah shout, "Joab will take the Amalekite to a private tent and place him under guard until *King* David is ready to pass judgment. Until then, let us all mourn and fast for the men of Israel who have fallen by the sword."

Jeering and taunts followed her announcement. I looked over my shoulder, ready to rescue the princess if my soldiers or their families refused her the authority I'd given her to speak. To my surprise—and satisfaction—my people's venom was aimed at the Amalekite, not at Maakah.

"Joab would never have allowed me to speak to the whole city." Nomy's expression was indecipherable. Was she jealous? Or did she admire Maakah for managing Joab so handily?

I glanced at Abigail, who seemed to be waiting for me to look her way. "Neither Nomy nor I would have thought to make such an announcement—though it certainly needed to be made." She gave a slight nod, as if she approved of both Maakah's and my willingness to assign her the task.

We entered our tent in silence, and I went straight to the partitioned chamber to be alone. I needed to consider what Saul's and Jonathan's deaths would mean for our future, but the moment I lowered myself to the reed mat, Maakah overshadowed every other thought.

She'd reacted quickly to the situation with the poise and calm of a queen. I'd been at a loss, overwhelmed with emotion. What I might have labeled presumptuous or invasive yesterday had today proven thoughtful and a rescue for my battered soul. If the Amalekite's report was true, and Israel had indeed suffered the loss of its king, crown prince, and a significant portion of its fighting force, my ascent to Israel's throne could be imminent.

At the mere thought, my belly flipped. *Thank You, Yahweh, for bringing Maakah here for a time such as this.* I could have no better teacher at my side than Geshur's sole heir.

FIFTEEN

MAAKAH

*They mourned and wept and fasted till evening for Saul and his son
Jonathan, and for the army of the LORD and for the nation of Israel,
because they had fallen by the sword.*

2 Samuel 1:12

I'd spent all day in our tent, trying to ignore Zulat's subtle disapproval of the continued wailing throughout the camp. When her deep sighs and fierce shudders became as distracting as the mourners, I could endure it no longer. "If you can't be respectful, you will leave the city and return only after these loyal people have mourned Israel's king and crown prince."

Her mouth fell open, as shocked as if a beggar had received a king's robe. "Do you hear yourself?" she scoffed. "These so-called loyal people are wailing over the death of a king who wished David ben Jesse dead for years."

"They mourn for the destruction of Israel and its leaders. They mourn for the upheaval that's sure to come in the void of leadership."

"There will be no void. Achish will name David as Israel's new king and—"

"Do you really think Dohd Achish or Abba will support David

196

as Israel's king when they discover what he's done to our southern kingdom?"

"I told you, Prin. They need never know." She splayed her hands as if explaining to a child. "It's a secret you can hold over David's head until you've been married for fifty years."

"First, I refuse to manipulate David like that, and second, do you think this nation of stiff-necked Israelites will follow a man they believe to be the Philistines' puppet?" I'd never considered the impossibility of David's situation. "Until I lived among these people, I had no idea how utterly devoted they were to their god and to their leader. Wouldn't those devoted to Saul and Prince Jonathan feel any less committed? How could Abba think the Israelites who served and fought for King Saul and his family would so easily shift their allegiance to the rebel David, a man accused of treason nearly a decade ago?"

Another loud wail rent the air. Zulat instinctively winced, but I never flinched, waiting for her to return her eyes to meet my hard stare. "That is the sound of commitment, of love for one's nation no matter what perceived wrongs have been done against you. That is the broken heart of lost love, deeper than duty or selfish gain. If you can't respect that, Zulat, I don't want you in my presence right now."

She sniffed, a sign of wordless disapproval. "I won't pretend to respect their overly emotional blubbering, but—because you command it—I will attempt to control my reactions."

For the rest of the morning, she'd done as she promised. I'd helped the effort by asking Zerry and Abital for the bread-making supplies so Zulat and I could at least make a few loaves for this evening's needs. We worked in silence, having no safe subjects to restore our once-close bond.

I rested at midday, awakened when Zulat nudged my shoulder with a plate full of dried figs, nuts, hard cheese, and bread. "Eat something. You hardly ate any of your yogurt this morning."

Noble

I didn't feel like eating after seeing how upset David had been upon hearing from the Amalekite. Even the word *Amalekite* set my teeth on edge. The fact that four hundred escaped from the camp was frustrating, but to have an Amalekite slave deliver the news of his best friend's death must have felt like salt in a gaping wound.

"I need to see if David is all right." Nudging the plate aside, I was on my feet before Zulat could object. "He seemed completely undone after hearing of Saul's death." My maid protested, but I spoke over her and kept walking. "He should remember he's soon to be king and must deal as a ruler, not as a warrior, with this Amalekite." I slipped out of the tent with a relieved sigh, ignoring Zulat's last indignant shout.

Pausing a moment, I turned in a full circle and was grateful that my feet had healed enough that I could walk with only a slight limp. Something else filled me with wonder: the deserted streets of a city in mourning. Geshur had never experienced anything like this, not even when Saba died, a beloved king of over forty years. Our people would have been too afraid of offending Abba, the incoming regent, to show such open grief for his predecessor. *But doesn't the predecessor deserve a day of mourning? At least some recognition for being the gods' choice to rule?*

A wave of admiration pushed me toward David's tent. The front flaps were closed, but they'd opened the sides—as we had—to let what little breeze there was blow through. I stopped at the front flaps, suddenly at a loss for how to begin my suggestion to Israel's next king.

David, in a public setting, a king never sullies his hands with a prisoner's blood. He orders his guards to execute the wrongdoer.

It sounded so arrogant. What did I know of other kings and kingdoms? I knew only what King Talmai of Geshur had taught me. I knew how Aramean royalty presented themselves at banquets and festivals. But what did I know of warfare? I'd never seen a man die until Abba beheaded that messenger in his throne room, and I wouldn't have seen that without disobeying his command. What if all kings didn't rule as Abba did? What if I was teaching David to rule Israelite people as would a Geshurite king?

The wailing inside David's tent paused as if he'd heard my thoughts. I leaned closer to hear lowered voices and then shuffling footsteps. One tent flap suddenly pulled back. David ben Jesse stood less than a step from me, his red-rimmed eyes puffy. With a sad but friendly expression, he stepped back and swept his hand toward their main chamber. "Come in, Maakah. I'm glad you've come."

My heart did a little flip at his warm welcome. Once inside, I looked for Ahinoam and Abigail, but the main room was empty. "Where are—"

"My wives have given me this time to mourn alone. They're grieving together in the partitioned chamber, but I can ask them to join us if you'd feel more comfortable."

"No!" I said too quickly. He tilted his head, questioning, and my cheeks instantly warmed. "I was hoping to talk with you. Privately." Perhaps I could explain what my heart intended in a more appropriate way if I could completely concentrate on only his reaction.

"Is something bothering you?"

"No—I mean—yes. Well, not really bothering me, but . . ." I was making a mess of it already. "Do you realize my dohd Achish could make you king over Israel upon his return from battle?"

He pursed his lips into a condescending smile. "Achish can give me a title, but he can't make me Israel's king. I must earn the right to rule Yahweh's people."

I nodded, pleased that he'd already concluded what I'd realized earlier. "True, but you have the opportunity today to show the people willingly under your reign that you have stepped into the role of regent. You are no longer merely a warrior chieftain, David. Today, your god has fulfilled his promise to you."

His expression shifted, but I couldn't read it. His back stiffened,

Noble

and his muscled shoulders looked like the rolling hills of my country. "Yahweh will fulfill His promise, but I dare not move too quickly ahead. I've learned three things in the years since I fled Gibeah of Saul. The first and hardest lesson: I can never anticipate the LORD's plan. Second, His plan is always better than I imagine; and third, His best for me always comes with a sacrifice."

Intrigued, I asked, "Can you give examples?"

"I never anticipated marrying again after Saul's daughter betrayed me. But Yahweh has given me two wives, which is far more than I could have imagined."

He smiled for the first time since I'd arrived, and I felt as if my heart leapt into my throat. How would it feel to make this man smile every day? To please him and see affection in his eyes for me—as I saw when he gazed at Ahinoam and Abigail?

My throat tightened, and I looked down, afraid he'd see my unbridled emotion. "And what did you sacrifice to accept those women as your wives?"

"I sacrificed the approval of some people who were important to me." The sadness in his voice drew me, and I found him rubbing hard at the calluses on his hands.

"Do you regret your decision to marry two wives?"

"Never." He looked at me, letting his hands fall at his sides. "Though the Law of Moses forbids a king from taking many wives, I believe the Law is a guardian over us to follow as if Yahweh Himself were standing over us and whispering to our hearts whenever we have a decision to make. Ahinoam, Abigail, and I prayed to hear the LORD's counsel clearly, and when He struck Abigail's first husband dead because of his wickedness, we all three felt it was Yahweh's clear approval that I was to marry Abigail and be her protector and provider. God's voice was as clear as if it had come from Mount Sinai—but it still wasn't easy to marry another when Ahinoam and I loved each other so thoroughly."

"But you three seem so content now. I can hardly believe it hasn't always been so."

This time he chuckled. "Surely you can imagine that my beautiful dagger-throwing Kenite was reluctant to share her husband with a lovely, elegant, capable manager of my household."

"You realize we can hear everything you're saying," Ahinoam said from beyond the partition. I joined the two women's giggles, feeling their camaraderie even with a curtain between us.

David shrugged. "It hasn't always been so amiable." He sobered, and the sound of mourning outside his tent brought us back to the moment. "You seemed as though you had something on your mind when you came here. Something about me having an opportunity to show those already under my reign that I'm not *merely* a warrior chieftain."

When he stressed the word, I realized how offensive it sounded. "I didn't mean—"

"I know." Another grin. "I'm growing accustomed to your . . ." He paused, tapping his bearded chin. "Let's call them helpful suggestions."

"That's how I intend them. I want to help as long as I'm here." The thought of leaving, of going back to Geshur with another failed betrothal, brought tears to the surface again. Looking down, I tried to gather myself before proceeding, but David's touch under my chin gently drew my focus back to him. "It's a day for mourning, Maakah. Don't be ashamed of your tears."

"But I didn't even know Saul or Prince Jonathan." My words came out on a whine.

"You know me, my wives, Zerry, and Abital. Cry for us, for our heartbreak." He brushed my cheek before dropping his hand. "Never be ashamed of your tears, Princess."

I thought my heart would burst. How different he was than Aramean royalty.

"I want you to become the greatest king Israel will ever have." My strangled words came out as desperately as I meant them. "You can become a regal king, David, not merely noble."

He smiled again. "Which am I—merely a warrior chieftain or merely a noble king?"

"Please don't mock me." Anger dried my tears. "I've trained my whole life to sit beside a king and help him rule more effectively. You seem to think ruling a nation is as simple as putting on a gold crown, moving into a new house, and sitting on a fancy chair."

"You have no idea what my anointing as Yahweh's king has cost me." I saw momentary frustration before he bowed his head and sighed. "Forgive me, LORD. I've gained far more than I've lost."

I'd done it again. While trying to be helpful, I'd crossed some sort of line and offended David beyond my ability to repair. He obviously had no interest in my advice. Maybe our worlds were simply too different. While his head was bowed, I turned to quietly slip out.

His hand gripped my forearm, startling me. But it was the look of pleading in his eyes that gave me pause. "Don't go," he whispered. "You still haven't told me your . . . helpful suggestions."

I looked down at his hand on my arm. He removed it as if he'd touched a boiling pot. I still felt the warmth of his touch, and I longed for its return. Fearing he'd see the yearning, I kept my head down and said, "I assume you plan to execute the Amalekite."

A slight pause, then, "Yes."

"It's a wise decision, given that your intent was to wipe out the entire Amalekite camp. Executing the slave who killed Israel's king will show both your people and all of Israel that your intentions remain unchanged. The Amalekites are still in your bow-sight. Your leadership is steady and dependable."

"I'm happy you approve."

Was he mocking me again? Frustrated, I looked into his handsome face but saw no hint of taunting.

"Tell me, Princess Maakah, what else do you suggest if I'm to reign as a regal king over my people?" His curved red lips were utterly pleasant, drawing me in rather than pushing me away.

"I . . . um . . . I . . ." I couldn't stop staring at them. His copper-colored beard rimmed those deep red lips with a lighter blonde. I was mesmerized, examining every handsome feature I'd overlooked before. Copper freckles covered his face. Deep-set eyes were intense, whether angry or concerned. A crooked, slender nose proved it had been broken at least once.

"Maakah?"

"Yes?"

His eyes, now crinkled at the edges, accompanied a smile. "Did you have other helpful suggestions?" he asked.

My neck and cheeks instantly flamed. "Order one of your guards to kill the Amalekite."

His smile disappeared. "Why allow someone else to avenge the blood of Yahweh's anointed?"

"Because you're now a king, and in public, a king presents himself as above violence and the baser human acts. A king delegates executions to the capable defenders he's chosen as his royal guard. Now they do whatever you, as a warrior chieftain, would have done yourself."

"But I'm still me." His brows lifted again, drawn together in utter confusion. How could a man so capable, so . . . *good* remain so humble?

"You must become a regal you." I wanted to brush his face as he'd done to mine, but I dared not—lest my heart fall over a cliff into unrecoverable emotions. I called over my shoulder. "I must get back to Zulat."

"Wait! Don't go!" Abigail's voice stopped me.

I felt a moment of panic and turned to face her as she stepped out from behind the partition. Would she know by simply looking at me how I felt about her husband? "I'm sorry. I thought I should probably leave you to your grieving."

"Don't go." Ahinoam appeared from behind Abigail. "You've given David sound advice."

"Advice we would never have known to share with him," Abigail added. "I'm sure it seems strange to you that David grieves so deeply for a king who betrayed him, accused him unjustly, and has been trying to kill him for years."

I looked at David, feeling rather awkward to have been called out on exactly what I'd admired in many ways but also struggled to understand. "It does seem a bit . . ."

"Unroyal?" David grinned again, and I realized he wasn't mocking. He was treating me with the familiarity I'd seen him use with his wives, his sister, and other family members and friends.

Finally, I could really laugh in his presence. "Completely unroyal."

"David, why don't you take your lyre and Maakah outside the city gates?" Ahinoam suggested. "Spend some time explaining your relationship with Prince Jonathan. I think it will help her understand why we all grieve Saul and Jonathan's loss." She stepped behind Abigail as if hiding from our reaction.

David's mouth dropped open, and he looked as shocked as I felt. "But it wouldn't be proper," I said.

"No one will think it improper if you remain within sight of the watchmen," Abigail assured me, then turned to David. "Nomy and I believe it's important that you gain as much wisdom as possible from Maakah before the messengers return from Geshur." David looked around Abigail to see his first wife. I glimpsed Ahinoam's single nod, affirming agreement, but also noticed her lips quaking. Her emotion seemed rooted in something deeper than Saul's and Jonathan's death.

"I don't think Ahinoam wants me to spend time alone with your husband, Abigail." I'd made a vow not to harm these women, and I would not break it.

Abigail turned toward her sister-wife, their whispers leaving David and me as awkward outsiders. After only a few moments, Ahinoam's frustration erupted. "I know," she said, then stepped away from Abigail and toward me.

Gripping my hands, she looked into my eyes so deeply that I feared she might read the secrets of my heart. "You must spend time alone with David so you'll be ready with an answer when Eliphelet returns with the message from your abba. If King Talmai wishes you to proceed with a betrothal contract, Maakah, you and David must decide if it's a match your hearts can also abide."

"But I . . . but you and Abigail . . ."

"Abigail and I believe Yahweh has brought you into our lives for a purpose. As yet, we're not certain what that purpose is, so today's time with David will help determine it." She turned a longing gaze toward her husband. "I thought it might be easier to share you with a second woman, but it's not. I'm sad that I'll need to give up more time with you, but at least I don't want to kill Maakah as I did Abigail." The hint of a smile pulled at the corners of her mouth.

"Stop!" Abigail chuckled, nudging her shoulder. "Maakah will think you're serious."

Ahinoam gave her a shameless grin. "Who says I'm not?"

SIXTEEN

DAVID

The LORD was with Joseph and gave him success in whatever he did.

Genesis 39:23

I kissed Abigail's cheek and captured Nomy's gaze. "Remember, I will never marry a woman who refuses to worship Yahweh alone." She made no effort to touch me, so I honored her vow to wait until the eighth-day ceremony before holding her in my arms. I hurried toward the door and picked up my lyre on the way out. *Give us all wisdom in this moment, LORD. How can marrying another woman— breaking Your Law again—be permissible to You?*

Timid footsteps behind me hurried to catch up. Did Maakah feel as torn as I did? There was no denying the attraction between us. The footsteps grew more distant. I glanced over my shoulder and noted her limping, only then did I remember her healing feet. Compassion slowed my pace—or was it more than compassion? My chest tightened, and I knew the answer. Maakah caught up and now walked beside me.

I looked down at the petite young woman whose long black curls bounced as she walked. She stared straight ahead at the city gate, her lips pursed into a worrisome line. After my initial distrust of her diminished, this young princess, who always had an opinion and an overwhelming need to share it, had intrigued me. Which made her silence beside me now even more unnerving.

"My wives don't waste time with subtleties," I said. "I hope you weren't offended by their directness."

She lifted a shoulder, still unwilling to look my way. "I'm quite relieved to find women who speak their minds."

"Would you be willing to speak what's on your mind right now?"

"Huh." Part scoff, part laugh, she shook her head. "I'm not sure what to think at the moment."

A long silence stretched between us as we passed through the city gate, receiving strange glances from the watchmen but no direct questions. I placed my lyre beneath my chin and began strumming a familiar tune to fill the space between us.

"That's beautiful." Finally, she looked at me. "From my tent, I've heard you singing. How did you learn to play?"

"I was raised by my abba's shepherds since I was five harvests old. They taught me to play several instruments. The lyre has always been my favorite."

I glimpsed a look of horror on her lovely face. "Why would your abba banish you to the fields?"

"It's a long story. Let me sum it up by saying Abba questioned Ima's faithfulness and labeled her an adulteress until I was born with Jesse ben Obed's ancestral red hair."

Her eyes grew misty, though I tried to keep my voice light. "I'm sorry your abba treated you so badly, David."

I shrugged. "Yahweh has used all my hard experiences for good. Had the shepherds not trained me to wield a sling, I would never have slain your dohd Achish's giant champion, Goliath. Had I not slain Goliath, my heart and Jonathan's would never have been knit together like brothers."

"So the crown prince wanted to be best friends with Israel's champion." A shadow crossed her features before she looked forward again. "I know the type. They want to be friends with the best warrior to bask in his glory."

I watched her profile as we neared the shade of an acacia tree. This was one of those moments when Maakah seemed older than her years. "I, too, have known men like you describe. After I fled Gibeah and Saul's assassins, the king took his daughter—my first wife, Michal—and gave her to such a man. Paltiel cared only about his rise to power in Saul's royal guard."

She halted and pinned me with a stare. "Was it your experience with Michal that made you never wish to marry again?"

No wonder Nomy and Abigail liked her. Maakah was as direct as they were. "Yes. Only Yahweh could have opened my heart, and only Ahinoam could have filled the emptiness in it. She's probably the only woman willing to dash from danger to disaster with me through the Judean wilderness for all those years."

"Hmm." Her eyes narrowed. "If Prince Jonathan didn't want a share of your fame, why suddenly become your friend after you killed Dohd Achish's giant?" She was as tenacious as a dog with a bone. There would be no steering her off topic.

"Do you know how I killed Goliath?"

"You said with a sling."

"*Only* a sling and one smooth stone. No armor. No shield. No other weapons."

Her eyes widened. "Did you use some sort of magic?"

"Better than magic."

"Well, whatever the source, it was effective and probably the reason Dohd Achish has given you sanctuary. A single warrior protected by the gods is better than a vast army without favor from the divine."

"You're very close to the real reason Jonathan and I became brothers."

Her brow furrowed. "I don't understand."

LORD, give me the right words. "Jonathan shared my strong belief that Yahweh would protect Israel from our enemies if we would only trust Him. So, after Goliath's threats kept Israel's army paralyzed for forty days, I came from Bethlehem with supplies for my brothers, heard the giant's blasphemy, and became incensed. I had no doubt Yahweh would destroy the giant to prove His power. Saul offered me his armor, but I refused. Instead, I took my shepherd's sling and grabbed five smooth stones from the nearby wadi—preparing to fight if all five Philistine cities produced their own giant. When Goliath saw me approach, he was furious that Israel would send out a mere boy to fight him. While he railed and insulted my God, I simply prayed that Yahweh would display His great power and defend His people. I wound the sling and hoisted one stone that sunk into the giant's forehead. He fell like a cedar of Lebanon."

I started walking toward the shade again, needing a distraction before I revealed the most vulnerable part of my story. "When I cut off Goliath's head and gave it to Saul as a battle prize, Prince Jonathan stood beside his abba's throne. Our eyes met. He was smiling as tears coursed down his cheeks. While others gathered to jostle my shoulders and praise my great victory, only Jonathan and I praised Yahweh for our miraculous deliverance. That's when our hearts were knit together. When I married Jonathan's sister, Michal, he and I were the only ones in Saul's household with hearts desperate for God. We became closer than blood relatives, dearer to each other than any woman." My voice broke, and tears began to flow again. I held back the wailing I'd indulged in all morning. Sitting down hard beneath the acacia, I began strumming my lyre once more.

Maakah sat across from me, listening, and I sang, "You are my strength. I sing praise to you, oh God. You are my fortress, my God, on whom I can rely."

I strummed the last note, eyes closed, and lifted my face to the

Noble

heavens. *Please, Yahweh, show me if I'm to move forward with Maakah, or if she is to return to Geshur and marry another.*

"My gods are important to me, too, David." The protest came as a whisper. I opened my eyes and saw her pallor matched the dusty earth on which we sat. "How could you ask me to abandon everything I've trusted my whole life?"

"You can be loyal to your nation, your Abba, and your ima without remaining loyal to the false gods they taught you to worship."

"False?" Her cheeks reddened with defiance. "How can you say my gods are false when you know nothing about them?"

"I know many things about your gods."

Her jaw hung open, seeming to have lost her words. I waited until she finally sputtered, "Wha—what could you possibly know about my gods when you're so thoroughly devoted to your own?"

"I'm also thoroughly devoted to my wives, but I'm aware of other women. The difference is, I *chose* to give my heart and allegiance to Nomy and Abigail—as I've chosen to give my whole heart to Yahweh. El and Asherah, Ea and Athirat—they're the supreme gods and goddesses of my ancient saba Abraham, but Yahweh proved Himself real and proved the other gods to be merely shedim—fallen angels wandering the earth. Yahweh called my saba Abraham out of Mesopotamia more than a thousand years ago and promised to give him the land we're seated on."

She was shaking her head before I finished speaking but with more wonder than defiance. "Ea and Athirat are even more ancient than El and Asherah. Do you also know the stories of Baal and Anat?"

"Of course, but that's all they are, Maakah. Stories." Though her excitement dimmed, I pressed on. "While living among the Chaldeans, Saba Abraham worshiped the ancient gods."

"He worshiped the gods of Babylon?"

"Yes, in the land given to Noah's son, Shem, after the Great Flood and the Tower of Babel."

210

"I know of the Great Flood! It's told in *The Epic of Gilgamesh*, but I've never heard of this babbling tower."

"It's the Tower of Babel, and, unfortunately, the story you've heard in *The Epic of Gilgamesh* is only a fable created by wealthy, powerful men to instill fear and assert control over the poor and weak. The Great Flood was Yahweh's judgment on all humans because they'd begun to mimic fallen angels who came to earth and conceived offspring with human women. These supernatural offspring became the Anakites—the giants—that your ancestors employed in battle."

Her face lit with wonder. "Like Goliath, who you killed with your sling."

"Yes, Maakah, but the Anakites were enemies long before they fought Israel. They deceived humankind soon after the Flood, coaxing developing nations to create false gods. Priests and priestesses eventually rose from among the common people, using the false gods to steal Yahweh's glory, hoard wealth, and secure earthly power."

Eagerness no longer lit her features. "I don't believe you."

"Then believe this. Only one man and his family survived the Great Flood: Noah, his three sons, and their wives. The giants also survived—because, at least in part, they were supernatural beings. When Noah and his descendants settled in Mesopotamia—the birthplace of humanity—the giants convinced Noah's descendants to build a tower to the heavens so they could themselves become gods. It was the same sin the first humans committed at the beginning of time that made it impossible for us to walk side-by-side with our holy God."

"Why must Yahweh kill people who displease him?" Her words clipped, I saw no indication of a softened heart. *Yahweh, give me the words* . . .

"At the Tower of Babel, Yahweh didn't kill the rebellious idolators. Instead, he confused their language and scattered them across the earth into tribes with different languages."

"Your Tower of Babel sounds very similar to *Enmerkar and the Lord of Aratta* in which the Queen of Heaven confuses the language of one kingdom to help Enmerkar conquer another. Are you sure your ancestors didn't lie to you and simply borrow stories from our common heritage and change the gods' names to Yahweh?"

"Our common heritage ended when Saba Abraham left the Land of the Chaldea's to receive Yahweh's promise. He believed the *truth* spoken to him by the one true God, and we're living out what Yahweh promised—you and me, right here and now. The difference between the true Tower of Babel and the story of *Enmerkar and the Lord of Aratta* is that Yahweh, at the Tower of Babel, directly intervened to frustrate human ambition that opposed His divine purpose. In *Enmerkar and the Lord of Aratta*, the goddess supported the human king, Enmerkar, to conquer Aratta's kingdom through trickery, magic, and confusion of languages. When Enmerkar was successful, the language confusion was overcome."

Maakah's angry features softened, giving me hope to finish with a plea. "Yahweh blesses and protects those who love and trust Him," I said. "I've broken His laws—sometimes inadvertently and sometimes because I succumbed to temptation. But Yahweh knows that my deepest desires are to please Him, to obey Him, and to love Him more every day."

"Love Him?" Maakah's whole body grew rigid. "How can you love a god, David? They're unpredictable and . . . and they take people away." She bowed her head, fidgeting with her hands.

"Who was taken away from you, Maakah?" Would she trust me enough to open that wound?

"His name was Kepha," she said without looking up. "He was the only one in my life who ever said he loved me."

"From what my wives told me, you seem rather close with your parents. Didn't they ever say they loved you?"

She shook her head and swiped at her cheeks with one hand. "I know they love me, but we don't speak of it. When Kepha looked into my eyes, he saw inside me. He knew how I felt about him, so he said it aloud to me—the night before he left for battle. It was the last time I saw him." She covered her face with both hands and wept.

I wanted to comfort her in my arms, to press my lips against her hair and whisper, *"You'll love again someday."*

She loves you. The words came quick and clear. Unmistakable. Undeniable.

"Uhhh!" Maakah swiped her face with both hands and glared at me. "Your wives want us to know if your god wants us to marry, and I'm telling you about the only man I've ever loved." She gasped as her eyes widened and spine straightened. "I didn't mean . . . he's not the only one I could love . . . I meant to say . . . uuuhhh!" Both hands went up again, hiding what had likely become a scarlet face. "If my feet weren't throbbing, I'd run back to the city and hide."

I chuckled and gently pulled her hands down to uncover her lovely face. "I'm glad you can't run and hide." I looked into those gray-blue eyes, the color of Geshur's Lake of Athirat. She tried to turn away, but I captured her chin and asked, "Will you allow me to see inside you, Princess Maakah?"

At hearing her formal title, her breath caught. Had I offended? When a spark of mischief brightened her eyes, I knew the bold princess had returned. "I have questions inside me, *King* David."

I, too, was taken off guard when she addressed me as *King*, but she continued before I could question her.

"What if I already believe in your god? Since Athirat and Asherah refer to a singular goddess whose name evolved over time—like the supreme god's name evolved from Ea to El—doesn't it make sense that your Yahweh is a further evolution of the supreme god's name?"

I drew breath to protest, but she continued, "In which case, I need not abandon my gods but rather add Yahweh to the other deities I honor."

Noble

"Yahweh does not evolve," I said. "Yahweh is the same yesterday, today, and always." Her excitement drained like an overturned wine cup.

I stood, raked a hand through my hair, and considered how to respond without showing frustration. Keeping my back to her, I said, "The God of my ancestors is a jealous God, Maakah. He requires our complete devotion. All of Israel teaches their children this prayer from the moment they're old enough to speak." I turned to watch her reaction and began reciting the words I prayed each morning. "Hear, O Israel: The LORD our God, the LORD is one. Love the LORD your God with all your heart and with all your soul and with all your strength."

Her lips pursed into a disapproving pout. "My gods may show their temper, but your god sounds like a selfish tyrant."

A tyrant? Bending to one knee, I released a calming breath and prayed for gentle words. "Do your gods come to you personally and comfort you?"

"Of course not. They have more important things to do than—"

"Maakah, Yahweh loves His people."

"You said that but I've seen no proof."

"He shelters each one like I would protect my firstborn son. He tends to our needs as Ahinoam nourishes our baby boy."

Her eyes glistened, but her features remained taut. "You tell pretty stories, David, but look around. Your god has failed you. He allowed your homes to burn and many of Ziklag's women to be defiled. You'll have no provisions for winter. Yahweh—or perhaps Mot, the god of the underworld—seems to be working against you, not for you."

I heaved a sigh and sat on the ground, facing her. Envisioning my dire circumstances from Maakah's perspective would indeed seem like a defeat to one who only had a pantheon of myths to explain the world. If I'd been raised in a pagan household and resolved every good or evil situation by a superstition or mythical being, I'd likely doubt Yahweh with as much vehemence as her clenched jaw proved. Under my perusal, Maakah turned away.

Yahweh, what can I say to open her heart to Your presence? Right here. In this moment. I sorted through the ancient stories of my ancestors. Was there a woman's story that might hold special meaning for this foreign princess?

"You've never mentioned any mercy shown by your god to a foreigner." Maakah spoke barely above a whisper. "Why would I give up my gods—sometimes capricious but at least familiar—for a tyrant deity who hates foreigners?"

Her question prompted the stories I needed to share. *Thank You, LORD.* "Yahweh loves anyone with a heart willing to open itself to Him."

"I'm sorry, David, but I don't believe you." She faced me, her lovely features twisted with doubt. "I fear you're the one who's been deceived all your life."

I bristled at the accusation but heard no malice in her tone. "May I tell you about a foreign woman Yahweh rescued with miraculous power?"

She sighed, but her features softened to a rueful grin. "Can I say anything to stop you?"

We laughed a little. "I'm afraid not." Our eyes held. She was listening. So I began two stories leading to one answer. "Besides the land Yahweh promised to Saba Abraham, God also promised that he and Savta Sarah would have descendants as abundant as the stars in the sky, and those descendants would bless all nations."

"*All* nations?" She raised a skeptical brow.

I pointed to the offending arch. She pursed her lips and donned an impassive expression that was totally wasted on her dynamic features.

"Unfortunately, Saba was seventy-five when he entered Canaan,

Noble

the land Yahweh promised to give him and his descendants, and Savta Sarah was ten years younger—having borne no children."

"She was past the age of childbearing." Maakah sat a little straighter.

"Yes, but Yahweh opened her womb and gave her a son when she was ninety harvests old."

She crossed her arms, that dynamic face showing obvious disbelief. "I'm not sure how this fantastical story relates to the rescue of a foreign woman. You said Abraham's wife traveled with him from Mesopotamia. Wasn't she of the same heritage as her husband?"

"Yes, but—"

"Tell me a story of a man like you who suffered at your god's hands and then married a foreign princess because—" She pursed quaking lips into a thin, taut line.

"Because what, Maakah?" I waited.

She slapped away defiant tears and said, "Because I see no scenario in which Dohd Achish will allow you to rule Israel. Your god can't give you ownership of Canaan because it belongs to Dohd Achish's gods and his giants."

I was wrong about her tears. She seemed more angry than desperate.

I continued with a second story. "Saba Abraham's blessing was passed down to his grandson, Jacob, who was renamed *Israel* after he wrestled with the angel of God. Israel had twelve sons. The ten older brothers were jealous of the eleventh son, Joseph. They sold him to Midianite traders, who took him to Egypt where Pharaoh's captain of the guard purchased Joseph as a slave."

"What does this have to do with—"

"You wanted a story about a man who suffered and then received his promise from Yahweh." I lifted my brow, waiting for permission to continue. She wound her hand in a circle, prodding me forward.

216

"Joseph served Potiphar, Pharaoh's captain of the guard, and was made overseer of the captain's estate. Unfortunately, Potiphar's wife also favored Joseph and relentlessly begged him to bed her." Maakah's barely audible gasp reminded me of her sheltered upbringing, and I hurried past those details. "Remaining obedient to Yahweh's laws, Joseph refused her, but one day, she trapped him. Joseph fled, leaving his cloak in her hand, which she used as evidence for her false accusation against him."

"Surely Potiphar had placed his whole estate in Joseph's care," Maakah interrupted. "He would have trusted Joseph over such a lewd and seductive wife."

"We can't know what Potiphar's thoughts were, but the stories passed down for centuries say Potiphar was so angry—whether with Joseph or his wife, we don't know—that the captain threw Joseph in Pharaoh's prison."

"No! It's unconscionable!" Fury thrust her to her knees. "You'd better not tell me he was executed, or I'll never let you speak of your god again."

In that moment, I saw what a devoted follower she could be and realized that to win this woman's loyalty would be a treasure beyond a king's wealth. "Relax, Princess, and trust me to tell you the truth about my God who rescued this good man and gives him a foreign princess as his wife."

Her breath caught, and a smile lit her face. "Keep going then."

My heart galloped, and I felt a moment of panic. *Oh, LORD, please don't let me love her unless You'll make her mine.* Her smile faded. My countenance must have given away my fear, so I continued with the story to distract us both. "Even in that dark prison, Yahweh proved He was with Joseph. The warden showed him favor by making Joseph his assistant. One night, when two prisoners—Pharaoh's baker and cupbearer—were disturbed by nightmares, Yahweh gave Joseph the ability to interpret their dreams. When

Noble

his interpretations came true—the cupbearer restored to serving Pharaoh and the baker executed—the cupbearer neglected to mention Joseph's unfair sentence as he'd promised."

"You'd better get to the good part quickly."

I grinned. "I'm sure Joseph felt the same. Two years later, Pharaoh also had nightmares that his magicians couldn't interpret through their false gods. The cupbearer finally remembered Joseph and mentioned him to Pharaoh. When Joseph was released from prison, he interpreted the king's dreams through Yahweh's power and saved Egypt and the surrounding nations with a plan for seven years of abundant crops followed by seven years of severe famine. That's one way Abraham's descendants blessed many nations."

Lifting her chin, she said, "In my extensive study of Egypt's history, there's no mention of your Hebrew god in their pantheon. They still worship their own gods."

"Yahweh doesn't need to be written in Egypt's meticulous records to speak to individuals. Do you remember what I said about Yahweh caring for each one of us, loving us personally?"

"It's nonsense."

I grinned at her stubbornness. She would indeed become a loyal follower if Yahweh ever snagged her heart. "Pharaoh appointed Joseph his new vizier and gave Joseph many gifts, one of which was an Egyptian wife." Maakah lifted her brow, engaged again in the story. "This wife was the daughter of a powerful priest. Do you think she worshiped Yahweh when they married?"

"Doubtful." She chuckled.

"Most of my ancestors agree that it's likely Joseph's wife eventually worshiped our Hebrew God because she would have named their two sons—and both bear Hebrew names. So Joseph's wife became the first foreign woman to embrace Yahweh as her own." I leaned forward and offered my hand. "And that's a true accounting of a godly man, rescued by Yahweh, who married a foreign princess, who inherited Abraham's promise and was blessed *individually* because Yahweh loves each one He creates."

She stared at my proffered hand as if it were a hissing snake. Slowly, she lifted her eyes to meet mine and pressed her small, trembling hand in mine. A myriad of emotions flashed across her features, making her even more beautiful. Hope. Doubt. Possibility. Dread. I looked deeply into the windows of her soul and saw the battle churning inside her. If she refused her gods and worshiped only Yahweh, her family might disown her. Any treaty agreement might be nullified, and my proselytizing could be interpreted as an act of war.

"To turn away from my gods is to turn my back on my people," she whispered, squeezing my hand more tightly. "You're asking me to abandon my identity as a Geshurite."

"No, Maakah." I cradled her hand between mine. "Geshur is more than its gods, and you are so much more than a representative of your city. Geshur's history stands separate from you and will endure long after we're in our graves. You and I have only this life to determine where our true allegiance lies. Will we be enslaved by earthly masters who demand more than they give? Or will we serve an almighty God who promises more than we can imagine?"

She pulled her hand away and looked toward the watchmen on the wall. "I shouldn't allow you to touch me. Your men might think—" Lowering her head, she whispered, "I'll consider all you've said, David, but I can't make such a weighty decision in a single afternoon."

"Again, you show wisdom beyond your years."

She looked up. "Thank you." Her tight, black curls hung in ringlets over her shoulders, demanding I run my fingers through them.

Instead, I looked down at my lyre and began strumming. "Perhaps you should return to your tent while I play a little longer. I'll consider your advice about how a king executes his enemies. Perhaps you'll reconsider what on this earth could prevent an all-powerful God from fulfilling His promises to His anointed king."

SEVENTEEN

MAAKAH

David said to the young man who brought him the report, "Where are you from?"

"I am the son of a foreigner, an Amalekite," he answered.

David asked him, "Why weren't you afraid to lift your hand to destroy the LORD's anointed?"

2 Samuel 1:13–14

I took my time walking back to the city, pondering all David had said about his god. Though his story about Joseph and the Egyptian wife sounded too idyllic—and as far-fetched as many of my own gods' antics—I trusted David's integrity. He had many opportunities to disrespect me or treat me with malice. Instead, after the first whiff of suspicion passed, he and his wives welcomed me like family. Somehow, I felt in my deepest being that David wouldn't lie to me. He'd encouraged my directness, and I felt I could depend on his in return.

Reaching my tent, I looked across the ten paces that separated me from Ahinoam and Abigail. Should I go over to speak with them? Their suggestion that they might accept me as David's third wife had come as a complete surprise. Could I face them now? I didn't really have any news except that I'd promised to consider all that David told me. Truth be told, I didn't want to face their disappointment at the news. They were so eager for me to embrace their God, but they had no idea the gravity of such a life-altering decision.

I ducked into my tent and immediately met Zulat's cool stare. "Humph. I can see by your starry-eyed look you were more concerned with strengthening your love life than advocating political advantage for Geshur." She stabbed both fists at her ample hips. "Have you completely forgotten we're here to help your abba's kingdom?"

"Have you completely forgotten you are my servant?" The last word escaped with a shout, and I remembered what Abba had taught me about royalty. *"The one with power never need raise his voice."* Regaining composure, I took three steps, halting close enough to see the surprise in Zulat's eyes. "I'm no longer the little girl you can bludgeon with shame and control with duty. I am your mistress, your princess, and possibly your queen, if Ima bears another daughter. You will speak to me with the deference my position deserves, or you will sleep outside with the goats."

She took a step back and produced the clay goddess from beneath her waist wrap, balancing it on an open palm, and ducked her chin to lower her voice. "Forgive me, Your Majesty, I only worry for our safety if David discovers the Mother Goddess. Or what if his wives discover it and betray you by telling David?" She reached for my hand and placed the goddess in it. "I fear grave consequences for you if anyone discovers it in your possession." Her eyes narrowed, folding my fingers over the clay doll into a fist.

I jerked my hand away and threw the goddess to the ground.

"Prin, stop!"

But I'd already stomped it with my sandal and felt the broken clay pieces beneath my tender foot. I stepped aside, revealing only worthless shards.

Zulat gasped and whispered, "You'll be cursed forever."

"I've saved our lives," I said with more confidence than I felt.

Noble

"Why worship a goddess who allowed our southern kingdom to be destroyed?"

Her head shot up. "How dare you blame the goddess for men's evil choices."

"Give honor where honor is due, Zulat. The Hebrew God empowered David's four hundred men to defeat over twenty thousand Amalekites. Don't you think their God gave that same power to fight our Geshurites? Don't you realize Abigail was likely telling the truth when she said our people were probably raiding other villages to survive in this desert? How else could they survive when Abba demanded such high tributes and never offered grain or livestock to help them endure the unbearable summers?"

Zulat's silent glare grew more intense.

"Well?" I coaxed. "Did Abba know the southern kingdom was starving? Did he know yet still refuse to lower their tribute or offer help?"

"I'll speak no more with you about King Talmai's governing decisions or David ben Jesse's Hebrew god." With teeth clenched, she continued in a whisper, "I have bribed a watchman at the gate to ensure we are first to read your abba's response when the couriers return from Geshur. We don't want David ben Jesse to steal the truth and substitute his lies to manipulate you further."

"He would ne—"

Zulat's lifted eyebrow stopped me. I'd almost said, *He would never*, which sounded utterly naïve and besotted. However, the David I'd spoken with outside the city gate was worthy of my trust.

Stiffening my resolve, I returned Zulat's defiant stare. "Enough talking. I'm going to rest until the shofar calls us to witness David's verdict against the Amalekite." I walked around her and settled on my sleeping mat. Turning on my side toward the tent wall, I ignored Zulat's grumblings and released a deep sigh. My body relaxed into the mat, and the soft sounds of mourning settled my soul.

Wakened by three successive shofar blasts, I shot upright and glanced around my empty tent. Zulat was gone, and a noisy crowd was quickly assembling outside our tent. I pulled my long, heavy hair over my left shoulder, separated it into three thick stalks, and plaited it into a loose braid. Was it possible that it had grown heavier in the few weeks since we'd left Geshur? Its weight often caused my head and neck to ache. Zulat had wanted to trim it before our journey, but I wanted to leave my hair long for my groom's first sight of me. Ima always said the curls were my best feature, which I presumed meant my only desirable quality. Neither David nor any woman in his family had mentioned it. Perhaps my hair wasn't so desirable after all.

"How silly you are," I whispered to myself and pushed up from my mat. Hurrying outside, I slipped through the crowd and stood beside Abigail. She offered a tentative smile and returned her attention to David, who stood in a tight circle with his nephews and other Mighty Men.

The prisoner knelt before the soon-to-be king, head bowed, and again offered up Saul's golden armband and crown. "After honoring the dying request of King Saul, I took these symbols to present to you, my lord."

"Where are you from?" David asked as if he'd forgotten what the man said this morning.

The slave looked up, confused. "I'm the son of an Amalekite."

"Why weren't you afraid to lift your hand to destroy the LORD's anointed?"

"But, my lord, I—"

"Uriah!" David shouted over the throng. "Uriah, I have need of you!"

"My lord," the slave continued, groveling, "if you'll let me explain."

Noble

As Uriah pushed through the crowd, David looked at the Amalekite once more. "I've heard your explanation and found it repulsive." He turned his focus to the largest of his soldiers. "Strike him down, Uriah, and prove you still deserve a place among my Mighty Men."

Without a heartbeat's hesitation, Uriah drew his sword and with a backhanded slice ceased the Amalekite's pleading. His head rolled very much like the messenger's had in Abba's courtroom, but his blood soaked the ground rather than staining a mosaic palace floor.

Before anyone could shout with victory or cry out in horror, David lifted his strong voice, attaching words to the melody I'd heard him strumming since early this morning.

> "A gazelle lies slain on your heights, Israel.
> How the mighty have fallen!
> Tell it not in Gath,
> proclaim it not in the streets of Ashkelon,
> lest the daughters of the Philistines be glad,
> lest the daughters of the uncircumcised rejoice."

People around us began to kneel, bowing their heads in the reverence of the moment. I knelt beside Abigail, realizing we'd witnessed King David's first regal act as Israel's rightful king.

> "Mountains of Gilboa,
> may you have neither dew nor rain,
> may no showers fall on your terraced fields.
> For there the shield of the mighty was despised,
> the shield of Saul—no longer rubbed with oil.
> From the blood of the slain,
> from the flesh of the mighty,
> the bow of Jonathan did not turn back,
> the sword of Saul did not return unsatisfied.

Saul and Jonathan—
in life they were loved and admired,
and in death they were not parted.
They were swifter than eagles,
they were stronger than lions."

As more people knelt, I glanced over the crowd and saw Zulat standing near the well and talking with one of the watchmen's wives. They whispered behind their hands, rolled their eyes, and then waved a hand in the air as if discounting something—or someone. When her eyes met mine, she straightened, and the other woman looked my way. She quickly left Zulat's side and found her husband in the crowd, but Zulat was unmoved. Her glare never wavered.

David's voice washed over me, drawing my attention back to him. His face lifted to the sky, eyes closed as the last rays of sunlight fell on his countenance in a bronzing glow. He looked more deity than human with the tears on his cheeks sparkling like gemstones. Yes, this was a man I could trust. A flutter inside my chest felt as if a hundred butterflies took flight. *I might even love you, David ben Jesse.* But could I believe in his god and turn my back on everyone I trusted before?

I looked for Zulat at the well, but she was gone. Scanning the crowd, I couldn't find her.

Abigail's hand reached for mine, and she leaned close. "David returned to our tent very hopeful after you two spent time together."

My heart nearly leapt out of my chest. "How do you and Ahinoam feel about it?" I leaned around Abigail to glimpse my other friend, but her eyes were closed, humming along with David as he repeated the lament. I realized how selfish I was to prolong the discussion while David still mourned his best friend. "Forgive me," I said, pulling away from Abigail. "We can speak later." She nodded her approval and bowed in reverence as David continued to teach the whole city the lament that would memorialize Israel's first king and a crown prince more noble than his abba.

Unable to concentrate on David's song, I studied the crowd, and an unexpected wave of loneliness washed over me. Where had Zulat gone? Until we left Geshur, I'd confided everything to her—even things I feared she might tell Ima. She'd proven as trustworthy as Geshur's iron prison bars and taught me the meaning of a deep and healthy relationship.

I bowed my head to hide sudden tears. *Healthy relationship?* Zulat insisted my relationship with Abba and Ima must be healthy to rule as Geshur's next queen. But how healthy could it have been if Abba had been secretly butchering people in his throne room and forcing our southern kingdom to become desert raiders by charging exorbitant taxes? And if Zulat, the person I'd trusted most in the world, added to the message I intended for Abba? What other conniving was Zulat planning with the watchman's wife?

David's clear voice broke through my worry. "Oh, how I loved you, my brother Jonathan. Our love was forged in the fires of faith and bound us tighter than the love of women."

I glanced up, startled, as if he had sung those words to me. *Our love forged in the fires of faith and bound us tighter than the love of women.* Yes, he was speaking of Jonathan, but his words felt like a promise straight to my heart. I had loved Zulat, trusted her with my happiness, my life, my future. But could love forged while ruling with David in obedience to his God somehow form tighter bonds than I'd experienced with my parents or Zulat?

As if sensing my question, David opened his eyes and looked straight into mine. He offered me a tender smile as he continued to sing, and I felt the warmth of it all the way to my toes. Was this part of Yahweh's personal comfort? Had I just experienced the individual attention of a God who truly cared for me?

Overwhelmed, I stood on shaky legs and bid a quiet farewell to

Abigail and Ahinoam. Their concerned faces lessened my loneliness as I weaved through the gathering to enter my tent.

Zulat was seated in the middle of the small rug where I had smashed the clay goddess. She stood as I approached, her brows more deeply furrowed. "What has vexed you so, Prin?"

I worked to keep my voice level. "Before we left Geshur, I trusted you with every secret of my heart, Zulat. I'm going to tell you one more secret even though you've betrayed my trust."

"I did *not* betray you, Maakah. I'm protecting you in ways you don't yet realize you need protection."

"Then consider what I'm about to tell you my way of preparing you to receive wisdom you don't yet possess." Her features hardened. "I'm considering marriage to David ben Jesse, and his wives have given their approval."

She nodded and heaved a relieved sigh. "Well, I thought you were going to tell me something awful."

"The marriage is contingent on my absolute devotion to the Hebrew God, Yahweh, and my complete rejection of all other gods."

Her face went ashen. "You can't."

"As I said, I'm *considering* the terms, and so far I've been more impressed by the Hebrew people and their God than the integrity of Geshur's gods, my own family, and the woman who professed to be my most devoted companion." My voice broke. I cleared my throat and swiped my eyes. "You've falsely represented yourself as my voice in an official missive to your king. You bribed a watchman to bring us Abba's message, insinuating David couldn't be trusted, when David has already proven we could trust him by revealing the hard truth about destroying our southern villages."

"Would you forgive these worms so quickly for killing our people?"

"Now you're angry they're dead?" I said. "You didn't shed a tear over them when I mourned for Alannah. And weren't you supposed

Noble

to teach me of Geshur's place among the nations? How we live at peace—and at war—with surrounding nations but also how we manage a north and south kingdom split by such a great distance and under Dohd Achish's care? Why didn't you tell me Abba's aggressive taxation turned our southern kingdom into raiders?"

"It wasn't my place."

"Wasn't your place?" I laughed at her duplicity. "You care for nothing but protecting yourself."

The force of her slap thrust my head to the side. Shock numbed the sting, but I instinctively laid a hand over my burning face and ever so slowly returned my attention to Zulat.

Eyes wide, she covered her mouth with both hands pressed together as if lifting a silent prayer for mercy. She would receive none from me.

"I saw you at the well," I said. "What are you plotting with the watchman's wife?"

Her hands fell to her sides, and something shifted in her expression. With cool defiance, she offered no reply.

Whatever bond I thought we shared was gone. "You may sleep in my tent tonight," I said, "but tomorrow David will order one of his men to install a partition in this dwelling. You'll have your space. I'll have mine. As of this moment, your service as my maid is over. You may, however, continue to help make bread for the city. Perhaps Zerry and the others will still tolerate your company."

"You're a selfish, foolish child." She spit at my feet. "I've taken too many beatings for you to allow you to ruin your life *and mine* with one lovesick, stupid decision. Your parents will reward me for protecting the honor of Geshur." She stormed from the tent.

"I'm no longer certain there is any honor in Geshur," I whispered as the tent flap closed behind her. After growing closer to David and his wives, my measure of integrity had risen considerably.

PART III

In the course of time, David inquired of the LORD. "Shall I go up to one of the towns of Judah?" he asked. The LORD said, "Go up." David asked, "Where shall I go?" "To Hebron," the LORD answered. So David went up there with his two wives, Ahinoam of Jezreel and Abigail, the widow of Nabal of Carmel. David also took the men who were with him, each with his family, and they settled in Hebron and its towns. Then the men of Judah came to Hebron, and there they anointed David king over the tribe of Judah.

2 Samuel 2:1-4

EIGHTEEN

MAAKAH

When the Philistines came to strip the dead, they found Saul and his three sons fallen on Mount Gilboa. They cut off his head and stripped off his armor, and they sent messengers throughout the land of the Philistines to proclaim the news.

1 Samuel 31:8–9

Had I not witnessed it myself, I might not have believed that an eight-day-old infant could change the schedule of every adult in his household. Just before dawn, at the time I normally walked across the path to join my friends' bread making, I stepped out of my tent and realized the whole city was awake and buzzing with activity. I waved at David, passing him as he left to begin rebuilding while the morning air remained cool. When I entered my friends' tent, both Abigail and Ahinoam were waiting. Ahinoam had chosen to remain at home this morning rather than getting sweaty and smelly at the forge.

Zulat followed me inside, walked straight to the oven at the opened side flap, and sat alone. Ahinoam and Abigail turned to me in silent question, but I shook my head as if to say, *Don't ask.* So they didn't. Instead, Abigail and I fell into our normal rhythm. I arranged mixing bowls, clay measuring cups, and wooden utensils while she gathered the necessary ingredients. Ahinoam tended her son and began explaining the details of today's circumcision ceremony.

That nauseous, spitty feeling started rising in my mouth. "Is the ceremony for the baby a private affair, or must the whole town witness it?"

Ahinoam gave me a sympathetic smile. "It's not as bad as you're imagining."

Before immersing my hands into the flour and goat's milk, I walked over to stroke the baby's downy-soft head. My feet had hurt terribly those first few days in Ziklag, but my pain was nothing compared to the injury this boy was about to endure. "Is my dread for this sweet boy's pain so obvious?"

"Dread?" Ahinoam chuckled. "Both you and Zulat are as gray as rain clouds." She looked over her shoulder at my maid, but Zulat didn't even acknowledge her kind teasing. Zerry and Abital approached the oven from their tents next door and greeted Zulat. The stubborn woman didn't look up and said nothing in return.

The two looked at me for an explanation. "I'm afraid Zulat and I have come to an impasse. She'll remain in my tent but no longer serve as my maid. Perhaps you two can coax a smile out of her with your cheery personalities."

Wide-eyed stares made the silence even louder. Though Zulat's head remained bowed, her knee bounced with the rhythm of a sparrow's wings.

Zerry sat across from Zulat. "If you need to mope, then mope. Sometimes we women simply need to stay angry for a while."

Zulat shot from her stool and toward the main street. Abigail hurried to the tent flap and called after her, "Forgive us, Zulat. Please come back, and we'll leave you to yourself."

"Don't, Abigail." I moved back to the bread-making table and immersed my hands to mix the first batch of ingredients. "I tried to reason with her last night. There's no moving her once she's decided."

Zerry released a deep sigh. "Stubborn old women are so frustrating, aren't they?" She held back her laughter for almost two heartbeats, and then we all agreed and teased her for the very same fault.

"All right, all right, ladies." Abigail pointed to her mixing bowl. "Today's bread must still be made." Everyone resumed their tasks, and she gave me several sidelong glances before speaking. "The circumcision and naming ceremony are beautiful memory makers, Maakah. Don't let your imagination ruin the good gift Yahweh is about to give you."

I nodded and gave a half-hearted smile, then glanced at the precious boy again. Ahinoam stroked her son's head, gazing at the bundle she'd worn strapped to her chest almost constantly for eight days.

"It's not about my baby's momentary pain," she said, "but rather the lifetime of purpose and love bestowed on him through his parents' obedience and our community's commitment to help us raise him."

I winced. "Is that why the community must attend?"

"That's why you're *allowed* to attend." Abigail swatted my arm with her dough-covered hand. "What are some of Geshur's birth rituals and infant ceremonies?" Her brows pinched together and lifted as if preparing to hear something hideous.

"I don't know."

Zerry leaned back on her stool to see around Abigail. "How can you not know? Surely you've witnessed someone in your family who's given birth or dedicated their infant to one of the gods in your temple."

I shook my head. "It's a highly valued secret ceremony that only abbas and their infant sons share under the priests' direction." I didn't dare confess that I'd heard infants had been sacrificed in the fire if Baal closed the skies and crops were failing.

Noble

"I've heard many foreign gods only allow abbas to be involved with their sons' birth rituals," Abigail said, "but Yahweh honors both abba and ima from the moment of birth throughout their son's lifetime. The commandment to obey one's parents—not just the abba, but both parents—is the only commandment with a promise."

"What promise?"

"That we'll someday inherit the whole land of Canaan," Ahinoam said.

"It seems like you offer a lot of blood and obedience before your god fulfills his promises."

Zerry cackled. "I like her."

"Do you say everything that comes to mind, Maakah?" Abigail asked with a wide grin.

I shrugged. "Why wonder when I can ask and get the answer?"

"Well, here's my answer." Ahinoam patted her baby's bottom and continued that constant swaying all imas instinctively inherit. "My boy's circumcision ceremony reminds us that he's included in Abraham's covenant and thereby inherits Yahweh's ongoing promises to our people. When I declare his chosen name, which is also an honor that Yahweh gives to Hebrew imas, my son will reap lifelong blessing from the character his name builds within him."

"These are the reasons the whole town will celebrate." Abigail turned out her freshly mixed dough onto the floured table, sprinkled a little more flour on top, and began kneading.

I labored beside David's wives all morning. At one point, Abigail whispered, "What sort of decision has Zulat made that has driven her away from you—and us?"

"I told her I was considering rejecting Geshur's gods and worshiping only Yahweh. We argued, and she showed gross disrespect. This morning, I'll ask David if he would have his men place a partition in our tent."

Hopefully, my explanation was enough to avoid more questions. I

234

hated keeping secrets from them. I hadn't been completely transparent about everything in our message to Abba or told them Zulat's disrespect included a slap. Though her actions had crossed the line of mere disrespect, I still wanted to protect her. And though my relationship with David and his household was growing stronger very quickly, how well could I know their true selves in only eight days? I still had much to learn about my new friends, and wisdom urged caution.

David's familiar lament drew my attention. We halted our work and meandered to the open tent flaps to watch the someday-king lead his tired, sweaty men toward some shade for a midday rest. David had sung loud and long into the night only ten paces from my tent, so I remembered every word of his lament. While Zulat had grumbled about the redundancy, I'd bathed in the smooth tone of his mesmerizing voice. I would never grow tired of David's singing.

Or David. My heart had already betrayed common sense, but until I could look into his eyes and honestly proclaim Yahweh as my only god, I couldn't agree to the betrothal or marriage—no matter what message Abba sent back from Geshur. *Can I wait for Abba's message about the betrothal or marriage if I'm convinced Yahweh is the one true God?*

"It's time." Abigail clapped the flour from her hands and laid her apron aside. "After David teaches the lament, we'll rejoice with the celebration of new life and circumcise our boy."

I turned to Ahinoam. "Do you mind if I stand with you and Abigail?" Was I being presumptuous to stand with David's wives? "I don't know where else I belong." My voice warbled a little, my throat tight with the vulnerable confession. Without Zulat, I felt more alone than I wanted to admit.

Ahinoam reached me first and took my hand. "Perhaps one day I'll call you my sister-wife."

Abigail flanked my left side and added, "If Yahweh has chosen you, He doesn't change His mind. Neither will we change our opinion unless Yahweh Himself proves His answer is *no*."

Both women looped their arms with mine, and we walked toward the shady spot where David was teaching the lament. With my friends on each side, the anticipation of discovering the name Ahinoam had chosen for her son had finally stirred enough excitement to overshadow my dread of his pain.

We stood at the edge of the gathered soldiers, all of them standing while David sat before them to break down each stanza of his poetic song. David shared the deeper meaning behind his word choice by telling stories about Yahweh's faithfulness during his and Jonathan's victories in battle. The strongest warriors I'd ever seen wept like children. Openly and unashamed, raising hands in praise to their invisible god, they joined their voices with David's.

Their loud, bass tones rumbled through my chest and pebbled the skin on my arms. I wanted to join the lament, but the moment felt too holy to spoil with a woman's high-pitched voice. Turning toward my friends, I realized Abigail and Ahinoam had removed their shoes and knelt. Abigail had bowed her face to the dusty ground, and Ahinoam had bowed as far as possible with a newborn attached to her chest. The baby remained silent, surrounded by his ima's worship.

I immediately followed their example, absolutely certain I was in the presence of their god. Knees tucked beneath me and forehead pressed to the ground, I listened. Waited. No incense burned. No blood sacrifices made. No priest prayed. How could any god be satisfied with the simple gifts of a song and a few raised hands?

Nine short blasts of a shofar raked against the sacred moment, and all other sounds ceased. Everyone bolted to their feet.

"To the walls!" David shouted.

A moment later, one of the watchmen cried, "A Philistine! Single rider. On camel."

Murmurs spread like a heavy wind, so David whistled to regain focus. "Mighty Men behind me. Soldiers, to your ranks!"

As he started toward the gate, Ahinoam reached for his arm but stopped herself—likely because of her self-imposed uncleanness. "Let me come with you," she shouted over the rising chaos. Having already reached beneath the generous folds of her robe, one hand rested on a six-dagger belt behind her back. How had I never seen it before?

With three long strides, David stood less than a handsbreadth from his feisty wife. "I need you to stay with Abigail and Maakah—in case the messenger is a ploy to draw me out of the city."

"Don't go!" I rushed toward him, heart pounding. "Please," I said more quietly.

His gaze softened when it fell on me. "Is that the advice of a princess or the fear of a soon-to-be betrothed?"

"Both?"

"While you decide, I should discover what this Philistine messenger has come to tell us." He winked before leaving us. I could barely stop my feet from chasing after him.

Both wives faced me. "It never gets easier," Ahinoam said.

"That's one of the few things we agree on." Abigail looked down at her dagger-throwing sister-wife. "You could obey David and still protect Maakah and me if all three of us moved a bit closer to the gate."

Ahinoam's mischievous grin gave silent consent. She unwrapped the swaddling cloth and called for Zerry, who eagerly accepted the baby into her care. Ahinoam led Abigail and me along the backside of the first row of tents, near enough to hear the soldiers speaking but in the shade and out of sight.

We reached the end of our cover at the same moment the messenger's voice rang out from the other side of the city gate. "I've come with a message from the five kings of Philistia. Open your gate to rejoice in our victory!"

Noble

Releasing the breath I must have been holding, I whispered, "It's not a ploy then?"

Abigail and Ahinoam exchanged an indecipherable look, then Abigail said, "It could prove worse than a ploy."

What could be worse than a surprise attack? But I kept that question to myself. Hiding a mere fifty paces from the city gate, we watched it swing open and the Philistine messenger advance to the gate's threshold.

David stood ten paces inside the city, blocking the dusty street with the thirty Mighty Men positioned behind him in a wide line. "You need not dismount," David said. "Give your report and go."

The man straightened his shoulders and lifted his chin. "The Philistines have triumphed over Israel," he said in a loud, clear voice. "King Saul and his three warrior sons died on Mount Gilboa. We severed their heads and stripped their armor to display in Philistine temples. Saul's body, however, will be fastened to Beth Shan's city wall as a warning to all Israel that further rebellion will be quashed swiftly and without mercy. All hail to our Philistine kings!" He lifted a single fist in the air and waited for an echoed reply.

None came.

David, you must at least pretend allegiance! I held my breath, waiting for David's reaction, praying to Yahweh that the man he'd chosen as Israel's next king would maintain the ruse that had won Dohd Achish's favor.

"You've delivered your message," David said with dangerous calm. "Now go."

The herald offered a devious smile. "Would you have me carry back a message to King Achish that explains your reaction to the good news?"

"Indeed, I would." It seemed as though every soldier leaned forward to hear David's reply. "Look at the condition of Ziklag and its people," he said, "and then tell Achish that while we were marching

238

with him to a battle the other Philistine kings refused to let us fight, Amalekites burned our city and took our families hostage. He'll understand that we're in no mood to celebrate when he realizes we have no homes, and our women have been ravaged by desert dogs."

Even from fifty paces, I saw the herald's visage change. He looked beyond David to the ruins of the small but once-thriving city and then back to its governor. Respectfully, he lowered his head. "You have my deepest sympathy, Governor. I will relay your message." He reined his camel to the rear and departed the same way he'd come. Our watchmen barred the gate behind him.

And I realized—the one God surely answered my prayer!

David looked up at the trumpeter and shouted, "Sound the shevarim. I want everyone to immediately assemble at my tent."

Abigail tugged at my sleeve. "We must be there when he gets back." Ahinoam was already retreating.

"Why is he assembling the whole city?" I asked Abigail.

"I can't be sure," she said, "but I'm guessing we're about to leave Ziklag."

"But we'll circumcise and name our son first!" Ahinoam called over her shoulder.

NINETEEN

DAVID

In the course of time, David inquired of the Lord. *"Shall I go up to one of the towns of Judah?"*

2 Samuel 2:1

When I entered my tent, Zerry was holding my son. Ahinoam, Abigail, and Maakah looked up as if they'd been caught stealing candied dates. I'd learned long ago that my wives seldom obeyed when my life was at stake.

Rather than scolding, I simply asked, "How much did you hear?"

"All of it." Ahinoam was first to confess—always—and with a defiant tilt of her chin.

I turned to Maakah. "They're already teaching you to disobey my orders?"

Her grin matched my wives'. "I would have suggested it if they hadn't." Of course she would.

I sighed. "And what would a politically savvy princess suggest as a wise strategy for my current predicament?"

She glanced at Abigail and Ahinoam, then raised both brows in silent question. My wives' eyes went wide, and both Ahinoam and Abigail began nodding like bobble-headed birds. How had Maakah

240

learned to speak their language in less than two weeks? I hadn't the patience for their games while Philistines plundered Israel and would soon discover I'd lied to Achish about destroying villages in my homeland.

"Someone tell me what you're talking about!" My harsh tone startled my son, who began to wail, which drew deadly glares from both wives. But it was Maakah who appeared wounded.

Now seeming timid, she said, "Perhaps there's a way to show your allegiance to both Dohd Achish and to Abba *before* Dohd Achish discovers the southern villages are gone." She hesitated, then added, "Before the messengers return from Geshur with Abba's approval for our betrothal."

Was she suggesting we marry—now? "I won't marry you until you've declared unwavering devotion to Yahweh."

Maakah instantly lowered her head. "I'm fully aware." The pain in her voice was like a dagger to my chest.

"Forgive me." I reached for her hand, but she took a step back. "I understand."

The two words were like a wall between us. I sighed and combed fingers through my hair. *Has she so suddenly decided to worship You? Is a hurried marriage what You have planned for us?* Hearing no inner reply, I bowed to one knee. "Truly, I ask your forgiveness for speaking sharply. I want to marry you as soon as possible—especially if you've decided to worship Yahweh."

Her lips curved into a hesitant smile. "I have decided," she said, "yet I hear a hesitancy in your voice."

I offered my hand, and this time she took it. "Yahweh has brought you here at a particularly precarious season in our lives. If I make one wrong decision, move too quickly or too slowly, it could cost every life Yahweh has placed under my care." I held her gaze, hoping she'd see I was telling the truth. "I believe we must leave Ziklag as quickly as possible. Yahweh is leading us back to Judah."

241

Noble

"No, David! Please don't." She squeezed my hand. "It will only be safe for you to return to your tribe if Dohd Achish pronounces you as his vassal king over all twelve tribes of Israel. If you go to Judah before that, he and Abba will interpret the move as a threat."

"Maakah, the Philistine army—including King Achish's troops—will continue raiding across Israel. They'll see the burned-out cities of Amalekites, Girzites, Geshurites and the thriving Judean towns. He'll realize my deception and return to inflict his wrath on me, these people, and Ziklag. He'll send messengers to Geshur, so neither your abba nor Achish will ever willingly make me Israel's king."

She didn't seem surprised. "I wondered if you'd realized the long-term political damage the destruction of our southern kingdom could mean."

"I do realize it, but I've vowed to Yahweh that I will obey Him, regardless of political gain or loss." She winced as if my words caused physical pain, so I tried to soften my harsh-sounding vow. "Judah is my home, Maakah. Many city elders became trusted friends after we destroyed the enemy villages that stole their crops and enslaved their women and children."

"Were my Geshurites among those who preyed on Judah's villages?"

Her pallor said she already knew the answer. "They were the worst offenders."

Her lips parted, as if to challenge, but her shoulders sagged instead. "I'm so very sorry, David. It would seem my abba hadn't prepared me to rule Geshur after all." How could her abba expect her to reign if he'd taught her only of bouncing eyebrows and hoarding spoils of war?

I tipped her chin up to reassure her. "You never knew of Geshur's sins against my countrymen, yet you were willing to forgive me and even embrace my God?"

She nodded, tears poised on her kohl-black bottom lashes.

"You are a wonder, Maakah bat Talmai."

"Please don't lead your people into Judah," she whispered. "The Philistines and my abba will interpret our move as an act of war."

"Didn't you hear the herald? The Philistines are already destroying Israel. They'll march into Judah next. I must help my tribe."

"And you would put everyone you love in danger?"

"Only after I gather the whole camp and ask Abiathar to inquire of Yahweh."

"Who is Abiathar?"

"My priest."

"You have a priest?" Her shock was endearing. "Why do you have a priest if Yahweh has no temple? Do you have a priestess also?"

"No priestess. No temple. Abiathar came to serve me when Saul had the rest of his family killed and stole the Tabernacle away from the city of Nob. Since then, Saul appointed a new High Priest and all of Israel's tribes worship at high places." I still couldn't believe Saul and Jonathan were gone.

"So you have the only remaining *real* priest of Yahweh?"

"Not exactly." How could I explain the complicated system that Saul had made more complicated by mingling in priests who weren't direct descendants of Aaron? "Abiathar wears the *true* linen ephod, which carries the Urim and Thummim worn by the High Priest who served at the one-of-a-kind Tabernacle."

"I have no idea what you're talking about."

"You will." I brushed her cheek, hoping Yahweh's decision through the lots would help strengthen her newborn faith. "Watch the process and ask Abigail or Ahinoam if you have questions." I turned to leave.

"Aren't you forgetting something?" Ahinoam's tone was lethal.

I rushed back to my wife, taking her off guard, and halted so close she stepped back to maintain the distance. "I would never forget our son's celebration day," I said, thankful I could soon brush her lips with a kiss. Her cheeks pinked as if she knew my thoughts. "As soon as we hear Yahweh's decision on our future," I said, "Abiathar will circumcise our son and you will announce his name. I'm eager to hear the character you and Yahweh have chosen for his life's path."

After a silent promise of soon-to-be restored intimacy, I left our tent and found most of the city already gathered. When my wives, Maakah, and Zerry joined them, I searched the crowd for the priest. As usual, he was standing in the back. "Abiathar, I have need of you."

While he shouldered his way forward, I explained, "After we celebrate today, we'll begin to pack our belongings. I believe the herald's declaration of Philistine victory was a sign that Yahweh wants us to return to Judah." A cheer rose before I'd finished the plan. It seemed my men and their families were as ready as I to end our deception and return to our homeland.

When Abiathar reached my side, I lifted both hands for silence. "Our faithful priest will inquire of the LORD to confirm our return to Judah and give us direction on a specific location."

Abiathar patted the linen ephod where the black and white stones rested in a pocket behind twelve precious gems. Those closest to us cleared a circle to make room to cast the lots. I leaned toward the priest and whispered, "We normally ask only yes or no questions, but today I need to know Yahweh's choice between multiple cities. How should we proceed?"

Abiathar pulled out the two stones. "Ask the first question. We'll seek Yahweh's direction with every step."

Inhaling a fortifying breath, I closed my eyes and exhaled the doubt that always accompanied a choice to completely trust Yahweh. "Shall we return to Judah?" I shouted my question to the Creator loudly enough for all to hear.

Abiathar cast the stones across the cleared patch of dust. The black Urim lay flat, and the white Thummim landed on its end, propped against Joab's big toe. My nephew raised a battle cry to celebrate, and I bowed my head in relief. *Thank You, Yahweh. You're taking us home.* But where?

I lifted my head and found Abiathar waiting with the two stones already back in his hand. "Perhaps you could choose two cities," he said. "Assign one to the Urim and the second city to the Thummim. Whichever stands upright is the city Yahweh chooses between those two. Then assign another city to the rejected stone, and see which Yahweh chooses. If it's the same city as the first casting, we can be fairly certain that's the right one. We could cast the lots a third time if you want another confirmation."

Squeezing the priest's shoulder, I nodded. "The LORD gave you wisdom for the task." I turned toward the crowd again, and they quieted without coaxing. "Abiathar has instructed me to assign the name of one city to each lot, and we'll know on the first casting which city Yahweh chooses between those cities."

"That method could take all day," Joab growled.

"Do you have a more pressing engagement?" My burning glare silenced my impatient general. I turned to Abiathar, who finished the explanation. "We'll keep assigning city names and casting lots until Yahweh makes it clear with multiple signs which location is His choice for our new home."

Abiathar directed the focus toward me, and I said, "For the Urim, Bethlehem; and for the Thummim, Hebron."

Murmurs fluttered through the gathering, and I assumed most were positive since nods accompanied most of the crowd's hum. Abiathar paused with his eyes closed and then tossed them once again. Everyone in the front row leaned forward to see how the stones landed.

"Hebron!" Abiathar shouted. His smile betrayed Hebron as his heart's choice—as it was mine. Though Bethlehem was the city of my birth, too many angry family members awaited me there. The priest

Noble

gathered the stones again, holding the white Thummim in a closed fist and offering the black Urim on an open palm. "Next choice?"

Some of my warriors began shouting out their hometowns, but the Mighty quieted their men. I closed my eyes, trying to be sensitive to any whisper from God. *Where would you have me establish my household, LORD?* But nothing came to mind. Was I to simply choose a random town of Judah and take a chance that the stones might choose it on their own? I pushed the thought aside. *Forgive me, LORD. The stones don't choose. You speak through them.*

"Jezreel," I said, glancing behind me at Ahinoam. The small city where she and her abba had lived before joining my army had been their refuge after fleeing the Amalekites. But she didn't look pleased. Perhaps she dreaded the hard memories of home like I had.

Abiathar cast the stones, and the Thummim stood tall for Hebron. This time, it stood alone on its own narrow edge in the uneven dust. A reverent silence settled over us, and I scanned the faces of my faithful people. They'd followed me to Moab, through the Wilderness, and then to Gath and Ziklag. Would they now follow me to a new home in Judah? "Does anyone need further evidence that Yahweh has chosen Hebron?"

"I do." A woman's timid voice came from behind me, and I turned to find Maakah's cheeks wet with tears. "If I'm to leave behind every god and goddess I once thought real and true, I must be absolutely certain Your God is more than the dice game of chance I played as a child."

Jeering erupted from the faithful, and terror washed the color from Maakah's face.

I backed up to shield her, lifting my arms to quiet the crowd, and shouted over their insults. "Can any of you say that you've never doubted Yahweh's voice through the lots?" The rabble faded to grumbling. "Didn't Uriah the Hittite boldly challenge the decision of the lots when we asked if we were to fight for Keilah? And didn't Yahweh graciously answer Uriah's doubt with a confirmation of His decision?"

All murmurs ceased.

I found Uriah standing only a few rows behind Joab and locked eyes with him. "Does a princess seeking the truth deserve less mercy than a Hittite who grew up among us—a Hittite who stirred dissension among our ranks but has since proven his loyalty and been forgiven? Did Yahweh not command, 'Do not mistreat or oppress a foreigner, for were you not once foreigners in Egypt?' Will we offer favor to Uriah because he fights yet mistreat a princess who has helped make bread for all of Ziklag since our victory over the Amalekites?"

Uriah shoved to the front of the gathering. "If Yahweh truly speaks through those stones, why not throw them again? Let the black stone say no, and the white stone say yes, to settle our move to Hebron."

I turned to Abiathar. "Does a return to a yes or no question seem right to you, Priest?"

With a single nod he gathered the stones again, giving me time to whisper a similar question to Maakah. "Will one more throw confirm in your heart that Yahweh speaks through His consecrated stones?"

Lips pursed, she nodded, looking at the stones as if they might bite her.

"Courage, Princess." I brushed her cheek. "Believe in the One who brought you to this moment so you could know Him—and so we would be wed." Her lips parted, drawing in a soft breath.

I turned toward the crowd and shouted over them once more. "Let the white Thummim confirm our move to Hebron and the black Urim restart our inquiry." The stones tumbled from Abiathar's hands, and Maakah nudged me aside to see where they landed.

For the third time, the white Thummim spoke God's affirmation.

Noble

Maakah covered her mouth with both hands and looked at me, eyes glistening. Unable to measure whether she was happy or sad, I gently tugged at her hands to see her unmasked expression.

I glimpsed a smile before she announced, "Whether my abba commands us to marry or not, David ben Jesse, I will worship Yahweh as my only God."

Unsettled murmurs fluttered through the onlookers, but my whole being was focused on Maakah. "Are you sure?" I whispered.

A nod forecast her answer. "I've never been more certain of anything."

"What about Zulat? Won't she try to lure you back to faith in Geshur's gods?"

Maakah's features darkened. "She's already tried, but I've released her from my service. Zulat no longer holds any sway over me." She turned to scan the crowd and then nodded toward a gathering of soldiers' wives at the back.

I followed her gaze and saw Zulat in their midst. "Your maid seems to be making friends rather quickly."

With a huff, she said, "I suspect she's building those friendships on a foundation of hatred for a Geshurite princess."

"Your abba would be less than pleased to hear of your maid's betrayal," I said, only then realizing the messengers we'd sent to Geshur wouldn't know we'd gone to Hebron. "I'll leave two of my Mighty in Ziklag to meet the messengers who return with your abba's message."

She turned her back toward the maid and the angry-looking women who sent visual daggers at Maakah.

"If you want anyone to remain for your son's circumcision celebration, you'd better begin now," Joab said over the retreating crowd. "People are leaving to begin packing for the journey."

"Sound the shofar to call them back," I ordered, then reassured Maakah. "First, we celebrate my son's name and Abigail's news. Then I'll deal with your traitorous maid."

"No!" she said too quickly and followed with a nervous laugh. "If you're to trust anything I say about ruling a kingdom, surely I should be able to deal with my own maid."

I touched her cheek, not caring who saw, then announced to those who ignored the shofar's call, "Would you disrespect Ahinoam bat Toren and ignore our son's circumcision covenant? Don't you want to celebrate the name Yahweh and my wife have chosen together?"

Though not all returned, most of the camp gathered out of respect for my wife, who had taught every woman to defend herself with some sort of blade. Nomy had been extraordinary since the moment we'd met, never the typical wife who mended, wove, and spun. I was certain our son would become equally exceptional.

"Abiathar," I said, handing him my newly sharpened dagger, "would you bless my firstborn by making him a son of Abraham?"

I stood at Nomy's side while she laid our son on a stool Abigail had brought from our tent. Abiathar's prayer was short, and the cut quick. The whole city shouted praise, partially drowning out our son's hearty cry. Zerry was ready with a healing ointment and dressing to soothe the pain. Nomy swaddled him as soon as the covenant wound was tended. And I raised my arms for quiet, nodding to my son's ima.

"Thank you, friends." She swallowed hard and blinked away tears. "I have prayed through long nights and difficult days, asking Yahweh what sort of name might produce a pleasing nature in Israel's eventual crown prince."

More raucous applause interrupted, and she bowed her head. Even as she said the words *eventual crown prince*, the gravity of the past few days settled more deeply into my heart.

Saul and his sons—likely all but Ish-Bosheth—were dead. But what about Abner, Saul's general? I should have asked the Amalekite slave who reported Saul's death if Abner still lived, but grief had overwhelmed forethought. Jonathan had always been in grave danger as Saul's firstborn.

Yahweh, when your promise to me is fulfilled, and I rule all of Israel, it will be Ahinoam's boy You must especially protect. I met Nomy's tender gaze, matching her smile, yet felt a terrible weight on my shoulders. Is this how all abbas feel?

The rejoicing quieted as desire piqued to hear the name Nomy had chosen. "Introduce us to the prince!" a woman shouted, beginning the good-natured banter.

Nomy tucked her chin, never having enjoyed being the center of attention. She'd bounced and shushed the babe enough to finally quiet his wailing, so I signaled for silence again so she wouldn't have to shout. Tilting him toward the gathering, she said in a strong voice, "Meet Amnon ben David. He will be both teacher and builder since he was born at a time while we were rebuilding Ziklag and circumcised while his abba taught us all to remember his dearest friend Jonathan." Immediately, she looked at me, uncertainty in her eyes.

"It's the perfect name, my love." I no longer needed to deny the overwhelming urge to hold her. Wrapping my arms around both ima and child, I placed a lingering kiss on Amnon's sweaty head and whispered to Nomy my heartfelt truths for her alone. How was it possible to love them both more today than yesterday?

Abigail joined our circle, adding her reassurance that Amnon's name showed clear wisdom from Yahweh in its choosing. Lifting my gaze, I found Maakah watching us. The small crease between her brows proved her deep in thought.

She noticed me studying her and smiled a little. I offered my hand and she came willingly to join our family's circle. Slipping between Nomy and Abigail, Maakah stood directly across from me—a wise position to keep gossips' tongues from wagging. Though we hadn't yet signed an official contract, Yahweh's will seemed abundantly clear. She would soon become my wife.

I rubbed my thumb across the back of her hand and noted the henna stains had nearly worn off since our first meeting. Lifting my eyes to peruse her features, I grinned at the desert sun's quick work. More freckles dotted her petite nose and tanned cheeks. She was so young, yet wise beyond her age. Stunningly beautiful yet seemingly unaware and not overly concerned with adornment. *Maakah is more noble than any king I've met and worthy of truth, Lord.*

In what other ways had King Talmai deceived his only heir? Or did his lack of teaching prove he'd never intended Maakah to become Geshur's next ruler? These were questions I needed to ask King Talmai in person—especially now that it seemed inevitable Maakah would become my wife. If he would betray his own daughter, I could make him a political ally, but I would never trust him.

"David?" Maakah quietly drew my attention. "Are you well?" The crease between her brows had deepened.

In that moment, I saw her as a wife to love and protect, not as a princess to debate or outwit. Maakah was no longer a problem to solve but rather the woman Yahweh placed in my life for His purpose and my blessing. Just as He had given me Ahinoam and her abba when my men needed weapons and Abigail when the women of our camp needed a kind but firm manager, the LORD gave me a regal princess who inspired me to become a regal king.

"I'm very well," I said. "Better than I've been in a long time." We continued the celebration with the announcement that Abigail was with child. More joyous shouts and cheers drew my people together and even brought some of those packing their belongings to rejoin their brethren. I scanned the happy faces and felt a joy I'd forgotten was possible. *Thank You, LORD, for Your goodness and grace despite our failings.*

"We have more good news to celebrate," I added. "Let it be known today that Princess Maakah bat Talmai denies every false god and worships only Yahweh as the one true God of all Creation!" The

Noble

few shouts of joy—mostly from my wives, Zerry, Eglah, and my nephews—sounded like clanging cymbals in an empty cave. Their praises cut short, my family glanced all around them at their silent friends and then back at me.

My gaze shifted to Maakah whose eyes were downcast.

I was wordless. Breathless. Ashamed of my people. Holy fury rose like a fire burning from my toes, up my legs, and into my belly, arms, and neck. As I opened my mouth to spew my wrath, Joab wrapped me in his arms of iron and shoved me aside with whispered warnings to remain silent.

"You're dismissed!" he shouted over the murmuring crowd. "We leave for Hebron in four days. Warriors pack all military gear and then help your women pack household goods. Women, see Abigail for food preparation assignments and keep your children's hands busy so they don't create mischief." As people began to disperse, he gave me a long stare and then turned once more to the meandering townsfolk. "We have only four days to prepare, people. Mind your attitudes and the conversations in your households. Listen well, I will impose discipline on anyone who seeks to divide us." Hushed grumbling replaced blatant complaints.

Joab pushed me into the shade of my tent, his expression as hard as granite. "Maakah's maid is as shrewd as the Garden serpent. I'm not sure what she's promised as a reward for some of our camp women, but she's thoroughly won their loyalty and turned them against the princess."

"Why? What does Zulat gain by stirring animosity toward Maakah?"

"For as much as you like women, you certainly don't know much about how they work." Joab shook his head. "If Zulat can't control Maakah, she'll protect herself instead. Which explanation would be safest for Zulat to report to King Talmai? That Princess Maakah is in constant fear for her life from hostile Israelites—which puts a target on our backs? Or will Zulat tell Talmai the truth—that Maakah rejected Geshur's gods to worship our god—which puts a target on Zulat's back for failing to control the princess?"

"And if I marry Maakah before we receive Talmai's message, he'll believe even more what Achish has discovered . . ."

"That I am—"

"That you are"—Joab finished the logic with me—"a deceiver who took Geshur's only heir for your own gain."

I raked my fingers through my hair, then gripped and pulled. Frustrated into silence, I fell to my knees. *Yahweh, what do I do to protect Maakah—and my people?*

"Vered has heard women talking," Joab whispered. "From our tent beside the central well, she can hear every conversation."

I'll bet she can. Fighting my aversion to Joab's wife, I said simply, "And what has Vered heard?"

He hesitated, which brought me to my feet to face my general. "Tell me."

"They haven't been specific, but I think we need to place guards on Maakah's tent to keep Zulat on her side of the partition."

I couldn't believe Zulat would harm Maakah, but neither had I believed the maid would turn women in our own camp against her mistress. "Should we place Zulat in another tent?"

"We don't have enough tents to give a Geshurite servant her own living quarters," Joab said. "I think we should put two guards behind the tent, and two at the front—one for each side of the partition. The princess will be safe."

"Do it," I said in a whisper. Watching my eldest nephew march away, I inhaled deeply, scrubbed my face, and called on the One who sees our past, present, and future. *Please, Yahweh, bring Your light into whatever darkness Zulat is spreading through my camp.*

TWENTY

MAAKAH

My companion attacks his friends; he violates his covenant.

Psalm 55:20

I stood in the dusty main street while David's camp dispersed. Though still surrounded by hundreds of people, I felt completely alone in my humiliation. When David had announced my gargantuan risk of choosing Yahweh, only he and his family had rejoiced. I'd taken a flying leap off Geshur's deity mountain and plummeted to the rocky cliffs without anyone—not even Yahweh—helping to soften the landing.

Then Joab announced the camp's plan for our move to Hebron, ending with a veiled threat to anyone who openly showed disdain for me. I'd seen the burning glares. Too many to count.

Now, David and Joab stood in the shadows. Whispering.

I bowed my head, unable to look at them. The whimpering of baby Amnon caught my attention, but I refused to look at David's tent, afraid to hear the very direct assessment of the friends I'd made in David's family. They were probably already busy planning for the move to Hebron.

Lifting my head, I glimpsed disapproving glances and heard

mumbled accusations from the townsfolk who were the last to leave the so-called celebration. I searched the dwindling crowd for the one who hated me most.

But Zulat was gone.

Where could she be? Why hadn't she remained to gloat over her victory? How had she persuaded so many in camp to hate me?

Unable to bear more invisible daggers, I started toward my tent. But confusion followed me. I'd felt such certainty in Yahweh's personal touch when He'd affirmed Hebron on that third toss. I wanted more of this God who had reached out of His invisible realm and proved to me—a Geshurite princess—that He existed. But did He hear me now? *If You hear me now, tell me why You allowed me to be humiliated in front of the whole camp.*

No answer came.

Entering my sweltering tent, I found Zulat on her side of the recently added partition, rifling through her large basket.

"Zulat?"

She snapped to attention, wide eyes making her appear guilty. "I thought you'd stay with David's wives all day." She nudged the basket aside with her knee. "Why are you here?"

"Why have you turned David's whole camp against me?"

"You're being ridiculous." She stormed past me toward the front flaps. "Is David trying to cook us? His men left the side flaps open, but we have no airflow with the center partition running lengthwise in this tent." She started tying up the front flaps. "You release the side flaps so they block the cross flow. Then we can get air from front to back. We'll see if that cools us enough to sleep tonight."

I did as she said but started on the side flap nearest where she worked. "What kept you busy all morning that you didn't already adjust the flaps?"

"Since I'm no longer in your service, you no longer command my activities or whereabouts."

I turned to face her. "Look at me," I demanded. She finished tying up the flap before obeying. Infuriated by her insolence, I seethed, "I am still your princess, and you will show me respect in private and in public. You will still be respectful in this tent, and when we are among David's people, you will represent Geshur, King Talmai, and his heir in a way that endears us to Yahweh's chosen king!" I ended with a shout—just as David appeared at our entrance.

"I've told the women of this camp," Zulat said, "that you and I only worship the image of our Mother Goddess." Her half-hooded eyes proved she'd intentionally spoken for David to hear.

David looked at me as if I'd shoved a spear in his belly. "Wha— what is she saying?"

"She's lying," I pleaded. "I smashed the only idol we brought from Geshur on the day you told me about Joseph and the Egyptian princess."

"But I told you about the consequences for idolatry before we left the Amalekite camp." His features hardened. "You brought an idol into my city and hid it from me?"

"Yes, but I didn't know you then. I was terrified and still believed a piece of clay could protect me."

Zulat bowed her head. "Master David, may I speak freely?"

"You are a conniving old woman," he said with no patience. "Only speak if you can prove it's true."

She nodded and kept her head humbly bowed. "Princess Maakah did *not* smash the idol we brought into your camp. In fact, she gave it to me for safekeeping, and we still worship the Mother Goddess when we're certain you and your wives won't see us." Zulat's words tumbled out, and the tremor in her voice made the confession more convincing.

David glared at me, waiting for a response.

Incredulous, I asked, "Must I really defend myself against a maid I dismissed from service who now seeks revenge?"

"I can prove it's true."

Zulat's words landed like a boulder in my belly. "You can't prove a lie."

Eyes narrowed at me, she said, "Master David need only look under the sheep's wool headrest beside your sleeping mat."

"There's nothing there," I said, following David, who already started toward my side of the partition. When I glimpsed the slight grin on Zulat's features, dread conquered confidence, and I rushed after David.

I halted as David rose from his knees, dangling a clay goddess like refuse between his thumb and forefinger. It was identical to the one I'd smashed.

His breathing ragged, he tore his gaze from the idol and locked eyes with me. "How could you deceive me?"

"No! I didn't!" Rushing toward him, I fell at his feet. But he stepped away as if my nearness would taint him, dropping the idol to the ground. I looked up, covered a sob, and tried to deny it again; but the despair on his features already shouted the guilty verdict.

I sensed Zulat's presence beside me and stood, backing away from my betrayer.

"Master David," she said gently, "I don't know how you intend to punish us, but might I beg your mercy for Princess Maakah? I beg you to send her back to Geshur, even though you clearly defined the penalty for idolatry since the first day we met you. I've worked in secret, telling the women of camp about Maakah's idolatry, in hopes the gossipers would reach your wives who would then beg mercy for my princess. Since you now know, I plead for mercy. If a life must be forfeit, Master David, take mine, not hers. Let my blood pay her punishment, and free her to return home to the royal parents who love her." She then made an overly feeble attempt to bow to her knees, which I thought David would surely recognize as manipulation.

Instead, he reached for her arm to assist the old woman back

Noble

to her feet. "No one will lose their life," he said. "I have no wish to instigate a war with King Talmai. However, you'll both be sequestered to this tent until we leave for Hebron. Hopefully by then, my scouts will have returned with a message from Geshur, and they'll be free to escort both of you to your homeland."

"David, please." I pressed my quaking lips, unable to form more words.

His eyes bored into mine. "I told you deception was the one thing I couldn't abide, Maakah. Yahweh is real, and He can forgive anything. You've seen His power. You've experienced His personal answer to your request. I hope your faith will be strong enough to help you actually crush that useless clay trinket."

Before I could beg him to hear a thousand more proofs of Zulat's lies, he turned and strode out of our tent. My legs felt like water, and I crumpled to the ground, numb. Every excuse I could offer would never erase all the deception I'd kept from David and my new friends. I hadn't even confessed the full contents of our message to Abba and that Zulat's secret addition had likely placed Eliphelet and the others in more danger.

"You'll thank me someday." Zulat stood over me, arms folded across her ample chest in triumph. "Perhaps now I can return to Geshur and care for your ima's newborn and hope he's a more obedient student than you ever were."

Rage fueled a quick recovery, and I bolted to my feet. "You'll never see Ima's child. As soon as we reach Geshur, I'll tell Abba of your treachery, and your life will indeed be forfeit—for treason."

She sneered. "Your threat is more proof that you know nothing of how King Talmai rules his kingdom. He'll praise my actions as shrewd and reward me for saving his only heir from the biggest blunder in Geshur's history." With a condescending scoff, she turned to go. "You stay on your side of the partition, little princess, and I'll stay on mine."

TWENTY-ONE

DAVID

From his dwelling place he watches all who live on earth—he who forms the hearts of all, who considers everything they do.

Psalm 33:14–15

When I'd left the confrontation with Zulat and Maakah yesterday, I'd gone straight to the flocks grazing on desert scrub outside the city. Snatching up my favorite ewe lamb, I waved at the shepherd. He'd delayed me only long enough to give me his cloak, anticipating my need against the night chill. Returning to my secret place, tucked away amid a rocky outcropping, I'd spent the whole night alone with Yahweh before facing my wives and family. Ahinoam and Abigail would undoubtedly wonder at my absence, but I didn't want to spoil their celebration. I knew they'd be as devastated as I when they discovered the truth about Maakah.

LORD, how can it be true?

I'd asked Him the same question all night and still hadn't received the shalom that came with divine confirmation. *I saw the clay goddess,* I argued with the God who knew. *Maakah admitted to bringing it into camp.* But she'd also insisted that she'd smashed the hidden

259

Noble

idol after our first real discussion about Yahweh's faithfulness. Why confess to one deception but hide another?

Equally puzzling was Zulat's motive for wanting me to believe Maakah still worshiped her gods. Why reveal the one thing that would end the betrothal—no, the *two* things: deception and pagan worship—when she'd seemed supportive of the match when I'd confessed to destroying their southern kingdom?

I glanced down at the little ewe that lay curled at my feet, sound asleep. Were my wives sleeping as soundly, or had they checked on Maakah and spent a sleepless night like me? Perhaps I should have gone home and tried to celebrate Amnon's Eighth Day, but how could I celebrate a landmark for our family when we'd lost someone I thought would become a part of us? Truth be told, I'd been a coward, simply too afraid to face my wives' tears while grieving my own broken heart. *Yahweh, didn't I ask that You not let me love her if You knew she would be taken from me?* Scolding God was never a good idea, but I believed He'd rather have my transparency than the lies we both hated.

"Come, little girl." I jostled the ewe awake before placing her gently around my neck. She only protested a little while settling into her familiar position on my shoulders. While dawn's amethyst promise shaded the eastern sky, I stepped sideways down the rocky incline. With my shepherd's crook in one hand and holding the ewe's feet securely with the other, I arrived at the sheepfolds and delivered my ewe to her caregivers.

Both yearning and dread filled me as I approached my tent. A quick glance to the left, and I noticed Maakah's front flap had been tied open. The central partition must have cut off the cross flow of air. I halted, seeing a single oil lamp shining inside. Had she, too, lain awake all night? I couldn't let my heart succumb to the temptation of loving an idolatrous woman as I'd done with Michal.

Turning toward my tent, I entered to the soothing sound of Amnon's suckling. Nomy sat on her mat in the corner, dozing. Two oil lamps burned on the large table in our gathering area. I removed my sandals, hoping to quietly walk past her. One, two, three steps toward the partitioned chamber and—

"Are you all right?" Nomy's eyes glistened in the dim light.

"Yes." It was a lie. "We can talk later."

"I can tell you're not all right," she said, patting the mat beside her. "We know what happened with Maakah. Abigail went over to check on her when she didn't join us to celebrate. She's not all right either."

I sat beside her with a long sigh. At the same moment, Abigail peeked out from behind the curtain. "I thought I heard voices. May I join you?"

"Of course." Nomy waved her over. "You should tell David about your talk with Maakah."

I brushed my son's cheek, then invited Nomy to the shelter of my right arm. She dissolved into tears and buried her face against my side. Abigail snuggled against my left, also weeping. I leaned back against a tent post, allowing their warmth to fill me as only they could. *Yahweh, please show us the way to peace. Give us wisdom in decisions for our family and the coming changes in our nation.* Finally, I released my tears. Time alone with my Creator had been good, maybe even necessary, for all three of us to process individually. But time with my wives was also essential. Bone of my bone and flesh of my flesh, through our covenant with Yahweh, He'd knit us together as one.

As Maakah will be one day. Was it my own desire or Yahweh's promise that birthed the thought?

I sat up straighter, releasing Abigail to sit across from Nomy and me. "Tell me everything about your interactions with Maakah."

"After the ceremony," Abigail said, "I went to her tent to invite her and Zulat to join the celebration of Amnon's special day. Zulat refused to speak to me, but Maakah talked with me for quite a while."

Noble

"Did Zulat remain on her side of the tent's partition?" I asked.

"Yes."

"The whole time you were there?"

"Yes, and I'm sure she heard all we said because she snorted and scoffed at nearly everything Maakah told me." Abigail's brow furrowed. "Zulat is really a difficult woman to like."

"That's a profound understatement," Nomy growled.

I almost chuckled but was too desperate for more information. "What else?"

"Maakah insisted the idol you found wasn't hers. She vowed that she had smashed the idol they brought from Geshur." Falling silent, Abigail exchanged a glance with Nomy, who prodded her with a nod. "Maakah then confided a few more things she hasn't confessed to you yet."

"Is there no end to her deception?" I released pent-up frustration, scratching my scalp though there was no itch.

Nomy pointed to my erratic itching. "And that's why she didn't tell you. If you flailed during her first confession, why would she divulge more truth?"

"Imagine how Maakah felt." Abigail interrupted my feisty wife. "She had no advocate in that tent with her. Her lifelong maid not only betrayed her but is now actively trying to turn a whole city against her. Didn't you think it odd when Zulat mentioned the death sentence for idolatry, then offered herself? When have you seen that old crone do anything selfless since she arrived?"

"At Besor Brook," I reminded them. "She would have used her own waterskin to wash Maakah's blistered feet. And hasn't the maid helped Maakah and you bake bread since—"

"Zulat comes to keep Maakah under her control," Nomy protested. "And she's acted more like Maakah's general than a submissive maid since we met in captivity."

"Nomy and I agree," Abigail said. "Maakah is telling us the truth,

262

and Zulat is trying to manipulate all of us. Not only is she lying about Maakah's worship of Geshur's goddess, but she's actively trying to turn this camp against Maakah to stop your marriage to her and exact revenge against the princess who dismissed her from service."

I tugged at my beard, considering everything Zulat and Maakah had said and trying to balance it with the wisdom of the women Yahweh had given me. How could I have felt certain yesterday morning that Maakah was Yahweh's choice to become the same sort of one-flesh partner as Nomy and Abigail yet doubted it within moments after Maakah had declared her unwavering faith in my God?

"David." Nomy placed her hand on my arm, sending a thrill through my whole body. "Maakah isn't Michal." Those simple words struck at the core of my emotion, dousing any warmth or desire.

"How can you know for sure?"

Abigail cradled my hand, drawing my attention. "You have two wives who love you, but death will someday take us away. There is only One whose love never dies. Only One whose love is stronger than an army and sweeter than a woman's touch. Yahweh will never leave you or deceive you, my love."

I lifted her hand to wipe my cheek, and Nomy placed a kiss where my tears left their mark. My wives had spoken as clearly as the voice of God. Memories of Michal's betrayal and my fear of a second princess breaking my heart had caused me to distrust a truth teller.

"Thank you both." I stood and said, "After a bit of rest, I need to talk with Maakah again and really listen to her this time."

My wives exchanged another meaningful look, and this time I knew they were concerned about Zulat's presence while I spoke with Maakah. "I plan to take Maakah outside the city to talk, as I've done before, so there's no danger of Zulat or anyone else overhearing our conversation."

"It's both Maakah's safety *and* yours we should consider now."

I let out a short chuckle, thinking they were jesting. They weren't. "Why would I be in more danger now than I always am?"

Nomy tilted her head, looking up from hooded brows as if I were a slow student. "Your warriors are loyal to the death, David, but only because they know you'll be a king who chases Yahweh's heart more than political gain. If this rumor about Maakah has spread through women's gossip, your men will soon hear it."

"My men know I serve only one God."

"Joab came to our tent late last night, looking for you. Upset." Abigail cleared her throat and stood to face me, her visage fashioned to appease. "One of your captains brought word that he'd disciplined a soldier in his contingent when the captain overheard the man railing about Maakah's idolatry and that you were too 'lovestruck gullible' to see it."

Was that Abigail's best attempt at appeasing? "What did you tell Joab?"

"We told him the truth. We had no idea where you were." She placed a steadying hand on my forearm. "But I think you should talk with Joab before you spend any more time in Maakah's tent. Nomy and I will provide meals for her and Zulat. I'll ask if Zerry, Abital, Eglah, and little Zeb would be willing to help pack Maakah's tent for our journey to Hebron. During the travel, we'll keep Maakah in the center of the family group. She'll be safe surrounded by those who love her and know the truth."

Nomy had joined us and reached behind her to twirl one of her six daggers. "Though I've taught all the women to use a blade, no one is as proficient as your wife. We love Maakah. She's one of us, though not yet legally bound."

Should I have felt encouraged or more concerned that my wives believed Maakah needed the heightened measure of protection? "I'll speak with Joab right away."

After a quick kiss on Amnon's forehead and a peck on Abigail's cheek, I hurried into dawn's new day. Joab's tent was the last in our family's row, nearest the center of camp and beside the well. No matter whether in Ziklag or setting up camps when we traveled, my general and the Three always guarded the water supply.

Since my nephew, Abishai, was captain of the Three, my sister didn't visit Joab's and Abishai's wives as often. She spent most of her time with Asahel's wife, Abital, since my youngest nephew always camped nearest me to ensure the captain of my Gadite scouts was available at a moment's notice. Zerry told me the one-hundred-step distance was the reason she seldom spoke to Joab's wife, Vered, and Abishai's wife, Raya. But we all knew the truth. My older nephews' wives didn't like Zerry any more than she liked them.

Vered's nasally complaints drowned out the morning birdsong as I drew nearer to Joab's tent. *LORD, bless Joab for loving that difficult woman.* Somehow, my eldest nephew adored her. When I reached the tent, I waited for a break in Vered's tirade but decided it might be midday before I'd talk with my general if I didn't announce myself.

"Shalom to this house!" I shouted over the noise and stepped inside. Three rowdy boys chased one another around a large table, which was similar to the one in our tent—the table, not the boys, all praise to Yahweh. Joab made eye contact with me, nodded acknowledgment, kissed his wife still in mid-sentence, and rushed me outside to escape the chaos.

"I assume you spoke with your wives, who told you to talk to me before visiting the princess."

"Is that how every morning begins for you?"

He halted in the street, eyebrows peaked with amusement. "Were you expecting a demure, obedient wife and three docile children to whisper reverent blessings as your maniac general left his sublime dwelling?" The eyebrows bounced.

I laughed and pointed to them. "Maakah said eyebrows give away too much emotion."

Noble

Joab sobered. "Do you believe everything Maakah says?"

"You know better." I started walking toward the city gate, refusing to speak of Maakah until we reached a more private location. Joab kept pace at my right. Neither of us spoke.

When we approached the gate, Joab lifted his right hand, and the watchmen hurried to lift the heavy bar from its multiple cradles. Our men saluted, and both my general and I returned the respectful gesture. I led my nephew to the tree where Maakah and I had quarreled, the place I'd also seen what a dynamic Yahweh follower she could become. *LORD, give me wisdom to hear Your voice over Joab's loud opinions.*

Glad I was still wearing the cloak I'd borrowed from the shepherd to shield me from the desert's morning chill, I sat outside the tree's circle of shade and motioned my nephew to join me.

But Joab was too busy pacing to sit down. "Do you believe the princess or her maid? Did you actually see a clay idol or not?" He kept pacing, not even stopping to hear my answer.

Only then did the thought hit me. Why hadn't I crushed the idol myself or taken it out of Maakah's tent? "Who do you believe, Joab?"

He stopped pacing and locked eyes with me. "I believe the princess. Now, I ask again. Who do you believe, *King* David?"

"I need to speak with Maakah this morning, to see if she's destroyed that second idol," I added. "But I'm leaning toward believing the princess."

"Leaning toward?" Joab threw his hands in the air and let them fall, slapping his sides. "Well, that's reassuring. I've always wanted to follow a king who leans one way . . ." He leaned right, hopping on his right leg. "And then leans another." He mirrored the same ridiculous action toward his left.

I bolted to my feet and grabbed his breast piece, pulling him close. "Keep your mocking to yourself, or I'll find someone else to do your job."

"And what job is that, David? Helping you *lean* one way or another?"

I shoved him away, glimpsing his scowl before turning my back to the most disrespectful general on earth. "If you've lost faith in my anointing, I'll find another general to help me fulfill God's calling."

"You won't find one today among your six hundred men." His voice was as soft as a dove. "Zulat knows how to fight, David, and her well-placed words could be more deadly than all the other weapons we've faced."

My head fell forward. *LORD, I was worried about the enemy outside my walls instead of one in the tent across the street.* With a deep breath and slow exhale, I prepared my heart for Joab's advice. "What is your plan?"

"I ask you again, my king: Do you believe that Princess Maakah worships her false goddess, or has she truly committed her heart to Yahweh alone?"

I whirled on him. "How can we know that, Joab? How can we be absolutely certain of anyone's heart? Only Yahweh can know the hidden places in a man's—or a woman's—heart."

He closed the distance between us, halting with our noses a few finger-widths apart. "Yet Ima said you planned to marry her. Tell me you were certain before you decided such a thing."

His misty eyes pleaded, digging into the deepest recesses of my heart—and that's when I knew. I'd hated Maakah the first time I saw her, assigning all the pain Michal had inflicted on me to the young princess from Geshur. But Yahweh had revealed Maakah's heart to me. More than that, Yahweh had revealed Maakah's heart to herself—and softened it to become His. And yesterday, He'd uncovered the viper who had deceived her since birth.

I pressed my forehead against Joab's. "I not only believe Maakah worships Yahweh alone. I *know* she worships the one true God and has been chosen as my wife to prepare me for Israel's throne."

Noble

He guffawed, releasing the odor of last night's onions into my face. As I winced, he shoved me away and said, "Excellent, my king. So, tell me *your* plan."

Thank You, Yahweh, for my crazy nephew and the lovely princess You've provided. With their bold challenge, my wives' encouragement, and Yahweh's wisdom, I would one day be a regal king.

"To keep Maakah safe, I should maintain the guise of my anger with her until we reach Hebron. There we can ask Jehoiada's warrior priests to help guard her."

"Agreed."

"For now, place guards around her tent to prevent any mischief or attempts at real harm while the rest of camp packs for the journey."

"I'll do it as soon as we return to the city."

I looked sideways at my suddenly cooperative general. "Why are you so eager to help keep Princess Maakah safe?"

He shrugged. "I think she's good for you, David." With a mischievous shove to my shoulder, he said, "What else?"

"Abigail and Nomy have already volunteered to care for her meals, and they plan to ask your ima, Abital, and her family to help Maakah and Zulat pack."

Joab brightened. "Maybe they'll find something to prove Maakah's innocence during the packing."

"When we return to the city, I want you to be the intermediary between the princess and me. Go to Maakah's tent and tell her the plan for their meals and packing. Make sure Zulat hears everything. I'll write a message, which you'll deliver to Maakah secretly, explaining our plan and my deepest regret for believing Zulat over her. Be sure the maid doesn't see you give her the message. We must keep our reconciliation hidden until we arrive at Hebron. By then, Eliphelet, Eliel, and Nakia will have returned with Talmai's response, and we can arrange the proper discipline for Zulat."

TWENTY-TWO

MAAKAH

Whoever digs a hole and scoops it out falls into the pit they have made. The trouble they cause recoils on them; their violence comes down on their own heads.

Psalm 7:15–16

I read David's message again in the dim light of a single oil lamp.

There are no words to express the depth of my sorrow and regret for believing Zulat's lies. I offer no excuse for my poor choice, only this in explanation. Improperly healed wounds inflicted by my first royal wife have left scars on my heart that are especially prone to defensive warfare. I pray the God who now unites us will show you a way to forgive me. Under no circumstance are you to enter Zulat's side of the partition or give any hint that we hope to reconcile. I love you, Maakah bat Talmai, and I want you to be my wife. But we must be cautious in these uncertain days.

How I had longed to hear his declaration of love. "But not like this," I whispered. Pressing the message to my chest, I squeezed my eyes shut. *Yahweh, he doesn't deserve my forgiveness. He hurt me* as deeply as Zulat—perhaps more because he knew the risk I took in a public declaration of faith and then didn't support me when I chose to follow his God.

His God?

The phrase stopped me. Wasn't Yahweh my God, too? Prickly flesh crawled up my neck and face, heat with it. Had I made my declaration of faith in Yahweh to please David or because I truly believed?

Yahweh, forgive me. I made that declaration because I truly believe in You, Your power, Your love. So why wouldn't I forgive David? He bore wounds from his past and had shared them freely with me. He asked for my forgiveness, and only time would tell if he repeated that same defensiveness in the future. We would travel to Hebron and wouldn't marry until after receiving Abba's message. I would forgive David ben Jesse and let him prove his desire to heal the wounds of his past. *Help me, Yahweh, by bringing the hurt I feel at his distrust into alignment with my decision to forgive.*

I returned the message to its hiding place beside the idol Zulat had used to defame me. Shattered now—as I'd done to the first goddess—I still wondered if the shards of the first goddess were what Zulat had hidden in her basket. I also wondered where Zulat had found a replacement goddess in David's camp. We'd only brought one goddess with us from Geshur. Setting aside another question to which I might never discover the answer, I kept to the shadows of my tent and peeked around the corner of the front right post.

A few people walked past on the main street between David's and my tent. Yesterday, I'd grown tired of nosy passersby who were slowing to peer inside our open tent flaps and decided I needed privacy more than airflow from front to back. However, we still needed to cool the tent. So I asked the two guards Joab had posted at the front to lower the flaps at the outer post corner, leaving each side of the middle open diagonally. I also asked them to open one

270

of my three side flaps. The guards, of course, needed Joab's permission. I played along, wondering if anyone except David, Joab, and I knew the contents of the small scroll tucked beneath my headrest.

My request to open the side flap was quickly approved, but Joab assigned two more guards to provide additional protection at the new entrance. His brother, Abishai, was one of the guards. I thought it strange that Abishai, captain of David's most gifted spies, would be assigned to guard my tent. Perhaps Abishai needed a rest from his usual dangerous missions.

Moving back toward my sleeping mat, I caught a whiff of my unwashed self and decided I should bathe and change clothes before Abigail arrived to break her fast with me. She and Eglah had brought separate pitchers of fresh water for Zulat and me with last night's meal. Zulat declined their thoughtfulness, saying another woman in camp had offered to care for her needs.

"Might I ask which woman?" Abigail asked.

"No, you may not."

I was mortified by Zulat's rudeness and apologized profusely when Abigail and Eglah came to my side of the partition. They were gracious, of course, and Abigail made the strangest request. "If you learn the woman's name," she whispered, "be sure to tell me."

Having found privacy a difficult feat in my new living arrangement, I'd saved both mine and Zulat's water for a morning bath. I stashed a small vial of lavender oil in my waist belt and carried both water pitchers to the shadowy back of my tent. Placing the pitchers on a table beside the medium-sized basin, I poured a few drops of oil in before filling it with water. I reached for a clean cloth from a small basket and slipped off both my robe and the tunic beneath it. The smell of lavender filled the air as I immersed the cloth and squeezed out the excess water, then wiped the fragrant, refreshing coolness over my whole body. *Thank You, Yahweh, for this simple pleasure in a difficult place and time.*

Noble

I was struck by the irony of the moment. Had I ever thanked Asherah for such a seemingly insignificant thing? I'd scoffed at David's invisible God, thinking Yahweh inferior because He inhabited no temple and had no priests or priestesses to offer my prayers through official sacrifices. How foolish I'd been. A god I can see with representatives who mediate my prayers would limit the God to whom I now prayed.

Yahweh, You are limitless. You always hear me. I sacrifice myself to You.

"Shalom to this tent," Abigail called. "Maakah?"

"Coming!" I said while she waited outside the front flap. I dried myself with a clean cloth and hurriedly dressed in a fresh tunic and robe. Thankfully, I hadn't attempted to wash my unruly black curls. *Without Zulat to help, how can I wash my hair?* The strange thought sent an unexpected pang of loss through me as I hurried to welcome Abigail for our morning together.

I pulled aside the angled front flap and moved back to make room for her to enter with the heavy tray laden with food. On my right was a guard I recognized as another of Abishai's three specially trained spies. "Shalom, Eleazar." He acknowledged me with a nod.

Turning to greet the other guard, I was startled to silence. There stood the watchman Zulat had bribed to ensure we'd see Abba's message first when the couriers returned. He nodded, as Eleazar had, and then looked away. I stepped toward him. "I'm sorry, but I don't know your name."

He glanced at Eleazar and then at me. "Phinehas." He held my gaze before his black eyes darted in all directions like a nervous bird.

"Shalom, Phinehas," I said and hurried inside to join Abigail.

She had already begun transferring food from the tray to my mat. Busy at her task, she didn't look up when I approached. "I won't be able to stay with you today to break our fast," she said.

"Ahinoam didn't go to the forge so she could help me pack our things at home."

I was still chilled by the way Phinehas's black eyes bored into mine. "That's nice," I said, barely listening. Wringing my hands, I wondered if Abishai and Eleazar were here to protect me from Phinehas. Heartbeat racing, breathing ragged, I shifted from one foot to the other. Should I mention it to Abigail? She was chattering on about something. If I told her, Zulat might overhear. I didn't want to put Abigail in danger.

She straightened and finally turned to look at me. Her face lost its cheery glow. "Are you all right? You look—troubled."

Placing my arm around her waist, I led her toward the front entrance. "I'm fine. You go back home and help Ahinoam. I have more packing to do, too, and you've brought enough food to feed me until we leave for Hebron."

"Well, it's not really enough for—"

I nudged her out of the tent. "You can tell me how the packing went the next time you come."

As Abigail walked toward her tent, Zulat's nasty friend, Dobah, arrived with a morning meal for them to share. Dobah paused beside Phinehas, who searched her waist belt and beneath her robe's sleeves for weapons, sharing an uncommon familiarity. I'd forgotten Dobah was the watchman's wife!

After the inspection, Phinehas nudged his wife toward Eleazar as if to say, *Would you like to search her, too?*

"Take off your belt," Eleazar said without hesitation. Dobah shot a glance at her husband, but Eleazar repeated the command and added, "Your husband won't save you."

Dobah removed her belt but held her robe closed with one hand while balancing the food tray with the other.

"Hand the tray to your husband." Eleazar's eyes never left Dobah's. "Now, lift both arms."

"But my robe . . ."

Eleazar silenced her with a single lifted brow, and she shot both arms up. While never breaking eye contact, Abishai's well-trained soldier squeezed every covered part of her from elbows to ankles, then said, "You may enter Zulat's side of the partition only."

Dobah picked up her tray, ignored me standing two steps away, and joined Zulat. I didn't dare look at Phinehas, but I mouthed a silent *thank you* to Eleazar. Hearing whispers on Zulat's side of the curtain, curiosity got the better of me. I stepped back into the tent and peeked around the partition. The two women's heads were bowed together, happily chattering like sparrows in springtime. Not exactly the response I would expect from Dobah after such a humiliating experience.

Zulat's laughter drew my attention. How long had it been since I'd heard her gravelly voice so joyful and refreshed? But there had been a time, when I was much younger, that we'd laughed and played. Had that also been a lie? Had she thoroughly hated me all my life?

As if she'd heard my questions, Zulat looked up. "Would you like to join us, Prin?"

Dobah grunted—seemingly as perturbed as I was surprised—which made me say, "I'd love to meet your friend."

But as I stepped around the partition, I remembered David's strict instruction in the message Joab had secretly delivered: *Under no circumstance are you to enter Zulat's side of the partition.*

Standing one step inside Zulat's private space, I created an excuse. "Perhaps I shouldn't. Abigail brought a lovely meal for me, and I mustn't let it go to waste." Turning to go, I noted both women launch to their feet.

"Wait!" Zulat rushed toward her large basket—the place I knew she'd hidden something. "I have a gift for you before we leave for Hebron." Dobah crowded Zulat near the basket while I waited.

I took another step forward, impatient to see what sort of gift my angry maid would have hidden on the day she'd betrayed me so completely.

Zulat straightened, hiding something behind her back, and Dobah moved closer so their hips and sides touched. Zulat looked at me with an overly wide smile. "I found it." She slipped the mystery gift behind her back to the watchman's wife.

Curiosity overwhelmed good sense. "I want to see what you have."

In one excruciating instant, a glint of metal hurtled toward me. Fiery pain seared my shoulder. A second dagger flew through our front tent flap and sunk into Dobah's temple.

Zulat screamed. Dobah fell. And darkness claimed me.

"David. David! She's waking up!" Abigail's voice was cheerful, but before I could open my eyes, unbearable pain stole my breath. A groan escaped with the searing fire radiating through my chest. Or was it my shoulder? Or my back?

I breathed out another groan and felt a cool cloth pressed against my forehead. "Zerry is bringing the poppy tea, love." Only one person had that clove and musky scent.

"David?" I forced my eyes open.

His handsome face was drawn, his eyes bloodshot and swollen.

"I'm sorry," I whispered.

He tried to laugh but only cried more. "Why would you apologize when two women tried to kill you?"

"You warned me not to go into Zulat's area, but when I heard her laughing with Dobah and they invited me to join them . . ." I closed my eyes, shame paining me as much as the wound. *Two women tried to kill you.* The words penetrated my consciousness, and I gasped. "David?"

Noble

"What, love? Is it the pain? Are you hurt somewhere else?" He spoke over his shoulder, "Did anyone check for other injuries?"

"David, no." The pain made it hard to think. "Dobah. Did she throw a dagger at me?"

"Yes." The answer came from a second familiar face. Ahinoam hovered over me, opposite David. She'd been crying, too. "I feel somewhat responsible," she said, swiping at her eyes. "I taught the women to defend themselves with a blade, but it was meant for enemy raiders." She bowed her head, deep sobs shaking her shoulders.

Abigail knelt beside her, whispering comfort to her sister. Then she turned to me. "It was Nomy's perfect throw that killed Dobah before she or Zulat could harm you further."

"How did—" A new wave of pain came with the quickening of my heartbeats. I sucked in a tortured breath and squeezed the hands that held mine until the worst subsided.

Zerry appeared near my head and tipped a steaming cup of something to my lips. I only drank the foul-tasting tea because I hadn't the strength to push it away. "This will be your best friend for the next two days," she said, then lowered the cup. She kissed my forehead and whispered in my ear, "Don't you ever scare me like that again, sweet girl." She darted away, leaving me alone with David, Ahinoam, and Abigail.

David repositioned, sitting on my right, his hip resting against mine. He leaned over me, supporting himself on one hand between his two wives. I felt surrounded by him, swaddled in the love of these three people. "Thank you," I whimpered, then glanced at the two women who would someday become my sisters. "I love all of you very much."

"We love you," Abigail said.

"I'll love you more after I teach you to protect yourself." Ahinoam slapped the tears from her cheeks as if offended by their presence.

"Your lessons begin on the way to Hebron. Your injured left shoulder won't impede your right-handed throws." We laughed together. Even I could offer a slight chuckle, feeling the tea begin its good work.

David brushed my cheek with his free hand, and I teased, "Were you brushing away flour again, David ben Jesse?"

"Not this time." A real smile lit his features. "Do you wish to hear the details of what happened?" He paused. "Or would you rather not know the consequences your conspirators face?"

Conspirators. Zulat was no longer my friend, my tutor, or my maid. "When we rule, we must set aside emotion to seek justice. You must show those in your camp what happens when conspiracy threatens someone—anyone—in your midst." I tried to sound brave, though I didn't want to know what sort of punishment awaited the woman who knew me better than anyone else on earth. "Tell me everything so I'm not surprised on the day of judgment."

Abigail and Ahinoam squeezed my left hand. "You're very brave."

I squeezed their hands back. "Abba taught me to be regal, but I'm learning that being noble is harder—and better." With a deep breath and cleansing sigh, I returned my attention to David. "What will happen to Zulat?"

He held my gaze. "Both Zulat and Phinehas will be among those who fall to the sword."

My mind immediately went to the messenger in Abba's throne room, whose blood filled the cracks between the mosaic tiles. Stanching my tears, I asked, "Who will execute the guilty?"

David sat up but his reassuring eyes held mine. "My Mighty Men."

"But there are thirty of them. How will you choose which of them—" David looked down, his hesitation stopping me mid-sentence. "What haven't you told me?" I asked.

After a heavy sigh, he met my eyes again. "The conspiracy was much wider than Zulat, Phinehas, and Dobah. The Law of Moses says, 'If troublemakers arise among you and lead the people astray to worship other gods, you must investigate it thoroughly. If it is proven to be, you must put to the sword all guilty parties.'" He slid his fingers through his hair and sighed again. "When Phinehas and Zulat were interrogated by Abishai and his assassins—"

"Assassins?" I squeaked. "Even through the fog of this tea, assassins sound much scarier than spies."

"We call Abishai and his men *spies* because we don't want to frighten the families in camp. Phinehas knew one of the Three would likely search Dobah before allowing her to enter, which is why she must have given Zulat her dagger sometime earlier to keep hidden in the maid's partitioned area."

I could barely keep my eyes open, but I remembered the basket. "Zulat hid something in her large basket on the day she lied about the idol. It might have been the broken pieces of the goddess we brought from Geshur." I yawned, feeling the tea doing its work. "But where would Zulat have found a replacement idol in your camp?"

"Joab is questioning Zulat and Phinehas again," David said. "When the Three interrogated them right after the attack, Zulat and Phinehas implicated forty of my foot soldiers and fifty women who also worshiped Asherah. Several of the fifty women are potters and could have easily fashioned the images."

"What?" I was wide awake again. "How could that be?"

"Zulat is shrewd," David said, his features returning to the sadness I'd seen upon waking. "She showed the image to Phinehas and Dobah—our camp's biggest troublemaker and gossip—when you first arrived. Phinehas and Dobah commissioned one idol to be made and then shared it with others. Others shared with more. Sin multiplies quickly, Maakah, which is the reason Yahweh's Law sounds so harsh but is exactly the discipline that's needed. Yahweh commands us to dig out the deep-rooted weed that grew so quickly among us so that it doesn't choke out the good fruit."

"Are you saying . . ." My mind had gone blurry again. "Will your Mighty Men also execute your own soldiers and the camp's women with Zulat and Phinehas?" I tried to focus on David, unable to believe the unthinkable.

His hand pressed against my cheek. "Yes, love. We must always follow God's Law of herem. We will completely destroy those things—or people—who are separated unto God by their sin. Their deaths are a holy act. A sacrifice done in faith even when our hearts and minds cry out against it." His voice quaked, but I could no longer see him clearly.

Unable to keep my eyes open any longer, I asked, "Have wu pazzd judjjjment yet?"

"Yes." His voice sounded far away. "All will die for their attempt to lead their brethren away from the one true God."

I wanted to ask more questions, to hear more about Yahweh's Law and David's adherence to it, but I could no longer fight the darkness claiming me.

The scent of musk and cloves overwhelmed me, and I felt a kiss on my forehead. "Sleep now, my love. Sleep."

TWENTY-THREE

DAVID

So David went up [to Hebron] with his two wives, Ahinoam of Jezreel and Abigail, the widow of Nabal of Carmel.

2 Samuel 2:2

I stood atop the watchtower with Joab and still felt sick. We'd burned the dead bodies overnight. Looking down in the valley where the flames had died to embers, I said more to myself than my general, "I'm grateful Yahweh turned the slight breeze to carry the smoke away from Ziklag so the stench wouldn't waft over our families all night."

He gave no reply. I hadn't expected one. His focus was on the caravan forming below us. Now that it was almost dawn, those left of our camp were gathering all they could carry to begin our journey to Hebron and its surrounding villages.

My heart and mind, however, were still fixed on last night's executions. The forty soldiers died while holding their wives. The other ten women died while begging their husbands to save them. Phinehas welcomed the blade, and Zulat's stony stare merely stoked Abishai's fury.

But it's what happens after punishment is meted out that tests a man's mettle. I returned home to check on my wives, who were tending Maakah, and found Geshur's princess weeping in her half-dazed state. Though Zerry had reduced the amount of poppy tea that day, hoping Maakah could attend the executions as she'd requested, the pain had been too overwhelming for her to bear. With poppy tea reinstated and without witnessing the executions, Maakah slipped into a tortured dreamland where everyone she loved was included in herem.

When I tried to calm her, she pushed me away and cried, "Assassin!" Zerry reassured me it was the poppy tea talking, but with every dead body I later piled into the valley, I'd felt Maakah's accusation like a blow.

"I believe everyone is gathered now," Joab nudged me. "Keep your comments forward-thinking. No mention of last night."

How could I do that when every person in our caravan lost a friend or relative to that pile of burning flesh?

I lifted both fists overhead to call for silence. The somber crowd quieted quickly. "I know last night's sorrow only added more angst to the uncertainties we face. I feel the same loss each of you is experiencing. Zulat was a viper among us, but I called the rest friends. Some of you even lost family members to the lies of idolatry. But *you* . . ." I pointed, panning my aim from the left side of the gathering to the farthest right. "Each of you made the choice to worship Yahweh alone. To trust Him only. To obey Him even when it hurts your heart." My voice broke, and I bowed my head, trying to regain control.

"Yahweh protected Princess Maakah," someone shouted, "because He knew we would obey His Law."

Surprised by their strength of faith, I cried out, "Yes!"

"We trust you, King David," someone else shouted. Then another, "We trust our king." The words became a chant. "We trust our king. We trust our king. We trust our king."

Noble

Joab moved closer and placed a hand on my shoulder, speaking so only I could hear. "Sometimes it's good that you don't listen to me." He pounded his other fist in the air and joined the chant. "We trust our king! We trust our king!" Little children danced below while also singing the chant.

Overcome by the moment, I lifted my hands to the heavens and sang with all my heart.

"LORD, our LORD,
how majestic is your name in all the earth!
You have set your glory
in the heavens.
Through the praise of children and infants
you have established a stronghold against your enemies,
to silence the foe and the avenger."

After repeating the new verse multiple times, everyone sang along, and I recognized it as Yahweh's gift to us. He had equipped us for the journey to Hebron.

Lifting my fists overhead, the gathering fell into a respectful silence. "Hebron's walled city is too crowded to shelter us all," I said. "Early this morning, I sent Attai, our fastest Gadite, ahead of us to alert Chief Priest Jehoiada of our coming and to ask which of Hebron's surrounding villages would welcome us into their communities."

"Respectfully, my lord," Amasai said, standing closest to the gate to lead the caravan, "I don't wish to be separated from my family." His son's chubby fingers curled around the devoted abba's left thumb, and his pregnant wife stood sheltered beneath his right arm. Joab had chosen the right man to be chief of my Mighty.

"No families will be separated," I vowed. The big man pulled his wife closer and tousled his son's dark curls.

Joab elbowed my side and whispered, "How can you promise

that? We don't know how much space Hebron and its surrounding cities can offer us until Attai returns."

I studied the caravan below and saw the joy and relief my simple promise had stirred among my somber people. "I did promise, Joab, and I will keep that vow because Yahweh is faithful to His faithful ones."

Smiling down at the children still dancing, I felt an overwhelming protectiveness for my whole camp—much like I felt for Amnon and my wives and now Maakah. They were my family, my tribe. Many of them had followed me since that day I took shelter at Adullam Cave and my family came to me begging for protection. Only four hundred men—who had left their wives and families to follow me in those early years—had been a band of misfits. But they'd turned into six hundred skilled warriors with their families, who had become dearer to me than many related by blood.

"Today's journey is mostly desert," I shouted, "but in the days that follow we'll begin introductions to new neighbors in the other eight cities of the Hebron colony: Eshan, Dumah, Arab, Aphekah, Humtah, Beth Tappuah, Janim, and Zior."

"What if we don't like the village you've chosen for us?" This from the wife of a captain. She'd been one of Abigail's maids and always spoke her mind.

An uncomfortable buzz rippled through the gathering, so I raised my voice to be heard. "Just as I promised no immediate families will be separated, I also promise you this, Sherah: You will almost certainly dislike the village chosen for you."

Quiet chuckles replaced the nervous buzz, but I quieted the mocking with a stern gaze. It wasn't my intention to shame Sherah but rather to teach everyone through her honest concern. "Living in an unfamiliar village will be difficult. Hebron is even more unique in its governance because it still serves as one of the Cities of Refuge prescribed by the Law of Moses. My friend, Jehoiada, is another in the long line of warrior priests who are trained to protect both the unintentional murderer in Hebron and protect outlying villages from enemy raiders. Jehoiada assigns his underpriests—also well-trained warriors—to govern your new hometowns as I've led Ziklag. I'm sure they'll do things differently than me, and I'm equally certain they serve and trust the same faithful God we worship."

I scanned the now-quiet crowd. "We're about to re-enter Israel—*our* Land—because Yahweh promised it to Abraham. We're returning to Judah—my tribe—because that's where I was anointed to become Yahweh's king. And we'll march with confidence because we're united under Yahweh's protection." Without providing an opportunity for more questions, I motioned to the watchmen to open Ziklag's city gates—for the last time—and lifted my sword above my head. "To Judah!"

My warriors responded with their battle cry, and the women began ululating. It was a wholly glorious racket that made the children run in crazy circles and the donkeys nervously toss their heads. I turned to Joab, shouting my question over the noise, "Which two Mighty have you chosen to wait here for our messengers from Geshur?"

"Maharai and Heled," he said. "They're single and can be placed in any of Hebron's colony villages after escorting the messengers to us."

I hooked a hand around his neck and pressed our foreheads together. "You are infuriatingly efficient, and I love you more than a brother."

He hooked my neck. "And your breath stinks."

I shoved him away, and we hurried down the tower stairs, eager to find our families amid the chaos.

Abigail and Nomy were perched in the front of an ox-drawn cart, Abigail holding the reins while Ahinoam cradled Amnon in the wrap she wore across her belly. Blankets cushioned the bed of the cart where Maakah leaned against Zerry. Abigail and Nomy had packed all manner of baskets, pillows, and clothing around them to protect Maakah's injured left shoulder. Since the injury, my wives and I had slept in Maakah's tent, allowing Zerry to sleep with Maakah in our partitioned chamber. When Abigail and I went over to check on our family this morning, Zerry had applied a fresh bandage to Maakah's shoulder and then immobilized it with a sling held in place with another bandage around her torso. My soon-to-be wife looked like the mummies of Egypt described in legends.

"Well done, husband," Abigail said, beaming as I approached. Nomy said nothing, but the gleam in her eyes told me she was also pleased with my final words as Ziklag's governor. I continued to her side of the cart where she lifted Amnon to be kissed, which I did. Then she whispered, "Kiss me long enough to taste the cloves on your breath." I happily obliged.

When I pulled away, I glimpsed Maakah watching us intently from the back of the cart. Her brows drawn down, eyes narrowed, her silence felt like judgment. Earlier, she'd spoken only to the women of my family and hidden behind others when I drew near.

Last night, while I piled dead bodies in the valley, I'd searched my heart. *How can I obey Yahweh's Laws to stone Zulat and others for idolatry yet willingly break His Law by taking many wives?*

My eyes remained locked on Maakah as I moved toward her. She never looked away, which seemed a good sign.

I stopped two paces from her. "Is your shoulder giving you much pain?"

She shook her head. "Not too badly even though Zerry is weaning me off the tea." The crease between her brows disappeared. "I heard no dissenters amid this morning's crowd. What do you think it means?"

I was fairly certain what it meant—that Yahweh had pruned our ranks for the next step in our difficult journey. But . . . "Tell me what you think it means."

Noble

A little smile pulled at the corners of her lips. "I think it only seemed as if Zulat had turned the whole camp against me. Perhaps only the fifty who worshiped Asherah hated me because I chose Yahweh." She looked into the distance. "My parents would have taken Zulat's side. Abba might have retaliated with violence against you if he'd heard you executed Zulat and convinced me to worship Yahweh alone. But when my parents discover Zulat tried to kill me, they'll—" She pursed her trembling lips into a thin, gray line and shook her head. "They'll still find a way to blame me." Bowing her head, she blinked a river of tears onto the blanket protecting her from the morning's chill.

"I won't let them blame you." Taking her hand in mine, I said, "None of Zulat's choices were your fault. She was sent by your parents to protect you, not to rule over you or deceive you, which she did from the moment you left Geshur. If she had obeyed you as her mistress and trusted in your authority over her, Zulat would likely still be alive."

She pressed the back of my hand to her cheek. "Maybe Abba would believe you if you told him in person. Like Zulat, they've never seen me as anything but a child."

I framed her face and locked eyes, wiping away her tears with my thumbs. "You are a beautiful and intelligent woman, Maakah bat Talmai, and I'm honored that you've agreed to become my wife and share your wisdom to help me become Israel's regal king."

Looping her right arm around my neck, Maakah pulled me close. I gathered her into my arms and found enough courage to ask, "Are you still angry with me?"

"Angry?" She released me and seemed confused.

"When I came to check on you yesterday before the executions, you . . ." I turned to Zerry who was shaking her head and giving me that *don't go there* stare. "I thought you might have been upset that you weren't able to say any last words to Zulat."

286

Zerry closed her eyes, and I could almost hear her sigh.

Maakah's features softened. "I have only spotty memories of the past two days. I remember that yours was the first face I saw after I'd lost so much blood and fainted. After the regular doses of poppy tea began, all I can remember are terrible nightmares until this morning when Zerry suggested we try smaller doses for the journey. So far, I've had very little pain." Her eyes were as clear as the springs of Ein Gedi. She truly had no recollection of anything she'd said. *Thank You, Yahweh, for protecting her from both the physical pain of her injury and the inner turmoil the executions would have caused.*

Though I didn't know what else had darkened her visions, I hoped to reassure her. "When Joab and I stood atop that watchtower and looked down at all the somber faces, I thought for sure those gathered would be angry that I'd somehow forced them to obey, but did you hear the shout that began our worship?"

Abigail and Nomy had turned around to be part of our conversation, and Abigail answered, "We were too far away to hear what was said before the chanting began."

My eyes remained focused on Maakah. "Someone said, 'Yahweh protected Princess Maakah, because He knew we would obey His Law.' Those who remain faithful to Yahweh—and to me—are very much for you, Princess Maakah."

TWENTY-FOUR

MAAKAH

David also took the men who were with him, each with his family, and they settled in Hebron and its towns.

2 Samuel 2:3

I was quickly reminded of the vast difference between marching with a shepherd-warrior versus caravanning with a royal escort. My Geshurite escort had traversed busy trade routes and meandered through friendly villages. David's caravan avoided crowds, keeping to shepherds' paths and desert plains.

David sent a dozen Gadites ahead of our slow-moving train to find a flat yet defendable campsite. By nightfall we'd reached the well-chosen location, and our faithful scouts had assembled tents for David, his wives, and me. They'd also lit several fires to cook the evening meal and provide protection against predators.

While Nomy lingered in her corner of our cart to nurse Amnon, Zerry and Abigail supported my right arm and waist while I scooted toward the wagon's back wall. Abigail unhooked the latches and lowered it. My stiff legs hung over the wagon's edge, feet dangling a cubit from the ground. Why make wagon wheels so tall? Zerry awkwardly supported me from the back while Abigail stood outside the cart and held my right hand. As I edged one foot nearer to the ground, the thought of landing hard and jolting my shoulder overwhelmed my courage.

"No, no, no." I scooted away from the edge at the same time Zerry tried to steady me by grabbing my left arm. I let out a shriek and curled onto my side. Zerry hovered over me, apologizing. I was trembling all over.

"Shhh. Let me take care of you." David knelt beside me, lifted my head, and cradled my right side against him, then offered his waterskin. "Drink," he said, "but slowly. I've been watching you today, and you didn't drink enough."

I wanted to both thank him and argue. I'd drunk as much as the rest of the women in our cart. He placed the waterskin against my open lips, then tipped it. The water felt cool on my throat.

When he lowered the skin, I said, "Thank you." My voice was hoarse—probably from lack of water. I was glad I hadn't argued.

"Drink often through the night," he said. "Zerry will stay with you in a small tent. Abigail will bring tonight's meal for you both. Make sure you sleep right after you eat. May I carry you to your tent?" He'd already set aside the waterskin, positioning himself to slide one hand under my legs and the other around my back.

Before I'd given permission or protest, I was in David's arms. He looked exhausted, too. How could I ever thank my new family for their tender care? They had to be as exhausted as I was. David stumbled over a rock, and pain scorched through me again. I sucked in a breath to keep from crying out, then buried my face against his chest.

"I'm sorry," he whispered against my head. "We're almost there." Finally, he stopped. "Can you stand?"

I tried my voice again. "I think so."

He sat my feet on a hillside as gravelly as my voice. Leaving one hand on my hip to steady me, his eyes roamed my features, then lingered on my lips. I stepped back and slipped. David caught my right arm, which sent another jolt of pain soaring through my left shoulder and down my arm.

"Zerry!" David scanned the bustling camp around us.

"Perhaps if I lie down . . ." I began.

"Zerry," he called again, ignoring my plea. "I told the scouts to have boiling water prepared when we arrived. Zerry!" he shouted again. "My sister should be here by now with your tea."

"David, please!" My tremulous words stole his attention. "Go. Tend to your people."

"But you—"

"Just help me into my tent," I said through pain-clenched teeth.

"Of course." He held open the flap and supported my right hand as I lowered myself onto one of the two sleeping mats.

Frustrated by my weakness, I grumbled, "I've lost so much strength in a few days of inactivity. I'm sorry to be a bother."

He tipped up my chin. "If that dagger had struck two finger widths lower, I would have lost you." He placed his hand on my cheek and brushed my lips with his thumb. "You are Yahweh's gift to me, Maakah. Caring for you reminds me of how precious you are to me—and to Yahweh."

"Here I am!" Zerry knelt behind David with my cup of tea and swatted him out of her way. "You're not allowed in there until after you're married. Shoo! Shoo!"

David winked at me and backed out, leaving me bereft at his absence. I laid back on my woolen headrest and heard him tell Zerry, "I'm sending four men to guard your tent. If Maakah has any difficulties during the night, send for me right away."

Zerry huffed. "And what remedy can you provide that I don't already know?"

"I'm going to marry her and love her as my own flesh, Zerry." His tone was playful. "Can you do that?"

"Only you can do that, brother." A slight pause—likely a hug—preceded David's retreating footsteps. Zerry returned to the tent with the tea, and I drank it, peering at her over the cup's rim. "It's good for David to feel a little helpless." She grinned. "He's always the one who fights the battles and makes the big decisions. He doesn't get as much practice as the women who wait in camp, trusting Yahweh to protect, defend, and then heal the wounds of those we love. My brother is learning a whole new level of trust because of you, Maakah, and it's a skill he'll need to rule our nation."

After finishing the tea, I handed the cup to her and asked, "David told me I could have died if the dagger had hit me two finger-widths lower on my chest. Why didn't you tell me?"

Zerry's eyes misted. "I didn't want to think of the what-ifs or face what your death might have meant for David's throne. Honestly, the way you were bleeding, I have no explanation for why you lived." She cupped my cheek. "I know only that Yahweh wants you here with us."

I tried to smile but could no longer feel my face. Zerry was beginning to look a little wavy. "I thingathe tea izz worgging."

"Sleep, my girl. Tomorrow will be a better day."

I'd awakened this morning to Zerry's snoring and the familiar pain in my shoulder. No longer a piercing burn as it had been after riding all day in the cart. The wound was still sore but manageable. I'd informed Zerry I would ride a donkey rather than fight the jostling cart today. She'd resisted at first, saying I wouldn't have the stamina, but with Victory's smooth gait and David walking beside me, I'd made it to our midday rest without yesterday's excruciating pain.

Unfortunately, I'd experienced a different sort of pain. We passed at least four large areas that had once been villages. One even had the remains of a city gate. When David lifted me off his donkey for our respite, I stood firm before him and asked, "Will you tell me which of the burned-out villages belonged to my Geshurites?"

His eyelids slid shut, and he exhaled as if he'd been holding his breath all morning. When he opened his eyes, they held sorrow as he stared into mine. "Two of the four were your people, my love." That was all. No *I'm so sorry*. No *I wish I hadn't done it*.

I walked away, joining Zerry, Abigail, and Nomy under the shade of an acacia tree. When I looked over my shoulder, David had gone the opposite direction, leading Victory to the nearby stream for water.

I sat down between Zerry and Abigail but didn't speak. Zerry leaned over. "Is your shoulder paining you?"

"No, I'm fine." The words came out much harsher than intended. I ducked my chin. "Forgive me. David just confirmed that some of the burned-out villages belonged to my Geshurites."

Silence answered.

I looked up and found only Abigail waiting to engage my sorrow. "Our love for you wants to say, 'I'm sorry, Maakah. We wish David and our men didn't destroy Geshur's villages.' But we've vowed never to deceive one another." Her words, though true, still wounded. "Instead, I'll tell you the hard truth and the reasons you know we obey Yahweh's commands. We obey because in the little time Zulat was among us, she coaxed nearly a hundred people to embrace a false god and nearly murdered you because you refused to believe her lies."

"But not all Geshurites are like Zulat. I'm not—"

"When there is proof among the plunder that they've raided Judean villages, are they not responsible for their actions?" Nomy's passion got the better of her, and the shrillness of her voice drew the attention of those around us.

Joab strode toward us and stood behind her, looking directly at me. "Is everything all right here?"

"When will we reach the first village?" I asked.

"Eshan is over the next rise." He pointed northeast, then returned his focus to me. "Are you able to climb with the other women, or should I prepare a wounded-warrior sling to hoist you?"

"I'll climb." Taking a piece of bread with me, I left the group to inform David I no longer needed his donkey.

Halting twenty paces from the small stream, I heard him before I saw him. With a voice lifted in praise, my soon-to-be husband knelt alone beside Victory with his hands raised to the God who possessed his whole heart.

> "When I consider the heavens,
> the work of your hands,
> the moon and stars,
> that you set in place,
> what are people that you would consider us;
> human beings that you care for them?"

The words drove me to my knees. *Oh, Yahweh, who am I to question Your commands and declare Your ways unjust. You, who created the heavens, the earth, and all that dwells in them, are gracious and good in all Your ways.* I covered my face with one hand in repentance and humility before the One God who spared my life and revealed Himself to me. *Who am I, Lord, that You would choose me to adore You?*

When conscious thoughts returned, I looked up and both David and Victory were no longer beside the stream. No longer hearing the cheerful buzz of our camp, I looked behind me and saw that the caravan had already begun its climb over the rise.

David alone waited for me about fifty paces away. "We need not rush," he said, smiling. "Yahweh is never in a hurry and seldom works on our schedule."

What sort of man have you given me, Yahweh? "I'm sorry I became angry again when I saw Geshur's burned villages."

He strolled toward me as if we were in a palace garden without

Noble

a care in the world. Anticipation made my heartbeat race, and I rushed toward him, flying into his arms. We both gasped, and I pulled away, staring into his wide eyes. "My shoulder doesn't hurt!" I said, wiggling it to be sure.

He gaped, then chuckled, then whirled me around. When he sat my feet on solid ground, he unwrapped my bandage and sling. We loosened the wrapping down to my robe, and I peeked beneath the dressing Zerry had changed this morning. Shaking with joy, I said only two words. "Turn around." I slipped the robe off my shoulder, removed the clean dressing, and gawked at where the wound used to be. "David, it's only a pink scar now."

He whirled, and I instinctively covered the miracle on my naked shoulder. He raised both copper brows, and I couldn't deny the silent request. Lowering the robe off my shoulder again, I revealed the pink, handspan-length scar just above my heart.

Wonder lit his eyes. David moved closer and ran one finger along the length of newly healed skin. "Yahweh did this," he whispered. Then he looked into my eyes and brushed my lips with a kiss. "Do you need any more proof of your worth to the Creator, my love?"

Now I was certain I could climb any mountain Joab put in front of me. Perhaps the LORD knew I'd need the encouragement to climb over the first real *hill* in Judah's hill country. When we caught up with Abigail, Nomy, and Zerry in the caravan, the delight about my healing had already dimmed by the reality of Judah's steep cliffs and outcroppings.

"Let me see!" was Zerry's first reaction. Abital and Eglah also heard the joyful squeals and joined us behind an outcropping to see what God had done. We raised more delighted cries but needed to keep the caravan moving. We'd planned to visit three villages today and needed to make up the time I'd cost us.

When we emerged from our hiding place, Zerry said to her brother, "You'll get to see the proof someday."

He winked at me. "That day can't come soon enough."

Thankful he hadn't divulged our secret, I brushed past him to continue the difficult climb. David's men, accustomed to scaling cliffs and descending desert ravines, focused on helping both animals and carts safely to the top and down the steep inclines. The women of camp helped one another through winding narrow paths and down the descents into lush, green valleys. The children considered it a grand adventure, and I was beyond grateful for my healing and my friends' help. I would never have scaled that hill without them.

When we arrived at Eshan, one of nine villages in the Hebron colony, a man dressed in a robe similar to Abiathar's met us on the road as we approached. Behind him was an unwalled city consisting of a cluster of ten or twenty mudbrick homes. As the governing priest drew near, I noticed variations between his priestly attire and Abiathar's. David's High Priest wore a twelve-gemstone breast piece, while the priest of Eshan wore a breastplate more like Joab's—a warrior's armor. Abiathar cinched his robe with a linen belt, but the priest approaching David with open arms wore a weapons belt with a dagger, sling, and quiver of arrows to stock the bow slung across his back.

"Welcome, David our king!" He turned toward the people who were following him out of the village and swung his arms like Amasai leading a chorus. "David our king! David our king! David our king!" The village's men, women, and children joined the chant, as did our whole caravan.

David lifted his arms, patting the air as if trying to silence their praise, but nothing could stop their joyous celebration. Thankfully, Joab grabbed one of David's arms, pulled it down, and whispered something that stopped the novice king's protest. *Oh, David, you must allow your people to adore you.*

Joab must have told him something similar to my thought because David took three running strides and leapt atop a boulder to address his people—at least that's what I thought he would do. Instead, he pressed his palms toward heaven and closed his eyes in silent prayer. My throat tightened with an emotion I couldn't quite define. Though David, Abigail, and Nomy agreed that I could teach him much about being a king, I must learn that David ben Jesse was to be Yahweh's king, unlike any other because Yahweh was unlike any other god.

As David continued his reverent response, the shouts faded. The Three and thirty Mighty Men bowed to one knee, their heads bent in respectful silence. The rest of our caravan and villagers followed their example. This time, with my head bowed and eyes closed, I felt as if I was returning to speak with a beloved Abba or trusted Protector. Peace washed over me with thankfulness at all Yahweh had done.

When I heard the sound of men's whispered voices, I looked up to see David crouching on the boulder. He spoke with the village priest and both were beaming. The Three then gathered around them to join the conversation, and finally Joab. I glanced at Ahinoam and Abigail, who knelt beside me. They, too, were watching intently.

"I'd give next week's bread to hear their conversation," Abigail whispered. Both Nomy and I covered our grins. I would guess we were equally curious.

When David stood, his men and the priest dispersed in a circle at his feet, a glorious display of the royal guard. "Thank you for your overwhelming support and kind welcome!" he announced. "While I have all of Eshan gathered," he added, "my first command is that all of Israel learn this lament for King Saul and Prince Jonathan so their memory will live forever."

"No," I whispered loud enough for his wives to hear.

Sideways glances showed their disapproval, but I needed them to understand and help me convince him before we went to the next village. "His first command as their new king in any village must be something grand and beneficial to the hearers." I still whispered, but the enormity of David's mistake made it hard to remain quiet. "We want people to forget about the previous rulers. Let the historians record the legacy of Saul and Jonathan but use the joy of David's new leadership to win the people's emotional attachment."

"Stop." Ahinoam's abruptness brought heat to my cheeks. "In matters related to Prince Jonathan, no one instructs David ben Jesse." Her stern gaze brooked no argument.

I withdrew my hand from her grasp. "I'll abide by your wisdom." *For now.* But I would speak privately with David about it.

The villagers provided four roebucks roasted on a spit for our meal. We dared not say we'd already eaten. Instead, we contributed crusty bread and hard cheese that had been packed for tomorrow's journey. It was midafternoon before we were ready to continue the journey.

"You have our gratitude and eternal commitment to lead you in the ways of Yahweh," David said in farewell. A cheer rose, drowning out whatever else he'd planned to say. Joab and the Three finally stood beside him and raised their swords, effective but inducing a nervous hum.

"And thank you for your enthusiasm!" David chuckled, shifting the crowd's uncertainty to joyful chatter. "Though I haven't officially been made your king yet, many of you know that Yahweh directed the prophet Samuel to anoint me when I was still a shepherd boy tending Abba Jesse's flocks. Though I believe Yahweh will someday place me on Israel's throne, I want to be patient and trust fully in God's timing. Until that day arrives, will you pray with me? Serve Yahweh with me—no matter what trials and tests come?"

"Yes!" shouted one villager. Then a cacophony of voices joined the chorus.

This time, when David lifted his arms for quiet, the noise faded without the officers' intervention. "Good, good. As your priest has explained, part of your help will be caring for sixty-six men from my army. Some are married with families while others are unmarried, either by choice or widowed."

"We've got plenty of maidens to remedy your warriors' loneliness!" came a shout and then a cackle.

David laughed with them but cautioned, "I suggest you get to know the new additions to your village before suggesting a wife. I'm not sure I'd let a daughter of mine marry these men who have been too long their own masters!"

I kept glancing at the sun's position in the sky. How much longer would we dawdle in this village? David chatted as if we had all the time in the world, but we had more villages to visit before he, his wives, family, and royal guards arrived in Hebron.

"Shouldn't we have gone by now?" I asked Abigail. Surely his administrative wife would agree.

She grinned and studied me before answering. "No one hurries David."

"We're leaving a portion of our flocks to help provide wool and milk for the extra population," David continued. "Let me introduce my men and their families to you." He began calling each soldier to the front, naming every warrior, wife, and child. I stifled a groan and prayed to Yahweh that he wouldn't introduce the sheep! Growing more frustrated every moment, I was sure my throbbing head would explode.

After the last family from our camp was welcomed by the people of Eshan, David opened his arms wide and shouted, "Whatever kindness you show the least of these, consider it a kindness that you've done for me." He offered a slight bow to the raucous cheers and retreated through the crowd with Joab, the Three, and the Mighty Men surrounding him. As they passed by us, David announced, "Put the women on donkeys and in the carts so we can travel more quickly to the next town."

Now he was in a hurry?

Without a word, Nomy and Abigail began walking in the general direction of the next town, and soon the donkey stable boys arrived with their mount and with Victory for me to ride. Zelek, one of David's Mighty who had guarded our tent last night, stood ready to help me mount Victory. He placed a sturdy basket upside down beside David's donkey, but when I tried to place my foot on it, my muscles rebelled. Stiff from the climbing and then standing all afternoon, simply walking would have been difficult—let alone climbing onto a donkey.

"May I help?" the guard asked.

"No. I'll do it." For leverage to pull myself onto the basket, I grabbed the blanket on Victory's back. It slipped off. My cheeks burned, and I wanted to scream my frustration.

Zelek took the blanket from my hands, replaced it on the donkey's back, walked to the opposite side of my mount, and—without a word—extended his hand for leverage.

I gripped his strong hand and strained against my sore muscles to mount the faithful, white beast.

"Well done, my lady," Zelek said with a slight grin but no hint of mocking.

He'd won my undying friendship. "Does David still plan to visit two more villages today?"

I noted his grin remained as he grasped Victory's reins. "Indeed he does, my lady." Thankfully, he couldn't see my expression while leading Victory into position behind David's wives. And I didn't dare voice my thoughts to anyone except Yahweh.

God of the heavens and earth, how will David ben Jesse become a great king? He was noble in every way, and I loved him deeply for those qualities.

But could he ever become regal?

TWENTY-FIVE

DAVID

This is the inheritance of the tribe of Judah, according to its clans . . .
In the hill country . . . Arab, Dumah, Eshan, Janim, Beth Tappuah,
Aphekah, Humtah, Kiriath Arba (that is, Hebron) and Zior—nine
towns and their villages.

Joshua 15:20, 48, 52–54

Aphekah was within sight. I signaled Joab to move the sixty-seven soldiers and their families who would live in the city to the front of our caravan. I wanted them to get the first glimpse of their new home so they could enjoy the welcome we'd received from the other Hebron colonies.

Yesterday, we'd successfully placed over 450 men, women, and children from our camp to their new homes in Eshan, Dumah, and Arab—three villages belonging to the Hebron colony. Though we'd arrived at Arab well past dark, they'd enthusiastically welcomed us into their midst. All three towns had eagerly learned the lament for Saul and Jonathan and showed wild approval for my reign as Israel's new king. The overwhelming cooperation and unity were miracles almost as great as Maakah's healing, considering most Judeans couldn't agree on the color of the night sky. This morning we would settle 150 more in Aphekah and enjoy our midday meal while getting acquainted with its citizens.

I lifted my fist in the air, signaling a stop, then looked over my shoulder to be sure the families assigned to Aphekah had begun moving forward. I glanced at Maakah, who rode between my wives today. The stubborn tilt of her chin accompanied the glare she'd given me since visiting our first village.

Last night, she'd retreated to her tent as soon as we'd reached Arab, forgoing the celebration with its citizens. I asked Nomy and Abigail if her shoulder had started paining her again or if I should check on her.

My wives exchanged another of their silent glances, which Abigail interpreted for me. "Maakah is frustrated by the length of time we're spending at each village."

I pondered the news, but for the life of me couldn't understand the frustration. "Am I unaware of an important meeting in Maakah's plans?" My razor-edged tone was unkind. Hadn't I waited for her at the stream when Yahweh was obviously doing his miraculous work on her shoulder? "Maakah should be pleased that I'm winning the loyalty of my future subjects."

"Your future subjects?" Abigail exclaimed. Both wives looked as if I'd grown a second head.

"You'll be a *shepherd*-king, David," Nomy said it as definitively as if she were a princess sent to train me. "Yahweh chose a shepherd to rule His people because you know His heart. Has Yahweh ever made it His goal to 'win loyalty'?"

"I didn't mean it that way."

"No," she said. "The answer is no. Yahweh pursues our *love* through relationship—as should the king He's chosen."

"Agreed." Abigail folded her arms across her chest.

Everyone seemed to have an opinion on how I should rule, but I was tired of hearing them. I had retreated to my tent—alone—and

Noble

skipped the roasted lamb from the spit. All I wanted was a sleeping mat, lamb's wool beneath my head, and the sweet oblivion of sleep to quiet my mind. What I received was a restless night of praising God for wives who speak wisdom into my life even when I don't like it.

Yahweh, help me to be more appreciative of Abigail and Nomy's wisdom in the moment, and teach me to seek loving relationships with those I rule rather than merely seeking their loyalty or approval. And please work in Maakah's heart to trust Your timing and direction. Work also in me to know the difference between being a king and a chieftain.

After that prayer, I was ready to apologize, but my wives and Maakah were surrounded by other women in the middle of the caravan, and Joab demanded my attention to lead us. He was determined to discuss how we'd divide responsibilities between our High Priest, Abiathar, and Hebron's chief priest, Jehoiada—who managed not only Judah's largest city, Hebron, but also managed the governor priests who served as elders of Hebron's other eight colonies.

"We must be sure not to offend Jehoiada," Joab said repeatedly. "He carries the favor of every elder in Judah. Win his loyalty, and we'll win—"

"We will win Jehoiada's respect," I said, "and then, through relationship and over time, we'll win Judah's love."

My general lifted a single brow. "You've been listening to your wives again, haven't you?"

"Two men approaching!" Abishai shouted from a cliff above us.

I turned and noted the two figures, both dressed in priestly garb. "Does Aphekah employ two governing priests since they're the closest village to Hebron?"

"Doubtful." Joab lifted a hand to shade his eyes. "Perhaps Jehoiada has joined the governor to meet you here so he can usher you into Hebron himself when we leave Aphekah."

My chest squeezed at the thought. I'd hoped for a little time in prayer and worship before seeing Jehoiada. Why was I so nervous? I'd met with Hebron's chief priest many times since fleeing Gibeah and Saul's assassins. He'd been among the few Judeans who had never turned his back on me. Even when most of Judah's elders feared Saul would kill anyone who aided me as he'd killed the priests and their families in Nob, Jehoiada and the people of these Hebron colonies still provided us with needed supplies during our years in Judah's unforgiving wilderness.

"David, I'd like to speak to you." Maakah suddenly stood at my right side, her eyes wide, lips trembling. "I should have spoken to you last night instead of pouting like a child, but I need to say this before we enter this larger village."

"Maakah, could we speak later?"

"I'll give you two some privacy," Joab interrupted as he backed away, making *hurry up* gestures she couldn't see as the oncoming priests drew closer.

"Please, David, I need to say this before I lose courage." She released a deep sigh as if she'd held her breath all morning. "Perhaps you believe that giving each village personal attention and homesteading each family from our camp is a royal act, but I assure you the things you've done in the last three villages will only weaken your leadership. Please consider amending your approach in Aphekah and especially when we arrive in Judah's capital. Knowing everyone's name when you rule a nation is not only impossible, but it's not royal. A king must maintain a sense of mystery about himself and about his wives. In the last three villages, you presented yourself more like a shepherd than a king, which proved you could be an effective chieftain or governor, but not a man capable of ruling a thriving nation."

My disbelief had bowed to anger after her first two sentences, but I dared not engage in a verbal battle with two priests approaching. I measured their progress and shot a panicked look at Joab.

My neck and cheeks felt like raging flames, so I reminded myself that Maakah was a treasured gift from Yahweh. He had miraculously healed her for this journey. Maintaining a steady voice, I said, "Please remember Who guides our path and that we're following Yahweh's plan, not yours." The last two words lit the flame in her eyes.

"You said you wanted my counsel, and I'm giving it!" Her voice carried, and the whole caravan grew silent. When Maakah glanced at the caravan, only then did she seem to notice Jehoiada. Her eyes widened as his pace increased, marching straight toward us.

"Who dares speak to Judah's next king with such gross disrespect?" The priest's question reverberated in the silence and sent a chill down my spine. He nudged me aside to face my soon-to-be bride. "You're barely a child off your ima's breast. What would you know about advising the king Samuel anointed?"

Maakah's face was ashen, as it should have been, but I took her hand and stood beside her to make the official introduction. "Jehoiada, I present to you Princess Maakah, daughter of King Talmai of Geshur, and soon to become my wife." When Jehoiada was left gasping for words, I turned to face my surly princess. "And I will remind *you*, my love, that you have knowledge of how one king rules the established kingdom of Geshur, one of five Aramean thrones. You have no experience of Israel's tribes, clans, and families, or how to build lasting relationships among so much history based on God's sacred calling on our forefathers. So let me make it clear that only Yahweh leads Israel, and I'm the one He's anointed to be His king for as long as it pleases Him. My task isn't to cultivate loyalty or become royal. I'm to care for Yahweh's people like a shepherd for his sheep. Have I made myself clear?"

Instead of the fiery reply I'd expected, Maakah bowed deeply. "I've never seen you more clearly, King David." She grinned at me when she straightened, then turned to Hebron's chief priest. "Forgive me for our awkward first meeting," she said. "I'm discovering Yahweh enjoys humbling me." Her cheeks were a lovely shade of crimson.

Jehoiada's mouth fell open, but no words came. He looked at me. I shrugged. He looked back at Maakah and then knelt before her with a full belly laugh. "I'm very honored to meet you, Princess Maakah of Geshur." He looked up, glancing at the both of us. "And I'm anxious to hear all about how our God made such a strange match, but first—"

Standing, Hebron's chief priest opened his arms wide, including both our caravan and Aphekah's villagers in his announcement. "I originally came to Aphekah to invite the village and David ben Jesse's caravan to Hebron for a special midday feast we've prepared to celebrate a historic moment in Judah's history." He gathered me under one arm and continued, "On this day, our tribe will witness the fulfillment of the prophecy spoken by our patriarch Jacob on his deathbed when he said to Judah, his fourth son, 'The scepter will not depart from Judah, nor the ruler's staff from his descendants, until the coming of the one to whom it belongs, the one whom all nations will honor.' The elders of Judah have cast the sacred lots to confirm that Judah will separate from Israel's other tribes and become an independent nation and—" Jehoiada placed his hand on my shoulder, drawing breath for the next logical declaration.

"Wait," I whispered, heart pounding. "Are you sure?"

He nodded and said in a booming voice, "We will lead David ben Jesse in a joyful parade to Hebron's city gate and there anoint him King of Judah!"

A deafening roar shook the ground, and I fell to my knees in worship of the only God who could have brought me to this moment. *Yahweh, nations conspired against me. Kings and peoples plotted in vain. They banded together against You and Your anointed king, thinking they could throw off the shackles You'd placed on them. But You, enthroned in heaven, laughed at them. You scoffed when their human attempts failed. You rebuked them with your anger and terrified them with your wrath, saying, "I have installed my anointed king!"*

Falling on my face, I laughed and cried, undone by the miraculous, generous, steadfast love of God.

Jehoiada insisted I ride to Hebron on Victory, the white donkey that had been my faithful companion during many battles. Maakah seemed content to join the women of my family, learning dances and songs celebrating the victories of our people since Moses and Miriam rejoiced over Pharaoh's drowned charioteers at the Red Sea.

As we approached Hebron's gates, citizens poured out of the city to join the celebration. I shaded my eyes from the late-day sun and could barely believe the sight. Elders from as far away as my hometown of Bethlehem had come to declare Judah a separate nation and to anoint me their first king. I searched the elders for my oldest brother, Eliab, but he wasn't among them. Why was I disappointed? My abba and brothers had begrudged Samuel's anointing the first time. Why would my blood relatives from Bethlehem bother to celebrate a second anointing?

Realizing bitterness had no place on a day of rejoicing, I silently laid my heart open to my God. *You know the wickedness within me, LORD. Root out the bitterness with your overwhelming love and help me choose forgiveness every day when past wrongs seep into my memory.*

Amasai's booming praise entered my consciousness, and I began to sing along as we approached Hebron's walled city. "Yahweh said to my king, sit in the place of honor at my right hand until I humble your enemies, making them a footstool under your feet." Eyes closed, I let Victory lead me into the melee of worship and praise, focusing on the One who had placed me on Judah's throne rather than those who chose not to celebrate the moment with me.

Someone tugged Victory's reins from my loose grip, startling me to attention. Joab grinned and led me into the city. The Three and my Mighty had created a path between them. Joab led me through their midst as they continued to sing with fists over their hearts. Every man I passed was dearer to me than blood family, closer than a brother. At the end of my captains, near the city's central well, stood my wives and Maakah with both high-ranking priests, Abiathar and Jehoiada.

As Jehoiada stepped forward, I dismounted Victory and waited, wondering for a fleeting moment if I was dreaming.

"We have gathered here this evening," Jehoiada began, "to anoint Yahweh's clear choice for Judah's first king." He stepped aside, inviting Abiathar to stand before the gathering. "I introduce Abiathar ben Ahimelek, the only living priest who worshiped before the Ark of the Covenant in the Tabernacle from the Wilderness." A reverent *ooohhh* spread through the crowd. Jehoiada motioned for silence and pointed at my priest's jeweled breast piece. "Abiathar escaped Saul's assassins with the original breast piece bearing twelve gemstones—one precious stone for each of Israel's twelve tribes. Behind the breast piece are the sacred lots with which we confirm David ben Jesse's calling today as Yahweh's king." Jehoiada stepped aside and motioned for Abiathar to continue.

My heart leapt into my throat, and I exchanged a panicked glance with my wives and Maakah. Had they known the lots would be cast to confirm my anointing? Before I could voice the question, Abiathar raised the two stones and sent them tumbling across Hebron's dusty main street.

I closed my eyes. *Yahweh, confirm me as Your king through Your Urim and Thummim.*

A great cheer was my answer. When I opened my eyes, the three women I loved had covered their tearful cries and were dancing—even after a full day's hike through Judah's hills and valleys. I searched for the stones and found the black Urim lying flat two paces from me and the white Thummim standing tall against my right big toe.

While the masses continued to roar, Abiathar removed the polished ram's horn full of sacred oil that he wore slung over one shoulder and placed it in Jehoiada's hands. The two priests held the horn of oil high, inciting another surge of celebration. Then Hebron's chief priest asked me to kneel before him. I did as he asked, but before he poured the oil, he leaned down to whisper, "I never imagined that Yahweh would give me this great honor, my friend." Without awaiting my response, he tipped the horn's full contents over my head.

Though my first instinct was to bow and wipe the slippery liquid from my eyes and nose, I resisted and hoped for the same sensations I'd felt during Samuel's anointing. Eyes closed again, I lifted my hands to the only Abba who ever loved me and felt the oil begin to warm as it dripped from my eyebrows and beard down my neck and onto my chest. The warmth continued to bathe me from the top of my scalp, where the oil first touched me, all the way to my toes, where the oil never reached. *Yes, LORD, You will do more in me and through me than the watching world will ever witness or comprehend.* It was a moment only my Abba in heaven and I would share.

All around me, people rejoiced with singing and dancing. Finally, secure in Yahweh's calling and steadfast love, I stood and received a cloth from my wives, to capture the sacred oil, along with their vows of enduring love and support.

A shrill whistle broke through the happy chaos. Instantly sobered, I scanned the main thoroughfare for Joab or one of my childhood friends to discover who signaled their urgent need. Instead, I found my nephews and all my Mighty rushing toward Hebron's gate. Approaching through the valley was one camel with a rider and my guards from Ziklag leading the camel running toward the city.

I joined the military rush toward the gate, straining to see more clearly who was on the camel. "Eliel?" I whispered in disbelief.

"The rider or one of the escorts?" Jehoiada shouted from behind me.

I slowed to let him come alongside me. "The rider," I said. "I sent Eliel, one of my best scouts. I sent him on foot with two other scouts, carrying a message from Maakah to King Talmai in Geshur."

"Aren't the runners two of your Mighty?"

Nodding, I said, "Heled and Maharai, cousins left in Ziklag to wait for the messengers and tell them we moved to Hebron."

Abishai, captain of the Three, passed us with his two men. His soldiers each spoke to Heled and Maharai while Abishai took the reins of Eliel's camel and led the mount toward us. He spoke with our courier, immediately garnering information though Eliel was clutching his ribs as he spoke. The Three were a special force of skilled spies who gained important information against our enemies and for our most delicate missions—both planned and unplanned.

When Joab reached the camel, Eliel slid off the animal's side, landing in the arms of my four best warriors. Gently, they carried him about ten paces to the shade of Hebron's southeast wall. The injured scout removed a scroll from his belt and placed it into Joab's hand. My general marched toward me at the same moment Maakah arrived at my side.

I immediately transferred the message to Maakah's trembling hand. "I'm sure his reply is meant for you."

She peered over Joab's shoulder where Zerry had begun tending Eliel's wounds. "I'm so sorry." She shook her head and broke the seal. "I'll read aloud so we can decide together what Yahweh would have us do.

King Talmai, ruler of all Geshur, the southernmost Aramean province
 To David ben Jesse, renegade deceiver of Gath's King Achish, my esteemed brother-by-marriage."

Maakah handed me the scroll. "It would appear Abba intended his reply for you."

I cradled the hands that held King Talmai's missive. "Then I'll read it aloud so we can decide together what Yahweh would have us do." She released it into my hands with a brave smile. Yahweh, please give me the privilege of killing the scoundrel who has disregarded his tenderhearted daughter. I brushed her cheek again and continued reading.

"After interesting conversations with my wife's nephew, Eliphelet, and your other scouts, I demand that you and your most valiant Mighty Men escort my daughter back to Geshur before the New Moon. I've sent a single scout back on one of my camels to expedite your return. If you do not comply, I will hang the headless bodies of your two scouts on Geshur's temple walls—as the Philistines did with Saul and his sons.

 Should you choose to retaliate, you and your fledgling nation of Judah will suffer the full military wrath of both Geshur and Philistia."

I wadded up the scroll and tossed it to the ground like the refuse it was. *LORD, anoint us with Your wisdom and righteous fury for the battle ahead.* "Do you understand what your abba's threats mean for us, Maakah?" Before she answered, I forged ahead. "As Yahweh's king of Judah, I must protect every man, woman, and child entrusted to my care against the aggression of any nation—including Geshur. I must lay aside every part of me except David, the warrior."

"No, David," she whispered, then met my gaze. "You must use every part of who you've become—shepherd, warrior, and king—to protect and lead your nation against Abba's threats and violence. I can't bear thinking of what he and his army will do to you or your family—my family now. I choose *you*, David ben Jesse."

I wrapped her in a ferocious hug, not caring who saw. "We'll marry as soon as we return from Geshur," I whispered against her ear, then released her. To all my Mighty gathered at the open gate, I restated King Talmai's demands. "Just as Yahweh healed Maakah's wounded shoulder, He will guide us safely to Geshur and then return us safely to Hebron with not only Maakah but also Eliphelet and Nakia. Yahweh will not only rescue us from Geshur's treachery, but our enemies will fall into the pit they've dug for us. We leave tomorrow before dawn to rescue our comrades." I thrust my sword into the air with a war cry. Even Eliel lifted a fist to show his faith in the One who could make the impossible possible.

"We have camels," Jehoiada shouted over the noise. "You're Judah's king, and we'll supply anything you need to fight our enemies."

I offered a respectful nod but declined. "Only Maakah and my Mighty will accompany me on this journey. We'll travel quicker on foot via shepherds' trails than on camels where Talmai's spies watch the trade routes." Gripping Jehoiada's shoulder, I added, "Your warrior-priests must remain in Hebron to guard my wives and your families. Talmai is obviously drawing my best soldiers away, so be wary of any unusual travelers."

He saluted, fist to chest. "We serve at your command, my king."

"Joab," I called my general from Eliel's side. He stood and helped the messenger stand to face me. "Joab, you must remain in Hebron to settle the remaining families in the surrounding Hebron colonies. Keep our watchmen on high alert."

I then focused on Eliel. "You paid a high price to deliver a madman's message. I'll escort you home and thank your wife for the price both of you paid for our nation's safety."

Zerry started putting away the herbs and potions she'd used on his wounds. "And tell your wife," she said to Eliel, "that I'll gather David's wives to help with your household chores so your family can spend more time with you as you heal."

I thanked my sister and chuckled inside. Hopefully, Zerry would give him some poppy tea to help him sleep amid the chaos of his house full of women.

In the fading light of dusk, I gave my final command of the evening. "Jehoiada will give you instruction on which families will settle in Hebron as your new home and which families will travel tomorrow to the other five Hebron villages. Tonight, we'll all camp here inside Hebron's high walls. It will be crowded, but I encourage you to enjoy this time with your family, if you have one. If you don't, share a cup of spiced wine with someone you respect. Then retreat to a quiet place and lift your prayers to Yahweh. Tomorrow, He leads us to snatch justice from a tyrant's grasp."

Another war cry carried us toward the city. Near the gate, Maakah pulled me aside, her pallor betraying her anxiety. She waited until I stopped in front of her to declare, "If Abba doesn't release Eliphelet and Nakia willingly, you'll never find them in his labyrinth of prison tunnels below the palace. You must use me to bargain with Abba, or you'll never get out of Geshur alive."

"I'll never use you to bargain with." I wanted to slip my arm around her waist but dared not—not until we were officially wed. "I refuse to put you in danger," I said, leaning close enough to smell the lavender oil in her hair.

She pushed me away. "Don't touch me or look at me that way. You must think of nothing but outwitting Abba and getting my cousin and Nakia back."

Frustrated, but knowing she was right, I studied the wounded princess. "I'm not sure you should go to Geshur."

She widened her stance and folded her arms. "I'm going to Geshur whether you allow me to travel with you or not."

"You will remain—"

"My king?" Zelek, my Mighty who had been assigned as her personal guard, stood three paces away. "May I speak plainly?"

"Why aren't you with your family?" I spat the words like an accusation.

"The Mighty are my family, and I'm waiting on my spiced wine to steep." The wry grin reminded me why I liked him.

"Speak," I said grudgingly.

"If you decide Princess Maakah would be helpful in Geshur, I might be qualified to make her travel more bearable. I was born among the Moabites, taken captive by Ammonites, then sold to Mistress Abigail's first husband, Nabal. On our way to Geshur, we'll travel through Moabite and Ammonite territories familiar to me, so I can help us avoid bandits and enemy patrols. I can also help choose easier routes for Princess Maakah to travel."

I held the man's gaze. He was shrewd, a man who had seen the opportunity for freedom after Nabal's death and fled the estate to join my Mighty Men. He'd proven a skilled warrior and devout follower of Yahweh.

"Do you believe Maakah will slow our progress?" I asked. "Can we arrive in Geshur before the New Moon festival if the princess comes along?"

His grin went from wry to beaming. "Absolutely, my king. Might this be the reason Yahweh healed her?"

I glimpsed Maakah's hope-filled eyes shining in the early evening

Noble

torchlight. "You see? Even Zelek agrees. Perhaps Yahweh healed my shoulder so I could join you on this journey."

I leveled a warning glare at Maakah. "Zelek isn't the Lord's anointed, nor does he carry the weight of a nation on his shoulders."

Zelek immediately bowed to one knee. "Forgive me if I've overstepped—"

"You did not overstep," I said, "but Princess Maakah did." She tried to look away, but I turned her chin to face me. "Never manipulate a situation to your benefit by using my soldiers against me. I make decisions through Yahweh's direction, and you will abide by them." Her shock and dismay prompted my next words. "I will listen to all my closest counselors, but Yahweh must always be first among them. Joab, my captains, and my wives—which you will soon become—are the earthly voices I give the most sway. So after hearing your reasons and the reminder of Zelek's heritage, I agree that your presence will be helpful on our mission to Geshur."

"Thank you, David!" She jumped and stifled a squeal. Did she think we were going to a feast?

"Maakah, your abba has committed an act of war against us. We're going to Geshur with every intention of righting those wrongs."

She lifted her chin and matched my intensity. "And I'm going to Geshur with every intention of protecting both families that I love."

TWENTY-SIX

MAAKAH

So my heart began to despair over all my toilsome labor under the sun.

Ecclesiastes 2:20

I endured a sleepless night contemplating my parents' reaction to the changes in me—and in our world—since I'd left Geshur. How would they respond to news of Zulat's death? Even more concerning, would Abba take off David's head when I insisted on marrying him? Or would he be even more angry when I confessed my sole allegiance to Yahweh?

Thankfully, our day of hiking through Judah's wilderness had occupied my mind. And the scowls from the son of Hebron's chief priest were more worrisome than the opinions of my parents three days away. "Why does he hate me so much?" I whispered to David after he'd hoisted me onto a high ledge.

He looked at me and then at Zelek, who followed me up the cliff by using handholds to climb. "Zelek doesn't hate you."

"Not him." I pointed to the young warrior behind Zelek. "Him!"

David waved off my concern. "Benaiah is just a boy. Jehoiada begged me to bring him along to give him some experience with my Mighty. Ignore him."

315

He reached for a handhold in the next cliff face, but I grabbed his arm and turned him to face me. "He's not just a boy," I whispered through clenched teeth. "And I'm telling you, he hates me."

Pausing, David searched my eyes. "You're afraid of him." It was a statement.

Relieved that I didn't have to confess my cowardice, I told him the reason. "You, Zelek, and Benaiah have been hoisting me up and over boulders and cliffs all day long. I sense care and caution from you and Zelek. I get only sneers and duty from Benaiah."

David took two steps to the ledge and gave Zelek his hand to help him up. "Help Maakah to the next peak," he said. "I'll wait for Benaiah, and we'll join you in a moment."

"David, wait." Had I made a mistake by telling him my fears?

Zelek blocked my view of him and extended his arm in the direction of continued progress. "This way, Princess." If I must proceed, I would walk slowly and try to hear their conversation.

"Take my hand, Benaiah." David's tone was friendly. That was good.

"Thank you, my king. Why have we stopped?"

"Because you have a choice to make, boy," David said, no longer friendly.

"Mistress?" Zelek offered his bent knee as a human footstool. I shushed him, but he grinned and said, "If the king wished for you to hear his dealings with young Benaiah, he wouldn't have sent you ahead with me." He slapped his proffered knee. "Up you go."

I growled my frustration but obeyed, knowing Eliphelet and Nakia's lives depended on it. With the fittest men in David's army driving me ever onward, I'd kept pace even when my whole body screamed its rebellion. Throughout our day, my eyes had remained on David's back as Zelek and Benaiah followed closely behind. Whenever we reached an especially difficult ledge or incline, David climbed it first. Zelek offered his knee as my first step. Benaiah's open palms

MESU ANDREWS

were my second step, that then lifted me to David's waiting reach from above. David hoisted me upward onto level footing where we repeated the process at every troublesome spot.

"Is that clear, Benaiah ben Jehoiada?" David's words came as Zelek's right hand boosted me to the top of a boulder.

I looked back at the king and his soldier, who was kneeling before him, head bowed. Though I couldn't hear Benaiah's reply, I watched as David offered his hand and locked wrists—a warrior's pledge—and then embraced as brothers. *Thank You, Yahweh, for Your intervention.*

I followed Zelek through a narrow cleft between two boulders and was relieved to find a wide, level expanse where we might rest for a moment. Both David and Benaiah arrived before I found a shady place to sit. David's Mighty were more mountain goat than man and more devoted to David ben Jesse than Azam, the captain of my abba's royal guard, was to my father.

As the sun was beginning to set, David stood atop a tall rock and pointed east. "We'll make Ein Gedi by nightfall." He disappeared down the next incline, as fleet-footed as any Gadite, Benaiah right behind him.

"What is Ein Gedi?" I asked Zelek.

"An oasis, mistress." He took my hand to help me over a fallen tree trunk. "While we were fugitives from Saul and hiding in this wilderness," he continued, "Ein Gedi was our paradise. We wintered there in peace until Saul and his army found us. It was the first place David had the opportunity to kill King Saul but chose not to raise his hand against Yahweh's anointed."

"But wasn't David also Yahweh's anointed? Didn't he realize a king must seize every opportunity given him?"

Zelek nodded, but his features gave nothing away. He'd make a good tutor for David on how to control those bouncy copper-colored eyebrows.

317

Noble

My chest tightened at the memory of when I'd told David that Abba had taught me that lesson at age five. The concern in his gold-flecked green eyes had been startling. He'd disapproved of training so young a child in the ways of court, but David knew nothing about raising an heir to the throne. Or was his desire to always put his family before his kingdom the better way to love—and to rule? Would little Amnon mature into a wise and capable crown prince and make his ima and abba proud someday when he inherited Judah's—or Israel's—throne?

"Mistress, are you well?" Zelek waited on a rocky ledge above me, his hand extended and waiting to pull me higher.

"Of course. Yes." I accepted the help, and we climbed higher, cresting the hill where David had made his announcement. I turned in a full circle, appreciating the rugged beauty in every direction. Before I could react, my foot slipped on loose gravel, and I slid down the steep incline, scraping my hands for at least the tenth time today. When I landed hard against a boulder at the bottom, tears threatened. Our endless ups and downs reflected the inner battle I'd waged all day. The thrill of chasing danger crashed against the pain and heartache awaiting me in Geshur. I could imagine no possible scenario in which Abba would allow both me and Eliphelet to return to Hebron. *Yahweh, this situation seems more impossible than healing my shoulder, but I will trust You.*

David skidded into the gravel beside me. "Are you all right, love?"

Zelek hurried to my left. "Mistress, forgive me. I—"

"It wasn't your fault, Zelek."

"Let me see your hands." David fussed over my bleeding palms, wiping them with the cloth he kept tucked in his belt. "I shouldn't have run so far ahead. Forgive me."

"Zelek said this was a special place for you and your men."

Joyful shouts erupted from the other side of the next hill. David looked toward the commotion with longing.

I pulled my hand from his ministrations and stood on wobbly legs. "Let's go," I said, delighted at the surprise on his features. "It sounds to me as if we're missing all the fun." Both David and Zelek helped me to the peak. An appreciative gasp stole my words. The setting sun sparkled off the lake east of Ein Gedi. It was the most majestic sight I'd beheld since leaving Geshur.

"It's called the Salt Sea," David whispered into the holy moment. "Though full of minerals and surrounded by life-giving springs, the water in the sea is briny and not fit for man nor beast."

How very different than my lovely Yam Kinneret, the sacred lake south of Geshur. I used to worship from Geshur's hilltop, waiting each new dawn to glimpse Asherah's reflection in the lake's crystal waters. Not once had I seen her face—because there never was a goddess. Now I considered the legends as briny as the Salt Sea's unfit water. How strange that a lake cloaked in false legends provided life; yet the Salt Sea, surrounded by inhospitable wilderness and unsuitable for drinking, saved the lives of David and his men. Since I'd met David ben Jesse and his God, my whole world had turned upside down. *Yahweh, do You always ask Your people to look at things differently?*

David placed his handsome face between me and my view of the water. "You look sad. I can have Zelek and Benaiah escort you back to Hebron."

"I'm not sad, just pensive," I said. "And I definitely don't want to return to Hebron."

He feigned a smile, but it didn't reach his eyes. "You've been a champion today, but I suspect the confrontation with your abba will be the hardest thing you've ever done." He cradled my hands and then pressed them against his heart. "I don't want to hurt you while gaining justice for my people."

"I belong with you, David. Abba needs to see that I'm staying by your side no matter what comes."

Noble

A slow grin hinted at mischief, and without warning, David ben Jesse scooped me into his arms with a "Whoop!" I threw my head back, laughing, as he carried me down the hillside toward a stream. Though every part of my body ached from today's journey, David's joyful abandon fought the inner foes of fear and sorrow.

He splashed into the stream and kept running, high-stepping toward a large pool that had been hidden by trees. I held on tighter. "David, I can't swim!"

"Hold onto me," he said at the same moment he leapt forward.

Submerged into what felt like a bottomless sea, I panicked, clutching at him as my head came out of the water. "David!" I shrieked. "David!" I heard others splashing but could only focus on getting out of the water. "David, please!"

His hands slid around my head and beneath my hair. "Shhh," he coaxed.

My flailing turned to blind whimpers.

"Look at me," he said gently. "Open your eyes and look at me." Still whimpering, I did as he said and stared into his calming presence. "Hold onto me, Maakah, and never let go." His voice was husky. Full of emotion. Passion, yes, but not desire. His eyes searched mine. Asking. Pleading. But for what? "Never let go," he whispered. Almost childlike, he seemed to need my assurance as certainly as I'd needed his moments ago.

PART IV

For God will bring every deed into judgment, including every hidden thing, whether it is good or evil.

Ecclesiastes 12:14

TWENTY-SEVEN

DAVID

For God does speak—now one way, now another—though no one per-
ceives it. In a dream, in a vision of the night . . . he may speak in their
ears and terrify them with warnings, to turn them from wrongdoing
and keep them from pride, to preserve them from the pit, their lives from
perishing by the sword.

Job 33:14–18

The stillness before dawn was my favorite time to worship. No matter how loud the thoughts in my head, the quiet surrounding me
proved Yahweh's calm.

"Do you hear the thundering inside me?" I whispered to the
heavens. "Save me from the dread of my enemy, LORD. Then I can
win the battle." I feared so many things about facing Talmai, but
what I feared most was losing Maakah. Her abba would certainly
discredit me and seek to turn her heart against me. The thought of
seeing disillusion or disdain aimed at me in those gray-blue eyes was
like shoving a dagger through my belly. When I was a commander
in Saul's army, Talmai's military savvy had been legendary. Could
I outwit a king with decades of experience when I'd been king for

three days? *Hide me from the secret plots of the wicked, O God, and from his horde of warriors.*

"No! Stop!" Maakah's desperate cry sent me dashing toward her. "Leave me alone!" she screamed as I rounded the corner of the large boulder that hid her from the rest of our camp. Flailing in her nightmare, she was weeping and fighting some unknown attacker.

I knelt distant enough to avoid her violence yet close enough to subdue her. "Maakah." I pinned her arms at her sides. "Shhh, love."

"Nooo!" She fought harder, now kicking and screaming even louder.

"Maakah, it's only a dream," I shouted.

Her eyes shot open. Confusion slowly gave way to recognition, and she relaxed in my arms. Trembling overtook her. "It was so real. We were approaching Geshur."

Goose flesh skittered up my arms and across the back of my neck. "Tell me."

She sat up, her eyes never leaving mine. "I thought you said you weren't a seer."

"I'm not, but tell me anyway."

She nodded and began, "We were in the wilderness under a starless night sky southeast of Geshur. You and your men had run too fast for me to keep pace, and I fell to my knees. The howls of jackals drew near. Ravens' caws joined the terrifying chorus. Hurriedly, I pushed to my feet, but I saw no sign of you and the Mighty. I was afraid I'd never escape the wilderness, but then a shaft of light shone down from the heavens highlighting a thorny acacia nearby. You taught me that where the wilderness bears life, water can be found. So I ran to the thorn tree and started digging." She squeezed her eyes shut as if reliving the moment. "As soon as my hands scooped away the earth, ravens swooped down and began their attack, their sharp beaks aimed at my ears, my face, my chest."

She opened her eyes. "I believe dreams have meaning, and this one seems rather ominous."

I agreed but worked to keep my features passive. "How do you interpret your dream?"

She swallowed hard, shaking her head as tears formed on her lower lashes. She circled her hand in the air, prompting me to answer. She seemed too frightened to guess.

I offered my hands, and she took them. Bowing my head, I prayed, "Yahweh, we're both frightened about what lies ahead for us in Geshur. Mine has manifested in wakefulness and Maakah's in a terrifying nightmare. If You're trying to speak to us through this dream, please make it clear to us both as we search the details and Your heart now." I lifted my head and said the most obvious detail. "Ravens typically mean death."

Maakah rolled her eyes. "Couldn't you have started with something more positive?"

"I believe every detail has meaning. You said the shaft of light came when you felt there was no escape, but it led you to a thorn tree."

She snorted a cynical huff. "The tree wasn't very helpful. I found no water and was still attacked."

It's about the thorns, not the water. That's when I understood. "Would water have helped you ward off the attack?"

A thoughtful crease formed between her brows. "I can't tell if you're criticizing me or trying to be helpful."

I grinned at this tenacious young woman. "What if you'd considered the *thorns* as a gift from the Light rather than digging for an immediate blessing with your own strength?"

"You are criticizing."

"I'm not," I said. "Think, Maakah. The answer is in the thorns."

Sobered, she looked away. "What good are thorns if I'm going to die of thirst in the wilderness?"

"What good is water if you're going to die by raven attack?"

She gasped and said, "Weapons! I could have used a thorny branch from the tree as my weapon!"

"Indeed." Her whole face bloomed with a smile, so I continued with what the dream taught me. "When we're guided by Yahweh's Light, He calls us to think differently. React differently. Even fight differently. When Yahweh guides us, Geshur's princess is safer with thirty Mighty Men than with a thousand Judean warriors. When I stand before your abba today, I'm to react differently than I normally would."

Her smile faded. "But what does that mean? What if he—"

"I don't know," I interrupted. "That's the thing about a wilderness. In the first year after I fled from Saul's assassins, I told Nomy the LORD said we were to hide in Judah's wilderness, and I didn't know for how long. She was terrified."

"Nomy? Afraid?" Maakah waved away my story. "I don't believe it."

"No one likes the wilderness, love. But I told her the same thing I tell you now: Yahweh uses these barren times and places to strengthen and shape us into what He wants us to become."

"Dawn is upon us, my king," Amasai's big voice announced.

I looked over my shoulder and saw him standing five paces away. "Zelek," I called, "when will we arrive in Geshur?" I stood and helped Maakah to her feet.

Zelek approached and knelt before me. "If we leave right away, we should arrive before dusk."

I kissed Maakah's cheek. "Today, we use thorns."

TWENTY-EIGHT

MAAKAH

They spread a net for my feet—I was bowed down in distress. They dug a pit in my path—but they have fallen into it themselves.

Psalm 57:6

After descending the desert mountains that separated Geshur from Ammonite territory, the terrain became easier to navigate. Even the protest of my aches and scrapes was muted as midday passed and Yam Kinneret came into view. I'd forgotten the calming effect of the lake on my soul. It was little wonder my people ascribed its peace-giving quality to a goddess, yet unfortunately they'd ascribed it to the wrong deity. Shading my eyes from the sun's reflection sparkling on the water, I could now worship the one God who created all things.

When Geshur's high walls came into view, my heart cried to the only God I knew would hear. *Protect us all, Yahweh, from the abba I once thought kind but now wonder if I ever truly knew.* Throughout the afternoon, David had sent out Gadite scouts whom he'd instructed to look for bandits or perhaps Geshurite troops sent to ambush us on the way. Tension rose with every step toward Geshur's city gate. When we were less than a hundred paces away, David lifted his fist, signaling our small company to a halt.

"Why stop now?" I whispered to Zelek. "We're so close."

Noble

"Any closer and we'd be within range of Geshur's archers." He glanced at me over his shoulder. "We're taking no chances with your life or ours."

When he faced forward, one hand was poised on his dagger, the other gripped his spear. Overwhelmed with gratitude, I could barely speak. "Why risk your life for mine?"

I heard a rare chuckle from my guard. "I serve Yahweh's chosen king, Princess Maakah, and obey his commands as if they're from God Himself." A quick glance over his shoulder revealed his lingering amusement. "I protect you because I know Yahweh has chosen you to be King David's bride."

My heart felt as if it might burst. I patted his back in a show of appreciation. Benaiah, who stood beside him, glanced at the innocent gesture and scoffed. I immediately removed my hand, prickly flesh moving up my arm. Would the chief priest's son accuse me of being too forward with my guard, a contrived flirtation? Heat raced from neck to cheeks, though I'd done nothing wrong.

David shouted at Geshur's watchmen. "King David of Judah, with his Mighty Men, has escorted Princess Maakah safely home."

We heard no verbal response, but the sound of Geshur's tree-sized wooden bar sliding off its iron brackets meant the two-story cedar doors would soon swing open. David's quick whistle called his men into a circle. I followed, eager to hear his precautions. "We've come to rescue Eliphelet and Nakia, gain Talmai's favor on my marriage to Princess Maakah, and return home."

"What about justice for Eliel?" Benaiah asked.

The terrifying vein in David's forehead began to throb and bulge as his silent stare sparked to flame. He drew breath to speak, but Amasai stepped between him and Jehoiada's son.

"The boy is young, my king, and he'll learn many things on this mission. Please, allow your Mighty Men and our God to teach him that he must obey without question."

"Teach him well," David said through clenched teeth, "or I will." Then, raising his voice for all his warriors to hear, he added, "No matter how King Talmai provokes us, we submit to his commands until Yahweh reveals His plan for vengeance. Understood?"

They replied with a unified *huuuh* and a slam of fist to heart, then moved back into perfect lines behind their king.

I wasn't sure where to stand, so Zelek extended his hand toward his right side. "Walk between Benaiah and me."

Jehoiada's son stepped to his right, placing plenty of room between us. Though his abba seemed ready to accept me as David's soon-to-be bride, Benaiah wasn't as welcoming. Before I could voice an objection to my reluctant guard, the whole company began to march. The disapproval radiating from the young man, who was likely my age or barely older, felt like it would scorch me by the time we reached Abba's throne room. If King Talmai suspected his hostility toward me—

I glanced at Benaiah, then forward again. "You clearly dislike me," I whispered, "but please don't let it show when you're in King Talmai's presence."

"Unlike you, *Princess*, I live by Yahweh's holy Law and will not be false."

"Does Yahweh's law prohibit David's soldiers from wiping all emotion from their features in a king's presence? If you'd like to show your pettiness to Geshur's powerful sovereign, then you'll die with your stubborn misinterpretation of Yahweh's Law."

He glared at me openly, his face as red as wine. "You would dare instruct me—the son of Judah's leading priest—on the Law?"

"Silence, boy!" Zelek hissed at his student. "The princess is trying to save your life. You've come to learn. Stop thinking yourself the teacher."

Zelek's defense boosted my courage to enter the city gates. Two lines of Abba's guards made a distinct pathway through the city, leading toward the palace. I was surrounded in the center of Mighty Men while David strode confidently at the front of our company. I watched every guard as we passed by, praying silently to the all-powerful God to protect him from a surprise attack.

"Forgive me, mistress" came the quiet whisper of the priest's repentant son.

Without turning toward him, I answered with equal discretion. "I applaud your defense of the Law, Benaiah. Perhaps someday I'll be able to study it as you do and know better what pleases my God."

I glimpsed his shock and hoped he'd recapture the soldier's placid expression before we entered the throne room and that he'd maintain it through all the uncertainties that lay ahead.

DAVID

Every Gadite I'd sent ahead of our company had returned with the assurance that Talmai's guards were positioned on surrounding hilltops, but only as lookouts. None waited with a contingent ready to attack, which was good news. However, none of them had been able to slip inside the city to spy out what awaited within the high walls. I felt as if I was leading my troop into a desert cave without first having tossed rocks inside to check for predators.

"None of the guards have a hand on their dagger," Asahel whispered without moving his lips. Marching at my right, he'd organized the scouts and agreed with my assessment that we must blindly move inside the walls—trusting Yahweh and the strength He'd provide if we needed to fight.

Did Samuel anoint me to be king of Judah for three days, LORD? With every step toward Talmai's lair, I felt Yahweh's reassurance that someday I'd rule over all of Israel. "We will not die here today," I answered my youngest nephew with the same covert whisper.

Finally reaching the palace, Asahel and I crossed the threshold and were abruptly halted by a man even larger than Uriah the Hittite. "I am Azam, Captain of King Talmai's guard." At least fifty Geshurites surrounded us in the hallway, each holding a weapon and ready to use it. Azam ignored me, stretching himself to a greater height to find our greatest treasure. "Princess Maakah, King Talmai will greet you privately in the throne room."

A soldier grasped her arm. "Don't touch me!" My feisty princess jerked her arm away. "I am your princess and may someday be your queen. Don't forget it."

The soldier shot a surprised look at Azam, then bowed to Maakah. "Forgive me, Princess. May I escort you?"

"No, you may not. I'm perfectly capable of finding Abba's throne room." With that, she strode to the front of our company and halted between Geshur's top soldier and me. "Azam," she said, chin held high, "David ben Jesse is the king of Judah. He is a royal guest who brings greetings from a newly formed nation. Treat him as you would any other sovereign ally."

Maakah strode toward the throne room without waiting for an answer. Two guards opened the double cedar doors as she approached, like the jaws of a great beast. She crossed the threshold, and the doors swallowed her whole.

Azam turned to me with a wry smile. "Well, King of Judah, you've given Princess Maakah an iron spine."

"Her confidence comes from Yahweh, the one true God."

His features clouded. "We'll see how strong your god is when you

Noble

and your men walk into King Talmai's court without your weapons." He spoke the next command for my Mighty to hear. "Divest yourselves of every weapon you carry before entering the king's presence. If my men discover any weapon on your person, you will be executed without further warning."

"It's a good system." I grinned into the captain's hard stare.

A dangerous smile matched my mocking. "We'll see if you approve after your meeting with King Talmai."

I reached for my dagger, and Azam drew his own blade in defense. "I'm only *divesting* myself." With two fingers, I pulled my dagger from its sheath and kept my eyes focused on the king's best warrior. I dropped the dagger into a basket and then thought it more practical to simply remove my weapons belt. After unlacing it, I tossed it into the same basket with my men's weapons, then removed the bow and spear worn across my back.

Turning toward my men, I emphasized what I'd said outside the city. "Remember, we're here only to retrieve our scouts and then leave in peace."

My Mighty slapped their fists to their chests again, which seemed to unnerve the royal guards. They forced my men into a single line, then formed two columns, flanking my unarmed warriors for the march into Talmai's court. Azam examined me. "I hope you enjoyed this morning's sunrise. It could be the last you'll ever see." He extended his left hand toward the throne room, and the double doors swung open. I marched into the same beast that had swallowed my betrothed.

King Talmai's court was far more ornate than Saul's meager palace in Gibeah. But all details fell away when I saw Maakah standing on the dais beside her abba with six guards around her. "Because Zulat was a traitor," Maakah pleaded, then turned to face Nakia. "And you're the worst traitor of all."

She lunged at Nakia, the Egyptian messenger we'd rescued on

332

our way to save our families from the Amalekites. He stood on the king's platform without a single sign of the beating Eliel had endured when he returned alone to Hebron.

My mind reeled with questions of what to do next. *Yahweh, where is Eliphelet? Had he been shown the same mercy Nakia was given?* Not likely. Eliphelet was no traitor. *LORD, show me how to escape Geshur with both Eliphelet and Maakah.*

"Welcome, King of Judah." Talmai opened his arms in mocking respect. "I've long wished to make your acquaintance, so today is especially rewarding since Nakia and I have much news to share."

Azam and I halted at the end of the central aisle, two paces from the elevated dais and very near my betraying servant. The young Egyptian took three steps to his right, moving away while aiming a triumphant grin at me.

I ignored the taunt and bowed to Geshur's king. "I'm honored to meet the man who raised such a worthy successor. Princess Maakah will make a fine ruler someday, should your wife bear another daughter."

When I straightened, Talmai was no longer feigning welcome. "You will not speak of my family, Hebrew."

"I'll speak of whatever you wish, King Talmai."

"Nakia revealed the lies you've told my brother-in-law, King Achish, since the moment he offered you sanctuary in his land. Maakah told me moments ago that you executed Zulat, the royal family's own dear maid." He stepped toward the edge of the platform, his eyes narrowed. "Tell me, King of Judah, how should I repay you and your warriors for killing my wife and daughter's dearest maid and destroying my entire southern kingdom?"

I glanced at Maakah, wondering if her abba's wrath had weakened her resolve to follow Yahweh—and love me.

She met my gaze with an affirming nod. *I'm still with you* came the silent vow.

Thank You, Yahweh.

Refocusing on the king, I felt a surge of God's favor. "I will go to war with *any* foreign nation that steals from Israel's towns and villages or tries to encroach on the boundaries that our God set in place four hundred years ago."

Talmai's nostrils flared. "And you'll fight with your mighty army of six hundred men?"

Again, I turned to Maakah before answering to read her emotions. She stiffened her spine and aimed her answer at her abba. "David only needed four hundred of his warriors to defeat the Amalekite camp of twenty thousand. Believe me, Abba, when Yahweh places David ben Jesse on Israel's throne, Geshur needs him as their ally."

His lips curled in a sneer. "You would bind Geshur's strength with a renegade chieftain who butchered our people and killed your own dear maid?"

"You mean the traitorous maid who tried to kill me?" She tore the neck of her robe, showing the freshly healed scar to prove Zulat's betrayal.

"Cover yourself!" Talmai lunged, pulling her robe over her shoulder.

"Is it more important to hide proof of Zulat's treachery than to expose her as the misguided traitor she'd become?"

"Misguided traitor?" Talmai's mocking laugh brought crimson to Maakah's cheeks.

"What else would you call a maid who intentionally enrages another nation against Geshur's only heir?"

"We'll see who becomes Geshur's heir."

Talmai's words were like a slap, the force of which left Maakah speechless. Without acknowledging his daughter's pain, Talmai turned his venom on me. "Answer me, David ben Jesse. Was my daughter in danger while she lived among your people?"

"Princess Maakah was in no danger until her maid incited several of our women to worship Asherah, which is against Yahweh's Law."

Talmai scrubbed his well-manicured chin. "Zulat converted your people from worshiping the Hebrew god to worshipping Asherah, our Mother Goddess?"

I nodded but said no more since Maakah hadn't yet confessed to her own change of allegiance.

He turned to his daughter, features as hard as granite. "Why would Judah's women, who began to worship Asherah, become a threat to you, who also worships Asherah?"

Yahweh, give her wisdom and courage to answer.

"I only worship one God, Abba."

His eyebrows drew together. "How can you worship only Asherah when she's the wife of El? Why worship only one god when the whole pantheon has various purposes and powers?"

"I worship only Yahweh." She straightened her spine and met his hard stare. "I've denounced any other god or goddess and believe Yahweh to be the only real God. He's not only the Creator of all things but He also cares about each of us personally." She pushed one of her guards aside and stepped closer to Talmai. "That's why Zulat wanted to kill me. That's why she recruited more Asherah worshipers in David's camp—who also wanted to kill me."

His face remained as unreadable as blank parchment. He turned to the guard she'd nudged aside and waved a dismissive hand. "Take my daughter to her chamber."

"No, thank you." She shrugged off the guard's grip and returned her attention to Talmai. "I will stay. I'm of age to make my own decisions and have no intention of ever obeying you again."

The slap came without warning, hard enough to make Maakah stumble back.

"Don't touch her!" I lunged toward the platform, but Azam caught my ankle and tripped me when my foot landed on the second step.

Noble

I fell hard, my ribs taking the full weight of my fall. How could I protect the woman I loved from an abba she'd once thought safe?

Maakah held her reddened cheek. "David, let Yahweh save us."

In that moment, we locked eyes, and her words settled into my soul like a direct command from our God. Distracted by the sacred, I had no strength to fight when Azam wrenched my arm behind me. He placed his knee in my back and pressed my chest to the steps and laid my head on the dais. My view was level with the platform, so I could see Talmai's satisfied grin.

"Don't touch her again," I gritted through clenched teeth.

Talmai's wicked chuckle infuriated me more. "I can see where my daughter gained her brazenness. Unfortunately for you, David, Maakah isn't a warrior. From her lips, any such threats are only impudence that I must purge before she marries Ish-Bosheth, Israel's new king." He stepped around her and moved my direction, stopping five paces away. "My daughter will never marry you, David. Maakah will marry Israel's new king and be well cared for. Nakia has been very helpful in carrying messages between Prince Ish-Bosheth and me these past few days. King Achish's troops have joined what remained of Israel's soldiers to escort General Abner and Saul's only surviving son to Mahanaim, Israel's new capital. When my spies reported that David ben Jesse had complied to my demands and both you and your Mighty escorted my daughter toward Geshur, I immediately renegotiated Maakah's marriage contract with Ish-Bosheth."

"Nooo!" I struggled under Azam's control, bringing his guards closer, weapons drawn.

"Nakia finalized Abner's and my negotiations this afternoon."

"Are you sure you can trust Nakia?" I paused, giving a moment for suspicion to take root. "He once vowed loyalty to me, too."

"I suspect Nakia becomes loyal to whomever is most likely to conquer his enemies." Talmai called four additional guards to join

336

him on the dais, then knelt in front of me. "It's too bad you won't live long enough to prove Nakia a traitor. Since neither Achish nor I have further need of your service, you will join your Mighty Men as Maakah's dowry, my gift to the bridegroom."

"You are despicable." Maakah spit at her abba's feet. Talmai's eyes narrowed. Calmly, he nodded toward the six guards around her.

With the dais steps still pressing into my ribs, my eyes at floor level, and six soldiers around her, I could no longer see the princess. I could, however, hear her breathing. Quicker. More sporadic. She was frightened but showing her strength.

"You *will* marry him," Talmai commanded.

"I'll never marry—" A terrible thud came immediately before Maakah could finish. She gasped for air, and I knew one of the soldiers had struck her abdomen.

I fought Azam harder, growling and groaning beneath his giant frame.

"David?" I heard Amasai's desperation in the single word.

He wanted to fight, as did I, but Yahweh hadn't yet given us permission. *Yahweh, please! Must I beg you to free us so we can defend my bride?* I heard only Talmai's indecipherable whispers in response. Nothing from the One I'd believed could rescue Maakah and my Mighty from impossible odds. *Yet will I trust You, LORD . . .*

"I will never worship Asherah again, Abba." Maakah answered her abba's whispers with a calm but determined voice. "I worship only Yahweh, now and always."

Talmai turned his back on her and waved one hand overhead. "Get her out of my sight!"

The guards broke formation, and Maakah's calm gave way to terror. Two grabbed Maakah's arms, and two gripped her ankles. "Release me!" She kicked and screamed against them, powerless against their strength and Talmai's authority. The two other guards led them to a hidden door behind curtains on the dais.

"Gag her so we need not hear her squawking." Talmai shook his head, as if disgusted, then returned his attention to me. "Somehow, in less than two months, your golden tongue ruined nearly two decades of etiquette training and all she knew about royal blood. Her ima has little time before the wedding to restore her to the obedient princess we raised."

Talmai grasped my hair, pulling my head up to meet his concerns. "But your smooth talk won't trick me, *King* David. In two days, we'll arrive in Mahanaim to celebrate my daughter's wedding to Ish-Bosheth. General Abner has planned the entertainment for the weeklong wedding feast to include the slow, painful deaths of your Mighty Men. We'll save your death until the end, of course, so you can watch your men die. Perhaps your first wife Michal will also be there to witness the justice she deserves as well." He used my shoulder to push himself to his feet and then pronounced, "But first, you and your men will spend a very dark night in my prison. We leave at first light for Mahanaim." He flicked his wrist toward Azam. "Take them away."

Azam jerked me to my feet. I met Amasai's intense gaze. He mouthed a silent plea. *Fight?*

I leveled my gaze and shook my head while being led past the single column of my warriors. *Yahweh, if you want us to fight differently, as Maakah's dream foretold, remind my men of my command and give us clear direction when the time comes to fight.*

Azam stopped me before we exited the courtroom. While using hemp rope to bind my wrists behind me, he said, "You disappoint me, Hebrew. I've heard tales of your valor and the Mighty Men's great victories. You're nothing but mewling lambs."

I would allow him to believe it until Yahweh's intentions became clearer.

TWENTY-NINE

MAAKAH

I cry out to God Most High, to God who fulfills his purpose for me. He will send from heaven and save me; he will put to shame him who tramples on me. God will send out his steadfast love and his faithfulness!

Psalm 57:2–3 ESV

Traversing the residence halls of a palace I once called home, I felt more and more nauseous as we drew nearer my chamber and Ima's. Why hadn't she been at Abba's side to greet me? Had he asked her to stay away, or was she so disgusted with all she'd heard of her only child that she refused to even look at me? What had Abba meant when he said, *"We'll see who becomes Geshur's heir"*?

Despair warred with humiliation, escaping in wild fits of temper against men twice my size. The more I struggled, the deeper their fingers dug into my flesh.

When my strength was spent, the shorter man at my right arm leaned close and whispered, "Keep fighting, Princess. When King Talmai removes his protection, I'll be the first to taste your royal lips."

I spit in his face, and he lifted his hand to strike me. The other guard shoved his partner away. "I shouldn't have tolerated your

Noble

disrespect, and I most certainly won't allow you to strike the heir of Geshur's throne."

"Her cheek is still red from the king's hand," the brute grumbled. "No one would know."

"We know." Ima's chamber guards emerged from the harem hallway. The larger man glared at my escorts. "Unless you'd like to join the brotherhood of eunuchs, neither of you are allowed to escort Princess Maakah any farther."

The mouthy escort immediately backed away, but the guard on my left said, "Forgive me, Majesty, for being silent too long." He extended his hand toward Ima's guards. "We leave you in capable hands."

"I accept your apology," I said, "and I hope the next time you witness wrongdoing, you'll have more courage to immediately stand against it." The man looked as if I were the one who slapped him.

I joined Ima's guards and started toward the harem hallway. One of them spoke quietly for only me to hear. "It appears Geshur's princess returned to us with more mettle."

"Am I disqualified for increased mettle if I feel like bursting into tears?"

He glanced at me with almost a smile. "I believe the mettle increases even more, Princess, when tears are held in check."

I proceeded toward Ima's door, the first on the right, but the guard stopped me. "I'm sorry, but the queen is otherwise engaged. She's commanded that we escort you to your chamber."

Rejection. Disapproval. What other unspoken reasons made Ima refuse to see her wayward daughter? "Otherwise engaged?" I scoffed. "How much does Ima know about what was declared in the throne room?"

"Nothing, Princess. Your Ima has been otherwise en—"

"Otherwise engaged." I finished the hurtful words. "It seems like a very broad description for a queen's activities."

"Indeed, Princess." He strode, eyes forward, as I increased the

340

pace toward my chamber—the last door on the left—where my familiar guards waited.

I'd trusted Haman and Zippor all my life but had never called them by name. Zulat said it wasn't regal. As we approached, their gaze remained fixed on some empty spot on the wall across from my door. "Welcome home, Princess," they said in unison. A note of happiness raised the tenor of their voices and warmed my heart.

I stopped in front of them, dismissed Ima's guards, and laid a hand on each of their large forearms. Startled, both men looked down at me, making eye contact for one of the first times I could remember. "Thank you, Haman, and you, too, Zippor. Yours has been the warmest welcome I've received. Thank you for your faithful protection all my life."

Haman, the older of the two, gave me a tentative smile. "It has been our greatest privilege." Both men bowed and opened my double doors as they straightened.

Hurrying across the threshold before tears betrayed my reunion, I stood two steps inside the doorway and scanned the chamber that had been my home only a few months before. The brightly colored carpet where Zulat and I sat for long hours on cold winter days wasn't as elegant as I remembered it. Taking a few more steps inside, I trailed one finger across the arm of my crimson couch. When had it become so worn and faded? A bronze bell sat on a tile-topped table with some of my childhood drawings.

When the door closed behind me, I jumped, feeling closed in. Memories assailed me of Zulat's lessons about foreign nations, Geshur's history, and life outside our high walls. She and my parents were my whole world not so long ago. I'd believed everything they told me as absolute truth. What a fool I'd been to remain in their prison so long.

"You're very pensive, my girl."

I gasped at the sound of Ima's voice and searched farther into

Noble

the chamber. When I reached the linen curtain that separated my bedchamber from the living space, I found her relaxing on my canopy-covered bed.

"Ima!" I ran into her arms, immediately sobbing as all the turmoil inside rushed out like a flooding wadi.

"Shhh." She stroked my hair as I burrowed into her comfort. "There's someone else here who wants to say hello."

I sat back on the bed and saw movement in the opposite corner. Eliphelet, almost unrecognizable from cuts and bruises, sat on a small settee. I scooted off the bed and rushed to my cousin. "What have they done to you?"

He lifted his left hand, three fingers visibly crooked, bruised, and swollen. "They'll do the same to David and the Mighty—and you, Maakah—if you refuse to marry Ish-Bosheth." He leaned forward, wincing in pain, and addressed Ima. "Was that convincing enough to keep my ima alive in Gath, Doda Raziah?"

Following his gaze, I saw Ima's eyes narrowed. "You did very well until your last question, nephew." She turned her focus on me. "Your abba and I knew you'd need a little convincing to marry the donkey farmer's fourth-born son."

How had I ever believed my parents to be good people? *When you know only darkness, you avoid Light.* The answer came as silent understanding, wisdom without my own reasoning.

"You're home now." Ima's gentle words felt like a viper approaching, smooth yet deadly. "You're safe, Prin. Your abba will take care of everything."

"No, Ima," I said, helping Eliphelet stand. He needed to get away from my parents as quickly as he could. Leading him toward my door, his arm came around my shoulder, and I heard every gasp and wince of this brave Mighty Man.

"What are you doing?" Ima asked, following our every step. "We're not finished talking, Maakah."

"I'm sending Eliphelet to Abba's personal physician," I said while opening my door. "Haman, take my cousin to Abba's healer and tell the man Princess Maakah wants a report on his injuries and prognosis before the moon reaches its zenith. You may then bring my cousin back to my chamber until Abba is ready to see us in his throne room tomorrow at dawn."

Ima huffed loud enough to snag her guards' attention at the end of the hall. "How dare you—"

"Thank you, Haman." Cutting off her poisoned words, I hurried Eliphelet out the door. Quickly closing it, I faced the angry stranger. "I *dare* make my own decisions, Ima, because I'm a grown woman who has been deceived most of my life by people who were supposed to love and protect me." When she drew breath to rail, I added, "Zulat is dead."

Her crimson fury drained, leaving only shock and sadness. "How?" she breathed out.

"Execution because of this." I bore my naked shoulder with its scar. "Last week she and a woman from David's camp conspired to kill me and almost succeeded."

"You're lying." She spat the words and turned her back on me.

"Should I assume by your reaction that you consider it *my* fault that your precious Zulat tried to kill me?"

She whirled and pointed to my pink scar. "It's impossible for such a large wound to heal in a week."

"That would be true if I still worshiped any of the Aramean gods."

We locked eyes in wordless labor until hers brightened. "If you wield the power of Ish-Bosheth's Hebrew god, your value as his queen has increased."

I let out a shuddered sigh. "Hear me, Ima. No one but Yahweh wields His power, and I refuse to be bought and sold as a commodity in Abba's political trade. I'm in love with David ben Jesse and will soon become his third wife."

Noble

"You will not marry a warlord!"

"True. I will marry Judah's new king and enjoy more love and freedom while worshiping Yahweh as part of David's family than ever before as the princess of Geshur."

Her features turned to granite. "You'll marry Ish-Bosheth, or many people will die because of you, Maakah bat Talmai."

"I will marry David ben Jesse, the current King of Judah and rightful King of Israel, and many people will *live* because Yahweh has promised it."

Ima scoffed and marched toward the door, tossing her robe's flowing train behind her. She flung the door open, startling Zippor, and left him staring at the wake of her flowing robe.

"It's all right." I patted Zippor's shoulder. "She's upset that I only serve Yahweh. He's the one true God, the Creator of all things, and His power is greater than King Talmai's and Queen Raziah's."

Both Zippor's eyebrows rose, but he offered no opinion. He never had. So I returned to my now-empty chamber for a much-needed rest. All that mettle Ima's guard admired suddenly turned to water, and I melted onto my faded rug. My left cheek still tingled from Abba's slap, so I pressed it against the soft carpet, closed my eyes, and called on the only One who knew my heart without speaking a word.

Yahweh, I understand now why You would command Your people to destroy their enemies completely.

The memory of Abba's glee when he described the planned executions at my proposed wedding sickened me. How could he renegotiate a marriage for me with Ish-Bosheth after all the terrible things he knew about Saul's surviving son? The gleam in Abba's eyes while commanding the throne room—that insatiable thirst for power and willingness to betray—broke my heart. He had bartered away his only daughter, and my mother willingly participated in the negotiations. For all I knew, the loving Ima who read stories of

344

Geshur's gods to me each night before I slept was as much a stranger as the Asherah priestesses who taught me of their so-called *sacred* worship. Today, I'd seen the underbelly of both of Geshur's regents.

Which was the mastermind behind the cruelty? Or were both of my parents equally wicked? Was it Queen Raziah who threatened Eliphelet's ima—her own sister—to get information? What if Ima had been the instigator of it all?

Hadn't such manipulation been the crux of my lifelong training? Yet I realized now that all the posturing and deception wasn't for Geshur's benefit, but rather to increase the reach of my parents' personal power and wealth. Abba cared little about the people of our southern kingdom, but he was deeply concerned about the lost tribute payments. His insistence that I marry Israel's new vassal king made perfect sense. If Ish-Bosheth was as inept as Joab and David reported, Abba would use me to gain control of Israel's throne and demand tribute from a nation whose capital was only a day's march from Geshur. I would become Ish-Bosheth's regal queen but never a noble wife like Ahinoam and Abigail.

I curled on my side and closed my eyes in the gathering darkness. Sleep would be slow to come, but I couldn't bear sleeping on a wool-stuffed mattress with fine linen sheets when David and his Mighty wallowed in the filth of Geshur's prison. *Yahweh, show them Your nearness.*

THIRTY

DAVID

My heart, O God, is steadfast, my heart is steadfast; I will sing and make music. Awake, my soul! Awake, harp and lyre! I will awaken the dawn.

Psalm 57:7-8

I'd never been in prison before. The darkness was almost worse than the stench and scurry of rodents. An occasional moan came from a neighboring cell, as startling as a bolt of lightning in the dead of night. *The dead of night.* I now understood that phrase. Total darkness felt like death. I couldn't even see my hand in front of my face.

"David?" Asahel's whisper was more like a shout in the void of sound.

"Hmm?"

"How do you want us to respond tomorrow when Talmai passes judgment, and his guards try to drive us like sheep to Mahanaim?" My youngest nephew was as direct as his older brother Joab, but much kinder. What he really wanted to know was, *Will I ever see my wife and son again?*

The silence was deafening, and fear began its slow wriggling up my spine. *Yahweh, what do we do without weapons against a trained army of soldiers?* As I gathered courage to answer, a door creaked on squeaky leather hinges. Pressed against the wooden door by thirty men squeezed into a room the size of my curtained bedchamber, I peeked through a small opening at the top of the low door.

"What is it?" The repeated question spread through the cell.

Before I could answer, the torchlight I'd seen bobbing down the narrow hallway shone through our door's opening. We shaded our eyes from the harsh light, gasping in a quick breath through clenched teeth.

"Sorry," a gruff voice said, then moved the light aside.

"Don't take it away!" Panic nearly overtook me.

"I'm placing it in a harness by your cell." His face appeared at the small, square opening. He glanced right and left, then pulled his sackcloth hood lower.

I'd never seen him before. "Who are you, and why would you offer us light?"

"I bring a message from Princess Maakah," he whispered. "I don't understand it, but she says, 'When you're guided by light, He calls you to think differently. Even fight differently.'" The man turned to go.

"Wait!"

He faced me again but didn't speak.

"Why are you helping Princess Maakah?"

Stepping closer to the tiny window, he whispered, "She's changed. Whatever you taught her inspired her to finally stand strong against Queen Raziah. Our little princess has become a warrior. She gave you and your god credit. I must return to her before I'm missed."

Return to her. He must be her chamber guard. I watched him disappear into the darkness and felt the warmth of Yahweh's anointing. When I turned toward my Mighty, sweat-drenched hair hung in stringy clumps around their expectant faces.

Noble

"Do we get to fight now?" Amasai asked like a boy hoping to play among the sheep.

After a slow nod, I controlled my growing fury through clenched teeth. "But we allow Yahweh to begin the battle."

Amasai's booming laughter filled the cell, and the next sound was his resonant voice singing the chorus Yahweh gave me after we'd escaped King Saul from the Ein Gedi cave. "Awake, my soul! Awaken the dawn. I will praise you, my God, among the nations and sing of you among my own people. For great is your love, reaching to the heavens; your faithfulness reaches to the skies."

Every Mighty Man sang along—even Uriah—lifting their voices to the one true God. Other prisoners joined the singing, learning the repeated Hebrew verses. We sang loud and long. Until our throats were dry and croaking. Until the words strengthened every mind, body, and soul.

When Azam and his men arrived at dawn, the joy in Talmai's dungeon drowned out their angry commands. Finally, they banged the handles of their swords against cell doors, threatening harm to those who continued singing. Men imprisoned too long immediately quieted. I suspected Azam had proven to be a man who kept his word.

"Who brought this torch to the dungeon?" Azam's anger deepened the silence. I peered out the small window and found him marching up and down the ranks of his soldiers, inspecting each man's somber features. "Bah! We don't have time for this." He motioned for someone to unlock our door.

I signaled my men to fall into two lines behind me. We would meet our enemy with the utmost respect—until Yahweh revealed how to end them.

Azam stood in the open doorway, narrowed his eyes at me, and sneered. "We'll enjoy killing every one of you." He strode away. "Follow me, Mighty King David." His laughter echoed in the hallway.

I hurried to catch up and whispered for only him to hear, "We

348

don't wish to kill you, Captain, so I certainly hope your king amends his plan."

The man looked down with a wry smile. "You have assaulted the king's only daughter, Hebrew. Nothing could make him hate you more."

"You lie," I said, heartbeat racing. Surely Maakah hadn't accused me falsely—as Michal had—to save herself.

"The princess need not testify to a truth so evident. Why else would she allow Zulat to be executed and turn her back on her gods if not for a lover who stole her heart and twisted her mind?"

I felt battle fury's first surge. Rolling my shoulders, tilting my head right and left, I was more than ready for the coming fight. *Make the Mighty and me fit for battle, LORD, and please protect Maakah.* I'd agreed to marry her because I felt Yahweh would use her knowledge of royalty to strengthen my reign, but perhaps His reasons for bringing her into our family were more similar to Abigail's. Maakah needed my protection as surely as a widow with no one to care for her.

I called in Hebrew over my shoulder to the Mighty, "Protect Princess Maakah."

"Yes! King! David!" They answered in our tongue.

Azam laughed. "Shout all you want while we're still in the prison, but once we reach level ground . . ." He halted me on the stone steps. "You will speak only when King Talmai addresses you. Understood, Hebrew?"

I answered with a nod and a thin-lipped smile, eyes penetrating past the amusement on his features. His smile died. He checked the hemp binding on my hands, still secured behind my back. "Keep marching." He shoved my shoulder, and I kept climbing.

We were paraded through the public entrance and into Talmai's throne room. Barely after dawn, the king's royal guards were awaiting our arrival outside the doors.

Yahweh, make me strong for whatever awaits beyond those doors.

THIRTY-ONE

MAAKAH

For you have delivered me from death and my feet from stumbling, that I may walk before God in the light of life.

Psalm 56:13

Haman and Zippor escorted Eliphelet and me through the palace hallways to the rear entrance of the royal dais. Abba waited at the closed door with six royal guards. I turned to my lifelong protecters and whispered to Haman, "Thank you for delivering the light to David and his men last night." To Zippor, I said, "And thank you for allowing me to leave my chamber door open overnight so you could testify that there was nothing untoward between Eliphelet and me." Zippor's cheeks flushed as they had when I suggested the slight amendment to Yahweh's modesty law that I'd learned from David when he'd come to my tent alone.

Though I wanted to kiss both guards on the cheek, I knew better. Remembering the two men who lost their lives by allowing me into Abba's court against his wishes, I dared not show the least impropriety toward my faithful chamber guards. Instead, I nodded a cool dismissal, and both men marched away. My heart broke that I couldn't free them when Yahweh freed us.

"Utter nonsense," Abba grumped. "Must you delay the whole day with your foolish sentimentality, Maakah?" He motioned to one of his guards, who opened the door behind the purple curtains.

"Where is Ima this morning?" I asked, though I was somewhat relieved by her absence.

"She's often queasy in the mornings, so I allow her to rest in her chamber until midday."

Did he allow it or command it? I followed him without further comment, and we took our places on the respective thrones—Abba on his padded, ornately carved golden one, and me on Ima's rather plain but comfortably cushioned seat.

"Before Azam escorts the prisoners into our presence, daughter, are you perfectly clear about the purpose for this morning's hearing?"

Suddenly aware that Nakia wasn't at Abba's side, bearing his gloating smile, I asked, "Have you sent Nakia on another traitorous mission?"

Faint lines appeared at the corners of his eyes, betraying his amusement. "Nakia fulfilled his purpose. Answer my question, Maakah."

I swallowed the implication of his words. *Nakia is dead.* What was the purpose of this morning's hearing? Would Abba execute me if I outlived my purpose? I glanced over my shoulder at Eliphelet, who was now surrounded by Abba's six guards, and then back at Geshur's heartless king. "The purpose of this hearing is to display Yahweh's power to you so you'll agree to release Eliphelet and happily agree to make me King David's bride."

He laughed and slapped the arm of his throne. "I've raised a stubborn one! Bring in the Hebrews," he said, motioning to his guards.

David's men marched in with their hands bound behind their backs and their heads held high. The courtroom filled with Geshurite guards who surrounded the thirty Mighty—hundreds of Abba's trained soldiers to manage David's legendary warriors.

Noble

Abba leaned over to whisper what he vowed would be my last chance to save my cousin and Doda Razin. "All the men before you will die during your wedding feast, Maakah. You can't save them, but you can save Eliphelet and his ima. After your confrontation with your ima last night, she already believes you to be a heartless, spoiled child who has forgotten everything we've taught you."

"Stop it." I glared into his manipulation and broke its chains. "I care only about the opinions of people I respect. You and ima no longer qualify."

Abba's snide grin never faltered. "Is that so? Well then, perhaps you no longer qualify as heir to Geshur's throne." He motioned to Azam, who dashed up the dais steps and trapped my arms at my sides. Though fighting was instinctive, I felt sudden peace. Submitting to Yahweh's overwhelming calm stripped away my current panic and freed me from the melancholy that had tortured me since our arrival. I leaned into Azam's strength, allowing him to support my weight as we descended the steps. Indescribable relief came when he shoved me into David's side.

I clung to him, and he whispered, "Did they harm you?"

"Get her away from him!" Abba groused. When I looked up, his cheeks were quaking, his lips trembling with barely controlled fury. "Maakah, you will marry Prince Ish-Bosheth tomorrow. You've changed nothing by your rebellious indignation. In fact, you've made things worse for those whose lives depended on you to sacrifice your selfish desires. You've forgotten the one rule we live by: Royal blood—"

"Means kingdom first—always," I recited with him. "I haven't forgotten, Abba. I've simply learned from David and his wives that putting kingdom first means putting *people* first, not the best interest of the royal family."

"May Mot and his shedim eat your liver." He spit on the dais and then motioned to the guards around Eliphelet. "Finish him."

352

"No!" David and I shouted.

I rushed toward the dais. "Take me instead."

"Absolutely not." David lunged toward me, but a wall of guards separated us.

I looked into his panic to prove my indescribable peace. Still, he shook his head, refusing to allow it. Yet he was helpless to stop me.

Returning my attention to Abba, I challenged, "Go ahead, Abba. Make an example of your rebellious daughter. Show that *you're* willing to put kingdom first by killing your firstborn." I couldn't believe I was saying it, but I was just so certain of his true motives. "If the real reason for my marriage to Ish-Bosheth is enduring peace with Israel and unfettered trade with Egypt through Israel's merchant roads, then break the betrothal contract with Saul's son. You know Ish-Bosheth is an imbecile. How long before Geshur must defend his nation or abandon their new capital to the Ammonites and Moabites that surround them? Why not join your daughter in a union with King David of Judah who will most certainly sit on Israel's throne within a few months—or, at most, a few years?"

I ventured closer to the dais, and not a single guard moved to stop me. "Or is your motivation for my betrothal to Ish-Bosheth more sinister? Perhaps you'll make Israel's new king your vassal, charge him exorbitant tribute payments—like the taxes you charged our southern villages and are now lost to you because David ben Jesse destroyed our people. Our southern kingdom repeatedly sent requests for grain, livestock, or a reduction in those tribute payments, but not once did you respond. It was you who made them into raiders and thieves in order to survive."

The courtroom was as quiet as a tomb. Abba wasn't smiling while he glared at the girl who once thought him noble.

"Talmai, please!" Ima's cry drew all attention to the balcony.

"Abishai, wait!" I shrieked. Though my parents had proven

Noble

despicable, I couldn't bear to watch them die. "David, please don't let your nephew kill her." When had the Three arrived in Geshur?

But David wasn't focused on me. Or Ima. His bonds had somehow been loosed, and his gaze was fixed on Geshur's king. "What was it you were saying, Talmai? Something about kingdom first—*always*?"

THIRTY-TWO

DAVID

[Abner] made [Ish-Bosheth] king over Gilead, Ashuri and Jezreel, and also over Ephraim, Benjamin and all Israel.

2 Samuel 2:9

Zerry's middle son, captain of my assassin spy force, stood at the balcony railing while Eleazar and Shammah held the valuable prisoner at the edge of their blades. Eleazar pressed his dagger against the queen's pregnant belly, and Shammah's blade was poised at her throat. I hadn't realized the Three followed us to Geshur, but such was the level of their skill. These men were masters of stealth and deft executioners.

"Don't harm my wife and child," Talmai seethed. "I'll do whatever you say."

"First, I'd like Azam and one other guard to remove my men's bindings while the rest of your men leave the throne room." I pointed to Eliphelet. "Of course, I'd like your wife's nephew to be freed and remain on the dais at your side—after he takes your weapons from you and returns our weapons to us."

Talmai hesitated, and the queen called down curses on her husband.

Noble

"All right, all right." Talmai launched from his throne, pointing at Azam. "Do as he says. Remove the bonds, return their weapons. Only you and one other stay in the throne room."

Maakah ran to my side and lifted on her tiptoes to whisper, "Shammah is holding the blade too tight. Ima's neck is bleeding."

My Mighty surrounded us, hiding us from her abba's prying eyes, so I leaned down and pressed my lips against her ear. "Just as you needed to make your own difficult decisions, my love, so must your parents make decisions in these moments that will affect their lives and Geshur's future. Can you trust the God who has brought us this far?" I stepped back to meet her gaze and saw the war raging behind her eyes.

Though misty, her gray-blue eyes sparked with confidence as she nodded.

I brushed her cheek, and she trapped my hand there, kissing my palm before releasing it. She then shouldered her way through my Mighty to face her abba again. I followed, not sure what my feisty princess would say or do next.

"Abba, please don't let them hurt Ima. David and his men aren't like the Amalekites, or even some of our own guards. I've lived among them, and they don't relish the kill. They only kill when Yahweh commands or when forced into a battle for their lives—or for the lives of those they love." She pointed to the balcony. "You can stop this nonsense right now, Abba. Simply let Eliphelet and me return to Hebron with David and his men. That's all we ask."

King Talmai no longer looked with pity on his daughter. The fiery red patches on his neck said he'd added her to his list of enemies, and she'd receive no mercy if captured again. "Listen to me carefully, Maakah. You and these men will never leave my city alive. Your lover has only thirty men. I have hundreds." He turned his attention to me. "We may be outnumbered in this courtroom, but the moment you step outside these walls, everyone with you will die."

356

"Perhaps," I said, no games this time. "But your wife and child will be dead now if I command it."

Talmai turned his rage on Abishai above us. "Release my wife immediately, or I'll have you flayed alive from your head to your toes!"

Abishai shrugged and then pointed his dagger at me. "You'll need to negotiate with King David. The Three take orders only from Yahweh and His anointed."

"If I order Shammah to remove the dagger from your wife's neck," I said to Talmai, "will you answer your daughter's question?"

"What question?" he said. "Yes, yes. Just ask me again."

I coaxed my bride. "Ask him again about his motivation for the treaty with Ish-Bosheth. You're a wise negotiator."

Her eyebrows jumped with her surprise, and I pointed at the lovely flaw. "Stop that," she said, swatting me. "I never should have told you to remain passive when I've never been very good at it." Turning to her abba, she said, "Did you arrange for me to marry Ish-Bosheth so you and General Abner could share the tribute Ish-Bosheth would pay? Or was the marriage strictly to ensure Geshur could freely travel through Israel's trade routes to Egypt?"

"You're a child trying to fathom the politics of nations." He waved off her question. "How could you understand the decisions of kings?"

Maakah gasped. "You had no intention for me to ever rule Geshur." The truth settled into her heart and reaped the rancid fruit of her abba's callous sneer.

"Talmai!" the queen shrieked again.

The king lunged toward the steps, but Eliphelet caught his arm and twisted from behind, halting Talmai where he stood. Azam raced toward the dais, but five of my Mighty subdued the big guard while five more formed a wall between the Geshurite captain and Maakah.

"My patience has worn thin." I turned to Abishai and lifted my hand to give the order.

"We'll answer!" Talmai looked up at his wife, pleading. "Raziah, tell them. Tell them."

The queen turned to Shammah, blood now dripping down her neck. "Lower your gods-forsaken blade so I can speak, you half-witted spawn of shedim."

Shammah looked at Abishai, who turned to me. I brushed Maakah's cheek. "I'm grateful you didn't pick up your ima's vocabulary."

She couldn't take her gaze off her ima. "I never saw her wickedness until last night."

How adept must the royal couple have been to deceive their only child for over twenty years. "Leave the blade where it is," I said to Shammah, "until the queen answers Maakah's question."

"The answer is both," Raziah said without hesitation. "We'll share Israel's tribute with Abner and gain clear access to Egypt through Israel's trade routes."

I waved my hand, giving permission for my men to lower their daggers. "You see, Talmai, that wasn't so difficult. I have only one more thing to say before I leave Geshur with your daughter, Eliphelet, and my Mighty Men."

"Never," he seethed.

In truth, even with our weapons returned, I had no idea how Yahweh would deliver us from this throne room with hundreds of trained warriors waiting in the hall to kill us. By now, they'd likely called for their Anakites—giants like Goliath—to help when we made our escape.

Our best chance was intimidation. "Not if, but *when* Judah defeats Abner's traitorous claim to Israel's throne, and I become the rightful king of Yahweh's chosen people, I'll never pay tribute to you or any other foreign king. Israel will be a free nation."

His wry smile reappeared. "Achish will be interested to hear that. As far as he's concerned, whatever nation you rule, he'll forever deserve at least half of your taxes for as long as you live—a penance for your betrayal of his hospitality." He flicked his wrist. "I'd never make a treaty with you, *King* David. I struck a contract with General Abner—a man I can trust."

Pounding on the throne room doors captured everyone's attention. I looked at Azam, who seemed genuinely surprised. "You alone can go to one door, and my Mighty will line up directly behind you. If anyone tries to push through the doorway, I assure you every single one of them will die."

"This isn't an ambush," he said, hurrying toward the double doors. "My men would never take a chance with the king's and queen's lives."

Azam reached for the door, and Amasai warned, "Slowly!" The Geshurite captain obeyed and held the door only wide enough to press his face through the opening and listen to the spokesman. Within moments, he drew back, and shouted, "Abner and hundreds of Israelite soldiers are marching toward Geshur!"

"How close?" Talmai asked.

Azam reached through the open door and pulled a dust-covered scout into the room. He said, "They've crossed the Yarmuk River, my king." Azam shoved him back into the hall and waited on Talmai's orders.

I calmly turned to the Geshurite king who had just been betrayed by a general he'd touted as trustworthy. "It appears General Abner intends to capture your daughter and the prisoners you promised as her dowry rather than waiting patiently, as he promised, in Mahanaim."

"We trust no one," the queen said from her perch. "But since we now have little choice, we should accept the man Maakah believes has earned the favor of his god. Perhaps we should reconsider King David as Maakah's husband and renegotiate the trade routes when he sits on Israel's throne."

"David, no." Maakah's fury strained her tone. "My parents proved they can't be trusted. Never enter into a covenant with them."

I pulled her into my arms and whispered against her curls. "For now, we agree to a *future* deal that helps us escape the present danger. If Abner lays siege to your abba's walled city, we have no way to send a plea to our Judean troops for help."

Releasing my soon-to-be bride, I inclined my head toward the queen above and the king on his dais. "We accept your promise of future negotiations and ask for your assistance for our safe escape back to Hebron. To avoid Abner's troops, we'll need a Geshurite escort to take us through the Jezreel Valley where the Israeli-Philistine conflict still rages."

"Are you mad?" Talmai scoffed. "I need every man in my army to fight for Geshur." He turned a forced smile toward Maakah. "I promise to return you and your future husband with his men safely to Hebron, but I want to hug my daughter to offer a proper farewell."

Was it another trick? I deferred to Eliphelet, who gave me an almost imperceptible nod. Releasing the king's twisted arm, Eliphelet escorted him down the three steps and remained at his side while the king faced the daughter he'd disinherited moments ago. "Remember your royal blood, daughter. You have the wisdom of a king, the beauty of a queen, and the heart of a warrior. Make Geshur proud." He lifted Maakah's hand to his lips and then let her hand fall back to her side. "We have loved you as much as royal parents are able."

Tears breached her lower lashes, falling down her cheeks. "You can only know love when you know Yahweh, Abba. So, for the sake of your next child, it will be my continuing prayer that Yahweh breaks your heart—so He can rebuild it with room for only Him." She threw her arms around his neck and hugged him like a little girl.

The king's eyes widened with surprise. For a moment, I feared he might push her away. Instead, he kissed his daughter's forehead and then commanded his captain, "Escort my daughter, her betrothed, and all his men to my stables. Eliphelet, too," he added. "Give them each a camel to ride to Hebron—the fastest dromedaries—and ten more loaded with Maakah's dowry."

He turned to me next. "Take the trade routes and ride fast. Abner hasn't been able to retrieve the camels from Saul's palace in Gibeah, so he'll never catch you."

Awed by his sudden generosity, I offered my hand in thanks. He waved it away. "I would give you half my kingdom if it meant keeping my daughter safe. Now, go!"

Forty camels were nowhere near half his kingdom; still, I was grateful for the unexpected way of escape . . . or was the offer another scheme to separate me from his daughter? I would never fully trust Geshur's king and queen.

Azam led us up the dais steps, and Queen Raziah called out, "I'll send word when your baby brother is born!"

Maakah looked over her shoulder and gave a conciliatory wave. Sheltering her closer to my side, I vowed to prove the steadiness of real love, the joy of a messy family, and the assurance of Yahweh's never-failing presence. We hurried across the platform and through the hidden back door, then ran through a maze of private hallways and finally emerged into what must have been the king's courtyard.

Azam commanded the stable boys to prepare the camels, and my Mighty helped while the Geshurite captain and I kept watch. Maakah remained at my side, leaned close, and whispered, "I'll be relieved to hear Ima's had a safe delivery, but I need never return to Geshur again. It's no longer my home."

I turned to face her. "I'm sorry, Maakah, but I know exactly how you feel. After I left Bethlehem to play my lyre for King Saul, it has never felt like home again."

"Where is home to you?" she asked.

Still keeping watch for a dust cloud rising that would signal the enemies' approach, I must have pondered too long.

Maakah turned my chin to meet the fathomless depths of her eyes. "You're my home now."

THIRTY-THREE

MAAKAH

Sons were born to David in Hebron . . . the third [was] the son of Maakah daughter of Talmai king of Geshur.

2 Samuel 3:2–3

We'd ridden hard and fast on the one-humped camels, stopping only five times in two days. Two stops were extended rest times, but only to refill waterskins, water the camels, and nap long enough to regain strength for speedier travel. Since I'd never ridden a galloping camel before, David had insisted I ride with him.

At first, I was uncomfortably stiff. Though we'd enjoyed such freedom and familiarity before arriving in Geshur, David had now witnessed the underbelly of Geshurite royalty. My parents weren't the regal leaders I'd imagined, and they were nothing like his loving family. Might Judah's king feel some regret for the betrothal promise he'd made to me?

Afraid to relax against his chest, my back took a pounding with every camel stride. David leaned forward, nudging my hair aside with his chin to whisper, "We'll marry as soon as we enter Hebron's gate, beloved. Lean back. Let me hold you." He pressed a kiss behind

363

Noble

my ear, held my waist tighter with one arm, and gripped the saddle's handle with his free hand.

I glanced behind us to see if Benaiah or Amasai—the two most devout Yahweh followers—might deem our actions improper. Both men grinned back at me and nodded kindly. No judgment. No condemnation.

David brushed his lips at the bend at my neck and whispered, "I love you."

"And I love you," I said, relaxing against his muscled chest. From that moment forward, our bodies moved together in rhythm with the camel's gallop, increasing my anticipation of our wedding night. *Yahweh, I want to please my husband in a way that honors the real and true love You've given us. Not as Asherah's priestesses trained me to manipulate.*

Our love would be an expression of the friendship Yahweh had given us, and our lives would include my two best friends. How could I be so happy in a life so different than I'd imagined?

DAVID

Asahel rode ahead of us with five other men. When they reached the crest of the last hill separating us from Hebron, Asahel reined his camel to a halt. "Yahweh, save us!"

"What?" I clucked my tongue, urging our camel to flank Asahel's right side.

Still staring at the valley below, Asahel was now shaking his head with a grin. "I suppose we can assume it's a friendly army that surrounds our new home since the city gate is open wide and no one is fighting."

Maakah stiffened in my arms. "An army?" Fear weakened her voice to sound almost childlike.

I held her a little tighter and scanned the tents, livestock, and soldiers that spread throughout the valley and around Hebron like a swarm of locusts. "Friendly indeed," I said. "If they'd come for war, the visiting warriors wouldn't allow Jehoiada and Joab to ride through their midst." The visitors waved at them as if they were all old friends, which sent a thousand questions racing through my mind.

"I count all twelve standards of Israel's tribes," Asahel whispered with reverence. "My guess, King David, is that all the tribes of Israel have come to make you their king."

"It can't be," I whispered reverently. "Abner would never allow it." My head snapped in Asahel's direction. "Perhaps these Israelites don't know Abner has already declared Ish-Bosheth Israel's king and Mahanaim their new capital."

We waited at the hilltop to meet my general and Judah's chief priest to ensure our guests didn't attempt a military advance upon my arrival. The swarm of Israelites below must have been the reason for Joab's and Jehoiada's beaming smiles. "Welcome home," Jehoiada said, halting his donkey beside my camel.

Maakah sagged against me with relief as palpable as mine. Instinctively, I kissed the top of her head and whispered, "I suppose this ruins our plan for a quiet wedding at the city gate upon our return." She didn't respond, so I feigned a disappointed sigh and added, "We might have to delay a little to prepare enough food for the extra guests."

My bride gasped and turned to hug my neck. "Thank you, my love." Her quiet squeal made my heart sing—until I glimpsed Jehoiada and Joab exchange a concerned glance.

Noble

Joab dismounted and stood beside my camel. "Our most recent census says 340,000 soldiers have gathered in Hebron's valley and surrounded the city." His brows lifted as if waiting for the number to properly shock me.

"Three hundred *thousand*?" Of all my racing questions, one seemed most urgent. "Why have they come?"

Jehoiada appeared at Joab's side. "Because they're determined to make you king over all of Israel." His smile returned, but my news would likely sober him.

"Abner has declared Ish-Bosheth as Israel's new king and established Israel's new capital city in Mahanaim." No one smiled now.

"How do you know?" Joab demanded. "Are you sure it's accurate?"

"Nakia betrayed us and helped my abba negotiate my betrothal with Ish-Bosheth," Maakah said. "Part of the negotiations was to make David and his Mighty my dowry and their executions the entertainment for the wedding feast."

Hebron's priest and my general gaped, so I continued the story of our rescue. "Instead of waiting for Talmai's troops to deliver us to Mahanaim, Abner grew impatient. He and his army descended on Geshur—in Yahweh's perfect timing—which proved Abner's duplicity. Talmai recognized that Judah's new sovereign was the best option to protect his daughter."

Jehoiada's eyes blazed with fury. "So it's Abner we must fight."

Joab slammed his fist to his heart. "Give the order, my king, and we'll be ready to march by dawn. We no longer fight with a few hundred or Hebron's few thousand." Joab turned toward the city, sweeping his hand toward the vast army below. "Hundreds of thousands have come from every tribe in Israel—even Saul's own tribe of Benjamin and tribes east of the Jordan, close to Mahanaim. They're determined to make you Israel's king."

Maakah turned in the saddle with a flinty determination in her jaw. "These soldiers have come as a gift from Yahweh. I want to marry you as soon as possible, but your throne and these soldiers' allegiance is more urgent. You must lead them while Abner faces the consequences of breaking a second betrothal with Geshur. Attack Mahanaim while Israel's troops are depleted from the Philistine war, and Ish-Bosheth commands only a few troops from Ephraim and Benjamin." She pressed her hand against my cheek, pleading. "You could take Israel's throne within the week."

Though Maakah's strategy was faultless, I felt nauseous at the thought of commanding Israelites to slaughter Israelites. *Show me plainly, LORD, how I am to honor the hundreds of thousands of Israelites who have come to pledge their allegiance.* From the height of my camel's back, I scanned the vast sea of fighting men, some who had even brought their families with them to Hebron. Children's laughter and protective imas' shouts proved they were the same as the imperfect yet loving families in my own camp. Though Yahweh gave me no audible answer—not even a whisper to reassure my heart—I knew. As surely as I'd known Maakah was to be my bride, I was certain Yahweh did not want me to divide His chosen people further with a civil war.

I held my bride's hand against my face and turned a kiss into her palm. It would be harder to refuse her plea than Joab's. She dropped her hand but kept her eyes locked on mine. "Do as Yahweh leads you," she whispered. Princess Maakah showed every sign of becoming my best advisor.

With a grateful nod, I turned toward my Mighty and spoke for only those on the hilltop to hear. "I won't—I can't—in good conscience instigate a civil war that could forever divide Yahweh's chosen people."

Joab and Jehoiada launched into a myriad of arguments to defend their opinion, but I quieted them with a lifted fist. The hilltop fell silent once more.

Noble

"I realize the military advantage of striking now, while Abner and his troops are weak and still reeling from Philistine raids. If I were advising a king, I would argue fervently for the shrewd military tactic, but I can no longer consider *only* what is militarily shrewd." I scanned my best warriors, whose expressions were a mix of confusion and comprehension.

I also glimpsed my bride's tearstained cheeks. "Because you are Yahweh's shepherd king," she said, "you must protect as well as rule. You can't prove your care for His chosen people if your first act as their king is violence." She had finished my speech for me, then swiped her tears before addressing my Mighty. "King David is more than a man after God's heart. He's also a noble king who tends the hearts of *all* Israelites."

While the Mighty roared their support, I framed my bride's face. "And I will be a husband who tends the hearts of the wives Yahweh gave me to love and protect." With a slight brush across her lips, I sat back and waited until she opened her eyes. "Shall we greet our wedding guests?" Only then did the details of such an enormous company settle like a rock in my gut. "Joab!" The high-pitched tone betrayed my panic. "How can we feed so many wedding guests?"

"No need," Joab said with a hint of satisfaction. "The soldiers' families sent them with enough food for three days."

"And some of their neighbors journeyed with them," Jehoiada added, "and brought even more food. With nearly 500,000 guests, we'll enjoy the largest wedding feast Hebron has ever seen."

Maakah's expression brightened with mischief. "With that many guests," she said to me, "surely no one would miss us if we left the feast a little early."

I laughed and drew her into my arms. Yes, Yahweh had most assuredly chosen this noble princess just for me.

368

AUTHOR'S NOTE

Noble: The Story of Maakah is different than other books I've written in that most of its characters are real people whose names are mentioned in the Bible—sometimes *only* their names with no other clues about their lives. *Noble* is unique because the character list mentions more people in Scripture than fictional characters from my imagination.

The fictional characters I've created fill in certain roles in the story that must have existed in David's time and culture. Geshur's King Talmai must have had a captain of the guard. Talmai likely had a queen who gave birth to his daughter, Princess Maakah. Eliphelet had a mother and Princess Maakah a nursemaid. And surely some of the Mighty Men were married and had children since the Bible mentions the Mighty having families (1 Samuel 27:3).

As for those mentioned *by name* in Scripture, I trust my sovereign God—who knows the number of hairs on my head and yours—to have a purpose for each name recorded. It's my joy and privilege to explore the Bible's Truth and historical data about the people history forgot.

Though I had lots of biblical names to work with, I found very little biblical or historical information about their stories or details

369

about King David's brides or their six sons' childhoods in Hebron. It's good news but challenging. With less Truth and facts to shape my book, I form fictional characters with the overarching Truths found in God's Word. Here's how:

1. I use supplemental Scriptures to connect concepts and family trees while forming characters' personalities and experiences.

2. I search Jewish literature, both ancient writings and modern websites, to discover what legends and traditions have been passed down from God's chosen people (these I consider helpful but not absolute Truth as is God-breathed Scripture).

   - *Ancient literature like the Talmud, Midrash, Herodotus's and Josephus's writings, and Louis Ginzberg's The Legends of the Jews*
   - *Modern resources like AlephBeta.org, BiblePlaces.com, Chabad.org, The Jewish Encyclopedia, and other reliable online Jewish sources*

By using biblical Truth as a foundation, historical facts as building blocks, and creative fiction as mortar to hold everything together, I try to create a story in which my readers feel like they're living in a cozy home *with* the very real people in the Bible. I purposely choose unknown people in Scripture who may have once been strangers to my readers but whom they can call friends after reading my books. So let's get to know some of the *Noble* characters . . .

Getting to Know Maakah

The name Maakah (sometimes spelled Maacah, Maacath, and Maachach) is mentioned thirty times in the NIV. Only twice does the name refer to Princess Maakah, the wife of King David and daughter of King Talmai.

Maakah is first mentioned as a location east of the Jordan River in "the territory of Og, king of Bashan, one of the last of the Rephaites, who reigned in Ashtaroth and Edrei" (Joshua 12:4). Remember the Rephaites? They were giants, kin to the Nephilim: half human, half fallen angels (Genesis 6:1–4). Called Nephilim before the flood, they also appeared after the flood by other names: Anakites, Rephaites, and Emites (Deuteronomy 2:10–11). Why do we care?

Enter the Philistine, King Achish, *the Maacathite* (1 Samuel 27:2; 1 Kings 2:39). Goliath, the "giant" David killed in his first battle, was from Achish's city of Gath (1 Samuel 17:4, 23). Those details we find in God's Word and historical data.

Where would King Achish find a giant to join his Philistine troops? We can answer this question only with a bit of fiction mortar based on a *logical* supposition from biblical Truth: Perhaps Goliath followed Achish from his hometown—Maacah, which is why Achish is called a "Maacathite"—where the Bible says descendants of Rephaites still lived.

Guess who else is a Maacathite? God's Truth says, in 1 Samuel 23:34, that Eliphelet, son of Ahasbai the Maacathite, was listed among David's Mighty Men. He first appeared in *Brave: The Story of Ahinoam* (Book #1 in the KING DAVID'S BRIDES series), but his connection to Princess Maakah (fiction mortar) comes to light in *Noble*.

Speaking of fiction, I found no record in historical documents or in the Bible of King Talmai's queen. Since their daughter was named Maakah, I gave Queen Raziah a sister, a Maacathite heritage, and made King Achish her brother to heighten the tension of the story. Zulat was also fictional, but every princess needs an evil maid because in every mystery . . . the butler did it, right?

Getting to Know Hebron

While writing my novels, I need to see the scenes playing like a movie in my mind. I tend to write whatever the people are doing and saying in their homes (or tents) and describe the landscape around them, the clothes they're wearing, and so on. If I can't see the movie, I can't write the scene.

So when 2 Samuel 2:2–3 said David went to Hebron with his wives and his men "and settled the men's families in Hebron and its towns," I could no longer see the movie. Hebron is one town. One. So what *towns*? If you check out the map in the front matter of *Noble*, you'll notice a pull-out labeled "Hebron colony." This label is my term, not found in the Bible, and in modern terms, the Hebron Colony might have been considered Hebron's "suburbs" and were ascribed to the Tribe of Judah when Joshua assigned portions of the Promised Land to all twelve of Israel's tribes:

> The allotment for the tribe of Judah, according to its clans, extended down to the territory of Edom, to the Desert of Zin in the extreme south . . . In the hill country: Arab, Dumah, Eshan, Janim, Beth Tappuah, Aphekah, Humtah, Kiriath Arba (that is, **Hebron**) and Zior—**nine towns and their villages**."
>
> Joshua 15:1, 48, 52–54 (emphasis added)

My picture-driven mind played the movie again, and these nine villages became "burbs" where David's men and their families found rest.

Getting to Know Hebron's Priests

Hebron priests and their warrior persona were another fictional concept reached through reasoning. Were Hebron's priests considered "warrior-priests?" Dunno. Joshua 21:13 says Hebron was Judah's tribal city of refuge. In the hundreds of years since the city had welcomed fugitives into their city, wouldn't it seem logical that their priesthood had developed into skilled protectors and discerning judges?

What about Jehoiada and his son Benaiah? Was Jehoiada really the head honcho in Hebron and in the tribe of Judah? Would his son have been privileged enough to be sent on such an important mission at such a young age? Later in David's reign—after he and his army overtook the Jebusites' city of Salem (later renamed *Jerusalem*)—the Bible describes in greater detail the Truth about Jehoiada and Benaiah:

> The third commander, for the third month, was Benaiah, the son of Jehoiada the chief priest; in his division were 24,000. This is the Benaiah who was a mighty man of the thirty and in command of the thirty; Ammizabad his son was in charge of his division.
>
> 1 Chronicles 27:5–6

Jehoiada is called a "chief" priest—not like Abiathar who was the only "high priest" remaining who had ministered in the actual Tabernacle built and used in the wilderness under Moses' leadership. King Saul killed all the priests of Nob (1 Samuel 22:19–20), Abiathar's whole family. Jehoiada was also a direct descendant of Aaron, from the line of Zadok, and at some time during David's reign was deemed "leader of the family of Aaron" (1 Chronicles 12:27). Since I found no historical record to clearly define how Abiathar and Jehoiada might have worked together in the early days of David's reign, I used research about designated roles later in David's rule to fill in those details.

What Comes Next?

In Book #3 of the KING DAVID'S BRIDES series, *Loyal: The Story of Haggith*, Jehoiada's pious daughter becomes the central story when she falls for Hakkoz, a young Levite who follows Yahweh's Laws as devoutly as she does.

Since the Truth of Scripture dictates how I shape the fiction, I'll tell you now that 2 Samuel 3:4 names Haggith as the mother of David's fourth-born son. In *Loyal*, I create a historically plausible and biblically accurate novel that imagines how the daughter of Hebron's chief priest (fiction) becomes David's wife (Truth). Want a sneak peek? Keep reading for a glimpse of who Haggith is and what her life might have been like before she became King David's bride.

If you'd like to follow the story's progress, become one of my "newsies" and receive monthly updates along with exclusive content and giveaways. Subscribe at: https://mesuandrews.com/#newsletter.

Happy reading, y'all!

DISCUSSION QUESTIONS

1. Early in the story, a character from the previous book in the KING DAVID'S BRIDES series, Eglah, steps into the picture. Eglah has suffered at the hands of her Amalekite slave owner since we saw her last, yet she reenergizes the faith of all the women present with her undying faith in Yahweh, even after losing her mother and becoming a captive. Name a time when Yahweh sent just the right person into your circumstances to encourage you.

2. David is described in the Bible as "a man after God's heart" (1 Samuel 13:14; Acts 13:22). But he was human and continued to make mistakes (sin), even as he was certain of God's guidance in his life. Do you think it's possible to walk closely with God and still make misguided decisions—sin?

3. Maakah was forced to swallow hard truths concerning her parents' identities. Unfortunately in life, everyone we love will at some time disappoint us. But there is One who always keeps His promises. Name one of God's promises that He has never failed to keep in your experience and describe its impact on your life.

Noble

4. David and his men are exhausted after years of destroying Canaanite villages, just as God commanded them to do. God's command was hard to digest for many Israelites—to kill so many men, women, and children. We don't always understand why God tells us to do what He does, but we are required to obey. Discuss a time when you felt God asking you to do something you did not understand, and how that situation turned out.

5. Maakah states, *"I needed time to sort out the harsh experiences of these past days so I could hold fast to the hard lessons they'd taught me."* Taking time to reflect after seasons of hardship enables lessons to be learned. What are some ways you deliberately take time to learn from mistakes and/or sins of your past?

6. While telling Maakah and Zulat about her time with Nabal, Abigail states, *"Sometimes we need only take one brave step, and Yahweh cares for the rest."* Reflect on a time when faith in God was the only thing that got you through a hard season.

7. David tells Maakah the truth about his destruction of her fellow Geshurites in the southern kingdom. Earlier, Joab had advised him to marry her and then tell her, or kill her so her father and uncle would never find out. However, David cared more about taking care of Maakah than trying to hide the truth. Have you ever had a time when in order to help someone, you had to hurt them first?

8. In a key transition point, David hears Maakah praying to her false goddess, Asherah. But instead of yelling at her, or rightfully killing her, David took the time to explain God's loving nature without demanding her allegiance. In this way, how does David foreshadow some of Jesus's earthly interactions with people?

376

9. David advises Maakah of the three things he has learned concerning the LORD: 1) That he can never anticipate the LORD's plans, 2) that His plans are always better than David could imagine, and 3) that the fulfillment of His plans always comes with a sacrifice. Would you agree or disagree? Why?

10. Toward the end of the story, David and his men surrender to King Talmai while David waits to hear from God what he should do. Discuss a time when you stayed still and waited for an answer from God before making a decision.

Read on for a sneak peek of

Loyal:
The Story of
Haggith

Book Three of the
KING DAVID'S BRIDES series

Available October 2026.

HAGGITH

*So to the descendants of Aaron the priest they gave Hebron
(a city of refuge for one accused of murder).*

Joshua 21:13

Hebron, Israel

I feared my head would explode if Ima criticized me one more time while grinding grain. *"An unwavering hand on the grinding wheel is good practice to steady your emotions."* She'd repeated that advice at least ten times since we'd started preparing flour for the wedding festival bread. Steady my emotions? I'd steadily loved Hakkoz ben Elasah for more than a year. How could my heart remain steady when Abba refused a betrothal with the only man I could ever love—without a word of explanation?

Yet he, Ima, and my brother Benaiah would celebrate King David's third marriage at dusk to a pagan, gentile princess. I stopped grinding and massaged my throbbing head. Abba had retired to his and Ima's bedchamber for an after-midday rest and to don his chief priest's wedding attire. Wasn't he—as chief priest of Hebron and spiritual leader of Judah—called to be the model of piety? Weren't we, his family, to walk in righteousness and obey every jot and tittle of Yahweh's 613 laws?

"Haggith!" Ima's shrill voice startled me and scattered kernels onto the floor. "You must keep grinding, or we won't reach our quota of bread to add to the others." She scooped the stray kernels into her hands, blew on them, and placed them back into the top wheel's center hole. Then, softening her tone, she tilted her head and coaxed, "Steady, my sweet girl. Steady, or you'll need to grind every handful of grain six times to make it fine enough for the wedding bread."

I kept my head bowed to hide my frustration. *All right, Yahweh. I repent. It's more than frustration. Help me to overcome the inferiority and shame I feel in Ima's presence.* Johanna bat Zabad was the most respected woman in Hebron and quite possibly the most stunning. Her red curls, slender curves, and strong but humble nature made her a godly example to every woman in Hebron—and an impossible standard for me to attain.

Seated only the hand-mill's width from me, Ima reached across the emotional divide to tip up my chin. Her perfectly sculpted countenance met my teetering turmoil on its sandy foundation. "I'm only trying to help," she said.

I wanted to shout, *Then why didn't you help Abba choose Hakkoz as my husband?* Instead, I smiled and pulled my chin from her grasp and tried to be steadier with my grinding technique.

Last year, she'd coaxed Abba to abandon the tradition that only brides painted their hands with henna, so he allowed both of us to decorate our hands on a gloomy winter's day. The year before that, she'd pulled me into the married women's dance at one of my friend's weddings. "Haggith's name means festive dancer," she'd shouted over the music before Abba could protest. Then she'd whispered to me, "As long as we don't break Yahweh's Law, it's all right to occasionally draw outside the lines of tradition."

Ima brushed my cheek, and I looked up, only then realizing she'd been watching me while I reminisced. "I should have been more sensitive," she said. "I know you're still grieving our answer to Hakkoz's request."

Our answer? "Are you saying you *agreed* with Abba's refusal?" My voice broke.

"Your abba and I always discuss decisions for our children's futures and would never give such a difficult answer unless we were in agreement. We even included your brother in our conversation, and he agreed. Hakkoz isn't the sort of man Yahweh would choose—"

"What does Benaiah know of love?" I choked out a mirthless laugh. "He's barely two years older and has never loved anything but his dagger."

"How do you know?" Benaiah entered the argument from his cushion in the gathering area. "I also love my sling and bow."

His low chuckle infuriated me more. "You think this is funny, Ben? This is my life!" I said through tears and then turned back to Ima. "You would confide in my brother yet refuse to tell me or Hakkoz the real reason you refused his betrothal request?"

"I did tell you," she said. "Benaiah agrees. Hakkoz is not the sort of man—"

"'Not the sort of man Yahweh would choose for me,'" I repeated the hurtful words. "Such a vague answer is at odds with what I've heard others say about Hakkoz. When he comes for his monthly leadership meetings, I've heard many describe him as a well-respected Levite who faithfully ministers to the people of Aphekah. What in that description disqualifies me—"

"You don't know everything!" Ima's raised voice jolted me.

"Then tell me." I was suddenly more steady than she was.

Bolting to her feet, she stood over me, her face crimson. "The fact that your parents forbade it is reason enough." Red curls, the color of anger, peeked out from her headscarf, and her hands balled into fists. She drew breath to say more, but in less than a moment's hesitation, she pursed her lips together and closed her eyes.

I exchanged a concerned glance with Benaiah, but neither of us spoke.

Ima inhaled a deep breath, held for several heartbeats, then released it slowly and relaxed her hands.

When she opened her grassy-green eyes, her cheeks were still a glowing pink, and that incessant steady smile had returned. "I must repent of pride, Haggith. My emotional outburst came from my own inner turmoil. I've been nervous about the quality of the bread we'll serve at the royal couple's wedding feast. Abigail has always been the better baker. Even as children, her bread was perfect, and mine was either left to rise too long or dense enough to be a slingstone."

Benaiah forced a laugh. I glanced at him but turned away immediately when he tried to coax a smile from me.

I reached for another handful of grain, poured it into the hole atop the runner stone, and steadily turned the wheel. *Fine. If my whole family conspired against me, I'll do whatever tasks I must to be obedient to the Law, but I'll never again trust them with my heart.*

Ima still stood over me. "Githa, my darling, please look at me."

I obeyed but let the pain in my heart kill any hint of emotion. Perhaps this was the only way to please Ima and become truly steady.

Ima's smile waned. "Please, won't you come to the wedding with us? Your absence will be noticed, and I don't want to explain to Abigail that my precious daughter is as stubborn as my abba's old mule." She lifted both brows as if more humor might somehow pull me out of the darkness I felt.

In truth, her words were another arrow to my heart. Neither my brother nor Ima seemed to comprehend the depth of pain they and Abba had caused by denying my marriage to Hakkoz.

I stood and turned to address both Ima and Benaiah and raised my voice so Abba could hear me in my parents' curtained bedchamber. "You may explain to whoever comments on my absence that my objection to today's wedding has nothing to do with your childhood friend or Mistress Ahinoam. My objection is wholly founded on God's Law, which clearly states that Israel's king must not marry many wives." I focused on Ima and said, "As soon as you discovered David's second wife was Mistress Abigail, you were certain God must have made an exception and ignored the ancient Law He gave Moses. Abba and Benaiah still held to God's Law and condemned King David's marriage to Abigail." I turned my attention to Benaiah. "But when you and Abba discovered King David's third wife would be a Geshurite princess who could bring political advantage to our fledgling nation, both of you were suddenly convinced Yahweh could make another exception to that same Law so our king could take a third wife."

Benaiah shot to his feet. "That's not true, Gith."

"Whatever allows you to sleep at night, brother." Surprised by the steadiness of bridled fury, I addressed Ima again. "Go to the wedding. Enjoy the festivities. Celebrate the king's sinful marriage. But Yahweh will judge between you and me for celebrating a law-breaker's union today and preventing a godly marriage yesterday."

Abba strode from the bedchamber. "Haggith, that's enough." He nudged Ima aside to loom over me with his intimidating height and build. "I didn't hear all you said, but the last of your speech dishonored your parents and made *you* the lawbreaker."

I lifted my chin to meet him eye to eye. "I said nothing to dishonor my parents. I merely said our God would judge between us. If you're certain your heart is right in the decisions you've made, Abba, why should that bother you?"

He released a huff and backed away, looking at Ima. "I've ruined her," he said. "She spends too much time with her nose buried in her scrolls and not enough time applying the Law to everyday life among our people." He returned his attention to me, but anger had succumbed to sorrow. "The Law is to be obeyed, Haggith, it's true, but I've never known a single person without sin. Our new king believes he's had Yahweh's clear direction to marry each of these three women. In each case, the woman has needed his protection, and he's needed her specific giftedness to endure a wilderness season of life. If the LORD is displeased with His anointed king, don't you think He would make it clear to the man He chose? The man God described through Samuel's prophecy as one who passionately seeks God's heart?"

"I think King David has a silver tongue," I said, "and he convinces everyone around him that Yahweh has given him the authority to supersede the Law with his own desires. I believe the Law is the only perfect guide for a righteous life, Abba—and I thought you, Ima, and Benaiah did, too."

"I also believe it's the only perfect guide. Unfortunately, I've failed completely if you think anyone can perfectly obey its commands."

"You haven't failed me, Abba. I'm grateful that you've taught me so well."

"Perhaps too well." He pursed his lips, examining the windows of my soul. Trouble brewed behind his eyes, so I didn't dare speak. Finally, he said, "When the royal wedding feast is finished, you will take a break from copying the Law into scrolls."

"Abba, no!" It was worse than I had imagined. Falling to my knees, I grabbed his hand and pressed it to my forehead. "I'll do anything. I'll never speak my opinion again. I'll be the steadiest daughter in Hebron."

His other hand rested atop my head. "I don't want you to stop speaking your opinions. I want you to experience more of life, get to know more people. Perhaps then you'll discover someone who could make a wonderful husband for you."

I dropped his hand, utterly offended. "How would you have reacted if your parents denied your betrothal to Ima and suggested, 'I'm sure you'll find someone better'?"

"That's not what I meant." His sad smile seemed almost compassionate. "Things were different with your ima and me."

"Because you loved her?"

"Actually, no," he said.

"What?" I glanced at Ima, waiting to see hurt or at least surprise in her expression. I saw neither.

"Your abba and I grew to love each other after we were married—as most couples do."

"So you're punishing me for loving the man I want to marry?" I glanced from one parent to the other. "When you denied our betrothal, you took from me the only man I'll ever love."

Ima sighed. "Haggith, you're too emotional about a young man you hardly know."

"I know Hakkoz's heart, Ima." Oh, how I wanted to tell her that for over a year Benaiah had chaperoned furtive getaways whenever Hakkoz came to Hebron for colony leadership meetings. But I would never betray my brother—though I felt like he'd betrayed me by siding with our parents.

"You don't know the *real* Hakkoz." Benaiah's voice startled me.

"Then why—" No. I wouldn't reveal his complicity by asking why he would provide the opportunities for me to be in Hakkoz's company. I would remain loyal to him though his vows to help me were meaningless.

Awkward silence gave hopelessness time to settle into my belly, and my love for Hakkoz had nowhere to flow. If Abba took my scrolls, too, what would I become? Like the Dead Sea, I'd be as bitter and useless as its briny water.

Lunging at Abba's feet, I wet them with tears. "Please don't take the scrolls. They're the one thing I love more than Hakkoz."

"Haggith, get up." Abba's commanding tone likely worked with his priests, but I had no strength to obey.

"I'll take care of her." Benaiah's voice was barely a whisper.

"You can't miss the wedding," Ima said. "Princess Maakah chose you to speak the blessing over her."

"I'll be there," he said. "Just let me talk to Githa alone."

Noble

I didn't want to talk to the one who had cut me deepest. In the absence of words, Ima hurried past me—likely to dress for the wedding. Sandals shuffled, the front curtain fluttered, and blessed silence followed. *Did Benaiah go with them after all?*

As if answering my thought, two strong hands gripped my arms and gently lifted me to my feet. Keeping my head bowed, I stubbornly refused to look at him.

"Ima took her wedding garments with her and is dressing with Abigail, so we're alone." He fell silent, waiting, but for what? Heaving a deep sigh, he said, "I know you're angry with me, but someday I'll tell you more about Hakkoz, and you'll be grateful for the family that loves you enough to protect you—even when it makes you mad."

Fury conquered stubbornness, and my head shot up. "What gives you the right to rule over me, Benaiah? I'm five years past the age of marriage. Instead of pursuing a husband, I chose to make Yahweh my Bridegroom and recording His sacred text my service of love. When I met Hakkoz, I found a man who wasn't threatened by my work—a godly Levite who also served Yahweh and His people wholeheartedly. He even vowed I could continue my work after we were wed."

Benaiah scoffed. "As I said, someday I'll tell you more about Hakkoz."

"Tell me now!" I stomped my foot and immediately felt foolish for the childish action.

He tried to hug me, but I pushed him away. With a frustrated sigh, he said, "If I tell you the truth about Hakkoz today, you won't believe me. Abba, Ima, and I are praying together that your heart will someday be open to see the truth yourself. That the facade he so artfully created for you and his fellow Levites will be broken and chipped away to reveal the true nature of Hakkoz ben Elasah." He kissed his fingertip, then transferred it to the tip of my nose—as my best friend and hero always had.

"We've closed the city gates for the duration of the wedding feast," he said, "so the city itself will be safe and quiet. The feasting outside the city will last no more than three days. Do you want me to come and check on you each morning?"

I was already shaking my head before he finished. "Please don't. I'm going to enjoy my quiet time. Maybe I'll even figure out a way to convince Abba that he should allow me to continue as his Law scribe."

"Together, *we* will find a way to convince him." My brother winked at me then silently slipped through our front curtain. No wonder he'd been deemed Abba's best scout.

As his footsteps receded, I scanned our empty two-room home. Somehow, it looked bigger with only me in it. Our main room was divided into three cozy spaces: a kitchen where we prepared the food, a hearth with a fire where we cooked our food, and a gathering area with lots of comfy cushions where we sat together and enjoyed eating the food Ima and I prepared.

My heart squeezed a little in my chest. I loved Hakkoz, without a doubt, but I couldn't bear the thought of becoming as brackish as the Dead Sea. Once Abba made a public declaration—as he'd done when refusing to accept Hakkoz's betrothal request—there was no changing his decision. But perhaps, with Benaiah's help, I could still pour out my love as Abba's Law scribe. If I stopped pushing Abba, Ima, and Benaiah away, perhaps I could pretend to believe they'd all recognized some deficit in Hakkoz that I couldn't see.

My beloved's handsome face came to mind, and the familiar ache weighed heavy on my chest. I remembered the first time I'd witnessed his full-belly laugh and closed my eyes to replay the memory. We'd decided to share a midday meal while hiding near some bulrushes beside Hebron's Pool. We were in the midst of asking getting-to-know-you questions when a bullfrog hopped into my lap. I screamed, leapt to my feet, and tossed the slimy creature right

Noble

into the meal I'd placed on our blanket. Hakkoz laughed so hard that his long, lean body rolled into a ball, and tears rolled down his handsome face. I chuckled at the memory, then realized memories would be all I had of my first love.

Needing a distraction, I returned to the hand mill and was determined to change Abba's decision by making Ima proud. Not only would I steadily turn the runner stone atop the bed stone and create the finest flour ever used to make wedding bread, but I would also make sure the bread dough rose just enough—and not too much. I lowered myself beside the hand mill, poured a half-full cup of barley kernels into the center hole, and began turning the handle more steadily than ever. I wasn't yet ready to expunge every memory of my beloved Hakkoz, but I could at least try to behave kindly toward the family that believed they were acting in my best interest.

As afternoon progressed to dusk, my arms felt as if they might fall off. I'd never ground three bags of grain by myself. Benaiah said he'd come back in three days, so he must have forgotten that our family had been asked to provide at least a portion of tomorrow's wedding bread. Would anyone come to help me? Would someone at least pick up the loaves so I wouldn't need to deliver them to a wedding I'd vowed not to attend?

Peering out the two windows in our main room, I estimated how much daylight was left and how long into the night would be required to mix the dough and let it rise, form the loaves and let them rise again, then bake the loaves in shifts until all this flour became delicious bread—better than Abigail's.

Perhaps I'd been a little too ambitious. With my hands covered in barley flour, I puffed some hair off my forehead and poured the last cup of grain into the runner stone's center hole. *LORD, if You would send me the help I need to accomplish whatever You have planned, I'd be very grateful.*

As if Yahweh answered my prayer before the last cup of grain was finished, I heard the shuffling of sandals approaching our doorway. Fear threatened, remembering I was essentially alone inside the city gates. What if it wasn't the help I'd prayed for? *Don't be silly.* I shook my head to clear my thoughts. I was too desperate for help to be afraid.

"Hello?" I crooned while standing to my feet. "Who's there?" The shuffling stopped. No one answered.

The hairs on my arms stood on end, and I grabbed Ima's kitchen knife. Because Hebron was one of six ancient cities of refuge, many of our citizens had committed an accidental murder and lived within the city gates as protection from their blood avengers. Robbery was the most common crime in a city full of bored fugitives. "You've chosen the wrong house, thief. Go now, and I won't report you to Chief Priest Jehoiada."

Every fugitive claimed innocence when appearing before Abba at the city assembly. If no evidence was found to prove malice, the blood avenger was sent away, and the fugitive was sentenced to remain inside our city walls until the death of the chief priest—my abba. Which was another reason Benaiah had secretly taught me to wield a dagger—actually, Ima's kitchen knife.

I took two steps toward the doorway and shouted again, "Leave now, or you'll tangle with my dagger."

"Haggith?" came the whisper from the other side of the curtain.

It couldn't be. "Hakkoz?" I dropped the knife and rushed toward the curtain.

I gasped at the sight of Hakkoz's blood-covered face and robe. "What happened?" came out in a gravelly voice.

He bowed his head, shoulders shaking, unable to answer. I fought for control, hoping to be the kind of woman that Ima always said would make a good wife: *"God's greatest gift to a man is a wife who remains steady in the face of adversity."* I still wanted to be this man's wife. Covering the distance between us, I tipped his chin up.

He startled at my touch.

"Shh, I only wish to inspect your injuries." He avoided my gaze but allowed me to lightly brush his bloodied lips, a swollen eye, and a deep cut above his left brow. Already emotional from today's earlier conflict, tears rolled down my cheeks. The longer he delayed explaining his injuries, the more uneasy I felt.

I stepped back, but he grabbed my wrist. "Please, may I hold you?" he asked, finally lifting his eyes to search mine. I saw fear in them and something else I couldn't name.

Benaiah's words haunted me. *You don't know the real Hakkoz.*

"What if Ima comes back to help with my bread making?" I asked.

"She won't." He circled my waist. "Please, Githa." The desperation in his voice dispelled all caution, and I allowed him to hold me tightly against his chest. I laid my cheek on the soft place over his heart, which was also the only portion of his robe without a bloodstain.

"Hakkoz, can you tell me what happened?"

"I can, but I need you to promise something first. Can you do that?"

"What must I promise?"

He held me tighter. "Promise you'll believe me *before* I tell you what happened."

MESU ANDREWS is a Christy Award–winning, bestselling author of biblical novels and devotional studies, whose deep understanding of and love for God's Word brings the Bible alive for readers. Her heritage as a "spiritual mutt" has given her a strong yearning to both understand and communicate biblical truths in powerful stories that touch the heart, challenge the mind, and transform lives. Mesu lives in Indiana with her husband, Roy, where she stays connected with her readers through newsy emails, blog posts, and social media. Visit her at MesuAndrews.com.

Sign Up for Mesu's Newsletter

Keep up to date with Mesu's latest news on book releases and events by signing up for her email list at the website below.

MesuAndrews.com

Follow Mesu on Social Media

 Mesu Andrews   @MesuAndrews   @MesuAndrews

Be the first to hear about new books from Bethany House!

Stay up to date with our authors and books by signing up for our newsletters at

BethanyHouse.com/SignUp

FOLLOW US ON SOCIAL MEDIA

  @BethanyHouseFiction